Dar
draw
runners. He glanced down. The form beneath the sheet was still without identity, and thus far he could take it. He gave the signal to uncover.
First impression; Oh God, help him! How she must have suffered! Nausea rose like a spume of gas to the back of his throat. Covering his mouth with his hand he started to turn away, but Turkel grasped him by the elbow. 'Can you identify her please, Mr Baker?'
He looked again, eyes glistening with brimming tears. Suppressing the need to be sick, he forced out his reply and fled the room, anxious to leave the horror and the clinging smell of death behind.

FINAL TWIST

SWIFT

Final Twist
a paperback published by
The Swift Press,
PO Box 9,
Manchester M21 7LQ

Printed and bound in the UK
by Short Run Press Ltd,
Exeter

ISBN 0 9517638 1 4
A CIP catalogue for this book
is available from the British Library

Originally written as:
The Kennedy Witness in 1982
rewritten in 1985, 1988 and 1992
inspiration sources; Rush to Judgement, Book & motion picture by Mark Lane
Oswald, Assassin or fall guy? by Joachim Joesten
On the Trail of the Assassins, Jim Garrison,
Farewell America, anon,
The Trial of Lee Harvey Oswald, Channel Four,
Howard Donahue,
The Assassination Chain, Leek & Sugar
Operation Mind Control, Walter Bowart
JFK: Man or Myth, Victor Lasky,
Conspiracy, Anthony Summers,
The Mafia killed President Kennedy, by David E. Scheim
Plausible Denial, Mark Lane
Crossfire: Jim Maars
Mortal Error, Bonar Menninger
and my own researches and travels.

Of course, a piece of work like this cannot
be the work of just
one man. Many thanks,
then, to the following
individuals for their valued
contribution.

Stephen Raw & Chris Clover
for a second brilliant cover.
Jack Spencer for the Dealey
Plaza illustration.
The Philadelphia Inquirer,
especially Carole Damiani.
The Associated Press.

For their enduring support,
heartfelt thanks to the following,
Jack and Margaret Spencer,
Lesley Shackleton (for pushing me)
Lawrence and Yvonne Mawn (for proof reading
and red wine)
Patricia Richardson (a friendly voice, there
when I needed it)
David and Susan Haykin,
John McCumesky,
Paul Harris and Joanne Davidson (For steering
me towards some very interesting material).
Jeannette Holmes,
Ken and June,
Tavia, Peter Spencer.

And Peng, who meant so much to
me during the early years of this
work.

BOOK ONE

1: Turning Point

The limousine cruised toward Daniel at a graceful speed and braked smoothly. Sleek and black, it had the look of a glossy predator, the dark tinted windows lending a sinister appearance. The rear door kicked slightly as an electronic lock sprang and he was invited to enter. The interior was dimly lit, and it took a moment for his eyes to adjust. A glass partition separated him from the driver, but he could see the man's outline. The experience would have been unnerving had the driver not turned to present a friendly smile. 'Sit back and enjoy the ride, Mr Baker. It'll take about a half hour to get to the Senator's house.'

Daniel thanked him, feeling himself start to relax. 'Help yourself to a drink.' The driver continued. 'There's always an excellent scotch in the bar just in front of you.' Daniel was happy to partake; his nerves were still shot. The small bar, illuminated upon opening, contained a small but select stock of superior quality liquor. There was ice in a frosted container, and he helped himself to a cube. Glass in hand he settled back on the lavish upholstery, visibly unwinding as the scotch banished his anxieties.

At length he caught sight of heavy iron gates swinging open, and the limo was streaking along a floodlit avenue neatly corridored with trees. He glimpsed a uniformed guard patrolling with a dog. The limo reached the end of the avenue and pursued a gentle arc, gliding smoothly to a halt before a large, colonial style house bathed white in the glare from floodlights positioned discreetly amongst the landscaped gardens.

Immediately upon stepping out he was surrounded by a group of stern faced men in dark suits. No ordinary heavies these, their movements were economical and their gazes moved constantly in a state of preparedness. He was escorted into a reception hall he would have described as opulent, complete with bejewelled chandelier and a vast sweeping staircase. He loosed a low whistle: 'The man certainly knows how to live,' he joked, but no one laughed.

A ramrod-erect butler with impeccable English manners and a disdainful way of peering along his nose took charge of Daniel, leading him away from the group and towards the study.

A set of huge, oak panelled doors closed behind him, and he was facing the great man himself. Senator Galbraith, a little shorter than imagined, and thinner, but as vital in life as his television image. His grip when they shook hands was firm, but on becoming aware of Daniel's bruised features his face registered alarm. 'What happened?'

Daniel smiled, gave a small shrug. 'Unrelated incident.' His natural suspicion was ignited momentarily; was it his imagination, or did Galbraith look relieved?

A drink was offered, and accepted, and both men retired to leather chairs by the fireside. The flames had been allowed to diminish, but the heat from the glowing coals still had a lulling effect.

'Very cosy,' Daniel remarked. The Senator nodded. 'The fire is not really necessary this time of year, but when the nights close in it can be a comfort.'

While the Senator was still settling into his chair, Daniel subjected him to a brief scrutiny. There was about him some enigmatic force that charged the atmosphere. At present that force was directed towards relaxation, but Daniel could imagine it being utilised to awesome effect in a serious confrontation. The Senator would be a hard man to stare down.

Galbraith rolled his brandy glass slowly between cupped palms. He smiled kindly, and that simple action seemed to drain away all of Daniel's anxieties. The effect was almost hypnotic. This was a man of unimpeachable integrity. A man he could trust. He cleared his throat. 'I'd like to thank you for agreeing to meet with me, sir. I appreciate your taking time out. I know you must be busy.'

'You are most welcome. Miss Rush hinted that the matter you wish to discuss is of national importance. I have learned to respect her judgement, and so feel duty bound to listen.'

'I hope you continue to feel that way, sir. Because I believe both our lives may be in danger.'

Another reassuring smile. 'That, as they say, comes with the territory.'

'I know that, sir. It's hard to know where exactly to start. Sometimes I feel the whole world is going crazy. All I know is that I can't stop the madness, and that is why I've come to you. If anyone in this country can do anything, you can.'

Galbraith smiled. 'I'm flattered to hear you say so.' He replied urbanely, and Daniel was reminded of Barbara's words. What had she called him? A man without vanity. A man who put others first.

'I really don't know where to start.'

'You mentioned madness.' Galbraith prompted him. 'Why not start at the beginning. What madness?'

Faced with the moment, Daniel felt haggard. He wanted to drink. God, he wanted to drink! But he had to make a start before fear seized his tongue. He swallowed, and his throat hurt from the dry movement.

'The madness that began the day John F Kennedy died.'

THE CONVENTIONAL WISDOM . . .

Says that on the afternoon of Friday, 22nd of November, 1963, President John F Kennedy was shot dead by three shots from a rifle fired by Lee Harvey Oswald, from the sixth floor of the Texas School Book Depository Building in Dallas, as the Presidential limousine, part of a motorcade, passed by.

Conventional wisdom says that one shot missed, a second bullet struck President Kennedy in the back, exited through his throat and passed into the back of Governor John Connally of Texas. The bullet exited Connally's chest, smashing his wrist and entering his left thigh. The third bullet struck President Kennedy in the head.

Within one hour of the shooting, Lee Oswald was picked up by the Dallas police after being reported for acting suspicously in an area close to a spot where a police officer, J D Tippett, had been shot dead soon after 1 p.m. Oswald was carrying a handgun when he was arrested in a movie theater.

A former marine who had defected to, and lived in, the USSR and who was then employed in the Texas School Book Depository, Lee had a Russian wife, from whom he was separated, and had been visible as a member of a pro-Castro group, Fair Play For Cuba.

On the following Sunday, the 24th November, while he was being transfered from the Dallas police building to a more secure facility, Oswald was shot dead by a citizen, local nightclub owner Jack Ruby. His reason for killing Oswald? He wanted to spare the late President's widow the pain of having to testify in court.

Within a few days the new President, former vice-President Lyndon B Johnson, had appointed a committee, under Chief Justice Earl Warren, to head an investigation into the death of President Kennedy. Almost one year later, after an intensive investigation involving the police, the Federal Bureau of Investigation and the CIA, the Warren Commission concluded that Lee Harvey Oswald, acting alone, had killed John Kennedy.

Earl Warren and his fellows were respected public figures, the FBI and the CIA were there to protect the USA. . . .

So why is it that eighty percent of Americans do not believe their conclusions?

* 1 *

Love Field, Dallas.
Friday, November 22nd, 1963.

One brief dreadful moment . . .

'There's the son of a bitch now,' Halstead said, touching the arm of the man at his side. His companion drew on his cigarette and did not exhale. Halstead swallowed, a trifle nervously, and raised the walkie-talkie to his lips. 'Talon to Rama. The caravan is ready to roll. Eleven fifty.' A terse acknowledgement barked from the instrument.

They were seated in the rear of a limousine, all but one of the windows covered by velvet curtains. From their vantage point at the edge of the airstrip they had an uninterrupted view of the President's aircraft. They watched the reception committee line up to shake hands with JFK and the first lady. A stray cop sauntered over to the limo and eyed the occupants suspiciously, but one look at the faked Secret Service ID's did the trick. Halstead's companion looked out at the sky and nodded his head in apparent satisfaction; the morning rain clouds had departed. 'It's going to be Kennedy weather,' he remarked sourly.

Halstead gave a crooked smile. 'Don't begrudge him that. Not on his last day.' He paused. 'In an hour or so he'll be dead, and . . .' He broke off, catching the merest trace of uncertainty on his colleague's face. 'Hey, not having second thoughts are you?'

He was quick to respond with an emphatic shake of his head. 'Not at all. The bastard deserves all he gets.'

Suspicion dispelled, Halstead nodded. 'That's right. If it gets hard to watch, remember your wife and keep her in mind. It'll make it easier.'

The other man nodded agreement and stared out of the window. There was nothing more to be said.

Danny.

'Aw, gee Pa, do I have to?' the boy whined. Almost automatically his father lifted a hand to lash out, catching himself just in time. Letting out a sigh of exasperation he decided to try reasoning with his son. He crouched down before him, and took gentle hold of his small shoulders. 'Yes, Danny, you have to go. It's a historic day, the President coming to Dallas. You'll remember it all your life.' The boy remained stoically unconvinced. His father swallowed his irritation. Turning to the basket on the floor beside him he drew back the red-checked gingham that covered it. 'Look, I've packed all your favorites. We have burgers, Oreos, a couple of Hersheys and four bottles of Coke. We'll have a great time!' He gave the boy's shoulder an affectionate squeeze. 'Now you be a big boy and haul this out to the pickup for me. I'll be right out.'

Heaving the basket from the floor with both hands, Danny tottered awkwardly out through the kitchen door and around to the front of the house where his father's battered '58 Ford stood. There he paused to catch his breath.

He was a bulky boy, overplump for his age, and so pale he almost always looked in poor health. His pallor was exacerbated by the rich carroty red color of his hair, and the bright emerald green of his eyes. Since the death of his mother, two years previously, he had withdrawn into a world of his own, become incommunicative and difficult. A lonely child who avoided other children, he would rather seek solace within himself. Rather stay home and read a book than play anytime.

His father came around the side of the house. His long arms swung loosely, and his lengthy, loping stride covered the distance to the pickup with surprising speed. Climbing into the driver's seat, he bounced to get comfortable, then looked over at the boy. 'Get in son.' He reached out and hefted the basket into a narrow space behind the seats. 'Close your door,' he muttered absently, once Danny had clambered in. He started the engine and soon they were heading west along the Thornton Freeway toward downtown Dallas.

Parking the pickup in a lot at the eastern end of Commerce, they walked the rest of the way. Crowds lined Main, and the noise and hubbub roused some dormant excitement in Danny. For the first time in ages he smiled, his eyes shone, and he looked about him in wonder, as though seeing the world for the first time. Noting his son's reaction, father felt warmed; he had done the right thing. He had no idea what magic was at work in Dallas that day, but it was good.

They had never been close, but since the death of Danny's mother the distance between Harrison Baker and his son had increased immeasurably. Harrison sighed; God, he had tried. There had been fishing trips, vacations to Miami beach. They never missed a county fair, and the previous summer he had almost bankrupted himself taking the boy to California, to Disneyland. But Danny remained cold and unresponsive, resisting all his father's attempts to pierce the screen of aloofness. At times, Danny's naive and innocent rejection of the friendly overtures would push his father to the brink of uncontrollable rage and he would beat the boy until he screamed. Later, guilt would always follow the anger, guilt and a sense of defeat that came from knowing he could only reach his son through pain.

Turning right onto Houston by the jailhouse, they looked about for a suitable spot, Danny following with difficulty as his father shouldered a path through the crowd. Under the scowling gaze of a cop on crowd duty, they cut across Houston to the fountains of the Bryant memorial, crossed the huge, grassy Vee of Dealey, and joined the crowd on the north side, beneath the trees in front of the Texas School Book Depository. A semi-circular Collonade built of white stone stood atop the mild slope, and Danny eyed this wonder with awe. He had not been to this part of the city before, and the sight of this corridor of gleaming white stone roused the vivid imagination that lay dormant within him. He longed to explore, longed to run along its inner length and peep out through the vast portals and the checkerworked openings cut into the stone walls.

The crowd was thinner here, and his father edged to the front, placing himself on the kerb. Putting down the basket he peered up the slope, to the corner around which, at any moment, the motorcade escorting the President, John F Kennedy and his glamorous wife Jackie, would appear.

Seizing his chance, Danny took off up the grassy slope with a war whoop and sprinted excitedly into the collonade. Along the corridor and back again he ran, then out and around the curved back wall of the structure, halting breathlessly by the wooden fence that separated the top of the grassy slope from the car park and the railroad yards beyond. There were cars in the lot, and beyond them, some one hundred yards away, he could see the railroad supervisor's tower. Inside, and just visible, could be seen the small figure of a man at work. Turning once more to the stone structure, Danny fitted his small fingers into the sill of the lowest aperture and hoisted himself up. His plimpsoled feet scraped for a grip on the wall. Panting elatedly he peered through the collonade and across Dealey. He could see the old courthouse, distinctive with its turreted rooftop, and his father, staring intently to his left. Danny's arms were aching, but before he lowered himself he caught sight of an open-topped car slowly rounding the corner.

He dropped to the ground and had started to take a deep breath when a loud retort, like a firecracker snapping, rent the air. The sound seemed to come from behind him, but before he could react another firecracker exploded. Puzzled about the origin of the noise he moved to the wooden fence and hauled himself high enough to peer over the top. The fence ran in an L-shape, and Danny was at the base. A number of cars were parked, front-end on, against the stretch of the fence that extended the length of the car park, separating the car park from the top of the small hill that sloped down to Elm Street. Some twenty feet distant, and peering over the fence, stood two men. One wore working clothes, with a white hardhat, the other was a policeman. The police officer watched as his companion squinted along the barrel of a rifle aimed over the top of the fence. He was concentrating, hard. The cop raised what looked like a walkie-talkie to his mouth and muttered into it. The rifleman's body was fixed, but not tensed as slowly he panned the weapon. From somewhere else came the sound of another shot, but there was no time to dwell on it because there was a louder explosion, an enormous boom, and a slight kick as the rifle fired. Immediately the weapon was passed to another man who had appeared. He walked quickly away from Danny, towards the railroad bridge at the far end of the car park. The police officer walked around to the front of the fence, returning in seconds holding what looked like some kind of camera. The construction worker threaded hurriedly between the parked cars, and as he passed Danny at a rapid walk his chilling, intent gaze fell upon the boy. It seemed to Danny the man had a fleeting moment of hesitation, but he dare not stop and he knew it. He sped past and vanished behind the tall, redbrick building nearby.

Tumult swelled on the air. Screams and cries. Danny ran to the top of the grassy embankment and halted, gaping. People, swarms of them, hundreds of them, were running across Dealey Plaza towards him. A cop on a motorcycle rode up the slope and, dropping his machine, ran, gun in hand onto the railroad yard. Redfaced and breathless he swung the gun around in an impotent gesture. The gunmen were gone. A second cop appeared. There was a rapid exchange, then the first wave of the panicked crowd surged up the embankment. The cops waved their arms to stem the crush, but to little effect. A man in a casual jacket appeared, waving an open wallet at the cops he seemed to take command. Orders were issued, and the cops set to work turning back the crowd.

'Danny! Danny!' His father's voice rang out. The boy ran crying into his father's warm, safe embrace. All around them people swarmed like ants, teeming across the Plaza and milling in hysterical bewilderment.

And still the motorcade rolled on, the vehicles slowed by the crowds. Most of the occupants of the vehicles stared around in confusion. They had no idea what had happened. Danny stared at the chaos that surrounded him, and was glad of the safety his father's embrace offered. Taking his son by the hand, Harrison led him away from the Plaza, past the depository building. A bleakfaced cop stood at the entrance.

Harrison approached him and had to shout to make himself heard. 'What the hell's going on?'

The cop jabbed a thumb at the building behind him. 'Some sonofabitch took a shot at Kennedy from up there.'

Danny's father looked puzzled. 'That's not right. I was over by that traffic sign. The shots came from behind me. From behind that fence.'

'That's what I thought,' the cop declared. 'I ran over there, but some Secret Service bull sent me here to watch this door. Listen, I better get your name.' He produced a pad and pencil.

After having his name and address recorded, Harrison led his son away. 'Well Danny, I guess I was righter than I knew when I said this would be a day to remember.'

'What happened Pa?'

His father shook his head. 'Someone shot the President, son.'

Evening. Danny was sitting cross-legged on the slatted porch of the house, flicking through his favorite comics, when the sound of an automobile braking made him look up. A dust-covered Rambler station wagon stood at the kerb. A man in a suit climbed out. He studied the house for a few moments, then his gaze descended, settling on the boy. Danny felt a rush of fear. He swallowed, then taking to his feet in alarm he ran into the house, shrieking: 'Pa! Pa! There's a man here!'

'Mr Baker?' The stranger inquired with a disarming smile. Harrison Baker was vague. 'Yes?'

The stranger glanced down at Danny, peering from behind his father, and he smiled. 'Fine looking boy you have there, Mr Baker. If you don't mind my saying so.' He crouched down. 'What's your name, son?'

Danny retreated a little, but managed to mutter a reply.

'Would you do me a favor, Danny?' The boy nodded timidly. 'I have to talk business with your Pop. Would you be a buddy and look after my car for a while? If you do a good job there's a Hershey in it for you. You'll find it in the dash.'

Danny peered up at his father. Harrison directed a puzzled scowl at the stranger, then nodded. 'Go ahead, Dan.'

Scrambling past them, Danny raced out to the Rambler. He patrolled around it, tutting impatiently at its coat of dust. It looked as if it had come straight from a trek across the desert. His father would never let the pickup get this bad! The plates were out of state, and a football pennant was just visible through the grime-covered rear window. Pulling open the driver's door he clambered in and bounced experimentally on the seat. By stretching out his toes he was just able to touch the pedals, then sudden recollection struck and he delved into the glove box to retrieve the Hershey bar. He was doing a good job.

Bored, he tore open the wrapper and ate the bar. At length he left the car and sauntered back to the house. Entering through the porch door he crossed the hallway. The sound of raised voices made him nervous. He pressed himself flat against the wall by the open lounge door. His father was speaking. He sounded angry. 'What exactly is it you're trying to say?'

The stranger's answer was elusive. 'The police will be contacting you for a full statement. We'd like you to reconsider what you told the cop at the depository. You've read the newspapers, you know as well as I do that Oswald did it. Your saying otherwise can only complicate things. He may even get off.'

'I don't care what the papers say. I don't care what you say. The shots came from behind the fence.'

The stranger sighed. 'You're wrong, Mr Baker. You misheard. Please, why don't you be reasonable? Why make things difficult for everyone? It's even possible that a little cooperation could be to your benefit. I happen to know you are behind with your mortgage repayments. Now, if you were to help us . . .'

'Just who the hell do you represent? Let me see some ID.'

'I represent official bodies that want this investigation cleared up quickly and the killer convicted. Oswald DID kill Kennedy, and we don't want any testimony being offered that might help the commie S.O.B off the hook. Did you know he defected to Russia? Lived there? Hell, he even married one of them! He's a danger to National Security, and he's got to be put away.' Harrison Baker said nothing. 'C'mon, Mr Baker, be reasonable. We don't want any trouble.'

'What do you mean?' Danny's father was growing angry. 'Are you threatening me? I oughta. . . .'

Danny smiled. He could just imagine his father raising one big bunched fist, could just picture the stranger taking a step backwards. 'Listen, Mister, I know what I heard. If the truth is a little inconvenient for you and your friends then that's just too bad. Close the door on your way out.'

Danny scuttled into the kitchen and took refuge behind the door. The stranger passed through without seeing him and went out, slamming the door shut behind him. Moments later the car could be heard racing away.

Danny stepped into the lounge. His father was leaning against a wall, one hand covering his eyes. He massaged his brow. Danny took a tentative step towards him. 'Pa?'

As Harrison looked down at his son, Danny saw something strange in his eyes, something that had not been there earlier. He was too young to recognise fear. 'Pa, what happened?'

Harrison looked confused. He rubbed slowly at the side of his head, then, as if exhausted, he sought his favorite armchair and sagged onto it. Motioning Danny to sit on the floor before him, he leaned forward and looked into those young, trusting eyes that so reminded him of his late wife. 'Danny, you're getting to be a big boy now. Sometimes I think you're older than you really are – you get so serious. . . .' He faltered, paused to collect his thoughts. 'Let's talk about this afternoon. You were at the top of that little hill weren't you, when the President was shot?' Danny nodded. 'Did you see anyone up there?' Again the youngster nodded. Harrison reached out and took one of his son's tiny hands. 'Go slowly, but tell me everything you saw.'

So Danny recounted everything he could recall; the man with the gun, the shots. The man hurrying away with the rifle. The gunman spotting him as he made his escape. There was a newspaper on the table; a late evening edition. Harrison unfolded it to show Danny the front page. Beneath a stark banner headline was a picture of a man, thin faced, with receding dark hair. 'Is he one of the men you saw?'

Danny stared at the picture, then shook his head. His father put down the paper. 'They're saying he's the one that killed the President, firing a rifle from the sixth floor of a building. There's no mention of men on the hill.' Harrison nibbled thoughtfully at his lower lip.

'I did hear another shot, or maybe two, but not from the men. From somewhere else. . . .' Danny strained to be helpful. His father digested this. 'So maybe this fella, Oswald, was involved. I just don't know.' He sighed.

'We can't have been the only ones, Pa. Other people must have heard where the shot came from. That cop, he said he heard.'

'Then why isn't it in the papers, or on the television? I spoke to Tommy earlier, he said the first flash on the radio claimed the President was shot in the front of the head. But now all the news is that he was shot in the back by this one guy, Oswald.' He tapped the newspaper. 'I don't know what to believe.'

Danny looked earnestly at his father. 'Pa, I didn't make this up. Honest. You saw how everyone ran towards where I was.'

Harrison smiled, reached out a hand to ruffle his son's hair. 'I know son. I know.'

'Pa,' the youngster suddenly brightened. 'If I tell the police what I saw they'll have to listen.'

Harrison shook his head. 'No. Definitely no. There's something funny going on. That man who was here, he threatened me. I can't risk anything happening to you. Say nothing, okay?'

Danny nodded. 'What are we going to do?'

Harrison pursed his lips and blew softly. 'I don't know yet.'

Sunday, November 24th.

Danny was hauled roughly from his sleep by his father shaking him. 'Danny, wake up!'

'What is it Pa?' the boy mumbled groggily. Lifting his son from the bed, Harrison carried him through to the lounge and lowered him to a chair. 'Look at the TV, someone shot him.'

The small screen was filled with harsh, monochrome images that Danny, still barely awake, struggled to focus upon. He rubbed at his eyes, caught a glimpse of the clock. Ten thirty at night! He'd never, ever, stayed awake this late before! His father's anxious excitement was infectious. He was instantly alert. 'Who? Someone shot who?'

'Oswald,' his father replied tensely, his gaze locked on the screen. 'Just now, I saw it on the news. A guy just leapt out and . . . shot Oswald. It happened today, while we were out at the lake. Watch, they might show it again.'

Wide awake now, Danny watched the screen entranced. The incident was rerun with a macabre voice over.

Oswald was being escorted from his cell in the Dallas police station. Being transferred to the safety of the County Jail. He was flanked by plainsclothes officers. As they neared the camera a bulky figure in a dark suit and pale hat shouldered himself into the picture, momentarily blocking the camera's view of Oswald. There was a shot. Then a pandemonium of sound. 'He's been shot!' The voice of the commentator at the scene exclaimed. 'Oswald has been shot.' Oswald had fallen. Fatally wounded, he was stretchered into an ambulance.

Harrison crossed to the TV set and lowered the volume. He turned to Danny. 'The man who got shot. Oswald. Was he one of the men you saw?'

Danny shook his head

The boy was halfway down the stairs the following day when the telephone rang. His father answered it, and Danny halted on the stairs to listen.

'You again. Listen, I will not change one word of that statement. Now leave me alone!'

Harrison Baker banged the receiver back into place. As he glanced up he saw Danny's frightened face peering down at him. 'Danny, what is it?'

The boy's face seemed to crumple. He started to blubber, and his shoulders shook convulsively as tears streamed down his face.

'I'm scared, Pa. I'm scared!'

Days passed, a week, ten days, and every day the telephone rang. It was not always the same voice, but the threats had been consistent. Harrison thanked God that Danny had not taken any of them.

He had not been into work for three days. He was being followed, he was sure. Someone was dogging him, biding their time. Nervously he nibbled at his ragged fingernails; a new habit. A strange feeling of foreboding haunted him. The die was cast; nothing he said would make the slightest difference now. Oswald WAS the killer of both President Kennedy and that police officer, Tippett. The official record would read that. And he now knew he had made a dreadful mistake, insisting in his statements that the shots had not come from the depository building alone. For he was a marked man. Odd things had been happening, a number of small events which, if taken individually, appeared trivial and unimportant, but, when one was able to fit together the pieces and gain an overview were enough to convince him that he had not much time left. All he could do now was protect the boy.

He had not been able to resist seeking others. Those who might also have a different tale to tell. And he had found two. A railroad worker who had seen a man with two rifles walking quickly away from the fence, dismantling the weapons and fitting the pieces into a black bag before walking to a car parked the other side of the triple underpass and driving away. And a woman, a black woman named Clarrissa who had witnessed the killing of officer Tippett. She insisted Oswald did not resemble the killer. When Harrison met her, she was packing a single case before leaving Dallas. She had been visited, she told him bitterly and after much persuasion, by a man in a suit who warned she might come to harm if she persisted in her story.

'So you're letting them drive you out?' Harrison declared with some impatience. She turned slowly to look at him, her eyes wide with astonishment and fury. 'What the Sam Hill is it to you? Of course I'm letting them drive me out. I want to keep breathing.'

'Go to the police,' he urged. She loosed a laugh. 'Police? Are you kidding me? Men in suits, no excuse me, WHITE men in suits, they OWN the police. A black life ain't worth a damm down here. The only one who values my life is me. So yes, I am leaving. Now do you mind getting out of here, I have a Greyhound to catch.'

Harrison had felt her fear, and it made him afraid. Now he stumbled into the bathroom and stared at himself in the mirror. He was looking haggard. He had not shaved, or washed, he stank, and his cheeks were covered with silvery bristle. For days he had not dared step outside. He could not face work, and was existing on beer and beans. He kept telling himself he ought to snap out of the haze, for Danny's sake, but though the beer had dulled his senses it could not completely bury the fear.

In a daze he carried a bottle of beer from the kitchen to the lounge and sank onto his favorite chair. The beer damped his spirits and made him think – more than was good for him. Morbid, fearfilled thoughts. He recalled how Danny had cried: '*I'm scared Pa, I'm scared!*' and how he had hugged his son and felt close to him. He had derived satisfaction from being able to offer hope, security and stability to the boy. Danny had been reassured by his father's bulk, his warmth. He truly believed everything would be alright.

He had neither courage nor words enough to tell his son that he too was afraid. There was no one to hold Harrison in a warm, womb-like embrace, no one to tell him that everything was going to be fine.

The sound of the doorbell chimed through the house. Harrison was tempted to ignore it – it might be the stranger returned, armed with that warning smile. There had been whispers, he had heard that others had altered their statements. He wondered if the stranger had visited them all . . .

The doorbell chimed again, and though the note had not changed there was this time a commanding ring to it. Harrison willed himself to his feet. He wavered unsteadily, striving for balance. From deep within him anger began to ascend. Anger ignited by fear, by the desire to hit back. If it was that smilin' bastard, he'd clean his clock for him . . . !

The hallway seemed to lurch and sway before him. He was forced to stop and take a deep breath. He gaped in astonishment; a cop stood on the other side of the screen door. He had a hand raised, poised to jab the bellpush again, but at the sight of Harrison he let the hand drop. In recent days Harrison had, irrationally, he told himself, taken to locking all the doors. Now he had to fumble thickly with the bolt on the screen door before he could hear what the cop was trying to tell him.

'Are you Mr Harrison Baker?' The cop spoke with a flat, nasal intonation. Harrison murmured a reply, and the cop went on. 'I'm afraid I have some bad news for you, sir.'

Harrison narrowed his eyes. He was confused. 'What do you mean?' he demanded, slurring his words, angry that he had let himself become dopey through drink. Then his heart plunged downwards and his face was animated with dread. 'It's Danny, isn't it?' he said in a soft voice, then louder: 'Is it Danny? Has something happened to Danny?'

The cop looked uncomfortable. 'Try to stay calm, sir. I know nothing about anyone named Danny.'

'Not Danny?' Harrison muttered thickly. He could not take this in. Danny was alright. Danny was okay. What then?

'Do you have a brother named Thomas? A twin brother?'

The obscuring ether in Harrison's mind started to clear. He was beginning to understand. 'My brother Tom? What about him?'

'I'm sorry to have to tell you he was shot dead earlier today. We do not yet know the reason for the attack, and the perpetrator has not yet been apprehended.'

Harrison's face registered pain. 'What? Why . . . How . . . ?'

'He was shot in the head by a thirty-odd six rifle bullet. Fired from a building. Death was instantaneous.'

Harrison stared fixedly. It was too much. It could not be true! His lips twitched into a sickly smile and he felt the swell of insane laughter bubbling deep within him. His head drooped as he suddenly saw things with an increased lucidity, saw the reason for it all. 'A thirty-odd six? Wasn't that the type of bullet Oswald used?'

The cop looked bored. 'I really wouldn't know about that.'

Harrison felt the laughter rising to the surface. 'No, no of course not . . .' He quelled a giggle. 'Of course you wouldn't.'

His mind's eye was already aimed at the distance, aimed at some lofty plateau from which at last he could see the workings of man. There was an irony in all this. A purpose.

Dimly he heard the cop ask if he was alright. Harrison cackled, said he'd never felt better; he was always on top of the world when a member of his family was murdered. The sarcasm was lost on the cop. Mumbling a vacant apology, he returned to his car.

On palsied knees he reeled back into the house. He fell onto the stairs and wept, each hurting sob wrenched from deep within his chest, each spasm rocking his heart.

He wept until he was sober; but even then, through his grief, he found himself asking questions, wondering why.

Still sniffing he forced himself upright and wiped a hand across his damp eyes. 'Tom's not dead. Tom's not dead. It's me. I'm the one who's dead.'

The telephone rang. In a trance he lifted the receiver to his ear and listened impassively to the familiar voice of his tormentor.

'Sorry to hear of your loss,' said the stranger. 'Just thought I'd call to offer my condolences. Still, I guess you ought to count your blessings. I mean, it could have been a case of mistaken identity, you being so alike. Yeah, I guess you were real lucky. Maybe you ought to change that statement while you still can.'

It was a little after four thirty when Danny came home to find his father's body slumped on the favored armchair. The wall behind the chair was streaked with blood. Harrison Baker had put the muzzle of his old service revolver into his mouth – and pulled the trigger.

*** 2 ***

2: Extracts from a conspirator's diary.

New Years Eve, 1962.
New Orleans.

'A dynasty stretching all the way to the 1980's? That takes some imagination, Drew.' The remark sent a ripple of polite laughter through the small cluster of people by the bar. The hostess appeared at Drew's side, looped her arm through his, and with an enigmatic smile led him away. The group dispersed into the larger crowd as the band struck up the last waltz of 1962. It was ten minutes to midnight.

Of the group there remained one man. He stood alone, and his forced smile contracted to a sullen line. One year earlier these same people had courted him, toasted his success. But now he was isolated, and he knew the reason for it. Failure. The air of it, the odour of it, hung over him, and everywhere hints were being left; he no longer had any right to move in these circles.

Damm them all! He cursed inwardly. They were showing their true colors. They had always resented his upstart wealth. His was not *old* money. Snatching a glass of champagne from a waiter's tray he sank it in one bitter swallow. His lips smacked, as though he had swallowed vinegar and not Krug, and he promptly returned the empty glass to the tray. He scanned the room in search of a friendly face, but by some peculiar happenstance every head was turned away and he felt solitude kick him in the gut. As always when on the defensive he took shelter behind cynicism. Drew's hypothesis was ludicrous. A dynasty. The very idea! Still, he had been right about one thing; there were indeed enough Kennedys to lock up the Presidency until 1984. Food for thought.

None of the Kennedy clan here tonight, thank God. They would be at Hyannisport, gathered like some ancient and separate race around the throne of the ailing old king, Joseph Kennedy. Paying homage to the man whose whelps held the fate of the most powerful nation on earth in their hands.

Couples filled the dancefloor, the mingled sounds of gaiety

enveloped him, and the bitter bile of being outcast cut something at the back of his throat. Impelled by his conspicuous isolation, he made for the dais where the flustered hostess and her helpers were working frantically. A net bulging with colored balloons was suspended from the ceiling, and they were loosening the tie ropes. Looking flushed, the hostess fiddled with the microphone, wincing as the amplifier beside her emitted a painful whine.

He stepped up onto the dais beside her. She returned his oily smile.

'You look exhausted,' he remarked with forced jollity.

Her response was cool. 'Thank God it only happens once a year.' Plainly she disliked him as much as ever. 'Did you ever see such a mess? There will be one heck of a cleaning job to be done in the morning.' Catching a rebellious strand of hair between two fingers, she impatiently threaded it behind her ear.

His smile broadened. He moved closer. 'If you ask me nicely I may volunteer to stay behind and help.'

She contracted, fractionally, as though afraid he might touch her, and when she looked sidelong at him a spark of contempt danced behind the fatigue in her eyes. 'Sorry darling, but I won't be here. Stringer's taking me to Italy tomorrow. But if you like I could put in a good word with the cleaning crew.'

The remark cut deep. He was straining to keep the unaffected smile on his face when she drove home the second blow. 'Where's your wife, darling?'

His stare broke. His eyes darted guiltily. 'She couldn't make it. She felt sick.'

'I can believe that,' she finished him off with acid charm, turning away before he could respond. But he was routed totally. As he stalked away she raised the microphone to her lips and warned the gathering that midnight was upon them.

The pompous pompous bitch! Biting down hard on his anger he shouldered a path through the revellers as they flooded onto the dancefloor. The noise had taken on substance, voices counting down in unison. '*TEN . . . NINE . . . EIGHT . . .*'

Abruptly he changed direction. He had to get away from there. Away from them . . . the fakes. The sons of bitches! '*FIVE . . . FOUR . . .*' Reaching the french windows he pushed them open as the tumultous roar, '*HAPPY NEW YEAR!!!!*' swelled behind him. He shut the windows to muffle the noise and sought the quiet of the terrace.

He found a low wall and sat upon it. The cold wind whistling across the landscaped gardens seemed to aim at him – and swoop. He pulled his jacket tighter about him and considered how ironic it was that he be on the outside, cold and alone on this, the most optimistic of nights, while indoors gaiety raged. The strains of Auld Lang Syne wafted from the big house, accompanied by peals of laughter and the sound of balloons popping. He snorted, to him the chorus sounded dirge-like. Funereal. A song about an ending. Reality was out on the terrace with him, being whipped by a rapaciously hostile wind.

Bitterly he lit a cigarette. As he puffed away he felt the jagged edges of his fury planed. He was a survivor, he reminded himself. A fighter. A winner.

As the thought struck him a particularly malignant gust of wind zeroed in on him. He shivered, and taking to his feet made for the shelter of the doorway. He was careful to avert his gaze. He was not ready to face the merriment that paraded indoors. He was not ready for that. Not yet.

He was cornered. He knew it and so did everyone else. He had bulldozed a path to the top, anger his mark, ruthlessness his style. Success had left him many enemies, and devoid of friends. He lacked the social infrastructure that might carry him through hard times. Now indoors a packed auditorium awaited his professional execution – or suicide. For a moment his guard was down, and despair lunged at the opportunity and almost took him. But in defiance he threw down his cigarette and forced himself to stare in through the window. It was useless to mope over the past. If he was bust, he was bust. Life had to go on, but he would go down fighting.

Pivoting abruptly he returned indoors. Once back amongst the noisy press he flung himself into the party spirit with a will, pecking ladies on the cheeks and shaking hands for all he was worth as he crossed the room, giving his own spirits a much needed lift in the process. Instinct guided him to the drawing room. He paused at the door to compose himself. The low murmur of masculine voices could be heard. Salvation lay beyond the door, he had decided, with the men of wealth. But he had to be confident, had to look the part. Taking a breath, he pushed open the door and entered.

In the crowded room an air of male propriety presided. In the hands of those gathered, the majority of whom were closer to seventy years than his youthful thirty-two, was preserved the real power in the State. The Brahmins. Old money. Financially and socially a buttressed elite, they sat on fat armchairs or stood in stoop shouldered groups, old men smoking Havana cigars and drinking fine Armagnac while discoursing on the decline of the nation. This was a Republican party, and though the new year was barely ten minutes infant the bile was already up for the party's favorite target; the Democrat President of the United States, John Fitzgerald Kennedy. Few glances were spared for the newcomer as he helped himself to a drink from a crystal decanter. Those who did recognise him frowned in disapproval; this was no place for failure to linger. But nothing was said and his presence was forgotten as a debate that flared in the centre of the room embraced the interest of those on the fringes. The newcomer watched from the periphery.

'To quote that old British king: Will no one rid me of this nuisance?' The speaker was Nathaniel Vincent, and the remarks brought hoots of clubbish laughter from the group. One man wagged a warning finger. 'Careful what you say, Nat. You know what happened there!' More laughter. The newcomer studied Vincent. The old man was sixty, squat and reptilian, with cold fish-eyes and a mouth never known to smile. His cutting wit and ruthlessness made him feared and respected, but not liked. He was a volatile, mercurial individual whose excesses were tolerated because his family had history. He had old boy status. A dangerous opportunist, his inclusion at such affairs was agreed upon with caution, the credence being it was safer to keep him where he could be watched. Vincent's steel plants had recently taken a financial pounding, the newcomer recalled, and the old man was rumoured to be in difficulty.

The newcomer was approached by one of the few young men in the room. He did not hide his surprise that the man should want to speak to him; being broke was like having a contagious disease amongst these people. Yet the fellow's handshake was firm, his smile wide. 'I heard about your trouble on Wall Street,' the man said through a brittle smile.

Hoping to minimise the damage, the newcomer shrugged. 'Just a temporary lack of confidence. I'd buy heavily if I were you – my luck's about to turn.'

The other looked at him sceptically. 'Are you up to something?' His eyes twinkled shrewdly as he probed for the con. There was a trace of smugness on his face, and the newcomer was reminded of the man's fondness for watching others squirm. 'Word is, the SEC will finish you for sure this time.'

The newcomer scowled. 'I know what I'm doing.'

'I've seen you stumble before – and bounce back, but this is serious. I just thought I'd let you know I'll be selling all my holdings before the bottom drops.' With a final, sly smile he drifted away.

Nathaniel Vincent's voice once more rose above the others. 'The son of a bitch is running us into the ground! And does he think I don't know why? I lost more in steel this last year than I made in the past five years!'

Another in the group, a tall, gaunt man with combed back silver hair that fell to his collar, intervened. 'Three times now we've lost face in full view of the whole world. And while young John's out at the nineteenth hole, partying with his Hollywood pals and telling the niggers they're as good as the whites, what's happening to the rest of us? I'll tell you: we're staring depression in the face. The worst since '29. And who'll get to bear the brunt of it? Why us of course, the goddam industrialists. The sons-of-bitches who keep the country moving!'

'Damm straight,' muttered a disgruntled Vincent. 'Craziest thing of all . . .' chipped in another, '. . . is that in Palm Beach, where he has a place, the segregation is the same as it ever was. The damm niggers get off the streets at sundown. The President doesn't mind them having their own restrooms and cinemas down there, boy, he just wants the rest of us to be equal.'

A sudden silence descended. The newcomer turned and saw that the hostess had entered the room. With her stood three men. One was an instantly recognisable movie star, his tanned face beaming glassily. The other two were swarthily complexioned, and each dressed in an expensive tuxedo. The smaller of them was in his fifties, and though he stood barely five feet tall, and was emaciated in appearance, he was plainly the leader. He emanated authority. In a calm sort of way he was menacing.

His colleague was a good twenty years younger, taller and with the handsome, elegant features typical of Mediterranean origin. His jet black hair was styled in the latest fashion, but it was his suit that shouted loudest. In contrast to the sober grey worn by his older companion, he wore a bold pinstripe with a waistcoat too loud to be anything less than a symptom of dandyism. A diamond clip shone on his wide tie and gold rings glittered on his fingers. His smile was gentle, but dangerous, and he had cold, shark's eyes that scanned the room with rapid flitting movements. Every inch the archetypical movie mobster.

The hostess cleared her throat, faintly embarrassed by the silence. She smiled as one who has made a social gaff might smile, and piped up: 'Gentlemen, three very welcome late arrivals. One,

I'm sure needs no introduction from me . . .' The Hollywood oaf beamed. Preened himself. '. . . and with him, just arrived from St Louis, Mr Giancarlo Giometri, and Mr John Rossi.'

Mention of the names sent a nervous murmur rippling through the gathering. His own interest piqued, the newcomer studied the two Latins as they circulated. Giometri and Rossi! Awed tension charged the atmosphere, and the newcomer had to smile. All these rich and powerful men phased because they were face to face with one of the best connected Mafia leaders in the United States, and his young henchman. St Louis was a long way away, mused the newcomer. What could have brought these two so far on a night traditionally given over to families? Then it was his turn to be introduced. He felt Giometri's small dry hand close about his own, felt the calm, watery eyes studying him with a frigid passivity. Then Rossi's grasp, warm and dangerous. The man was reputedly insane. He laughed at death. Challenged punks to try their luck against him at Russian roulette before he despatched them in gory style. His eyes glittered arrogantly, and in them the newcomer saw something unclean. He felt relief when the two men had moved on.

Introductions completed, the hostess guided her risque guests into the next room, and the Brahmins collectively heaved a sigh.

The tall man with the silvery mane, who had been discoursing so loudly earlier, appeared at the newcomer's side. 'Unusual taste in party guests our hostess has.'

The newcomer nodded. 'She has a rosy-eyed view of life on the other side of the tracks. All real life is to be found in Hollywood.'

The other man nodded, he had heard the rumours. 'Still, I expect her husband will be disappointed at her lack of discretion.' He moved away.

The two Italians returned with the movie star. Huddled over their drinks, they hovered on the edge of the group where Nathaniel Vincent still held court.

'If he gets that second term there'll be hell to pay in the south. Cuba's made him a lot of enemies and it's not going to go away.'

'Damm right!' A raucous southern drawl sounded from the back. 'There's a lot of nice little family casinos sitting empty right now. Castro wants his ass kicking off that island.'

A murmur of agreement greeted this last diatribe. Not knowing what reaction to expect, the newcomer glanced at the Italians and knew that though they were looking elsewhere, their attention was on the debate.

'Castro don't scare easily.' The single dissenting opinion in the room was rapidly quelled by a curtain of abuse.

'We don't scare either.' Vincent took up the mantle once more. 'I'm telling you the people who matter are getting tired of waiting. He's cutting the balls off anyone that wants to do this country any good. Are we expected to just sit back and let the Russians and the Chinese carve up Asia? We have the resources, I say let's get the Commies out of there. Damn the consequences, leave the place barren if we have to, just make sure Moscow and Peking get the message!'

It was only when Vincent finished speaking that the newcomer realised just how quiet the room had become. The group stood in rapt silence. A few looked uncomfortable; off the rein Vincent could be embarrassingly forthright, daring to speak what others only dared think.

Vincent glared around at the company, his stare inviting challenge and finding none. Then the full baleful force of his glare focused upon the newcomer. 'What are you looking at, boy?'

The newcomer felt himself shrivelling under the onslaught. He made good his exit, grateful to be out of there and away from that crazy old man.

The party had moved to the upper floors. The older guests had either gone home to bed, or were gathered in even more clubbish groups, playing cards, drinking hard. Younger partygoers were gathered in small rooms, jiving to a gramophone player, or taking refuge in the gardens, or the bedrooms. . . . The newcomer wandered, idly taking it all in. Turning into a room where he spied a liquor cabinet, he fell into conversation with a stunning brunette in a low cut tight dress. She ran a hand through her dark tresses and sipped at a brandy. 'Some party, huh?'

He nodded 'I've been to worse.' He raised his glass. 'Happy New Year.'

She smiled wanly. 'Here's to nineteen sixty three.' Her voice was velvety soft. He introduced himself. She nodded. 'I know who you are.' In response to his look of surprise she giggled, then went on to explain: 'A coupla years ago I was dating a Wall Street lawyer. He advised me to put money into the market. Some of the stock I bought was yours.' She mockingly waved a finger at him. 'You cost me a lot of money.'

He smiled. 'I hope you won't hold that against me . . . ?' he left a space for her to fill.

'Julie,' she purred. 'Julie Starr. I'm an actress.' she added. 'You may have seen me in *Life's a Dream*, last year.'

'I don't get to the movies much. Business, you know how it is.' He studied her, taking in her beauty. She was shapely, face narrow, her eyes set at an intriguing tilt had been accentuated by skillfully applied makeup.

'Are you here with someone?' he asked. She nodded, mentioning Todd Fletcher, the Hollywood star he had seen earlier, then added: 'But he's just bearding me.'

'Excuse me?'

'A beard. You know, an escort there to cover for the married man I'm really with?'

'Oh, I see. Am I allowed to know who he's bearding for, or is it a secret?'

'I guess it doesn't matter really. It's Giancarlo.' She took a deep swig from her glass. She had dropped the bombshell for maximum effect, and enjoyed seeing his reaction.

'You mean Giancarlo Giometri, the. . . .'

'The Mafia boss. Yes. Does that bother you?'

'I don't know. Should it?'

'Maybe. A lot of men get scared when I tell them that.'

'So why are you down here alone?'

She grimaced. 'With Carlo, business always comes first.' She drained her glass. 'Will you pour me another drink?'

He smiled. 'Sure, that is, if you don't think you've had enough.'

She pulled a tart face. 'It's New Years Eve, and I'm standing here miles from home, talking to a complete stranger. I intend to get well and truly smashed. You can join me or you can go to hell.'

He nodded once more. 'What are you drinking?'

'Vodka, anything. Got a cigarette? What are you doing here, no family?'

'None worth mentioning. I guess if I'm honest I'd say I didn't want to be alone.' She sipped from the refilled glass. Pouted her rosebud lips. 'Poor baby.' Moving forward she kissed him with her full soft lips, taking him by surprise. He inhaled her perfume, the heady mix of cigarette smoke and Chanel, and felt moved. 'I guess no one likes to be lonely.'

Within an hour they were in a darkened room, making frenzied love. She straddled him, and he watched her silhouette as she raised a glass to her lips and tilted back her head. She let the drained glass drop with a thud to the carpet, and lowered herself, letting her dark tresses brush his face. 'How was I?'

His chest was heaving from the exertion. His body was coated with a fine sheen of perspiration. He gasped. 'Brilliant. Perfect!' He had a feeling she was smiling in the blackness. She clambered off him, pulled on her panties and started to slither into her dress. 'I better be going.'

He levered himself up onto one elbow and switched on the bedside lamp. He studied her, his heart still pounding. 'Will I see you again? I'd like to see you again.'

She ducked to peer into the dresser mirror and arranged her hair. She said, absently: 'That might be difficult. Carlo can be so jealous. He's on the move all the time and he likes me to be available.'

'But there must be times when you can get away. What if you're making a movie?'

Digging into her purse she uncapped her lipstick and deftly coated her lips. 'There's always someone. Listen . . .' turning to him, she peered earnestly into his eyes '. . . It was lovely. You were great . . . why don't we just leave it at that. I have to dash.' She planted a kiss on his lips and turned for the door. He loosed a laugh. 'I don't believe this.'

At the door she glanced back at him. His laughter was infectious, she smiled. 'What?'

'I actually feel used.' At that she did laugh. 'Now there's a change. See ya.'

Once she had gone, leaving only the trace of her perfume in the air, he lay flat on his back. The room grew chilly, and he drew a crumpled sheet over his naked body. From somewhere in the great house a clock chimed, the sound reverberating. Through the window he heard sounds of laughter, and gathering the sheet about him he crossed to the window and parted the curtains. Below in the gardens he saw a group chattering on the landscaped terrace. He was reminded that this was not his house, and he had no idea whose bed he had been using. In the lamplight he dressed, then opened the door and stepped onto the carpeted landing.

Down the long spiral staircase he descended to the ground floor. He strolled, peering into different rooms where the few remaining guests were gathered in late night cliques. Cigar smoke tainted the air. His mind was in a whirl. Whatever else happened, he knew he had to see her again. Finally he caught up with Todd Fletcher. A lean and bronzed individual who sported swept back blonde hair and wore a stylish tux, the movie idol stepped from one of the rooms, gently closing the door behind him. He and the newcomer knew each other slightly, and engaged in light conversation. The movie star's eyes were glassy, from drink or drugs, and his conversation was animated. 'You got anything important to do. You going home?'

'Not yet. Why? You got something going?'

'Party. We have a private aircraft waiting. Giancarlo's parties go on for days. You wanna come along?'

'Sure.' Inwardly our man was gleeful. He might get to see her again. He was curious to know how she would behave in the company of others. What spell did the ageing gang boss hold over her?

'Come on,' Todd summoned him. 'I have to get the coats.'

Between them they ferried a dozen thick overcoats, including a sumptuous mink, from the drawing room to the reception room where the mafia boss and his group, including her, awaited. Todd held out the mink for Julie to slip into, then she turned, and the newcomer saw the momentary flash of horror and uncertainty dart across her face as she recognised him. Giometri scowled as his stony gaze fell upon the newcomer, but Todd glossed over his sudden appearance by introducing him as an old friend. Giometri held out a hand, his rheumy eyes flinty hard as they bored. His grasp was hard and dry.

'Nice to meet you . . .' the newcomer said, swallowing the hard lump nervousness had propelled to his throat. 'What do you like to be called? Giancarlo? Johnny? Carlo?'

The voice that replied was savage with contempt. 'How about Mister Giometri,' he rasped.

The small man brushed past the newcomer, leaving him shaken to his toes. Coats were donned. John Rossi swaggered by, mouth warped into a cruel sneer. Then Todd was at the newcomer's side. He was sweating. 'What the fuck are you doing? You can't jerk these guys off like that. You're likely to be taking a walk in concrete shoes.'

The newcomer smiled 'C'mon, you sound as though you're reading a bad script.'

'Laugh all you like, pal. It's your neck. Just as long as you know these guys are from the old school. They value respect.' He pulled on his own coat. 'Come on, the aircraft will be waiting.'

They piled into one of two waiting Cadillacs and were ferried the four miles to the nearest airstrip. The newcomer sat next to Todd, who, for safety's sake gave him a rundown on who was who and what behaviour was permissible. 'Giancarlo likes to be addressed by his surname. Only his very closest friend call him anything else. He's Top Don, up there with Carlos Marcello and Santos Trafficante. He's close to Hoffa. Tremendously powerful. He's a bad man to have against you.

'Johnny Rossi is a killer. A fucking psychopath. He'll rub you out if he doesn't like the way you ask him for the time. He likes to draw people into crazy games. Likes to play with people. The best advice I can give you is keep him at a distance. You can get hurt.'

'If they are so dangerous, how come you're mixing with them?'

Todd opened a gold cigarette case and lit up. The newcomer could not help but admire the man's elegance. Graciously he smiled. 'I have family connections.'

Realisation dawned on the newcomer. 'That's right, your wife's family.'

Todd nodded. Inhaled and exhaled. 'That and my Hollywood image ought to be protection enough. But apart from that, if you want to know why I hang around with them, it's because they're good people. Lots of fun.'

'Are you serious?'

'Oh yeah. They're exciting. In the movies I get to play guys like them, and for most people watching that movie is as close as they'll ever get. But I get to hang out with the real McCoy. It's fun.'

The flight to the west coast was arduous, but when they landed in Los Angeles and were driven to a private palatial house, the partying began in earnest. The newcomer was shown to a room with a sea view. He showered, then on an impulse decided to call home. His wife, the bitch, for all her faults, was entitled to know where he was. Business had called him away, he battled to explain against the tide of abuse and vindictiveness that flowed down the telephone line. It was with relief he was able to replace the receiver. He did not give her a contact number. There came a knock on the door and Todd entered. 'Hiya buddy. How are you doing?'

'I'm fine, except for the fact I've only the clothes I arrived in. When I went to the party last night I was expecting to go home afterwards.'

'I'll have one of the boys take you into town. You can pick out a suit.'

'On New Years Day? Will there be anywhere open?'

'For Giancarlo the shops open on a telephone call. You can

put the suit on my account.' He good naturedly raised a finger. 'But you owe me.'

'Why are you doing all this?' the newcomer asked. 'Last night at the party I got the cold shoulder from just about everyone except you – or haven't you heard my news?'

'About your business? I heard. Let's just say that maybe I know what it's like to be on the outside. Be ready in thirty minutes. I'll have a car waiting.'

Once more alone, the newcomer towelled dry his hair. He found a thick bathrobe in a wardrobe and donned it. There came a knock at the door. He opened it to find Julie standing in the corridor, an anxious look on her face. She did not wait for an invitation but pushed past him. 'Close the door.'

He did as bid. 'Well, this is a nice surprise. What ever happened to hello?'

She rounded on him. 'What on earth do you think you're doing? Do you have any idea what you're risking? What you could do to me?'

'I just got invited to a party.'

'I'm not stupid. I've had this trouble with men before. Why couldn't you just leave well alone? All we did was fuck, for Christ's sake! Why does it have to be such a big deal?'

She put her head on her hands and turned away. 'Why was I so stupid? I'm going to ruin it. You're going to ruin everything!'

Stepping nearer, he placed his hands on her shoulders. She juddered, then relaxed, turning into his embrace.

'I'm sorry,' he cooed. 'I just wanted to see you again.'

She looked up into his face. 'Well you musn't. Understand me, I've worked hard to get where I am. Carlo can open doors for me and I won't risk that.'

He swallowed. 'Okay . . . I promise I won't spoil things for you.'

'Promise?'

'You have my word.'

She produced a handkerchief from a sleeve and dabbed dry her eyes. Then after a quick look in the mirror she walked to the door. Watching her rapid recovery he shook his head; sure he'd been taken, somehow. 'Can I see you again?'

She paused, hand on the door knob. 'I'll be at the party tonight. You'll see me there.'

His face was a mask of bewilderment. 'You really are some piece of work, you know that? You suckered me. You're quite an actress.'

She smiled, said: 'Why, thank you.' And then was gone.

The party that night was a success. The newcomer, knowing that the problem of his dwindling fortunes could not be solved, put the difficulties to the back of his mind and concentrated on enjoying himself. He and Julie had no more than the fleetest contact, instead he found himself being drawn into a different world. He sat in on conversations made up of veiled references, his presence accepted on the basis that he was a friend of Todd Fletcher. He became intrigued by Giometri, the enigma, and the empire over which he ruled.

Other men arrived, paid their respects and departed. Card games were played, and the days merged into a blur. Girls were available. Beautiful girls. Experienced girls. And the newcomer acquired a taste for a world he had never known existed. He stood on the fringes of real power and felt its intoxicating influence.

Then, on the third night, he left his bed and the blonde sleeping in it. He walked downstairs and stepped onto the enclosed terrace into an atmosphere charged with tension. Voices were raised, insults and warnings traded. The lights were low, bottles littered a table, and the air was heavy with the taint of cigar smoke. But when his shadow fell into the room the noise stopped dead, and hostile stares were directed at him. He looked around, nervous, sure he'd stumbled into something he was not supposed to know about.

From the group stepped forward Todd Fletcher. 'Hi . . .' he began, glancing anxiously about him. 'We er . . . we all thought you'd gone to bed. Is there something wrong with Kitty?'

'No, she's asleep.'

'Whoa,' Todd feigned enthusiasm. 'Way to go. She's a girl who can take it. Some guy, huh?' He glanced around, looking for a decision.

'Todd,' a grizzled voice rang out from a darkened corner. 'Why don't you explain to your friend that this is a private meeting?'

Todd nodded nervously. 'Sure Vinny.'

The newcomer held up his hands. 'I'm sorry, I didn't mean to intrude.' He started to back away, but was halted by a word from Giancarlo Giometri. 'Wait a minute.'

The newcomer paused. Giometri took a fat cigar from his mouth and with a half turn of his head addressed both the gathering and the newcomer. 'He's okay. Get a drink and take a seat.'

He found a seat close to the door. Todd brought him a bourbon and settled beside him. The disgruntled murmuring continued, but soon the newcomer's presence was forgotten.

Against a background of raised voices, Todd whispered. 'Boy, are you one lucky son of a bitch! Giancarlo has been watching you these past days. He's asked a lot of questions. He must like what he heard.'

'Who are all these people?' the newcomer whispered back.

Todd paused, an arcane smile drifted onto his face. 'A fraternity, of sorts, a kind of informal club. Ordinarily their paths wouldn't cross, but they all play golf and afterwards they drink together. Believe me, the mix you have here would make sensational news copy, if a couple of high powered newspaper owners, editors and TV execs weren't on the fringes too. You see him over there . . . ? That's Max Valentino, the crooner. And the guy drinking from the brandy bottle? He's Dino Wise, the TV comic. The smoothie in the shiny suit, he's CIA. Used to be in the OSS during the war. Liaised between the military and the crooks hired for their specialist skills. Now he runs weapons to Cuban emigres. The guy with the square head and the crew cut, he's an admiral with a liking for young girls. Giancarlo can provide.'

'Jesus, an admiral. What am I getting into here?'

'Well look at it this way. He's a strong active man whose wife happens to be trapped in a wheelchair. He does not love her less for that, but he does have needs. No one gets hurt, so what does it matter?'

The newcomer did not answer. He was distracted, staring at the comedian, Dino. Watching the man's antics on television recently, he had laughed until he cried. It was not easy to reconcile that memory with the image of the drunken figure slumped in the chair opposite.

Todd reached under his chair and produced a bourbon bottle. He refilled his glass and raised it to the newcomer in a toast. 'Welcome to the underbelly, my friend. To life under the stone.'

The debating continued heatedly. The newcomer absorbed references he thought he understood, but did not want to believe. Talk of business. Of removing a menace.

A vindictive tone crept into the proceedings. Finally, when there came a lapse in the conversation, he chanced a question. He had to know. 'Who are they talking about?' he whispered to Todd, getting quietly drunker at his side. With the whisper the silence became complete; he had spoken too loudly. Todd was too far over the edge. He stared dully at the floor. The newcomer glanced up to find every stare in the room upon him. Todd slurred something incomprehensible, and another voice muttered something about the newcomer minding his business, but Giometri cut in:

‘That’s okay. I’ll answer the question.’ He looked directly into the newcomer’s eyes, and the man felt the fear return.

‘You want to know who we’re talking about?’ No response was forthcoming, just that terrified gaze.

‘Well I’ll tell you.’ The Italian hissed. ‘We’re talking about that fuck in the White House!’

* 3 *

One month later.

President Kennedy ended his speech on a typically dramatic, analogous note, and drew back the forthright thrust of his head. He beamed as the vast auditorium swelled with the sound of rapturous applause, then stood back from the podium and characteristically patted a side pocket as though checking for some item. Ushered by his aides he turned along the aisle and hastened down the steps from the stage. His path was corridored by serried ranks of outstretched hands, each and every one of them straining for a handshake, or at least a talismanic contact from this most enigmatic, most magical of men. Touching as many palms as he could he descended to the ground, then he was gone, shepherded away to a waiting limousine.

His departure began a vast migratory shift in the auditorium. Hundreds filtered towards the exits, but in a row high up at the rear a small knot of men remained seated. In the centre of this small group, disgruntled but calm, sat Nathaniel Vincent. He was deep in thought, gaze aimed intently at the distant stage. He awaited the return of a messenger, a man sent to seek help for the ailing Vincent company. Around him, his gathered aides eyed him warily, tuned to mirror his every shift in mood and react accordingly. But the smouldering vindictiveness of the man was never far below the surface, and even the calmest of his aides felt uneasy.

At last the messenger was sighted, ascending the steep slope of the aisle. The errand he had been sent on was vital to the survival of the Vincent Company, but from the downcast set of his head it was plain he was not returning triumphant. Halting before the old man, he raised his head to meet the stare and felt himself shrivelling before the baleful intensity of it.

'Well?' Vincent gruffly demanded. 'I . . . I tried . . .' the man stammered. 'But it did no good. They're not listening.'

The old man drew in a breath that swelled his chest and infused his frown with renewed ferocity. 'Did you speak to him personally, or one of his flunkies?'

The man looked apologetic. He shuffled from foot to foot.

'I couldn't get past Salinger's office, but it was made clear the decision originated at the top. Project Pontoon is a no-go. It doesn't matter how low you set your tenders, you're going to bust. He said to pardon the pun.'

The old man's face was a mask of fury. Abruptly he snapped orders. 'Get this man a last paycheck and have the airplane made ready. We go home tonight. And call the plant; shut it all down. There's nothing to be done now.' Heaving his bulk out of the chair with an effort, he turned to leave. Like multiple shadows the group followed, one by one passing the dismissed man without a glance. Unable to comprehend that he was suddenly out of a job and hundreds of miles from home, he gaped helplessly after them until the very last man was passing him.

He grasped at his arm. 'Jim . . . Jim, you have to help me.'

There was desperation on his face. 'What about Lois? The new house? You know how extended I am?' Meeting indifference he dried up. The man, whom five minutes earlier he would have called a friend, would not now even look at him.

'Help me . . .' It was an involuntary utterance. Jim pulled free his arm and without a backward glance followed the others.

The distraught man clapped a hand to the back of his head. 'How am I going to get home?' His anguished cry rang feebly in the vast open space.

'Greyhound bus,' called out a joker in the pack. Cruel laughter pealed.

The last man in the auditorium collapsed onto a seat, placed his head on his hands, and wept.

Houston.

Nathaniel Vincent paced uneasily. The boardroom on the fifth floor of his company headquarters had been the scene of many triumphs as he struggled to construct one of the nation's largest producers of steel from the tiny foundry he had inherited from his father. But now, as he paced the thick pile carpet, surrounded by oak panelled walls on which hung priceless paintings, he was nervous. The company was in trouble, the meeting scheduled for later that day was going to be difficult, and for once he was not sure his iron will would be enough to prevail.

At the window he gazed down at the car park and recognised a brand new Cadillac parked by the entrance. The owner of the car, an old friend and major shareholder in Vincent's company would be on his way up.

Vincent felt tired. He was sixty now, he ought to be thinking of retiring while he still had a few good years left. Instead he was fighting for financial survival. He looked inside himself for inspiration, and found none. He was not sure he had much fight left in him.

The Cadillac belonged to an old friend. Martin Lowther was a partner in a brokerage firm on Wall Street, successful, but not glamorous, and he penned a weekly column in the financial pages. His family creed had been '*Prudence Pays*' and for him it certainly had. He had cultivated a knack for knowing when to put money into a venture – and when to take it out. To many in the city, to the even more prudent institutional investors, the banks and insurance companies who owned major portions of many companies, he was viewed as a barometer to the health of a company. If he was bringing the news Vincent thought he was bringing, then Vincent Steel was going to go under. The thought was a bitter one.

The door opened and Martin Lowther entered. He was small and slim, with thinning dark hair and piercing brown eyes. He wore a cheerful face, and greeted Vincent with a firm handshake, and as always he was dressed casually. Something of a maverick, his writings were often critical of a financial world where irreverence was something that attracted extreme disapproval, but he was so often right he had become a name to be respected, a pundit to be listened to, and a man whose opinions were feared by the financially unsound.

Vincent warmly returned the greeting and offered a drink.

Lowther drank only seltzer, and Vincent made it his business to ensure his favorite brand was always available. As he watched Lowther sip, Vincent decided on a strategy of bluff. He had to find some way to persuade his old friend to write a glowing piece about Vincent Steel. Something subtle, but strong enough to take the edge off the fears expressed by the banks. His mind worked quickly, desperate for a solution.

Lowther began the conversation. 'So, Nathaniel, how is business?'

Vincent beamed. 'Fine. We just pulled off a large European order. Not a word to anyone, but . . .' he tapped the side of his nose with a fingertip, '. . . It will mean substantial expansion.'

Lowther grinned 'Save the crap for the board, Nat. Vincent Steel is about to go belly up.'

Vincent frowned. He considered trying to continue the bluff, but the look on Lowther's face told him that to do so would be pointless. 'It's not like you to gloat.'

Lowther put out a hand and gave Vincent's arm a squeeze. 'I'm not here to gloat, my friend.'

'So what does bring you here? No, don't tell me, I think I can guess. You've decided to unload your stock. I can't say I blame you, our financial position is bad, but you know as well as I do what the result will be once word is out you sold at the current price. Vincent Steel will fold, and I will be finished.'

'I don't have to sell just yet, but I have a question, and I need an honest answer from you. You have a ten million dollar interest payment due in nine days. Do you have any hope of meeting it?'

Vincent inhaled, then deflated. 'Not a hope. The well is dry.'

'So whether I sell or not is irrelevant to the future of the company. By selling today, or tomorrow, I would merely be accelerating the inevitable.'

Vincent was defeated. 'I suppose so.'

Lowther left a pause. He had finished his seltzer and was staring into his empty glass. Vincent suddenly remembered his manners and offered a refill. While he was pouring, Lowther stroked his chin as if deep in thought.

'What you need, Nat, is a new line of credit.'

Vincent dropped an ice cube into the seltzer and handed over the drink. 'There are lots of things I need. A new line of credit is just the most improbable.'

'No, hear me out. You need a new line of credit. Some kind of revolving fund large enough to retire your existing arrangements and give your credibility a boost. News like that would refresh your share price.'

'There's no doubt about that, but where would I find a bank crazy enough to give it to me?'

Lowther levelled his gaze. 'I know of one.' He left another pause. Vincent's head jerked up as he snapped alert. Had he heard correctly? Lowther continued talking, his tone measured and deliberate.

'Suppose I could get you all the money you needed. The question I've been asked to put to you is this: how badly do you want to save the company? How far will you go?'

Vincent swallowed the knot that had swollen in his throat. Martin Lowther was not a man to joke about such a thing. If he said he knew a bank crazy enough to save Vincent Steel, then that bank existed. 'I . . . er, I guess I would go pretty far. Dammit Martin, I'd do anything.' The pause was infuriating. Vincent snarled: 'Goddam it, what do I have to do?' Then he laughed. 'Who do I have to kill?' A wave of relief doused him; he could sense salvation. He grasped Lowther by the shoulders. 'Can you do this, can you really do this? Who is it, who is it, which bank?'

Lowther's face was pink. He was faintly embarrassed. 'Yes, the money is there. One hundred million dollars, if you can make Vincent Steel fit the bill.'

For Vincent the first alarm bells rang. He was prepared to ignore them, but he had to ask. 'Okay, just let me calm down some.' His husky voice levelled. 'Listen Martin, I know there are bound to be conditions, but I have to know. Where is the money coming from?'

'From a Lebanese bank interested in purchasing a foothold in an American company.'

Vincent grimaced. 'What do you mean, Arab money?'

'The money comes from many places. It ends up in the Lebanon and comes to you via a bank in the Caribbean basin. Also, before you get too high minded, you ought to bear in mind that there is not a bank in America that will touch you. This is a last resort, but it is also a last chance.'

'You don't mind my asking? It's nice to be offered a chance for survival, but I needed to know.'

'That's quite alright. You had a right to ask. You asked about the conditions, well of course there are some. You can receive the money in ten instalments of ten million dollars over the next year. In exchange you must let a man of their choice assume the post of Chief Executive.'

Vincent's response was immediate. 'No, dammit, no! I built up this company from a draughty blacksmith's shop into the third largest operation of its kind. I will not give up control.'

'Nat, Nat, will you calm down. This is not what you think. They want you to stay as Chairman of the Board, but you have to accept a new hand at the helm. You know it. It is the very least an American bank would expect in the circumstances, and without it, frankly, there will be no deal, and you know the consequence of that.'

'Let me talk to them. Let me deal direct. I can make them see my point of view.'

'That is not going to happen, Nat. If you want this deal you have to accept that it comes with strings. I asked what you would do to save the company. All you have to tell me is yes, or no.'

Vincent inhaled, deeply, mind in a whirl at the thought. One hundred million dollars! A way out! Another chance! But his cautious side called out a warning. What would it all cost?

'What are the other terms? Repayment schedule, terms, interest rates, what time scale?'

Lowther shook his head. 'That, I do not know. I will simply pass back your answer. I imagine that if you agree there will be another contact.'

Vincent nodded. In his mind, conflicting thoughts battled for prominence. He desperately wanted to ask the right questions, but to buy time, to stall, he smiled, gave a little shrug. 'I must admit, Martin, at my age I thought nothing could ever surprise me again.'

Lowther agreed. 'I felt the same way when I heard. If you don't mind my saying so, Nat, this could just be the opportunity you are looking for. In your position I'd grab it.'

'Why you, Martin? Why ask you to come?'

'The answer to that would seem to be pretty obvious. I have some small influence, I know you, and they thought that coming from me you would accept the offer as genuine. And of course, I do have a financial stake in the company.' Seeing Vincent tangled in a web of indecision, Lowther decided to prompt him 'Nat, you've always been a shrewd man. Your negotiating skills have never been in doubt. Agree to the terms. Once you get into the clinches you know you'll be able to mould the deal to suit yourself. What do you say?'

One last moment of anxiety, and Vincent took the plunge. Grasping Lowther by the hand, he firmly shook on the deal. The tide of relief left him perspiring heavily under his expensive suit. He was glad to have it all behind him. God, that had been hard.

While Vincent was at the small bar pouring drinks of celebration, Lowther watched him. His eyes glittered. So far so good, the columnist made a mental note. His part was done. The rest was up to the others. . . .

* 4 *

Nathaniel Vincent was at his desk, poring over company reports. They made dismal reading; five major plants closed, two more teetering on the brink of shutdown. But all of that suddenly did not matter anymore. The contracts had been signed. He had the money. Vincent Steel, the colossus he had built from the dirt, was saved. He had stared over the dark precipice into the depths of disaster, and been pulled back from the edge. Life was sweet, and he savoured the taste.

Years of politicking and business in-fighting had left him with a near-perpetual scowl, which now intensified as the intercom on his desk buzzed. He jabbed at the answer button. 'What is it?'

'Mr Vincent . . .' the voice of his secretary piped from the speaker. 'The gentleman you are expecting is here.'

He swallowed, suddenly nervous. The moment had arrived. Inhaling deeply, he told his secretary to escort his visitor in; the man had to be shown respect.

Before signing, and knowing his position was weak, he had insisted upon knowing the name of the man to whom he was effectively assigning control of his company. It was a risk, but he reasoned that anyone willing to unlimber their wallets to the tune of one hundred million dollars for what amounted to a slice of Vincent Steel, must want that slice pretty badly. The name had duly been supplied, and for one hundred million dollars and the saving of Vincent Steel, and, dammit, the saving of his face, he had been forced to sign away a virtual mountain of stock. If push came to shove, he knew, his greatest fear would be realised and he would lose control. And that was something he could not bear even to think about. Vincent Steel was his creation, his alone, and giving up that stock had been the hardest morsel to swallow. But he had a plan in mind, and had that very afternoon instructed his brokers to start buying Vincent stock on the exchange. They were to buy, with utmost discretion and through intermediaries, as much stock as they could lay their hands on. He would be in hock to his eyebrows, but he had to win back control. No one, no matter how desperate he became, could be allowed to have a hold over him. He had worked too hard to be beaten now. . . .

The man who entered the office was a little over six feet tall, slim and dark haired. He wore a bright smile and he met Vincent with a firm handshake. Vincent, upon learning the name of the man who was to replace him as Chief Executive, had ordered research done, and read the prepared file from cover to cover. The visitor too had built up a business from modest beginnings. A brokerage house that had enjoyed success. Recently he had suffered a run of bad luck, or bad business, and there had been hints of scandal, illegal trading. His name had been cleared, but his business had been forced to close. Vincent could not work out why this man, of all those available, had been selected to run Vincent Steel, a business he plainly knew nothing about.

As they shook hands and exchanged smiles, each gauged the other. The old man peered hard at the other's face and was struck by the familiarity of it. 'I know your face . . .' he said with quiet force. 'No, don't tell me. Let me . . . got it! New Years Eve, The Hendersons' place!'

'Quite correct, Mr Vincent.'

'Well this is a surprise. I hadn't put a face to the name. I was reading about your little problem with the SEC, and frankly I was surprised at your inclusion in this deal. Given your recent record I would have thought you'd be the last man on earth to be offered a job like this.'

The other man settled on a chair. 'But you must have come to some conclusion.'

The old man's voice verged on the hoarse. 'I can only conclude you have some connection with the bankers, and used it to set yourself up. Let me warn you now, if I see you driving my company to the wall I guarantee I will find a way to get rid of you. It won't matter a damn to me whose bed you shared to get this job, I will destroy you, and believe me I make a powerful enemy.' Vincent habitually used his gruffness as a weapon to unbalance others and gain the higher ground.

The newcomer was not perturbed. 'I think I can assure you there are no worries on that front. I want success as much as anyone.'

The old man continued to stare hard at the younger man. His arrogance might be enough to save the company, he sensed, but he still had to probe . . . 'Why are you interested in coming here? What makes you think there is any future to be had?'

'I've studied and admired you and the way you have built up Vincent Steel. The company stands as a model of mid-twentieth century success. I know things have been hard recently, but I have a gut feeling that the best is yet to come. As to the future, well, I watch the world, and I see all the unease that is out there, and I remind myself that business is a cyclical entity and that history, if it proves nothing else, proves that windows of opportunity will always open to those who stand prepared.'

He continued speaking, his voice silky smooth. 'It may be the demise of Vincent Steel is inevitable. Your plants are poorly sited, relatively speaking, and the competition from similar plants in California is strangling you. Put simply; the times are against you, and that is why you failed.'

This calculated slur struck a nerve. Vincent exploded: 'Failed? Preposterous!' he bellowed, almost forced from his seat by the heat of his anger. 'Take a look around you, look at these offices, the plants. If this is failure, what do I have to do to succeed? Business is about to turn, so help me. All I needed from your friends was a lifeline, and that is exactly what I got.'

In sharp contrast to Vincent's volatility, the visitor was impassive. 'Don't bust a gut, Mr Vincent. You don't have to impress me. I have read the secret reports. I know the truth. The market for your steel is shrinking fast as you lose ground to the Californians. The recent labor disputes have left you vulnerable. You have two plants operating where previously you had seven, and your cashflow last week would not have covered your wage bill. You would have been dead by the end of the month.'

Vincent's shoulders dipped, pretence pointless. It hurt that others knew how exposed he had been.

The newcomer changed the subject by asking for a drink. Vincent led him to the bar in the corner and the newcomer studied the bottles arrayed there. 'Interesting selection. I'll take a scotch rocks please.'

'You want out of steel production alone, and into other areas. No, for Vincent Steel, the time to diversify could not be better.'

Vincent mumbled something about just getting his head off the block, adding: 'I'll be looking for opportunities. My only regret is the early tooling up we did for Pontoon. Still, we may be able to offload the plant.'

The newcomer nodded in sympathy. 'That,' he declared firmly, 'is the very last thing we should do.'

Vincent glanced at him, gaze cutting. 'What are you up to?' The old man poured the drinks, then passed one to his guest.

The newcomer held the glass beneath his nose and inhaled. 'Nice.' He savoured his first sip before speaking again. 'Tell me about the feud between you and Joe Kennedy.'

The question came like a dagger thrust under the heart, taking

Vincent by surprise. His habitual scowl intensified. 'What has that to do with anything?'

'You own a small munitions plant, yes?' Vincent agreed.

The newcomer continued: 'You were banking on getting a slice of Project Pontoon. A contract of that size would have solved many of your financial problems.'

The newcomer was smooth. With subtlety he had manoeuvered the conversation until it was he leading the way.

Vincent was cornered, his questions becoming defensive responses. 'So?'

In a voice that was silky, the other said: 'So, I know the attitude of the President during the labor crisis drove you almost to a coronary.'

Vincent spat. 'That whelp! He's as poisonous as his old man!' Vincent felt the burn of anger in his gut. The visitor was goading him. He contained his ire by planting his hands in his jacket pockets and bunching them into fists. 'It's no secret we hate each other's guts. What of it?'

'I find the two of you interesting. So alike, both starting from fairly humble beginnings to build business empires worth millions. You are the type of men who might ordinarily find each other's company desirable, yet you do not. I want to know why.'

'It's not relevant.'

'It's a factor. If not for him, you might have gotten the slice of Pontoon you wanted, you might have avoided signing away great chunks of the company.'

'. . . Yeah, yeah, and Joe's brat shot me down. You think I don't know the old man's behind it? He wants me on my knees, the son of a bitch.' Vincent's gruff voice rose in hoarse pitch as he attempted to browbeat the other. 'What is all this? I signed a banking contract with your Arab friends, and that's the end of it. Your presence here is something I will have to live with, but that's as far as your involvement goes.'

The newcomer remained unfazed. 'I don't see it quite that way, but let's not argue over semantics. I think you'll find I have some good ideas. I'm sure that together we can turn Vincent Steel around. . . .'

'And no offence to you . . .' Vincent blustered, 'But I won't be needing your ideas. I got this far by myself and I intend to go on doing just the same.' He approached the newcomer, who stood half-a-head taller, and stared up into his smiling face. 'I read about you. You like the high life. Why don't you stay home and collect your salary? I won't tell if you don't.'

The newcomer smirked 'What if I were to say you did not have to waste all that tooling up you did?' The old man's ears pricked up. He sensed something. . . .

The newcomer, seeing that he had gotten through, continued patiently weaving his web. 'And what if I were to say we could have a slice of Pontoon after all. Not the scraps you were hoping for, but a major slice. Would you be interested then in hearing my ideas?'

'You already know the answer to that, but I doubt you could deliver on it.'

'I understand your scepticism, so let me tempt you further. What if I say we have a chance to turn the Vincent Company into one of the largest defense contractors in the country. Would you call that delivering? What would that be worth to you?'

The old man licked his lips. Did the smug bastard know something, he asked himself, quickly deciding that the newcomer did. 'It would be worth a lot,' he admitted in a broken voice. 'And you know it.' He cleared his throat: 'Go on.'

The newcomer took his time now. Playing. 'And just suppose,' he teased, 'that as a bonus, I could arrange to tear the heart out of Joe Kennedy for you. Ruin him at a time when he believes he finally has it all. Would that interest you even more?'

Vincent's eyes narrowed. He had long ago learnt not to rush into commitment – however tempting the offer. There was no such thing as a free lunch! He forced his face into a mask of heavy jowled scepticism. 'Possibly, but I'm not so sure you could do it. I'm no fool, certainly you're no smarter than I am. I can't imagine you finding a way to beat Joe that I haven't already tried.'

'You're right. I am no smarter than you. So for now let's just say you are humouring me. Tell me about the feud between you and Joe.'

'Why?' Vincent was not the type of man who allowed his weaknesses to show. The secret would have to be prised from him.

The visitor hesitated barely a second. 'I'm interested in knowing what set you at each other's throats. I know you worked together in the 'thirties. You must have been reasonably close. What happened between you?'

At length Vincent sighed, a weary, rusty sound. When he spoke his voice was softer, but still reluctant. 'It's a very long story that stretches back to the end of prohibition. I was bright and pushy, he was already wealthy. We did some work together. I had a few ideas, he helped me with them. Property mainly. It was the depression, and there was money to be made if a man was smart enough to see the openings. Joe was sharp, and cunning, and a lot more ruthless than I ever was. He made my ideas work better than I could myself. In fact, if I was being brutally honest, I would have to admit that to some extent I rode on his coat tails. We were never great friends, so don't get any ideas about that, but we did socialise. Being Irish meant there were doors closed to him, no matter how rich he was. Just as if he were Jewish, or black. My background may have been humble, but it was the kind that found acceptance. So I guess you could argue he used me too.

'At first there was a friendly rivalry between us; when it came to business, to women, a particular woman, but eventually the rivalry became serious, and . . . How can I say this? Do you know what happened? How it all ended?'

'All I know is that each time the two of you have clashed you've gotten savaged. And now, while he enjoys almost unassailable wealth, even though he is in a wheelchair, you have just avoided Chapter Eleven by the skin of your teeth.'

Vincent was suddenly weary. He was not sure exactly how he had allowed himself to be drawn out, but the words were coming, and kept on coming, in a cathartic outpouring. 'I had an idea I proposed to a small syndicate. Joe took it and made millions. Well, that was it. A barrier of bitterness grew up between us and never healed. Each year we didn't speak the rift grew wider, until there was no way back.'

'You never did marry?'

Vincent shook his head. 'That was probably the bitterest issue between us. . . . A woman he could have, but I could not.'

'But still,' the visitor declared, 'you didn't do badly. You built all this.' He gestured at the window. Beyond could be seen the expanses of office buildings, massed sprawlings of steel plant and acres of parking lot. 'And there will be more.'

Vincent mulled over all that had been said. When he spoke it was in a measured tone. 'What is all this about? Are you telling me you can deliver Pontoon, despite everything the President has said, despite the competition from the major contractors, the corporations who have spent years building up good relationships with the appropriation boys at The Pentagon? That's a large pill to swallow.'

'In a word: Yes. I can deliver.'

Vincent glowered. 'What makes you think there will be a demand for arms on that scale?'

The younger man paused tentatively; this was the crucial moment, when he was at his most exposed. The ice upon which he stood was perilously thin, and he was risking much if the old man refused to entertain the idea.

Vincent turned away from the visitor and stared out of the window. He was adept at manipulation, but in the present situation he felt entangled and helpless. He knew he was being managed, led like any dog on a leash, and he wondered how much of it he could take.

Still not looking at his guest, he decided to chance a question. 'What is all this really about? And spare me the cute answer, because I can't stomach hearing again how much you admire me. You're not here to pay me compliments. I must have something you want. Tell me the truth.'

The visitor inhaled. He had hoped subtlety would do the trick. 'You own a small munitions plant.'

'Ah, now we're getting to it. Go on.'

'You asked me why I believed there would be an increase in demand for armaments. Well, I have some inside information, and I see a chance to make a killing. But to make that killing I will need some major changes in Vincent Steel.'

Vincent interrupted. 'And to make those changes you need my cooperation. What happens if I don't like your ideas?'

'Then I'm sunk. And so, incidentally, are you. If you stay in steel production alone you will merely postpone your demise. Once you fail to meet the financial targets necessary to maintain your new line of credit, your new bankers will foreclose.'

Vincent knew this was undisputable. To stay in business he had, in effect, traded the confines of one prison cell for another. He had gained time, a breathing space, but he was no more in control, except . . .

'I control the board and the shareholders. Your friends the Arabs hold stock – a lot of it, but the rest is held by supporters of mine.' The old man filled his chest before declaring proudly. 'I still run Vincent Steel.'

'Absolutely right.' The visitor conceded. 'And that's as it should be. I don't want to undermine your position, but I have a fair idea what it will take to keep the banks backing you. I want to keep you in business, and with my information we can both build our fortunes.'

Vincent's face glowed. 'So what is this *inside information* you have?'

'There are people in the know who strongly believe opportunities are about to open up in the defense field. There is unrest in Asia; Laos is still a problem, an escalation of hostilities is inevitable in Cambodia and Vietnam. There will be a need for armaments on a scale not seen since Korea.' A sly glimmer shone on the newcomer's face. 'I believe that with the right guidance, Vincent Steel can become a colossus.'

'And the piece about Joe Kennedy? Your offer to tear the heart out of him, what was that about?'

'For the answer to that, you have to wait.'

'And if I choose not to?'

'Really, Mr Vincent, for that you do have to wait.' He glanced at his wristwatch. 'I'm short of time. I'm afraid I have to be going.' He outstretched his hand, and Vincent took it.

As the visitor moved for the door, the old man called out: 'I'd still feel happier knowing what you meant.'

The man paused, his face a mask of indecision. 'You put me in a difficult position. But I'll give you this much. What I'm offering is a complete change in the political environment. Chew on this for a day or so. Think about how we all might benefit if a more sympathetic ear resided in The White House. Then go over what you know about US foreign policy and take a look at South East Asia. Think about what it would take to guarantee a change in Washington – overnight. Then, when you've thought it through, ask yourself if you really are willing to pay the price. Ask yourself if you really do want to hurt Joe that badly.

'We'll talk again. You will be contacted and invited to a party. An informal gathering. You'll be given a time and place. If you're interested, just turn up. Good day Mr Vincent.'

Spinning on his heel, he was gone, leaving Nathaniel Vincent speechless for the first time in his life.

* 5 *

April 1963.

With a crunching of tyres on dry snow, a black limousine drew to a halt before the palatial residence of the new Chief Executive of Vincent Steel. The snow still swirled, but had slowed considerably. From the interior of the limousine Nathaniel Vincent eyed the residence with an impressed, downward turn of his lips. Then the rear door was opening, and the driver stood ready with an umbrella to escort the old man to the portico.

Indoors, and relieved of his heavy overcoat, the old man was guided to the drawing room where his host awaited. He was reminded of the ironic circumstance; at their first meeting, eight weeks previously, in his office in Houston, he had been the host, the titular head of the company greeting a man he believed to be a new employee. How wrong he had been! The man had moved through the company like a hurricane, cutting a swathe through the upper levels of the organisation, pushing ahead with radical reforms that seemed almost calculated to enrage the old man. Two plants had been shut down and the inventory sold off. An ordnance factory had been purchased with the proceeds, all with barely a hint to Vincent. To Nathaniel Vincent the rapid actions were a taunt; without the presence of the newcomer the Vincent Company would be dead, and everyone knew it. He knew that bluster as he might, he dare not directly challenge the authority of the newcomer. The company meant too much to Vincent, and the newcomer knew this. He knew he could proceed with his plans almost with impunity, for he was safe from the old man's fearsome wrath.

The old man had heard the admiring whispers, prompted by the man's dynamism, circulating amongst his staff. He had heard the nickname given to him. They called him the Executor. He was a man who got things done. Who tied up the loose ends, and, some of the crueler jokers amongst them claimed, knew how to deal with the effects of the dead. Vincent among them!

A slow fire burning in a vast grate and a couple of table lamps were the only sources of light in the room. The shadows thrown onto walls and ceilings by this flickering ruddy light were enlarged and distorted. As his eyes adjusted to the gloom Vincent saw his new Chief Executive approaching, hand held out in greeting. 'So,' he said gruffly, in a tone meant to convey his scepticism. 'You are the Executor.'

The man smiled. 'I'm glad you could make it, Mr Vincent. The first time we met you treated me to a good scotch. Let me return the compliment. Water? Ice?'

'Just a little water will be fine.'

The newcomer had ignored the specific mention of his nickname. He was not embarrassed, in fact he felt slightly flattered. The Executor! It had a ring to it. He had heard that Howard Hughes, the legendary billionaire, liked to be known as The Stockholder, and he felt that by letting the nickname be applied he might be considered in the same league. From small acorns do such legends grow!

'Take a seat,' the Executor invited, and Vincent did as bid. The old man began. 'I've been wanting to speak to you. You talked a lot about getting our foot in the door of the Pentagon. So far I've seen nothing except the systematic butchering of my organisation.'

'Hasn't the value of stock in Vincent Steel risen by over two dollars?'

'What has that to do with anything?'

'Everything. You know, Nat. . . .' The Executor chanced the flippant abbreviation, knowing the old man demanded respect. He wanted to keep him off balance. 'You ought to lighten up some. The wonderful we can do overnight; witness the stock price. Miracles take a little longer.'

'I don't like being on the outside. I need to know what is going on.'

'No, you do not. Everything is going according to plan, so why don't you take the advice you gave me back in February; sit back and let me make you rich.'

'Goddammit! I built that company! I have a right to a say in what happens! You think you can barge in . . .'

'With my one hundred million dollars and rescue you? Yes!! I do have some nerve don't I? Look, I made you some promises. Give me the chance to keep them will you?'

The old man rose from his chair. There was a burning sensation in his chest, but he disregarded it. 'I warned you not to cross me. I'll have you thrown off the board!'

'Really? Shall we put that to the vote?' The Executor's gaze bored into Vincent, and in that instant the old man knew he had lost his company. The son of a bitch had him by the balls. He was doing something positive with Vincent Steel. Ripping up the deadwood and winning new business. The board, faced with death or growth, would put sentimentality aside. They would go for the new blood. No one liked being a loser.

Nathaniel Vincent was history. Both he and the younger man knew it. Sensing the clashing emotions tearing at the older man, the Executor offered an olive branch. 'Trust me. I can deliver everything I said I would. We can build Vincent Steel into something new.'

The old man shook his head. You don't have control of events. How can you make such a promise?'

The Executor paused. Unsure of how much he should say, he settled finally, for the simple words: 'Trust me.'

The old man knew he had little real choice. Sentiment was something he could not afford. He owned a twelve percent share in a company whose stock was rising. He ought to bide his time, wait for the stock to peak, and bale out. He was old, and tired.

'Dinner will be served in twenty minutes. Come on through to the dining room when you are ready. I think you'll find my other guests interesting.'

The old man nodded. He felt drained. There was nothing he wanted to say.

Dinner was a strain for Vincent. He sat, alone and friendless, amongst a group of gregarious individuals who drank and joked. The others all seemed to know each other, and between the laughter there was much circumspect conversation conducted. The old man had plenty of time to study his fellows at table. Opposite sat an individual he thought he recognised – but could not put a name to. He was stocky, with rough hewn, square-jawed features and silver hair trimmed short. He had the bearing of a seasoned veteran. Aware of Vincent's scrutiny at one point, he shifted uncomfortably on his seat. He looked like a man who felt naked out of uniform. A soldier.

Another at the table caught Vincent's eye. He was much younger, in his late thirties, slim and immaculately preened in a suit of European cut. He had the stylised, perfectly groomed look of one of the newly emerging breed of television politicians, those who had what the TV people termed *Presence*. But to the old man's jaundiced eyes he appeared merely clean and seamless, devoid of any notable characteristic. Vincent disliked him on sight.

The younger man at one point returned the stare with a polite yet challenging candour that needled Vincent, causing him to growl: 'Do I know you?'

The response was a flattering smile. 'We have not formally met, sir, but who hasn't heard of Nathaniel Vincent?'

The old man snorted.

Others at the table Vincent did recognise. There was an Italian he was sure had been at the New Years party. Dressed in a loud suit, he had greased black hair and wore thick rings on his fingers. He was drinking heavily and joking crudely. What was his name? Rosetti? Rosselli . . . Rossi! That was it! There had been something else about him. What could it have been?

There was a showbusiness contingent at the table. That fading English actor, Todd Fletcher, known these days more for his marriage to a society queen rather than film roles, was badly and pathetically drunk. Fletcher was slotted between the bobby sox idol and singer Max Valentino, and the comedian, Dino Wise, who had recently made a splash in a hit Hollywood picture. These three formed the nucleus of a show business group, dubbed *The Gang* by the sensational press, which was noted for its excesses of drink and drugs and women. Vincent found their crude in-jokes and raucous laughter distasteful. They noticed this, and played to it, their childish, dope-enriched giggling enraging him even further.

Dinner broke up soon afterwards, and the twenty or so individuals at the table dispersed into small groups. Nathaniel Vincent seemed to be, and felt, the odd one out. He drifted from room to room, a glass of fine brandy in hand, listening to the buzz of conversation, catching the odd whiff of illegal cigarettes, and admiring the works of art dotted around the house. He spent time in a library whose shelves held a treasure trove of first editions.

Then he wandered into a room in a distant wing of the building. He heard voices from inside, and, on an instinct, stepped quietly up to the door and listened. . . .

'Here you are, gentlemen.' The voice was that of the Executor. Vincent, feeling inexplicably intrigued, moved slightly closer and peered through a crack in the door. He could see three men at a long table. The Executor was one of them. He passed drinks from a tray to the two others, then he joined them at the table. The two were the men Vincent had tagged as the soldier and the New-Politico.

There was a fire burning in the grate of this room too. A log on the fire broke and fell with a soft 'whoosh', sending upwards into the grate a shower of sparks. The Executor sipped his drink, then broke the silence. 'Shall we get to business?'

The soldier peered over the rim of his glass. His eyes glittered. The younger fellow lit a cheroot and drew on it deeply. The air was infused with a pleasant herby fragrance. The soldier rumbled impatiently. He had a large bourbon in hand. Rotating his jaw contentedly, he sipped, and felt the spirit settling in his belly. He was not comfortable with small talk; 'Get on with it.'

'You have been given hints. You have some idea what we are trying to achieve. No doubt you are wondering why you are here, what your roles will be, and what will be the subsequent rewards. But before we go on, I think you ought to know each other a little better.'

'What is this?' the soldier sneered. 'Some kind of sorority house? We don't have to be friends, just move along.'

At the Executor's elbow on the table lay two slim files in buff covers. Taking up the top one, he passed it to the young man, saying: 'Here you are, Senator. A little background on the General.' As he passed the second file to the General, he added: 'You could call it a job recommendation.'

The two men read the files, then, faces blank, they exchanged them. A gasp from the Senator made the others glance at him. 'Where the hell did you get this? It's lies. All of it. Lies.'

The Executor smirked. 'Turn the page, Senator. The camera never lies.'

The man did so, and his face blenched white. 'Job recommendation? This is blackmail!'

'You catch on fast,' came the smug reply.

'Oh my God,' whispered the General, staring in horror at the contents of his file. Then his face hardened, and he hurled a vicious glance at his host. 'Okay, you made your point. Let's have it.'

'Good. We all understand each other. No doubt you can see why you were selected.'

'You want something from us,' the General growled. 'What is it?'

'In your case, General, I want some sympathy. You are responsible for millions of dollars of government spending, in certain areas you head the decision making process. My company, Vincent Steel, is moving into heavy ordnance. We want your business.'

The General quietly fumed. He knew he was caught. Knew there was little point in resisting. There was danger inherent in rigging the allocation of defense orders, but the danger of exposure of his secret, and the resultant loss of position, honor and pension, would devastate him and his family. He immediately knew he had little choice.

But still he tried to resist. 'I don't really have that kind of power. The thinking from the White House is determined to trim our spending. I'll try my best, but I can't promise. . . .'

The Senator was furious, his face beginning to turn a baleful pink. 'And what exactly could you want from me? I do not control vast amounts of money. I simply represent the people who voted for me.'

The Executor raised a quizzical eyebrow. 'You underestimate yourself, Senator. You have a reputation for genuine integrity, and, you are often appointed to committees. You could conceivably sit on committees that operate to the benefit of my company. Your job is to be my friend. When I need you there, I want you to be there.'

'Well, that was brutally frank,' remarked the Senator with an edge to his voice. 'Supposing we agree to your proposal, which, incidentally, I'm not saying I will, are we expected to provide these services *gratis*?'

'Oh no. You will be amply rewarded. In your case, Senator, play the game and I think I could safely promise you a period in the White House.'

'When?'

'Within a decade, twelve years at the outside.'

The General chipped in. 'What are the specifics? What are you aiming at? If you've done any homework at all, you must know the White House is against an increased arms build up.'

'Then JFK has to go. Is that specific enough for you?' The General nodded. 'Get on with it.'

Vincent listened in a mood of growing amazement to the conversation as the Executor outlined a scheme to destroy a man's reputation. It was plain the others had an inkling of the plan, but though the details did not surprise them, there was, for the Senator at least, a moral dilemma. His face wore a worried frown as he listened.

The Executor was on his feet, and pacing. He thought more fluidly on the move and it was vital he think well, and speak even better. He had to convert these two men to the cause with little more than infectious enthusiasm, had to haul them into the net before they had time to rationalise themselves out of it. 'There is a sizeable groundswell of support. We will have all the co-operation and resources we need. And because I am the sole link, the risks to you will be eliminated. Let me stress that.'

The Senator leaned forward and screwed the butt of his cheroot flat in a crystal ashtray. 'Let's stop going around in circles, shall we? I understand that in some . . . communities, it is common practice to talk in riddles, but let's have all this out in the open. Unless I'm mistaken, we're talking about destroying the President of the United States.'

'That's rather a strong term. I prefer to use the word *remove*.'

'For God's sake, he's the President!'

'He's just a man.' The General growled.

'He wouldn't be the first to fall to a scandal.' The Executor continued. 'And the country does need a shot in the arm. I've heard you say so yourself in the Senate. Nobody asked him to fuck around. He's left himself open. We cannot risk him winning another term. We cannot afford even two more years of the New Frontier. The dream has to end. Can you think of a better, short term way to make the changes that you, even more loudly than I, have proclaimed necessary to haul the country back on course?'

'There is the ballot box!' The Senator dammed him forcibly. 'He won't fool all the people all of the time. He'll fall at the election.'

'I disagree. My information is that even more money, even more organisation, will be pumped into the next campaign. His advisers have learnt an art they are calling "*Trial by television*," and we already know the voters can be swayed by the man with the better image. Up against Nixon on TV, Kennedy looked the part, and that is going to become increasingly important. He has the glamour, the movie star friends. The public will lap it up. And unless something catastrophic happens, or unless we stop him, he will win.'

The Senator remained unconvinced. 'It all sounds much too dangerous. The figure of Joe Kennedy is still powerful, even in a wheelchair. If this all backfires, I could be ruined.'

The Executor leaned forward. 'We need you with us in this. For the good of the nation. A second term half as eventful as his first will be disastrous. We are in decline, and if you don't believe me, go out to the party and talk to Nathaniel Vincent. Ask him how a man with an empire valued at two hundred million dollars can stumble to virtual penury.'

From his vantage point, Vincent felt his blood simmering. *They were plotting to get Kennedy out of the White House!* Once again that dreadful feeling, that he was being invisibly manipulated, descended upon him. He had been drawn into something unpleasant, he was sure. Something beyond his control, that could get him into trouble. Realising that his chest was feeling tight, he took a tiny bottle from a pocket, spun open the cap, and swallowed a pill. He thanked his stars he had stumbled onto this meeting. He was going to get to the bottom of this. Going to find out . . . . His face settled into its habitual scowl.

The Senator looked to each of the two men in turn. 'Just supposing you get him out. How do you propose to administer this . . . shot in the arm?'

'Defense spending,' declared their host. 'Pumping money into the economy. There are entire communities being torn down by Kennedy's defense cuts, company towns where thousands are out of work. There are massive corporations teetering on the brink of collapse. We can turn all this around. A strong country equals a strong economy.'

With a snort, the Senator turned to the General. 'You can't actually believe this?' But it was plain the General did. The silence in the room was oppressively heavy. Anger swelled in the Senator's chest, and thoughts surged through his head. Then the answer occurred to him, and a smile of derision divided his face.

'This is just an excuse, isn't it? A means to some end. Tell me . . .' he aimed a fierce look at his host. 'What is your part in all this, and the General's?'

The Executor pursed his lips. The initiative had been taken from him, but he was cornered. He recognised the need for a moment of candour. 'The General occupies an almost unique position. Because of a mistake he made, many years ago, his once promising career has been twenty years on the backburner. He wants more. He deserves more. Unfortunately for him, if things do not change he will remain unfulfilled. He has worked hard to get to where he is, and now has final say in many of the contracts awarded to industry by the Pentagon. He is in a position to award contracts to what are called: *non-competitive bidders*. Happily, the company I have just taken over is expanding into heavy armaments. . . .'

The Senator broke in: 'And you're in for a percentage! That's wonderful, real . . . American of you.' His chest was heaving, so worked up was he. 'So why am I here?'

'I told you. Know your own worth. You are viewed as a politician with a big future. A man of unimpeachable reputation.' The Executor smiled, pointed a well manicured finger. 'Who knows when we might need a friend on the hill?'

The Senator drew back slightly, took a breath. When he spoke it was in a tone heavy with bile. 'It won't work.'

The Executor straightened. Then slowly, calculatedly, he allowed a triumphant smirk dawn across his face. 'You'll be the man we put in the White House. Join us, and I guarantee it.'

'Do you have any idea what you are going to be up against if you go ahead with this? You think you can control it all, the FBI? The CIA? And later on, the voters?'

'I think I mentioned earlier a groundswell of covert support.'

'What are you trying to say, the FBI and the CIA are with you? I don't buy that.'

'Let me just say the President is unpopular. We do not need help so much as we need lack of action against us. Bureaucratic inertia is fairly simple to organise.'

The Senator stared down at the desk for long moments. Then he steeled himself, and glanced up. 'I can't do it. I'm sorry but I cannot afford to get involved in anything so . . . immoral. Thanks for thinking of me, but . . .' He smiled feebly.

The Executor nodded, face assuming an expression of resignation and regret. 'I am sorry to hear that. I had hoped I would not have to sink to this level.' He lifted one of the files and passed it to the Senator, who reacted with a slightly worried look of enquiry 'Now what?'

'Take another look.'

The Senator took the file and placed it on the table before him. He slowly opened the cover and read the contents. Once more horror crossed his face, then his expression hardened into one of purple outrage and he glared fiercely at his host.

The Executor strolled to the bar and leisurely refilled his glass, deliberately omitting to offer refills to the others. He returned to the table and stood over the Senator. The man was there for the taking, still in shock, the file open at the incriminating photograph.

'I want you to step down from your pulpit and cut the morality speech. I'm not asking you to participate in our scheme. All I want is a commitment that when the time comes, your efforts will be to our cause.'

'What do you mean *our* cause. You keep saying US, WE. Who the hell else is involved? Who is behind you?'

'That I cannot say, for your safety as much as ours. Remember, I am the sole link. I am your protection.'

The Senator's mind was in a whirl. The man meant everything he said – the existence of the file proved that much. There was no length they would not go to. They! Now he was thinking *They*! Who could *They* be?

He was torn, a man on the brink of a momentus decision. It occurred to him he may have been unwise to voice his objections. If they were determined to destroy the President, surely they would not hesitate to silence him. And if he was not with them. . . .

His chest rose and fell as his conflicting emotions swelled. Of all the emotions, anger grew tallest, with a furious energy all of its own. Then, decision made, his shoulders sagged. When he looked to his host there was an air of resignation on his face. 'Well, I'm sorry but, flawed as the system is, I have to believe in it. If we reject it we're no better than the dammed communists and we stand to lose everything. So, I'm afraid I must decline your invitation.'

The Executor's expression became cold. 'A pretty speech Senator, but you're not fooling anyone. I know you are ambitious. The White House is in your sights. Join us.'

The Senator rose slowly to his feet. Now he had decided on a course, he wanted nothing more than to leave the house.

The Executor raised his voice. 'What about the file? Are you prepared for public exposure? Are you really prepared to be ruined?'

'You would really do that? Make all that public?'

'To get what I want? Yes.'

The Senator narrowed his eyes. 'Then you are the lowest scum I've ever met.'

'That may be, but are you prepared for what will happen if the file comes out?'

Beads of perspiration blossomed on the Senator's brow. 'If it comes out, it comes out. What you are planning is wrong and you know it. Nothing you say will gloss over that.'

The Executor nodded. His lips pursed as he cogitated. 'Senator, might I suggest you leave now.'

'Yes.' Almost faint with relief, the Senator turned, in his hurry striking his knee against the chair. Though he fought hard to hide it, the fear showed; he could not believe they were letting him walk away.

He was halfway to the door when the Executor called to him. 'I must ask you to respect the confidential nature of our discussion.'

Almost in a swoon, the Senator nodded. Then on trembling legs he walked towards the door.

Nathaniel Vincent, not wishing to be caught in the act of eavesdropping, turned suddenly to make an exit. As he spun, he came face to face with the mobster, Johnny Rossi. Rossi stood extremely close, leering at him. Vincent felt fear close around him, felt his heart accelerate. He took a step backward, swallowing the lump of congealed dread that swelled in his throat.

'Keep still old man,' hissed the mobster. His breath was heavy with garlic, and his complexion was ruddy, as if flushed with drink.

The silence was disturbed by the sound of a shocked exhalation as the Senator arrived at the door and saw them. With barely a pause he burst past and hurried away along the corridor.

Johnny Rossi gave Vincent a nudge. 'Why don't we go inside?'

The old man allowed himself to be prodded into the study where he felt the piercing gazes of the Executor and the General upon him. Rossi said: 'I found him listening at the door.'

The General frowned. 'Who's this?'

The Executor replied. 'Mr Vincent, I think you have heard of. John Rossi is a business associate. He has agreed to oversee the organisation.'

Leaving Vincent's side, Johnny Rossi fitted a toothpick between his thin, sneering lips, and sauntered arrogantly to the head of the table. Gripping the back of a chair with bejewelled fingers, he nodded to the Executor – as if to convey a signal. The others picked up on it, and tacitly received the message that the Senator was not destined to get far.

'The guy was never cut out for politics.' Johnny joked. 'Too decent.' He slowly panned his cutting stare from left to right, that flat, expressionless gaze settling upon each man in turn. They felt the venal concentration, the morbid arrogance, of the man.

'Rossi.' The General repeated the name. Outwardly giving no sign he had ever heard it before, he consigned it to memory. 'And what exactly is he going to do for us?'

'John is well connected. He knows people who can be of use to us.'

'What exactly is going on?' Vincent growled the question. The Executor replied. 'Surely you heard.' His tone was cold, aloof.

'I heard you talking about getting Kennedy. I heard the Congressman, or whatever the hell he was, tell you it was too risky even though you were blackmailing him. What the hell are you up to?'

'We are putting JFK out of office. That simple. It's time for a change. We need . . .'

'Save the soft soap. *What are you going to do?*'

The Executor had never before witnessed Nathaniel Vincent in full angry flow. He was perturbed by the thrust of the old man's question, but he retained his composure 'Do you recall the day we first met, and I asked you about Joe Kennedy? I asked what it would be worth to you to hurt him at a time when he thinks he has it all. Well this is the time.

'All his life Joe wanted recognition, to stand at the top of the social tree. Society doesn't get much higher than the White House. Now, while he is virtually incapacitated we are going to take all that away from him. Stuck in that wheelchair his power to hit back will be limited, and his fury and frustration will be more than he can bear.'

Vincent did not feel any pleasure hearing this. Emnity had existed between he and Joe Kennedy for over twenty years, but whether he would really want to hurt the man . . . physically hurt him, he was not so sure. Hoarsely, he asked: 'How?'

'Information. President Jack has been a naughty boy, we hear. Bedding women, consorting with undesirables; mob figures. He was running with a fast Hollywood crowd, some of whom are here tonight, until he upset a couple along the way. Then there was all that fuss last year. Monroe. All kinds of rumours; an unusual death.'

'But just rumours?'

'Perhaps. Perhaps not. Hoover, the FBI Director, has a huge collection of files. He is obsessive about cataloging people, did you know that? Well, he and John Kennedy do not see eye to eye, and whenever Hoover finds himself in that position he goes on the offensive. He has a file this thick on the President's indiscretions.'

'For what possible reason? He could never release such a document without hurting himself.'

'Quite correct. Hoover is proud of his public image as the guardian of American morals. But the Kennedy brothers want him out of the FBI, and the file is his way of making sure he stays.'

'You mean he is blackmailing the President?'

'To the best of our information.'

'And where do you come in?'

The Executor shared a complicit glance with Rossi and the General. 'We have access to the file.'

'What are you going to do with it?'

'We are going to explode it across the world's press. The scandal will force him out of office, and Johnson will become

President. He shares our ideas about keeping America strong.'

'You make it all sound so easy.'

'Yes I do, but that is because you need not worry about the technicalities. There will be problems, but nothing we cannot overcome.'

'Where do I come in?' Vincent at last asked the question.

'Vincent Steel, in its new incarnation as a supplier of ordnance to the US military, will be a major beneficiary.'

'And what is in all this for Mister Rossi?' cut in the General, eyeing the mobster critically.

Rossi's lips twisted into a sour curl. 'I'll be well paid.'

'Which brings me to a second point.' Vincent said. 'This must all be costing something. Who is paying?'

'Why you, Mr Vincent. Or rather, Vincent Steel. But look at the other side of the transaction; Kennedy is gone, and Johnson sits in the Oval office. Traditional influences prevail. We expand the number of advisers in Vietnam. Without our help the communists will take that country. Kennedy is soft on communism, we know that after Cuba. There are still missiles over there, you know. The Pentagon will increase its ordering capacity. The forces in Asia will need lines of supply in addition to weapons, and Vincent Industries, as we will be known, having sealed the Pontoon deal, will be a major player. If you like, later I will show you a few business projections. If they are only half right the Vincent company will turnover between five hundred million and a billion dollars a year. The imminent conflict in Vietnam will be a hard war to win; we are not a race of jungle fighters. The fight over there might last twenty years, and if the history of military expenditure is to be believed, my projections will turn out to be underestimates. We will make billions, Mr Vincent. Billions.'

Vincent swallowed his protest, as the Executor knew he would. *Up to one billion dollars a year!*

The Executor walked around the table and gripped Vincent's upper right arm in a friendly gesture. 'It's a lot to take in, I know. Why don't we re-join the party. They'll all be wondering where we've gotten to. We can talk more later.'

In the corridor, Johnny leading, the General questioned the Executor's fitness to run the operation. He added: 'You've already made a mistake. The Senator.' His tone was mocking. 'What made you choose him.'

The Executor shrugged. 'It might please you to know that of the three of you, I considered him the weakest link. If he'd come through he would have meant a lot to us in the future.

I'm just glad we found him out this early in the game.'

'What will happen to him?' Vincent fished. 'Surely he won't be allowed to spoil your plans.'

'Quite correct.' The reply was emphatically, and finally, brief.

'What about the files?' the General asked. The Executor paused, then handed them to him, a look of wry amusement on his face. 'They are in your hands.'

As they rejoined the party, the warming glow of laughter and fragrant cigarette smoke embraced them. Vincent studied Johnny Rossi. He recalled seeing him at the Hendersons' New Years' bash. He knew something about him, and his patron, Giancarlo Giometri, who was rumoured to be boss of bosses in organised crime, and was featured often in the campaigning press. The man's presence, at the home of the Chief Executive of Vincent Steel, caused him to worry anew about the plot. Surely the government, the FBI and the CIA, would not sit back and let this happen? In his experience, men like Rossi brought trouble . . . the sort of trouble he did not want to be involved in.

'You're asking a lot,' the old man said, his shoulders shifting uncomfortably as cold seeped into his coat.

'You're getting a lot,' replied his host.

They were standing at the open front door, eyeing the snow-covered drive. Vincent eyed the younger man, noted how confident he appeared, and shelved his own doubts. 'You know, a lot of people think I'm ruthless. Joe Kennedy and I have a lot in common.'

'He cost you a lot, and I don't mean money.'

The old man sniffed. He hoped he wasn't coming down with a cold. 'Your idea could work, but I'm wondering about the expense. I'm asking myself; can I do this without you? Will it cost me as much if I do?'

The Executor's warm regard stiffened. 'Believe me, it would not be safe for you to go ahead without us. Your involvement would be hard to deny.'

Careful to keep the look of satisfaction from his face, Vincent studied the face of the younger man. 'Tapes?'

The Executor nodded. 'And more.'

Vincent was pleased; his ploy had resulted in exposing the younger man's defenses. If he was cunning enough to build defenses to keep his co-conspirators in line, he was probably smart enough to pull off the crazy scheme. To appear beaten, he let out a sigh and allowed his shoulders to sag. He was a patient man, that was his strength. He could wait.

He stepped over the threshold, where the driver awaited with an umbrella, having drawn up in the limo moments earlier. Vincent turned back to his host for a final word 'When does it get under way?'
The Executor smiled 'It already has.'

The Executor stood at the door and watched the swirling snow blot out the shrinking tail-lights. He closed the door. Most of the guests had gone, and those who remained were partying determinedly in the games room. Rossi was still in the drawing room, and the Executor rejoined him. The lights were up and the Italian was unsteadily helping himself to more drink. Noting the disapproving scowl on the face of his host, he grinned inanely. 'Satisfied?'

The Executor indicated he wasn't sure. Throwing back his head, Johnny drained his glass and belched lewdly. Another look of disapproval and he erupted into crude laughter. 'Don't worry about a thing. They'll play ball. They have to. It's just that so far, none of you have realised how rich the pickings are gonna be.'

The Executor poured himself a drink. 'I was worried. Thought it might be too rich for their blood.' He glanced at the Italian. 'It's a risk. The biggest.'

Johnny flexed his shoulders, then unbuttoned his jacket and reached for a refill. Replete with alcohol, his dark good looks took on an evil, brooding cast. The Executor was struck by the incongruity of the man's behaviour, his loud clothes, extravagant hand gestures and loose, big talk. The archetypical movie hoodlum who could play with your kids one minute, then cut out your heart with a dull butter knife the next.

'You did the right thing, coming in with me,' Johnny declared with peasant sagacity. 'You're gonna need help. You don't know how complicated things are going to get. You are going to be owed favors by some pretty important people, you dig?'

Signalling that he dug, the Executor finished his drink and refused a refill. He wanted a clear head. Doubts about Rossi and the others presaged him. Had he known about the man's tendency to overdrink and overbear, he might have reconsidered getting involved. He thought back to the party after New Year's, at Giometri's house. The *Hollywood Gang* entertained. They were in full swing, joking, and breaking out into impromptu song. As the night wore on and the gaiety waned, the conversation darkened. The talk turned to a game *The Gang* called: *People We Hate.* Among those whose names came up was that of the Attorney General, Bobby Kennedy, whose efforts against the mob were tearing up the fabric of organised crime. He was proposed by Johnny Rossi. The Executor listened through a drunken haze to talk of having Bobby Kennedy 'whacked'.

'Nah,' Johnny Rossi, sluggish with drink, had blurted out. 'That wouldn't get you the result you wanted. If you cut off the dog's tail, the head can still bite you. But you hack off that sonofabitch's head, the tail will die right along with it.'

Heads nodded sagely. Later, as dawn crept over the horizon, and most of the group had fallen asleep where they sat or lay, the Executor watched as Rossi fitted a single shell into a revolver, spun the chamber, and, placing the muzzle to his temple, pulled the trigger three times. The Italian had laughed, crazily, each time the hammer clicked on empty, and the Executor needed a drink just to stop his hands from shaking. Stories he had heard since had confirmed the myth. The Italian was completely insane. The problem now was; how to handle him?

Johnny was pacing, drink in one hand, free hand rolling over and over as he rambled to himself. 'I'll negotiate with Castro directly. I still have friends over there who can get me in to see him. Once the casinos reopen, they'll all know exactly who they owe it to.'

'That's not the reason we are doing all this, Johnny.' Rossi flicked a hand, as though shooing a fly. 'I know that, jeez, will you quit reminding me? There are more things going on here. You throw a rock into a lake, there are always ripples. Dontcha understand that? Everyone has his hand out. Everyone has a stake. The people we need, the ones who will help, they have needs to be taken care of. And when this job is done, there will be markers to be called in.'

'I still don't understand,' the Executor lied. He did know, or at least suspect, what was going on, but he did not want to face the responsibility of admitting he knew what kind of web was being woven around him.

Johnny grinned morbidly. 'All I'm saying is that there are bound to be benefits, and it's up to us to make the most of them. Nobody is gonna give us nothin' unless we deliver, but once we do, once we do. . . .' He rambled on, speech slurring to an almost incomprehensible mush. 'Ripples. That's why you need us. To take care of the ripples.'

Hiding the contempt he felt for the man's state, the Executor asked about the specialist Rossi had found to run the operation. 'Tell me about him.'

'Halstead's a good man. Ex-Company, he came out of the Bay of Pigs a very angry guy. He's been training some of the CIA's pet Cubans down in Florida. Pretty involved in the hits on Cuban shipping. He comes highly recommended by Ed Wilson himself. He'll do it.'

'Can we trust him?'

Johnny chuckled. 'About as far as you can spit me.' At the startled expression on the Executor's face, Johnny burst into coarse laughter. 'Don't worry. We can always get rid of him once the job is done.'

'You mean kill him? I'm not sure I want this job to get that complicated.'

Rossi stared at him, caught midway between scorn and incredulity. 'You're kidding me, right? No, I can see you're not.' He shook his head. 'Man, you have no idea how complicated all this is going to get.'

'What do you mean?'

Johnny banged his empty glass on the table, then throwing his host an odd, slightly dangerous look, he shambled from the room.

* 6 *

The Executor found himself walking the landscaped terrace that adjoined the dining room. He was worried, besieged by doubts. The more he thought about what he was doing, and who he was involved with, the more anxious he became. Now he awaited reassurance from a man he knew, in his heart, could not give it to him.

Todd Fletcher opened the french windows and stepped onto the terrace. He was wearing casual, light coloured slacks and a thin, collarless jacket. He shuddered against the night chill, then spotting the Executor, walked towards him. 'You wanted to see me?'

'Yes,' the Executor replied. While he gathered himself, tried to assemble the appropriate opening words, Fletcher opened a gold, monogrammed cigarette case and took out a cigarette. He lit up and inhaled. In the half light cast through the nearby windows, the Executor was struck by the man's good looks. He was almost impossibly handsome. No wonder women flocked to his bed. The actor shivered. 'Come on old chum. Spit it out. It's bloody cold out here.'

'Todd, I need to know what I'm involved in here. Who I'm involved with.'

Fletcher winced, averted his gaze. 'You know. . . .'

The Executor grasped him by the arm. 'No. I can only guess. I'm standing out there, sucking other people into something I'm not too clear about myself. I have to know for sure what all this is about!'

Todd glanced around. 'This is not a good time, or place.'

'Come on,' his host urged him. 'Let's take a walk. No one will see us.' Todd was reluctant, but allowed himself to be led along the terrace and down a shallow flight of bedrock steps. They crossed the lawn and strolled along the edge of an ornamental lake. Fletcher smoked furiously, the glowing tip of his cigarette flaring and dimming. The Executor, normally the most confident and forthright of men, was out of his depth, and willing to let that be known if by doing so he could find the answers . . .

'I need some background. Help me . . .'

Fletcher murmured something under his breath, then said, louder: 'Okay. You know the aims, to drive JFK out of office? Well, that is the truth. He has made enemies amongst some of the most powerful people in the country, and they are bearing grudges. One way or another they are determined to ruin him.'

'But why? What on earth can that madman Rossi, or Giancarlo Giometri, hope to gain?'

Fletcher paused in mid-step. 'Look, I'm like you; an outsider. I am English, I'm not a citizen here, I can't vote and I have virtually no interest in American politics. I'm only here because of Max. He's the one who is friendly with the mob. I'm just one of the gang. They don't talk to me. Anything I've picked up is by chance. Odd remarks I've heard, coupled with my putting two and two together.' He drew in a sigh. 'For some reason, Giancarlo and his associates think that JFK has betrayed them.'

'What?' The Executor exclaimed. Fletcher nodded, drew harder on his cigarette. 'Oh yes. That basically is it. The others I've seen around, the military, the spooks, the Cubans, them I can understand to a degree. With military cut-backs, disenchantment over the Bay of Pigs and the sacking of intelligence chiefs, Kennedy is seen as a threat.'

The Executor mused. 'Robert Kennedy is after organised crime, we all know that, but how on earth could they think Jack Kennedy betrayed them? It doesn't make sense!'

'Not to you and me it doesn't, but like I said, we are outsiders. I've seen and heard a lot of strange things around Giancarlo. I don't think anything could surprise me.'

They walked in silence. The air cool, the snow dry and soft underfoot. His voice crisp in the cold air, Todd Fletcher delivered a final, chilling statement: 'I've met Jack Kennedy. I like him. But he's been careless. He is vulnerable, and he is in danger. Dammit, these people are at war with him!'

A lump arose in the Executor's throat as an uncomfortable thought descended. 'What if it doesn't work?'

Fletcher glanced at him. 'Meaning?'

'This file of damaging evidence; the affairs, the links to Monroe. What if it doesn't work? If Kennedy stays in office, what happens next?'

Fletcher looked away into the night. His shoulders rose and fell, expressing his feelings more eloquently than any words. The same thought had occurred to them both.

The Executor softly whistled. 'Jesus.'

Fletcher dropped his cigarette butt into the snow. 'It will work. Don't worry about that.'

On some unspoken signal they started the long walk back to the house. The Executor's mind was in a whirl of confusion and fear as he realised the position he was in. The only visible member of the plot! The sole link. The fall guy.

'You be extremely careful,' Fletcher muttered to him as they ascended the terrace steps. 'You don't want to end up the patsy.' Before they entered the drawing room, the Executor grasped Fletcher by the elbow, and thanked him for having the courage to talk. 'I appreciate your taking the time. No one is asking anything of you, you don't need this, why don't you get out before it all blows up?'

Fletcher's expression was grave. 'Because after Johnny Rossi, Max is the most vindictive man I've ever met. He is a powerful figure in showbusiness, and it's considered a privilege to be in his group. He demands loyalty, and if he thinks he's been crossed, he will get you.' He smiled, wanly. 'So you see, unlike you, I have no choice.'

The Executor sympathised. 'Seems we are both somewhat trapped.' He paused. An idea had germinated in his mind, but it was a subject that needed broaching delicately. 'Look, how can I put this? I need an ally, I need a buddy, a pal. How do you feel about helping me?'

Fletcher was suspicious. 'What exactly do you mean?'

The Executor went on. 'You are in closer than I am. I want you to keep your ears and eyes open. Find out more. The more information I have, the better prepared I will be if all this goes bang.'

Fletcher was vehement in his refusal. 'Oh no, old buddy. I'm not that crazy. These are dangerous people. Rossi can kill you if he doesn't like the way you ask for the time.'

'I'll make it worth your while.'

Fletcher laughed bitterly. 'You are surely not offering me mere money, old boy. You forget, I'm a movie star. I have money.'

The Executor wanted to be kind, but knew there was not really any easy way to continue. 'Todd, come on, I read Louella. Your career has been in tatters since Paramount let you go. These last ten years you've struggled, and the little work that has come your way has been due to the largesse of studios hiring Max Valentino. Do I have to remind you what happened when you fell out with Max that time? Three years without work. You have marital problems; the word on the wire is that you will divorce soon, and your financial situation is parlous to say the least. Mere money is going to be a valuable commodity in your life, Todd, and I have plenty. Be my pal and you'll be taken care of. I guarantee it.'

Fletcher stood in silence, absorbing this. The mask fell away and he was suddenly much less handsome. He was reminded of his mortality, and he was scared.

The group had gathered around the lulling fire in one of the great rooms of the house. A grand piano stood in one corner, Max Valentino leaned on it and crooned a few songs from his new long player. The Executor helped himself to a drink and took his seat on a chaise longue upholstered in rich leather. Closing his eyes he settled back and let the music wash over him. He heard Dino join in, his voice a resonant, drink tinged timbre that flowed under and over Valentino's.

The audience, a dozen men and women including Julie Starr and Todd Fletcher, watched and listened, entranced, by Valentino's magic. He was the world's most renowned vocalist, having successfully made the transition from small time jazz singer, to bobby sox idol, to international multi-million selling recording artist and Oscar nominated actor. He lived hard and played hard, and the company he ran with kept him on the fringes of the scandal pages. He was known to be vicious when crossed, and overly generous when pleased. He had power, the kind of power that meant other, seemingly more powerful men, respected his word. If he was making a film and wanted a friend included in the project, he got his way. And because of his associates, the mobsters he was known to party with, he was feared.

The singing slowed, then stopped, and the Executor lazily opened his eyes. The group members had drifted away. He looked around for Julie, but she, and Giancarlo, had gone. In fact besides himself, only Johnny Rossi remained.

The Italian grinned at him. In the firelight his eyes glinted evilly. 'I waited until you woke up. We have to talk.'

The Executor nodded, not quite knowing why he had. Johnny went on: 'You been pumping Fletcher. You didn't have to do that; any questions you had you coulda asked me.'

'Not so much questions. More . . . reservations. I'm scared Johnny. I don't mind telling you. I'm out of my depth.'

'No need to feel that way. You don't actually have to do anything. You just have to sit back and let the money roll in. So, what's your problem?'

The Executor hesitated. If there was one thing he had learnt about Johnny Rossi in the twelve weeks since their paths had first crossed, it was that one had to be careful what one said. The Italian hung by a short fuse, and had a temper that the Executor had no desire to test. 'Well, I know that you and Giancarlo have helped me a lot. You got me back on my feet and I'm grateful. But all I know about you is what I read in the papers, and I'm nervous about being involved with you. I could be ruined if my connection to you were made public.'

'Bullshit. You just got no balls.'

The Executor blushed, stammered a protest. 'No, really . . .'

Rossi overrode him with brutish vehemence. 'No, you listen, you shitfilled fuck!' His face glowed as anger suffused his face a violent pink. 'You're scared! So what? You are in now, and you're staying in, you hear me?' Rising from his chair he moved with a soft, sprung tread to the other man's chair and grasped the Executor by the throat. The man started to choke. 'This is big, you son-of-a-bitch. Bigger than you, bigger than me!' Johnny's crazy gaze burned into the other's eyes, probed like searing hot needles into the other's soul, searching for a weakness. 'There's gonna be no backing out. No walking away. You're in for life.' Breathing heavily, Johnny released the grip and stood back. He straightened his jacket and walked to the bar where he poured himself a drink. 'You know that Senator you were talking to, the guy who didn't want to be in on this? You're gonna be reading about him in the papers tomorrow.'

Shock registered on the face of his host. 'What does that mean?'

'Think about it. And learn; in our business we never talk specifics.'

The Executor listened, and absorbed, knowing he had been given another message – and another chance. 'Okay. Okay I understand. I'm sorry.' He was dizzy. His body still fizzed with fear, his heart pounded wildly and the rushing feeling continued to surge.

Rossi inhaled, his large chest swelling his jacket. 'Tomorrow, Halstead will come to your office and introduce himself. I want you to make sure he meets Vincent. I want you to make sure the old man feels that Halstead believes he is a major player; the secret money behind the set-up. Is that clear?'

'Why?'

Rossi grimaced, his hands rose, half clenched, and for one dreadful moment the Executor feared the man was about to erupt into terrible violence. That sense of danger, the frightening aura that emanated from Rossi even when he was good humored, now surged, transforming him into the very image of evil incarnate. Then the mood eased, the hands were lowered, and Johnny spoke again, this time in a tone guttural, and taut with anger. 'Just do as I say, will ya?'

The Executor stared blankly at him for a few moments, then nodded.

Rossi watched him. His eyes, shaded by his thick eyebrows, were in darkness. When he spoke it was in a tone heavy with menace. 'You will not contact Giancarlo again. You will not mention his name to anyone who might become involved. Anything you have to say to him, goes through me. If I were you, I'd keep away from Max and the boys, too. And that faggot Fletcher. You have to stay clean – you said so yourself. They are linked to us. This is serious business now.' He lifted his glass, drained it.

'I'm going to bed. I'll be seeing you.'

As Johnny walked away, the Executor called to him. The Italian paused, made a half turn, and returned the stare. 'What?'

'Why, Johnny? Why are you and Giancarlo involved in this? Why do you want to destroy Kennedy?' When the answer did not immediately come, he pressed further. 'I need to know?'

Johnny considered a moment longer, then said: 'The son of a bitch owes us.'

The Executor left his desk to shake hands with Halstead. The man was of stout build, balding, and sporting a dark moustache. The bags under his eyes aged him, but the eyes themselves were alert, rapidly appraising the Executor with a look that showed he knew who he was meeting. They engaged in light conversation until the office door opened and Nathaniel Vincent burst in. The old man barely glanced at Halstead, focusing his glare instead at the Executor. 'You asked to see me?'

The Executor rose from his chair. He swallowed, nervously, then gestured towards Halstead and introduced the two men.

Vincent took the proffered hand. 'And who are you?'

The Executor cut in with the reply. 'He's the specialist taking care of our file on the President.'

Vincent paled noticeably, Then his ferocious frown gathered stormlike, on his face. 'Halstead. . . .' he managed to mutter in a civil tone. 'Would you leave us alone for a few minutes?' The man agreed, and left closing the door softly behind him.

'What are you thinking of?' Vincent glared. His voice fierce. 'Bringing him here, letting him see me! I am NOT one of your plotters, I'm not in your *gang*! I do not intend getting involved with all this!'

The Executor smiled. He was astounding himself, how well he was doing this! 'You're right,' he agreed, managing a slightly foolish smile. 'I made a mistake. I apologise.'

There was nothing Vincent could say, he was marked and they both knew it. Still, rage burbled inside of him. 'I do not want to know *anything about it. You hear me? I don't want to know!*'

The Executor held up his hands in apparent acceptance of his error. Vincent remained for a few moments longer, trembling with rage, before spinning on his heel and storming from the room.

The Executor lit a cigarette and engaged in a languid study of the man seated opposite. 'So,' he said at last. 'You're Carter.'

Carter was painfully thin, with neatly cropped brown hair. His suit looked worse for wear. According to Halstead, things had been tough for Carter since the Bay of Pigs abortion. He'd trained many of the Cuban refugees that had made up the invasion, and had been riding shotgun that night, watching helplessly, furiously, from a high powered launch off the Cuban coast as his men were cut down by machine guns waiting on the beaches.

The Executor briefly consulted an open file on his desk. 'You were rated very highly when you worked the Dominican situation. But things have changed. Tell me, why should I employ you?'

Carter gave a puzzled, half-hearted shrug. 'Well, I heard . . . that is, Ray told me you had something coming off. You might need someone like me.'

The Executor frowned; there was no fight in the man. He looked completely beaten. 'Someone like you, yes, but why you in particular?'

Carter swayed before the penetrating gaze. He could not hold up his head and stare back. His eyes were sunken, haunted. 'I . . . I guess I don't know. I can do most things.'

The Executor held the look a little longer, then loosed an exasperated sigh and, moving slowly upright in his chair, took his cigarette from his mouth and impatiently crushed it in the ashtray.

'You know what I think, Carter? I think you're a bum. You've had it tough for a while and you can't take it. You're finished. Washed up.'

Carter sat, dumbfounded.

'You know what else I think, Carter, I think you're —'

As he launched into a tirade of abuse, anger flickered like lightning flashes around Carter's eyes. Then he was out of his seat and across the desk, hauling the Executor back over it with immense strength and slamming him flat against a wall.

'Washed up am I?' He hissed. 'Is that what you think? Mister, I could tear you apart the best day you ever saw.' The Executor looked at the face so close to his, into the eyes so suddenly alive, and felt satisfaction. His blood raced, and he was breathless, but he kept his voice level.

'Halstead said you ran on a short fuse. Listen to me Carter, the way you feel now, that anger, that power, that strength, that's the way I want you to be for as long as you work for me. Understand?'

Carter was breathing heavily. A puzzled frown creased his brow, to be soothed away as understanding flooded onto his face. With embarrassed suddenness he released the grip and stood back. The Executor straightened his tie and his jacket, then with a forced calm returned to his desk. He fiddled with the blotter to still the trembling of his hands. 'Three hundred dollars a week. For that I expect complete commitment and discretion. Are you in?'

Carter was still rooted to the spot. He hestitated only a moment before accepting the offer, adding: 'Why did you do that?'

'Halstead told me you were good, but you'd fallen into a rut. You've been drinking too much. You hit your wife.'

Humbled, Carter looked down at his hands.

'I discovered that your mortgage payments are in arrears. I took the liberty of paying it off in full.'

Carter blenched in astonishment. 'Why?'

'Because I require your full attention on the job ahead. No distractions.'

Carter sighed, showered with relief. He was buzzing. 'Thanks. Thanks a lot. You got yourself a good man, mister . . . I don't know your name.'

The Executor smiled. 'Let's keep it that way, shall we?'

Halstead and Carter were recruiting, but they were selective. The man they met in the waterside bar came well recommended, but they were naturally wary. The waitress brought three large bourbons, skipping nimbly away as Carter squeezed her fanny.

Davis was thick-bodied and athletic looking, with a ruggedly handsome face and sandy hair. He sipped his bourbon, then put down the glass and stared across the table. 'I've heard of you,' he said to Halstead.

'S'at so? How did you do that?'

'I had a buddy worked with Wilson. You were under him for the routine Cuban fuck-up.'

'You're well informed.' Carter slipped in. Davis gave a non-committal nod, then took up his glass and drained it.

Halstead signalled for refills. 'You had a soft number in the Kennedy camp. Why'd you quit?'

Davis snapped: 'None of your goddammed business!'

'Don't go off at half cock, Davis,' Halstead said soothingly. 'We've heard some good things about you, but our employer insists we ask a few questions before we make any proposition. We have to know why you quit.'

Davis averted his head, a look of utter disgust on his face. 'You don't need me for that,' he muttered sourly. 'Talk to a few people at Hyannisport, almost anyone could tell you.'

Halstead pressed. 'I want to hear it from you.'

There was a pause while fresh drinks were placed before them. The waitress glared pointedly at Carter, then stalked haughtily away. Davis peered into his drink. He was having difficulty getting the words past the lump in his throat. 'That son-of-bitch screwed my wife.'

Halstead and his partner exchanged a glance. 'You can always get another woman.'

Controlling his distress, Davis gave his head a quick shake. 'Not like her. It was my own fault. I worked my butt off for the brothers. I was always tired. She kept pushing me to spend more time with her, so on the last job I took her along. I had to check out security at the hall we were using the next day, so I left her at a party JFK gave for the boys. We were all checked into the same hotel.

'I got back before dawn. She wasn't there. I felt sick to my stomach. I took a walk along the corridors. Next time around she's in bed asleep. I woke her. Hello darling, she said, you're back at last. I asked what time she got back. Midnight, she said.' His shoulders gave a convulsive shudder. 'I lost control. I laid into her like a crazy man. Screaming . . . she damm near woke the whole building. The guys had to bust in to pull me off, but I got it out of her.'

He paused to take a fortifying swallow of bourbon. 'She had a special invitation to *his* suite. I tell you, my blood ran cold when I heard that. Of course she lied at first, said nothing happened. But I threatened to hit her again and she spit it out.' He was panting. 'He laid her . . .' his fists rose, in frustration, and fell. 'Right there in the same hotel. The fuckin' President!' He dropped his head onto his hands.

'She said it never would have happened if I'd been home more. . . .' His shoulders shook as he silently wept. 'Hell,' he lifted his head at last, eyes dry but still red-rimmed. 'He's got that other broad, Julie Starr, he's sharing her with that mob geek, Giometri. He's puttin' it to every woman he can. And that little bastard Bobby's just as bad. I swear, I coulda killed both of them, right there and then, but I didn't. When I left, they didn't even ask why I was going. I loved that woman. Now I've got nothing.'

Halstead looked to Carter. A spark of accord passing silently between them. Davis was bearing exactly the sort of cross they could use.

'Davis,' Halstead reached out and touched his arm. 'How would you like to get back at the both of them?'

Davis narrowed his eyes. 'What do I have to do?' he asked, suspicious.

Halstead shrugged; it was too early for total confidence. 'Nothing too definite yet, but when the time comes we'd like you along. We're going to fix him, and that Bobby son-of-a-bitch too if he becomes too much of a nuisance. We're gonna pull the fuse outa that Kennedy machine.'

Davis stared at them. His mind worked fast. It was a huge and dangerous undertaking, for if he'd read between the lines correctly they were planning to waste the President of the United States. And if he wasn't in . . . Maybe he already knew too much to say no. Grimly he realised he was trapped.

'Pays good.' Carter chipped in.

Davis decided. 'I don't care how much the pay is. I'm in.'

An apartment overlooking the Potomac . . .
September 6th, 1963.

The Executor greeted Halstead with a warmth the former CIA man was unaccustomed to. Bourbon was offered, and accepted, then they went out onto the terrace that overlooked the river.

They sipped drinks in silence, each man locked away with his own thoughts. The wind coming across the river was gentle, fresh and damp, the passing waters rustled gently and the noise of city traffic was a distant and not unpleasant vibration.

Halstead eyed his employer and wondered what he was up to. This was the first time they had met without the insane presence of Johnny Rossi. The Executor seemed nervous, hesitant. But finally he mustered the courage to break the silence. 'I've been wanting to talk to you alone, Halstead. How are things coming?'

Halstead shrugged, but his face could not hide his misgivings. 'Okay I guess. Keeping busy. Carter and Davis are down at the point. I've been spending a lot of time at the range.'

'Anything else?'

Halstead glanced around furtively. 'I was surprised to see that Johnny wasn't here.'

'Does that bother you?'

Halstead gazed across the river. When he replied it was in a subdued voice. 'I guess not.' He paused. 'Are we talking frankly?'

'If you want. What's on your mind?'

The Executor was nervous. His palms were slick with sweat but he successfully held a tight rein on his fear. Sure that Halstead and the others could sense his inexperience, he was convinced they were laughing at him behind his back. That thought, and the attendant feeling of humiliation, cut right through him. He hated the idea with a vehemence that burned.

'I have a strong feeling that things are going on without my knowledge. That bothers me. I am, after all, supposed to be running things around here. I'm looking to you to let me in on what's been happening.'

Halstead moved uncomfortably on his seat. He strove to look noncommital, but could not carry it off. The Executor stared hard at him, knowing in his heart that he was not strong enough to browbeat Halstead. The best he could hope for was that Halstead himself did not realise it.

As he pondered, Halstead moved his jaw in a lazy, chewing movement. The Executor, a new set of senses honed to a fine pitch by his recent proximity to intrigue, saw an opening and on instinct decided to press him. 'Come on Halstead. Better to have me as a benefactor than an enemy. Work with me, and when all this is over I'll make sure you are looked after.'

Halstead mulled over his options, then opened up. 'There have been a few problems. With the plan to blackmail JFK out of office.'

'Oh? I've heard nothing. I thought we were still compiling the information.'

Halstead shook his head. 'That was finished a couple of months ago. You remember that weekend we were away, me, Carter, Johnny and the others?' The Executor nodded. He felt the heavy stormclouds of foreboding gather. Halstead went on: 'We were all out at a private house on Malibu; that's a surfers beach in California. JFK was out there, staying at the Lawfords. Giancarlo had arranged a clandestine meeting via a special courier. An actress, named Julie Starr.'

'I've met her.' Even now, the Executor felt his heart quicken at the mention of her name.

'Well . . .' Halstead faltered. 'This is kind of hard to explain, but, Julie's been fucking Kennedy for a couple of years.'

'But I thought she was Giancarlo's girl.'

'She was. Still is. She's been doing the both of them.'

The Executor was aghast. 'Does Giometri know?'

Halstead sighed. 'He knows alright. He was the one arranged it.' He left a pause for this to sink in. 'It's a long story, and I don't know all of it, but it has something to do with the election in 'sixty. Kennedy was going to come up short a few hundred thousand votes. He needed Chicago. His father had connections going back to the thirties. A few strings were pulled, Giancarlo made Chicago safe, and JFK fell over the line. After a favor of that size, Giancarlo assured his business associates, the pressure on them would decrease. But when Bobby Kennedy became Attorney General the reverse happened. The pressure was stepped up, Bobby has dozens of investigators and lawyers putting the squeeze on. Hoffa, all the rest. Then in April 'sixty one, the millions of dollars the CIA had spent building up a force of anti-Castro Cuban refugees to kick Castro out of Cuba, went to waste at the Bay of Pigs. Kennedy refused the aircover for the invasion and as the rebel force landed on the beach they were met with massive resistance and took heavy casualties. Those that didn't die were imprisoned and tortured.'

'But I remember this,' interrupted the Executor. 'Didn't

Kennedy state publicly he would not support the use of American military force against Cuba? Wasn't there some kind of legal directive that prevented him?'

Halstead nodded. 'National Security Directive 5412. That's true, but he was kept aware of the actions being planned, and the agency people believed that when push came to shove he would get behind the assault. When he didn't, he left a lot of pissed-off people. CIA, Cubans. There were a lot of reckless individuals involved in the campaign to remove Castro. Hotheads. Crying out for blood.'

'So where is this leading? Tell me about the weekend in Malibu.'

'JFK was given a message, a plea really, to have Bobby and his justice people back off. When he refused to play ball he was shown the contents of the file, including explicit photographs of him and Julie, and told that if he did not play along they would be published, if not here then in Europe. He refused to listen.'

'He was prepared to risk exposure? I don't believe it.'

'Believe it. He was probably sure he had enough clout to persuade the press not to take the material. America is a fairly prudish society, don't forget.'

'So it was all for nothing?'

Halstead paused. 'That part of it was. Then came the getback at us; two days ago Giancarlo Giometri was seized at his home and taken to the nearest airport. He was put on a scheduled flight to Costa Rica. He had illegal alien status. He was deported.'

The Executor felt goosebumps rise on his skin. 'Deported? Why Costa Rica?'

'Giancarlo holds a Costa Rican passport. He had the place earmarked as a bolthole, someplace he could run to if the need arose. There is no extradition treaty between the USA and Costa Rica. The Justice department had him flown there, and dumped on the tarmac.'

The Executor was breathing heavily. His skin felt inexplicably clammy. Halstead swallowed the last of the bourbon. 'Giancarlo has lost a lot of face in front of his associates; *la familia*. He is furious. He wants blood.'

The Executor was pale. 'What are you telling me?'

Another pause. Then: 'I'm telling you that I had a telephone call from Johnny Rossi. He has heard from Giometri. He told me to tell you this is no longer about publishing a few dirty pictures. Now we hit back.'

The Executor felt fear tingling, trembling through him. 'I am still not following you.'

'You called me here to tell me a new man is being put in charge of the operation, right?'

Taken aback, the Executor agreed. He asked Halstead how he knew. 'Johnny told me too,' came the reply. 'This is now something more serious.'

'What are you going to do?'

Halstead took in a breath, then exhaled – heavily. 'I don't know.'

Fear, accumulated like steam contained to bursting point in a boiler, escaped from the Executor in a hiss of anger. 'Of course you know! Don't fool with me! What is going on?'

Halstead looked at him, expression blankly innocent, and shook his head. 'I really don't know.'

The Executor felt exasperation bind him. His heart was pounding. He had the feeling of being lifted up, snatched from a sure footing by a lethal whirlwind, and being carried, an unwilling and helpless participant, on the back of the wind. He was trapped.

His heart sank.

The doorbell rang. The two men reacted instantly, Halstead by becoming alert, the Executor by jerking like a startled rabbit.

'That'll be him,' he said, voice weak. Halstead rose to his feet. He left the room, returning moments later accompanied by a man taller than he, taller and broader, with square-cut handsome features and a slightly stooped athletic build. He wore a suit of immaculate European cut. He looked like a French banker.

He shook hands with the Executor, introducing himself as he did so. Halstead poured drinks, and the new man led the toast. They chatted inconsequentially, the new leader of the operation making an effort to put the others at ease. Then, it was on to business.

'First of all,' he said. 'I must make a stipulation. From now on we do not use my name. For all purposes I shall be known by a code name.'

The Executor grimaced. 'Code name? What for?'

The new man stared levelly at him. 'It is an operational necessity. From here on in I shall be known as Rama.'

Halstead, smiled. 'That's apt. I suppose if I'd thought about this, I might have guessed it would be you.'

Rama looked at him. His voice was smooth, and cultured.

'You have me at a disadvantage. I know far less about you.'

Halstead returned the stare. 'I was offered work at Metrotel, and at the Five Eyes, but I'm careful who I work for. This job is a little anti-establishment for you, isn't it?'

'Not at all. I'm used to being on the winning side.' His manner and mannerisms, some of which might in lesser men have been construed as signs of an effeminate nature, here served only to reinforce the tough gentleman image. 'Let's get to business, shall we?'

The Executor cut in. He made an extended speech about the roles each man would play, stressing that he was in charge of the operation and expected to be kept informed of all developments. Rama listened politely, his face wearing an expression of faint amusement. Then he replied. 'You will be kept informed, if you wish, though I have a feeling you won't like what you hear. We'll meet privately sometime to talk about the project and your role in things.'

He turned to Halstead. 'We'd better be going. We have a lot to talk about before your flight leaves.'

The Executor was startled. 'Flight? Where are you going?'

Halstead glanced at Rama. It was the bigger man who answered: 'Ray has a message to deliver for our client on a matter unrelated to your project.'

The Executor look stung. He cast around, mentally, for a put-down, some witty line guaranteed to put the cocksure Rama in his place. But there was nothing. He was forced to settle for a demand: 'I insist we talk.' He asserted himself. 'Meet me at the Manhattan tonight at eight.'

Rama agreed, then he and Halstead left. As they took the elevator down, Rama broke the silence. 'Everything is in place for you. You'll be met at the airport. The men you need will be in place. Just do the dry run, make sure everyone knows what they are doing, and wait for the call.'

Halstead nodded. 'Don't worry about me, worry about Johnny. He's a crazy son of a bitch. He's not gonna take kindly to your taking over.'

'He drinks too much and talks too much. We'll handle him when the time comes, just as we'll handle our friend back there in the apartment. You know the drill; we cover everything, complete plausible deniability. No compromising connections. No mistakes. This is one we cannot afford to let get messed up. I want clockwork; simple, organised and effective.'

Halstead felt a surge of confidence. Rama was the man they

had been missing; the professional edge the project had so far lacked. It felt good to be part of a team again!

That night the Executor lurched unsteadily into the mens' room in the Manhattan club, and steadied himself on the edge of a basin. He stared at himself in the vast, gilt framed mirror that extended the entire length of the tiled wall. In the bright glare reflected on him from a lamp in a concealed housing above the mirror, he gazed in horror at the gaunt visage that confronted him. His eyes were sunken, haunted, as he pondered on the enormity of the deed these people were planning. On the size of the hole he had been sucked into.

'What kind of people are you?' He had gasped after Rama had explained the plan.

'We are specialists,' came the impassive, chilling reply. 'Professionals. This is what we do.'

In the mirror he could see that behind him two men stood at the urinals, cheerfully exchanging laughter. He gripped the sides of his head in an attempt to shut down the dreadful knowledge that filled his mind. He wanted to scream at the men – *do something! Don't you know what is going on?*

He retched into the bowl, dimly aware that the men, now washing their hands at the basins adjacent, were directing looks of disapproval at him as he shamed himself.

In seven days time they were going to kill the President! What should he do?

Seven days.

Chicago!

* 7 *

October 1st.
New Orleans.

The Executor sat behind his polished desk and idly cleaned his nails with a small file. He glanced at the clock on the wall, watched the second hand as it swept in a smooth radius around the face.

Rossi was late. He had summoned the Italian, and Rama too, because his nerves could no longer take the strain. He was being excluded, and that knowledge made him anxious. He had decided he had to find a way to fight back, but the only weapons he had were his wit, and what was left of his nerve. . . .

The two men arrived together. There was a silence between them, a tangible animosity. Rossi glowered at the Executor, but in the calming, dominant, reasonable presence of Rama, the Executor, surprisingly, felt no fear of the man.

Johnny growled. 'What is all this about?'

Gathering his inner resources, The Executor threw the latest batch of expense chits onto the desk and focused a scowl on the Italian. 'All this is what it's about. This isn't realistic, Johnny. You're squandering thousands —'

'LISTEN!' Rossi howled, raising a fat fist. 'Stop giving me this shit! If you want to bring these people in you have to entertain them, and entertainment costs!'

'I expected certain expenses. I anticipated a reasonable drain on resources, but I was expecting cars, salaries, equipment. Not casino notes.'

Rossi turned his eyes upwards. He muttered under his breath. Rama casually moved to the desk and lifted a few of the chits. He eyed them, then let them fall. Rossi sneered at him. 'What is this? This is nothing to do with you. Get your nose out of there!'

Rama lifted his gaze and met Rossi's stare full on. 'I'm running things now, John. This is my show and I'm holding the purse strings. So tell me, you're the man with the connections. You've had six months, what have you managed to *connect* for us?'

'That's none of your damm business. I take orders from Giancarlo.'

'And he takes orders from me.' Rama was firm. 'I'm here to

tell you that unless I am satisfied to the validity of future expenses, they will not be paid.'

'You. . . .' Rossi snarled, taking a step as though to attack, but halting as the big man positioned himself to respond.

Rossi growled. 'You son-of-a-bitch, you can't do this to me!'

'You're a risk, John.' The Executor interceded, feeling bolder with Rama in the room. 'You drink too much, and when you drink, you talk. Now we don't want to lose you, we believe you have a lot to offer. We just want you to keep your nose clean until the job is done.'

Madness glimmered in Johnny's eyes. His fists clenched spasmodically and his chest heaved under his loud jacket. Then he appeared to gain control, his fingers relaxed and he straightened. 'You're just sore 'cause you fell on your butt in Chicago.'

Rama was still. His stare frigid. In a cold tone he replied. 'Things went wrong in Chicago because someone talked. You better pray I never find out it was you or I'll be handing your head to Giancarlo on a plate. Now pick up Halstead and get back here. We're looking at Miami in two weeks. I want you to scan the area and report back here in four days.'

With a stiff nod to mask his fury, Johnny left them. The Executor watched, chin cupped in fingers, as Rama paced the room. The more he saw of the man, the more impressed he was by his professional attitude. 'What about Rossi? Can we depend on him?'

Rama shook his head. 'He's a wreck waiting to happen. Sooner or later we'll need a decision on him.'

At the mention, the hint of intrigue, the Executor felt a thrill ruffle the hairs on the back of his neck. Then something Rossi said returned to him. 'What was that about Chicago?'

'Nothing.'

'Come on. Stop stonewalling me. Let me in.'

Rama heaved a sigh. 'Believe me, you don't want to know.'

'I could probably make a pretty good guess. I'm already in deep. Why don't you come clean with me?'

'How secure are you?'

The Executor peered at him. 'I don't understand.'

'Are you dependable?'

The Executor held the stare. 'Yes.'

After a pause, Rama opened up and told him. The Executor listened, enthralled and terrified, to the awful truth; The Plan, and the things that had gone wrong. With an attack of guilt he realised he was becoming something of an excitement junkie!

A man could get used to almost anything.

Four weeks passed before the two men met again. On this occasion Rama was candid; someone had blown Miami! Someone had talked. The Executor commented that all they had to do was find the loose lips – and close them. Rama nodded, adding that it was easy closing lips. Finding them was the hard part.

'So where do we go from here?' The Executor posed the question. Rama noted the *we* and, with a raised eyebrow, deliberated. 'We go again. Probably in the south. And this time it will run.'

'What makes you think the next time will be any different?'

Rama cut back: 'Because this time I will cut away the deadwood. I will delegate less, and reduce the amount of information available beforehand. Only six people, including myself, will know the plan. And if anything goes wrong, I will personally kill each of the other five.' He grinned starkly. 'Welcome to the six.'

The Executor took it all in – and swallowed.

November 10th.
Dallas, Texas.

Johnny Rossi leaned back on his chair and sucked on his cigar. He blew out a cloud of smoke and stared, glassy-eyed, at his drinking companion, a man he had known slightly for some months. The man savoured his drink, then said, in a voice rich with drink: 'How in hell d'you think would be the best way to get him?'

Rossi exhaled again. 'From an office building with a high powered rifle.'

'You think he knows he's a marked man?'

'Sure he does.'

'They are really gonna try to kill him?'

'Oh yeah, it's in the works. Brown and Rome are favorite to pull the trigger. They already tried to get King. I tell you, Bill, this is really gonna happen.'

His companion, Bill, wearily rubbed at his eyes. He was a skeletal figure, a railroad worker with a prison-pallor complexion. He spoke in an easy drawl. 'Well, you may have figured out a way to get him, the office building and all that. I don't know how the secret service agents cover all them office buildings everywhere he is going. Do you know if they do that?'

Rossi was expansive. 'Well, if they have any suspicion they do that, of course, but without suspicion, chances are they wouldn't.'

'But how would you go about it? You wouldn't just walk into a building carrying a gun.'

'You would disassemble it. All those guns come knock down. You can take it up in pieces.'

The conversation proceeded at a gentle ramble, their voices slurred. Rossi, once drunk, had a tendency towards wanting to impress others by parading his knowledge. He could not reason. He was unstable. 'We have got to be ready, we have got to be sitting on go. There ain't no countdown to it, we have just got to be sitting on go. With Countdown they can move in on you, and on go they can't. Countdown is all right for a slow prepared operation. But when timing is tight, you've got to be sitting . . . you know, on go.'

'Boy,' Bill sighed, with a shake of his head. 'If that Kennedy gets shot, we have got to know where we are at. Because you know that will be a real shake. . . .'

'Nah,' Johnny replied, with a shooing wave of a hand. 'No way. They will pick somebody up within hours . . . just to throw the public off.'

'They won't leave any stone unturned. Oh boy, someone is going to jail if he gets killed.'

Johnny nodded. 'Just like Bruno Hauptmann in the Lindbergh case, you know.'

An hour later, Bill stepped outside and flagged down a cab. Once home, which was a single, dilapidated room situated over a late night deli, he stripped off his jacket and loose shirt to reveal the bulk of a tape recorder and microphone device strapped to his torso with sticking plaster. Grimacing at the pain he peeled away the plaster and dropped the recording device onto the bed. Connecting a tiny earphone, he listened with some satisfaction to the playback, knowing he was on to a big one! He lay back on the mattress and closed his eyes. He would take the recording into the office the next morning. For now, he had to sleep off the drink.

That same night Halstead and Carter were in the drawing room in the Executor's house, poring over maps of Dallas, when Rama burst in. 'The wop son-of-a-bitch!' he raged. The two men looked up in surprise. Neither had seen him this angry before. He was normally the most controlled of men. In answer to their looks he waved a piece of paper. 'Another damm bar bill! from a club in Dallas! Two thousand dollars blown by Rossi. What is he doing down there? We're all in place!

He's pushing too hard now . . .' He muttered breathlessly. 'If he keeps this up. . . .' He stopped, and impatiently thrust the bill at Halstead. 'Get down there. Pay the bill. Give the money to the owner personally and tell him we're paying for no more. From now on, Rossi buys his own drinks.'

Halstead said he would leave immediately. Rama halted. He looked tense. 'We're getting close.'

Carter asked if they were any nearer a fixed timetable. Rama shook his head. 'Not yet. I've a feeling we'll be waiting until the last minute on that. But there are possibilities, and probabilities. You'll know when I know.' He ran his gaze over the map outstretched on the table. 'The likeliest route will be this one through the centre of the city, leaving here, through Dealey Plaza, and on to the Trade Mart down here, where we at least know there is a luncheon planned.' He glanced up at Carter. 'Get me everything you can on this area. Good sites will be here, here, and here.' He indicated with a finger. 'It's wide open. In the meantime . . .' He looked to Halstead. 'You get down to Dallas and muzzle Rossi.'

When Halstead and Carter were alone once more, Carter picked up a pen and drew a circle around Dealey Plaza on the map. 'So, we have our killing ground.'

His partner murmured. He was deep in thought, scanning the drinks bill.

'The Carousel Club,' he read aloud. 'Proprietor, Jack Ruby.'

Lee.
Dallas.
Monday, November 11th.

He was tired, but glad he'd made the effort to visit the camp. Things had not developed quite as planned, but the bureau ought to be pleased he had gotten anything at all.

Entering the Deluxe diner on the corner of Elm and Field, he settled onto his favorite stool at the counter. Allie, the waitress, greeted him with a wry smile and asked how he was. As she poured him a cup he studied her, wondering if he could score. Certainly he could use the break; Marina was being difficult. She was still in Irving, and the isolation was beginning to weary him.

Thinking about Marina brought back the emptiness, that inner vacuum, the *Hole in his soul* as he had once jokingly referred to it. This led him to wondering what it was made him different from others; what marked him out. All his life he'd been an outsider; as a kid, growing up with his Ma. In the marines. It was being a loner brought him to the attention of Naval Intelligence, and later, after Russia, the FBI. For six months he had lived with promises. Done all they had asked of him. He had wormed his way into Bannister's organisation in New Orleans, kept the bureau informed about the activities of Ferrie and his Cubans. But they kept stringing him along, keeping him waiting for the promised payoff.

Allie brought him two donuts. He picked one up and was preparing to bite when a large, warm hand settled on his shoulder. He started, spilling coffee. He shot a look over his shoulder.

'Hiya boy!' a deep voice rang in his ears. It was Johnny Rossi. 'Still hanging out with those faggots?'

'Hi John.' Lee answered. He had met Johnny in the Carousel Club in Dallas one night. The talk between each set of dancing girls had been politics, and Lee relished the chance to be a feed. 'What are you up to?'

Johnny topped off his broad smile with a secretive wink. 'Makin' money.' He slid onto the stool beside Lee. 'I got some time to kill, you wanna real drink?'

Lee shook his head. 'It's a little early for me.'

Rossi's eyes glinted. He smiled wolfishly. 'So how about later? I have something I wanna talk to you about.'

Lee thought for a moment, then agreed. 'Tonight?'

Halstead arrived at the Carousel early evening and glanced quickly around him. The place was fairly low rent, a stage, a bar and a couple of dozen tables grouped across a plain wooden floor. At sight of Rossi his heart fell. The Italian was in a booth against one wall. He had each arm laced around a pretty girl, and wore a wide smile on his face. Dammit, Halstead cursed to himself. The jerk was holding court! Turning away, he asked one of the girls where he could find the boss. He was directed to Jack Ruby, a man of stout build, with a face that looked like it had seen some action. The two men shook hands and then Halstead guided him into a corner. After a brief consultation, during which Ruby began to look concerned, an envelope containing the cash settlement for the bar slate changed hands. Ruby ran a thumb over the bills, then folded the wad and tucked it into a pocket. He turned to move away, but Halstead put out a hand to stop him. 'You understand now, Johnny's no longer on expenses?'

Ruby scowled. 'You guys . . . And I get to tell him, right?' He sighed. 'Y'know, there are times I wish I'd never heard of you all.'

Halstead stared hard at Ruby; if the man was going to buckle, they needed to know. 'We'll be having a few friends coming down to Dallas in a couple of weeks, Jack. We want you to take care of them. You know the drill.'

'What dates? I might be out of town.'

'The twentieth and twenty first. That's Wednesday and Thursday. Choose a motel, somewhere just out of town. Let me know what it all costs.'

'But then I'm finished with you.' Ruby declared. Forcefully enough to appear abrupt. Halstead studied him calmly, then replied. 'You got a lot of nerve for a man who owes money.'

'When this is done I won't owe nobody nothin', and that's just dandy by me.' He strode away.

Halstead made his way to the bar and ordered a scotch. In a mirror he watched as Ruby comically remonstrated with the Italian.

'Come on Jack,' he heard Rossi say. 'Give me a break!' Halstead smiled, and turned his attention to his drink.

The following morning Rossi sought out Halstead at his hotel. The Italian was furious, humiliated by the order given to Ruby.

'I have respect down here, Ray,' Johnny snapped as they walked down to the hotel lobby. Halstead listened patiently before replying.

'Look John. You know I'm just acting on orders. We can't talk here. Come on, we'll find somewhere more private.'

Aston Park was two blocks away. As they walked, Rossi continued to complain. It was clear he felt cheated by Rama, and disappointed by the lack of support he was receiving from Giancarlo Giometri. 'We go back a long ways, Carlo and me. I can't believe he's keeping me in the dark on this.'

'He's probably busy keeping the Justice department at bay. He's back in the country illegally,' Halstead reminded him. 'And they want him.'

'But that son-of-a-bitch Rama, he's undoing all the good work I've done here. They've forgotten it was me put all this together. They owe me.' They neared the entrance to the park. 'Come on Ray. . . .' Johnny protested, tired of the attempts to reason with him. 'I don't need this. Let's go back to Ruby's place and tie one on.'

Halstead grabbed his arm. When he spoke his exasperation showed. 'What do I have to do to get through to you John? You're running out of steps. You can't go on this way. They won't put up with it.'

Rossi snorted. 'Those chicken-shits. I'm a made guy, they won't do nothin'. They need me.'

Halstead let out a weary gasp. There was no talking to the man. They were at the park entrance. Glancing in, Halstead paused, a puzzled expression on his face. Two men, engaged in absorbed conversation, sat side by side on a bench. He nudged Rossi. 'That guy there, the younger of the two, on the bench, he was in Ruby's club last night. Do you know him?'

Rossi nodded, a cocky, half-smile dividing his face. 'Sure, that's Lee. Lee Oswald. I seen him around Bannister's in New Orleans. He lives here in Dallas. He's one of ours.'

'You mean he's in on this?' Halstead reacted with horror.

'Why sure. I meant to tell you about him.'

'And what about the man he's with, do you know him?'

Rossi turned down the corners of his mouth. 'Him? Nope.'

Halstead was breathing heavily as the adrenalin of anger surged. For the first time his patience with Rossi had run out. He now understood Rama's position. 'Well I do know him,' he said bitterly. 'I met him a year or so ago at a seminar. His name is Savage. He's FBI.'

The look of horror on Rossi's face went unnoticed as Halstead's thoughts struggled upstream against a current of conflicting fears and emotions.

Halstead took an afternoon flight and broke the news to Rama. The specialist took it calmly – at least outwardly. Inside, he was seething. The spic bastard!!

'I did some work on Oswald,' Halstead was saying. 'I called a friend in the agency. Get this: *They already have a file on him!* He was a marine with ties to ONI. He spent time in the USSR, out on a limb for the agency. He knows a few of the oddballs hanging around Guy Bannister in New Orleans, and has been seen out at the camps they are using in Operation Mongoose.'

'Anti-Castro program,' Rama muttered. His gaze was vague as he stared ahead. Mind working fast. Halstead was continuing the breakdown. 'Rossi was telling me about the old days, the thirties, when rival mobs used to hit each other, or senior cops and officials who refused to look the other way.'

Rama nodded, but absently. Halstead went on. 'In 1933, in Miami, the Mayor of Chicago, Cermak, was attending a political rally with President Roosevelt. As they mixed with the crowd, a man with a gun stepped out and fired a few shots. Five people were wounded, one of them Mayor Cermak. He died three weeks later. But the gunman, Guiseppe Zangara, was tried, convicted and executed in less than two weeks. He had said he was aiming for Roosevelt, but though he was an experienced marksman, he managed to miss the President's party and hit the people clustered around Cermak instead.

'Now, the interesting thing is this; the way Johnny tells it, Mayor Cermak of Chicago was making trouble for the Capone mob. While Zangara was blasting away, a lone gunman, working for Capone, stepped out of the crowd and put the fatal bullet into Cermak. The proof: Zangara was firing a .32 calibre pistol, but it was a .45 that killed Cermak. The point Johnny was trying to make was this; we kill Kennedy, and there will be uproar. Someone will have to take the blame.'

Rama nodded. 'I've already been thinking along similar lines. 'You'll be pleased to know that Rossi got at least that right. But now I have other problems. Look at this.' Taking a folded sheet of paper from inside his jacket, he passed it to Halstead. The paper was a teletype, and as his gaze scanned the page, Halstead's jaw dropped.

URGENT   1:45 AM EST   11-10-63   HLF   1 PAGE

TO   ALL SACS
FROM   DIRECTOR

THREAT TO ASSASINATE PRESIDENT KENNEDY IN DALLAS TEXAS
NOVEMBER TWENTYTWO DASH TWENTYTHREE NINETENN SIXTYTHREE
MISC INFORMATION CONCERNING

INFO HAS BEEN RECEIVED BY THE BUREAU
BUREAU HAS XXXXXXXXXXXXXXXXX DETERMINED THAT A MILITANT
REVOLUTIONARY GROUP MAY ATTEMPT TO ASSINATED PRESIDENT
KENNEDY ON HIS PROPOSED TRIP TO DALLAS TEXAS XXXXXXXX
XXXXX NOVEMBER TWENTYTWO DASH TWENTYTHREE NINETEEN
SIXTYTHREE.
ALL RECEIVING OFFICE SHOULD IMMIDIATELY CONTACT ALL CIS
PCIS LOGICAL RADICAL AND HATE GROUP INFORMANTS AND
DETERMINE IF ANY BASIS FOR THREAT. BUREAU SHOULD BE
KEPT ADVISED OF ALL DEVELOPMNETS BY TELETYPE.
SUBMIT FD THREE ZERO TWOS AND LHM
OTHER H – OFFICE HAVE BEEN ADVISED

'Where did this come from?'

'New Orleans office of the FBI. Originates from Washington.'

'Coincidence, you think? Or a leak?'

'I'm not sure, and I need to be sure. I'm having a friend of mine chase it up. He's ex-bureau. He'll get me the answers I want.'

'We have ten days. What is the trigger point?'

'The morning of the twenty second. I'm prepared to go right to the wire on this one. We can't afford another foul-up like Chicago.'

'Do you still think it was Johnny's loose talk that sank us there?'

'I'm almost certain,' replied Rama. 'We were lucky in Miami, even luckier in Chicago; Giometri's friends got our men out of jail. But we can't keep banking on that kind of luck.'

'No, as far as Rossi is concerned, the jury's still out. Get back to Dallas and keep him out of trouble for a few days. I'll call you if I need you. I'll have Vincent's private aircraft made available to you. Keep it on standby.'

Halstead hesitated, he had doubts and questions he wanted voiced. Rama noted the reaction, and urged him to open up. 'I have a lot of time for you, Ray. You do a good job. If there's something on your mind, I'd prefer it out in the open.'

'Okay, I gave Ruby your message – about guests visiting Dallas on the twentieth. And I couldn't help noticing some of the calls you've been getting.' Once more he hesitated.

'Come on, what is it. What's bothering you?'

Halstead grasped the nettle. 'Are there two operations going on here? I sometimes feel that me, and Carter and Davis, are involved in one scheme, and a group of others, people I know have connections to the CIA, are involved too, but in some other way.'

Rama's smile became rather fixed. He whistled softly. 'No fooling you, eh, Ray?'

'If you don't want me to know, I can accept that.'

'Well, you've brought the subject up, so I guess I owe you something. The short answer is that the operation is running on more than one level. The degree of compartmentalisation is pretty extreme – for reasons of safety; you know yourself this is a dangerous undertaking we are engaged in. And that is all I can tell you. It is all for the best.'

Halstead loosed a wry smile. 'You know what's really weird, what is such a strange coincidence it makes my hair stand on end?'

Rama raised one eyebrow in inquiry. Halstead went on: 'This guy I checked up on, Lee Oswald. *He works in a building on Dealey Plaza!* What do you think of that?'

Rama rewarded him with an enigmatic smile.

Sunday.
17th November.
New Orleans.

Rama greeted Halstead and Carter at the impressive entrance to the Executor's home, thanking the former for flying up from Dallas at such short notice. Halstead shrugged; it was nothing, Rama was, after all, his boss. Leading the two men into a study where maps and photographs were spread on a polished table, Rama offered drinks, then started the conversation. 'Where is Rossi?'

Halstead replied. 'His car was waiting at the field. He's driving up himself. He'll be here soon.'

Rama nodded. 'Well, I wanted to talk to the two of you alone first anyway.'

For the first time since he had known him, Halstead noted that the leader looked nervous. Rama turned away and peered out of the window. The gardens were a lush expanse that extended half a mile to an ornamental lake. Beyond the lake was planted a border of trees, skeletal, as befitted the season, the earth around them carpeted with a rust red layer of autumn leaves.

He spoke: 'We have a problem. A serious problem. First, I had a call from Jack Ruby in Dallas yesterday. That was the reason I called you back here. Johnny has been talking. Jack had a panicked call from one of his waitresses first thing Saturday. Johnny talked his way into her bed and told her about the operation. She was panicked. She told Jack she believed it was dangerous for her to know about this, and she was leaving town. Jack asked her what she intended doing with the information. She said she didn't know.'

The silence he left was ominous. The two men felt uncomfortable as they watched their leader, standing still, at the window. He was tense, but in control.

'What do you want doing?' Carter posed the question.

'I'll tell you later. For now let me tell you what else has come to light. Ray, I showed you an FBI teletype about a rumoured assassination attempt by a radical group in Dallas. My information is that a police informer, thinking he was involved in something entirely different, recorded a prediction that Kennedy was going to be hit from a tall building when he arrived in Dallas. The informer passed the tape onto the cops, who passed it on to the FBI. The man doing the boasting was Rossi.'

'Oh, fuck!!' Halstead exclaimed. 'They got this on tape? I don't believe it!' He raised his hands, touched the sides of his head with his fingertips as he fought to contain his anger.

'That son of a bitch.' Carter breathed an appropriate response. 'He's gonna put us all in jail.'

Rama turned to face them. 'The man is a walking disaster area. But you haven't heard the worst of it. Ray, that guy you told me about: Oswald, the marine who'd been to Russia? Well he is on the FBI payroll. He's been working on a covert infiltration of the Cuban anti-Castro groups for the bureau. Feeding his findings directly to Washington.'

The bombshell dropped. A new horror dawned on Halstead's face. 'Jeezus! And Johnny's been talking about having him in the group!'

'Right,' Rama countered. 'Oswald is Hoover's pipeline to us. The Director of the FBI *already knows about the plan!*'

Halstead fell silent. There are no expletives eloquent enough to convey the horror, the numbness, he was feeling.

Carter though had a challenge. 'How good is the source of your information?'

'You ever hear the name Frank Rome?' Rama asked him. Carter had. 'Well he's the provider of this information, and his sources are as good as they come. Johnny has fucked us.' He waited for the implications to sink in. 'If we want to avoid going down, we have to find a way to turn this around. Otherwise, Hoover will have us cold; if we don't go to jail we'll spend the rest of our lives in his pocket. Rossi really screwed up this time. The crazy expenditure was bad enough, but to rope in an FBI informer . . . . that was pure carelessness. He has to go.'

His words rang with a chilling finality, and, as though on cue, they heard Rossi's voice echoing through the house. 'Hey, anybody home? Where are you, you schmucks!'

Carter and Halstead looked to Rama. He said: 'If he talks this much before the action, how long do you suppose he could keep his mouth shut afterwards?' One more pause, then: 'He has to go.'

'Ray, you lazy son-of-a-gun! Where are you?' The voice was nearer, they could hear footsteps in the hall.

Rama nodded at Halstead. 'Take him into the kitchen. We'll meet you there.' He moved to a set of drawers, and from the top drawer took out a wide bladed knife and placed it on the table. Next came a wicked looking machete and a garrotting wire. The blades glinted as they caught the light.

Glancing up, he saw the uncertainty on the faces of the two

men. Taking up the wire, he slowly wound one end around the fingers of his right hand. He asked: 'How about you two. Are you secure? Are you dependable?'

Carter started to speak, but Halstead overrode him.

'We are professionals. We don't concern ourselves with personalities or moral issues. We do what we're told.'

Rama managed a grim smile. 'Then let's go.'

'What are you going to do?' Carter chanced the question.

Rama met his stare full on. 'You'll find out. Come on gentlemen, let's see just how professional you are.'

Halstead called out to Rossi, told him he would see him in the kitchen.

Johnny looked up as the three men entered. He had been drinking, his face was flushed. Noting their serious expressions he burst out laughing. 'Come in boys. Why, Mr Rama, you do look unhappy.' He chuckled as he opened the refrigerator door and made a pretence of looking inside. When they did not respond to his jibing, but just stood staring at him in chilly silence, he sensed something. He closed the door and frowned back at them. 'Say, what's going on here?'

Rama stepped forward, the others just behind him. His hands hung loosely at his sides.

Sudden knowledge settled with a dead weight in Rossi's gut. 'You sons of bitches,' he said in a gravelly, almost guttural monotone. He raised a hand to lash out, but they were upon him, Rama grasping one arm, Carter the other. Halstead held the knife in his hand. There was a noise, Johnny shouting and swearing as he struggled. He lashed out wildly with a foot, kicked out again, then gasped as a frigid cold scythed his thigh. He felt strength seep from his leg, and looked down to see a neat slit in his pants and a deep cut in the flesh of his thigh. A glut of crimson, horribly, darkly red, flowed from the wound. He felt it journey along his leg, he saw the fat blade, dripping blood, in Halstead's hand. With an angry roar he swung left in an attempt to free a hand and strike out, but the grip on him held and he could only watch in furious horror as Halstead twice thrust the machete blade up under his ribs.

'JEEEEZUUUSSSS!!' Johnny screamed as Halstead two-handed the blade around in his gut, and with a strenuous effort ripped it across Johnny's gashed belly. Beads of sweat blossomed on Halstead's brow, and not just from the physical effort of gutting. His own stomach churned, and he knew he would be lucky to hold it.

The grip was released, and Johnny fell to his knees. His face was bloodlessly pale, and he weakly clasped his hands over his spurting belly in an attempt to hold in the seeping contents. 'Oh God . . . .' he whimpered, looking down and catching sight of purplish intestines leaking into his hands despite his desperate efforts to contain them. He started to topple forward, but his head was jerked viciously back and he found himself fighting frantically for air as the wire looped in Rama's hands snapped tight around Johnny's throat. And as the big man hauled on it, the wire began to cut through flesh and muscle.

Tears poured from Johnny's eyes as the wire was drawn remorselessly tighter towards the centre of his neck. Vision dimmed, his face swelled and purpled, and his tongue lolled in an ugly spasmodic fashion between his lips. Rivulets of blood trailed down his chest.

At last he was allowed to fall to the floor. The wire still embedded deeply into flesh. His head swam with the effects of the pain, but with some relief he told himself it was over.

Then he heard Rama say: 'Finish it.' And he could not believe the message the nerve-endings in his body screamed at him. Swamped by waves of nausea he lay there, helpless and in indescribable pain as his legs were hacked off at the crotch.

Halstead leaned his head against the bathroom wall and spewed into the basin until not even bile came. His stomach ached from the contractions, and his nose was clogged. He cleared it, and doused his face with cold water.

Carter was beside him, towel and glass of cold water at the ready. Halstead dried his face, drank, then looked at himself in the mirror and shuddered. 'God, that was hard. That was the hardest thing I've ever had to do.' Gripped by cold, he rubbed at his upper arms. 'Jesus.'

'You okay now?' Carter asked.

Halstead looked at him. 'You want the truth? I'm more scared than I've ever been. I don't ever want to be a loose end in this organisation.'

His friend nodded in sympathy. 'He's one tough bastard. I never would have guessed.' He paused. 'Better pull yourself together, Ray. You have to be strong now. If he thinks you're not up to the job. . . .' The unsaid put across the point most eloquently.

Halstead stared at himself in the mirror. His face was gaunt, haunted. The image of the machete blade, gleaming as he struggled to hack through glistening bone, would not go away, but with a great mental effort he thrust it aside and straightened. 'Okay,' he breathed. 'Let's go see what he wants done next.'

New Mexico.

Halstead and Carter were hunting. The search had been conducted in urgency, but their efforts had borne fruit. Marie Soper, the hostess who had fled Jack Ruby's Carousel Club, had found work in a bar, and they had found her.

It was after two in the morning when Marie left the bar and climbed into her little foreign car. The puny headlamps flickered on, and the bug-like auto buzzed out onto the freeway heading north.

Halstead's powerful black Buick hung behind the bug, crouched low to earth like some preying jaguar. When they struck a desolate stretch of road he forced the accelerator to the floor and effortlessly overhauled the smaller car, drawing dead level as they took a curve above a sheer drop.

Marie glanced right, saw Carter's face staring, skull-like at her in the dim light, and was gripped by sudden stark terror.

Halstead swung the wheel and the Buick lurched left, nudging the bug towards the edge. Marie's screams, and the screech of scraping metal, cut through the quiet night air as she fought to stay on the road. Then Halstead, his face viciously distorted, swung the wheel again, and the bug vanished over the precipice.

The world outside the windows whirled. Marie let go the wheel and clapped her hands over her ears. She screamed as the bug bounced and crunched and rolled to the bottom of the rocky incline. The windows imploded, the horn bleated madly, and as the earth rushed forward to meet her she closed her eyes and cringed into a ball. . . .

Blackness.

Hospital, she guessed from the sounds and the sterile odour. A cry burst from her as she recalled the nightmare.

'Doctor, she's coming to,' a female voice echoed softly. A man replied, brisk and competent. 'She's not ready yet. Sedate her again.'

Her mind screamed: *NO!* But in truth she was becoming aware of the pain and was glad when the prick of the needle brought relief.

* 8 *

Final briefings. Two days to go. Rama eyed the men gathered in the room, some two dozen of them, a mix of Caucasian and Hispanic, and his gaze settled on the thin faced individual in the front row. 'Can you handle that, Lee?'

The little man mumbled. He seemed self conscious, almost shy, in company. 'Sure. As long as that's all I have to do.'

'Of course,' Rama assured him. 'Great stroke of luck for us, you getting that job in the depository.'

Lee mumbled once more. 'Yeah, well, like I said, a friend arranged that. I didn't have —'

Rama smiled. 'Whatever. The devil looks after his own, right?' A nervous titter rippled through the gathering.

The event was gone through, stage by stage, each man reciting his role and exhibiting a detailed knowledge of the timing of the anticipated sequence of events. Rama wound up the meeting, dismissing them with a cry of 'Good Luck!' when a voice piped up: 'When's Johnny coming back?' A chorus joined in; the Italian, generous to a fault with the boys, was popular.

Rama, hiding the strain well, smiled, then looked askance at Halstead. 'You want to tell them, Ray, or shall I?'

Halstead gaped. 'Er . . . be my guest.'

Rama clapped his hands together. 'Okay, but I want to make it clear that what I tell you goes no further than these four walls. We all agreed?'

There were exchanged looks, uneasy mutterings, then a general assent.

'You all know John. We all love him, but sometimes he goes over the top. The truth is he's having a little medical treatment right now. He's down with a case of syphilis.' This was met with a number of blank stares. 'In plain language, a dose of the clap.'

Laughter; then animated chatter. Wasn't that just like Johnny. 'A piece of tail is a piece of tail.'

'I told him the poon would get him in the end!'

Rama raised his voice: 'He sends his regards and promises to share his experiences with you when he gets back.'

The meeting broke up, the men drifting away content with the explanation. Halstead joined Rama at the drinks cabinet and whistled softly. 'I'm impressed.'

Rama poured drinks and handing one to Halstead. 'Health.'

Halstead echoed the sentiment, then asked: 'Do you think Lee suspects?'

Rama shook his head. 'No, I don't think so. He believes he has me fooled, and that leaves the advantage with us. Once the hit is in motion we have to maintain that advantage by mobilising everyone and hoping to Christ the police shoot him dead.'

Halstead voiced a doubt. 'That's the only piece we can't completely cover. The only weak spot.'

'And Ruby.' Rama reminded him. 'The man's nervous. He could go either way. I wouldn't be surprised if he cracked.'

'He'll be okay,' Halstead countered. 'I've spoken to some of the guys who knew him in Chicago. They all say Jack's standup. He'll keep his mouth shut. He knows better than to cross you.'

At that instant Carter appeared at the door and entered. His face was flushed. 'Bad news. I had a friend in the police follow up the Marie Soper accident. She survived. She's in hospital.'

Halstead cursed. Rama restricted himself to a sharp intake of breath. 'How bad is she?'

'Miraculously – for her, only superficial wounds. Don't ask me how – that was a two hundred foot drop in a spinning vehicle. Beats me how she didn't break every bone in her body.'

'Well, Halstead?' Rama challenged. Halstead held the stare, saying to Carter: 'Go back and finish her, and be sure this time.'

Carter signalled his understanding, and hurried out.

Lee.

Damn Hoover! The son of a bitch was never available when you wanted him! Turning out of the telephone booth in the Deluxe diner, he returned to his seat. In his absence Allie had refilled his cup.

Morosely he sipped at his coffee, the narrowness of his face intensified by the frown. He was concerned about the difficulty he was experiencing in contacting the Director of the FBI. This was the plot of the century! The man had demanded to be kept informed, dammit! And Lee had so much to tell.

On sudden impulse he called to the waitress and asked if she had a piece of paper and a pen. 'I have to write a letter.'

Pausing in the motion of wiping the countertop, she replied, with sardonic good humor: 'I suppose once you've written it you'll want an envelope too.'

A grin shrugged onto his face. 'If you have one.'

Procuring the items from a drawer, she placed them on the counter before him.

'Let me have another donut will you?' he asked, taking up the pen. She did as requested, flashing him an inviting smile as she placed the plate at his elbow. He seemed not to notice. With a sour puckering of her lips she turned away.

Scribbling frantically, he wrote an update report containing everything he knew. Names, times, locales. He finished with a plea for guidance; time was short, and though he had no doubt Hoover would intervene to prevent the killing from going ahead, the lack of visible activity worried him.

Signing his name with a flourish, he folded the paper and fitted it into the envelope. He glanced up; Allie was leaning on the counter, a postage stamp trapped between thumb and fore-finger. 'You'll need this,' she beamed, a suggestive glint in her eyes. 'Unless you plan to deliver that by hand.'

He swallowed nervously. 'Thanks,' he said hoarsely. 'But I plan to do just that.' Pausing only to dunk the donut and cram it into his mouth, he hurried out.

The sun outside was bright, hot. A glance at his watch told him he was going to be late back for lunch. He would have to deliver the letter to the FBI office later.

November 21st.
New Mexico.

Marie opened her eyes to a flood of bright sunshine slanting in through window blinds, and felt warmth stream over her. The whisk of crisp bedlinen being changed on the next bed caught her attention. She was clearheaded for the first time in days, and the reality snagged in her mind.

Quickly, she had to tell . . . before they sedated her again. Darting out a hand, she clutched at the nurse's skirt. The nurse spun to look at her and, seeing she was awake, smiled kindly. 'Hi, how are you feeling?'

Marie's throat grated rustily. 'Fine, I think. Just a little weak. I have something to tell you . . .' She paused to clear her throat.

'I'll fetch you some water,' the nurse said. She started to move away but Marie snatched at her wrist. 'No wait! I have to tell you something . . . first.' She hesitated, ran her tongue around the parched interior of her mouth. She had to tell, get out the words . . . first! 'What day . . . what date is it?'

The nurse gave a perplexed frown. 'It's Thursday. The twenty first of November. Really, you haven't been out that long, just a couple of days . . .' She broke off as Marie invested more force in her grip.

'Listen. This is important. I came here from Dallas. The President is going there on the twenty second. He is going to be shot. They are going to kill him. Do you understand?'

'Shot?'

'Killed.' Marie was breathless from the effort. 'You have to tell someone . . . the cops, the FBI, anybody . . . you must.' Her grip failed. She slumped back onto the bed.

Assuring her patient that she would return in a few moments, the nurse hurried out.

Marie closed her eyes. Her chest rose and fell in tune to her labored breathing. She hoped she'd been in time.

A sharp, pricking sensation between the two largest toes on her right foot brought her up with a start. A kindly faced intern in a white jacket stood at the end of the bed. As she slowly focused on him he deftly thumbed the plunger on the hypodermic between her toes, then withdrew the needle from her flesh. He smiled in a relaxed fashion, then winked an eye.

She forced herself up, arms locked straight behind her, and in a nervous husky voice demanded to know what was going on.

He gave her big toe a friendly tweak, and it was at that instant her head began to whirl. Vision blurred and cleared, blurred and cleared. The room tilted, then started to revolve around her, slowly at first but picking up speed. It was as if she was seated in the static centre of a hurtling carousel.

Carousel! The word flooded her mind with horror-filled associations. The intern was on the merry-go-round with her. As he passed, he smiled, and she heard him softly say: 'It's better this way, Marie. Really.'

Fear. Her nerves were suddenly jagged, raw-edged. She grasped the mattress, hung tightly onto the bed, willing the spinning to stop. The intern had stepped off the carousel, somehow. She caught a last blurred glimpse of him as he strode for the door. Reaching out she clutched feebly at the air.

'Help me . . .'

Nausea had hold of her. Faster the room spun, and faster still. Her stomach spasmed, hurled a gust of bitter fluid to the back of her throat. She shut her eyes to blot out the sensation, but the nausea worsened. She retched, throat seared by bile, then, the drug immobilising her limbs, she fell backwards and lay unable to move, unable to prevent the spasms, too weak to do anything to prevent the puke filling her mouth.

Gurgling, and clawing weakly at the bedsheets, she choked to death on her own vomit.

The nurse returned to find her, grey-faced and still. Her mouth a well, brimming with thin, bitter fluid. Her face spattered and hair matted with milky globules. Her terrified gaze fixed on the ceiling.

Thursday night.
21st November.
Cabana motel, Dallas.

They were in a non-descript motel room. Sparsely furnished with twin beds, a wardrobe, and a TV set in one corner. Their guests had gone, things were finally moving. A celebratory drink was poured and a toast offered, and Rama and the Executor settled back on their chairs and stared at each other.

'The last night,' the Executor repeated the toast. 'To tomorrow.' He left a pause. 'Are you confident this . . . pawn, Oswald, will never make it to trial?'

'Very confident. Frankie will take care of him.'

The Executor nodded. 'I have to hand it to you, you've done one heck of a job. A thoroughly professional piece of work. What about the other arrangements, the *tidying up*?'

'A minor detail.' Rama replied with an airy wave of a hand. 'That will be the simplest part of the entire operation.' He adjusted himself on the chair, and cleared his throat. 'Well then,' he said, tentatively. 'We arrive at the moment of reckoning. My payment.' He knew this was a delicate moment. He noted that the other man was oddly taciturn, peculiarly uncritical. He was the kind of man who would normally probe for weaknesses. Rama continued: 'Everything is set, as per our deal, and I'm ready to receive my fee. In full settlement, and in cash.'

The Executor pulled a reluctant face. 'What do you plan to do with your money?'

Rama smiled. 'I'm going to disappear for a few years. I'm a great believer in the ripples theory. I drop a stone in the ocean today, and some time later, months later, maybe years, when I'm standing at the shore one day, looking out to sea, the ripple comes in to swamp me, and I drown. I'm going away long enough to let all the ripples fade.'

'If I pay you now, and you take off, my operation might falter for want of a good commander at the last moment.'

'Halstead knows the drill. He could do it without me. And Frank Rome, he'll take care of the tidying up. But you know me better than that. I'll see this thing through. Quit stalling.'

'Well, if that is the case, and the operation really can go ahead without you, perhaps it's time I did this . . .' The Executor's hand rose from behind the desk, and in it he held a gun. The weapon's evil single eye peering at Rama. 'It's been a pleasure watching you work,' he said smugly. 'You really are a professional.'

Rama stared blankly at him. 'You know, I . . . er, I thought you might do this. But then I thought, no, he's okay. I can trust him.'

The smile on his employer's face widened. 'Just goes to show how wrong you can be. I rather thought you were a good judge of character.'

'Oh I am, normally.' Rama's shoulders dipped. 'Do I have time for a last cigarette?'

The Executor cautiously agreed, adding: 'But move slowly. If anything that isn't a pack of cigarettes comes out of your pocket, I'll shoot first and ask questions later.'

Moving with deliberate steadiness, Rama took out cigarettes and a lighter. He lit up, then said, conversationally. 'Why are you doing this?'

The Executor did not hesitate to reply. 'Because I've heard you blithely talk about tidying up. I know what happened to Johnny Rossi, and I've no intention of letting the same thing happen to me.'

'What makes you think the same thing might?'

'Because I know too much. I've seen you, and I know about the others, Giometri, Frank Rome. To them I must represent a danger.'

'Killing me won't change a thing. If they want you dead, you will die.'

The Executor was panting, sweating. He was not the sort of man who had ever pulled a trigger. He was nervous, and they both knew it. 'Maybe not, but if I remove enough of the people who are a danger to me, perhaps I can isolate myself. Survive despite you all. I'm new to this. What else can I do?'

'Before you do anything rash, I want you to let me make a telephone call. It will be to your ultimate benefit.'

'How so?'

'Remember how you got involved in all this? Remember just who you are crossing? My feeling is that you ought to make yourself valuable to those people. If they believe you are worth more alive than dead, you could be secure. May I?' he indicated the telephone on a small cabinet by the bed.

The Executor nodded, once more warning him to make no sudden moves. Rama dialled, spoke quietly into the handset, then held out the receiver. 'They want to talk to you.'

Moving slowly, the Executor reached for the receiver. Of what happened next, he was never completely sure. As his fingers closed around the receiver, Rama's own fingers moved with deft speed. Gripping the Executor by the wrist, placing a thumb against the back of his hand for leverage, Rama gave the hand a savage twist. The Executor squealed, in surprise as much as pain, and in an instant found himself face down on the bed, one arm twisted up his back, the gun removed from his hand.

Rama was breathing heavily. That had been a hairy moment. He straddled the Executor, placed the muzzle of the gun behind his ear, and muttered: 'How do you like this, eh? You want to know what its like, dying?' His finger tightened on the trigger. To his credit, the Executor did not plead for mercy. He shut his eyes tightly, waiting to die, expecting to die, without ever hearing the fatal shot . . .

Rama reined in his temper. Getting up, he hauled the man off the bed and slammed him up against the wall. The Executor winced. The fear showed on his face. He swallowed. 'Are you going to kill me?'

'Would you blame me if I did?' Rama answered quickly.

The Executor stared vacantly, mouth slack. He looked dishevelled; tie knot loose at his neck, shirt crumpled. Rama stepped up to him and placed the gun beneath his chin. 'What will you promise me if I don't?'

The other man gulped. 'What do you want?'

Rama licked his lips while he thought. Then he spoke, and his voice was hoarse, far from confident. 'I want us, just you and me, to go into partnership.'

'Partnership? Why?'

Rama stood back, calmed himself. He pocketed the gun. 'I'll level with you. You need me if you want to live. What you were saying is right; you are a danger. You could put Giometri away. You can embarrass the government by revealing what you know about Frank Rome, and the others. You see, when I took on this job I was told one thing. The mission has to succeed. It doesn't matter what it costs, or how many people have to die. For them, this mission has to succeed – *no matter what.*'

What are you saying, I'm a dead man?'

'I'm saying that both you and I are dead men, unless we take steps to protect ourselves. Who knows more than you? Me!'

'But you are one of them! You're ex-CIA, they know they can trust you.'

Rama shook his head with a rueful smile. 'It doesn't always work that way. Believe me, Kennedy will only be the first to die.

Look at the lengths we are preparing to go to protect ourselves; we have a whole tidy-up scheme planned. Now look at the people behind you; Giometri and his friends, the CIA people behind me. They have a lot to lose. They want protection as much as we do. If we don't take steps, we'll be dead within a week.'

The Executor moved slowly away from the wall and settled onto the bed. 'What can we do?'

'I have it all safe. Tape recorded conversations. Film. Transcripts. Receipts and signatures. Teletype copies. I let them have a copy of what I have. They know I'm not kidding. The stuff stays in button-down —'

'What?'

'Button-down. A kind of dead man's handle. As long as I'm alive to make a telephone call each day, the stuff is secure. Once I don't make the call, the stuff is released to the press. The result? Catastrophe. It's a fairly normal pattern.'

'Will that be enough to keep us safe?'

'I think so.'

The Executor sighed with relief. His shoulders sagged. Then he turned a sceptical eye to Rama. He wondered what the big man was up to?

Rama asked if he wanted a drink, then filled two glasses from a bottle of bourbon. The Executor finally mustered the courage to voice his misgivings: 'Why would you care what happens to me?'

'What do you mean?'

'I'm as much a danger to you as I am to the others. Why would you want to keep me safe?'

'Call it my good deed for the day.'

'Excuse me if I don't sound too convinced. You don't do anything for free. What's your angle?'

Rama gave a resigned sigh, then passed the other man a drink. 'Okay, I'll tell you how I see things. I talk to our associates. I make them aware that we are in partnership. I let them see the material we are holding, and then I convince them that you are much more valuable alive than dead. You know where the money has come from to save Vincent Steel. So do they. It is in everyone's interest to keep the Vincent company in business. They'll see that.'

'Are you sure?'

'I'm sure. You'll be fine.'

'I know I'm repeating myself, but, what's your angle?'

'I told you. I'm going away for a while. But when I return I want a slot, a well paid slot, in Vincent Steel. I want you to guarantee my financial security.'

'And this is in exchange for . . . ?'

'Your life, right now. And my silence regarding your part in all this. If anything happens to me, you'll be doing hard time too.'

The Executor absorbed all this. He felt uneasy; he was as good as writing a blank check for the man. But what choice did he have? Rama still had the gun.

'Okay,' he agreed finally. 'But one more thing. How do I know I can trust you?'

'I'm willing to show my good faith. In fact I have a gesture planned, an alteration to the plan. I will be on the knoll in Dealey Plaza tomorrow. I will take up the last shot position, and I will personally put the last bullet into JFK. Only you and I will know. It will be our secret.'

* 9 *

The Final Day

Carter and the Corsican, Raoul Samartino, clambered up the final flight of stairs to the sixth floor of the Texas School Book depository building in Dallas, and paused to make sure the way was clear. They wore the pale blue, boilersuit-type uniforms of a locally known vermin extermination company. Lee was waiting on them. He looked nervous, glancing around as if afraid of being seen with the two, though their appearance was innocuous enough.

'This way,' he motioned to them, leading them around a mass of stacked boxes to a partially open corner window. Lee licked his lips, and Carter felt a rush of annoyance. What was up with this guy? No one was asking *him* to kill anyone. If he hadn't the balls for the job he ought not to have gotten involved!

He snarled. 'You brought the rifle?'

Lee had, and he nodded. He ducked behind a nearby box stack and brought out the weapon, a type Carter recognised as being of Italian origin; Mannlicher Carcano. Firing a powerful, 6.5mm cartridge, with a muzzle velocity of 2234 feet per second, the Mannlicher was capable of killing an elephant with a single shot to the head. An ill-fitting sling and a cheap looking Japanese four-power scope had been attached, the scope badly.

Raoul took the weapon without a word and quickly examined it. He fitted the stock into his shoulder and frowned as he squinted through the scope. 'Is loaded?' he asked Lee in a thick, heavily accented voice. Lee nodded. Raoul shifted his aim. 'The telescopic is shit,' he muttered with a glower.

Lee shrugged. 'It's all I had time to get.' He leaned towards the window and peered at the street below. 'It isn't too great a distance. A hundred, hundred and fifty feet.' He glanced at the Corsican. 'You gonna take him coming along Houston?'

Raoul ignored the question. He was re-acquainting himself with the rifle sight, but still seemed unhappy. Lee looked to Carter and was dismissed with a nod. He walked to the elevator and called down the shaft. 'Hey guys, close the door will you?' There came the clanging of a door slamming shut, then the sound of heavy winding machinery. Carter looked at his watch; eleven fifty.

Raoul busied himself, moving boxes to provide cover, then settled to wait. Carter raised the walkie-talkie to his lips and checked in. 'Sunray to Rama. Sunray to Rama. On site and secure, over.'

A terse acknowledgment barked from the handset. He took a deep breath, filled his chest and slowly exhaled. He was tense. This was the big one. They didn't come any bigger.

The Corsican stiffened, ears pricking up at the sound of heavy footsteps. *Someone was coming up the stairs!* Acting quickly, Carter and Raoul moved away from the window, threaded between alleyways of stacked boxes and crouched down in a corner. Peering around the edge of a boxstack, Carter watched as a stocky black man entered from the stairwell. He was carrying a lunchbox and a bottle of coke. He sauntered lazily to the very corner window Raoul was supposed to shoot from and sat down on one of the boxes! Placing his coke bottle on the window sill, he opened his lunchbox and started to gnaw on a chicken leg.

Carter covered his face with his hands and pressed hard. Jeezus! Who could plan for a depository employee wanting to watch the motorcade from a high vantage point?

He cursed. It was so damn obvious. Why the hell hadn't they thought of it? They had planned so much, to the last detail . . . hundreds of details. Everything but this. The silence in the room was soundtracked by crowd noise, a gentle burbling, a simmering excitement. Carter switched off the walkie-talkie. He did not want anything to attract attention. He had to think.

On Dealey, Rama paced the area behind the fence that ran along the top of the little hill. Dressed as a construction worker, complete with hard hat, he had arrived two hours earlier in a car he had hired in New Orleans. The other cars had appeared at eleven thirty, circled the parking lot that backed onto the railroad yards, and moved on to park in their designated spots. One by one the other teams checked in. Two teams of two men. One team in the records building, and one in the Texas Book depository building. He and Davis, and four men primed with fake Secret Service ID, formed the last team; the hill shooters.

He stepped into the depository, found a payphone on the first floor and dialled Halstead, who was waiting in a callbox at Love Field. It was confirmed; The President was on his way. He glanced at his watch. Eleven fifty five.

In the railroad supervisor's tower, one hundred yards from the parking lot, Railroadman Tom Boland watched the activity with interest. Men in suits patrolling, had to be FBI or Secret Service. He noted the cars arriving. They looked dusty, as if they had come in straight from a hard drive over desert. One had what looked like a political pennant stuck to the rear window, and he could see that each car had out-of-state plates.

One of the drivers had a walkie-talkie held to his face.

He had watched the tall man, wearing a suit, who seemed to be in command, pace the area. He noted that the three others, one wearing a check sports jacket and pale slacks, one dressed like a police officer and another like an auto mechanic or building worker, appeared to be taking orders from him. Boland glanced at his watch; five minutes past noon.

Lee went down to the first floor canteen to eat his lunch. The food was dry and tasteless, and butterflies fluttered in his gut. He had made the call. Now all he could do was wait, and hope Savage was as good as his word. He watched as his colleagues in the building drifted outside to watch the Presidential parade. One of the secretaries, a girl he knew faintly, peeked in and smiled hello. He wanted to wave back, but his nervousness got the better of him. And then she was gone and it was too late. He desperately wanted everything to appear normal, but his hands, anxious for something to occupy them, were interlaced, wringing each other.

On the sixth floor, Carter was becoming anxious. The Corsican made frantic hand gestures, indicating he wanted to kill the black man who was still quietly enjoying his lunch. But Carter demurred with gestures equally graphic. It was fifteen after twelve, and the Presidential car was due within seven or eight minutes. Pretty soon he would have to make a decision; handle the black employee, or abort his part in the action. But not yet. He wondered what Rama was making of the radio silence.

Below, on Dealey Plaza, Rama was furiously clenching a fist at his side. He knew that Carter was a good man. If he was not talking there would be a good reason, but knowing this did not make him any less nervous.

The Corsican was getting itchy. He had a narrow bladed knife in hand and was itching to use it. He had not come half way around the world to be thwarted. Carter was frustrated; was this going to be Chicago all over again, the stunt aborted with only minutes to spare? He breathed a sigh of relief as the black worker finished his lunch, got up and left. Carter and Raoul moved rapidly to the corner, Raoul taking up his position at the window. He practised aiming down at Houston Street, swinging the rifle in an arc until he was sighting at Elm Street, sloping away beyond trees and vanishing under a triple railroad overpass.

Carter switched on the walkie-talkie and checked in. Rama sounded relieved. So far the operation was green.

Jack Ruby had met Rome and Carter outside the Dallas police building early that morning. They had sized up the place, discussing an escape route through a side door leading to the basement, to be used if any of the team were taken by the police. There were enough Dallas cops on the payroll to be of help if executing an escape became necessary. Jack then spent the rest of the morning in the offices of the Dallas Morning News, placing ads for the Carousel. The deadline for placing the ads passed at noon, but he lingered in the building.

Walking up to the second floor, he settled in a vacant chair at a desk by a large window that overlooked Dealey Plaza. He had a perfect view of the spot the Presidential car would pass. He glanced at his hands and noticed his palms were damp. So far he had been calm. He had done a good job. He was calm. . . .

Northside, Dealey Plaza.
12.20 pm.

Davis still patrolled the length of the fence that ran along the top of the hill. These were crucial minutes, they could not afford any mess. He was startled by a figure in uniform approaching from the far end of the fence where the car park ended and the railroad track passed. He moved quickly forward, seeing clearly now that the man was wearing the uniform of an infantryman, and guessed him to be a soldier on leave. Taking his Secret Service ID from his pocket, he decided on an offensive approach and called out to the man. 'Hey, you can't come back here. Get outa there.'

The soldier stared back at him. 'You and which army is going to move me?'

Davis lifted the open wallet to the soldier's face and let him see the ID. 'Presidential Security. This whole area is off-limits.'

The soldier took a breath, then sighed. 'Well, I guess that's good enough for me. If you don't mind I'll just leave this way.' He brushed past Davis as another of the team, a man named Donahue, came walking up. Donahue was the team member dressed as a Dallas police officer. Beyond him, Delvecchio, the fourth man in the hill team, who wore the casual checkered jacket and slacks, glowered at the soldier's back as the man passed by. Donahue approached Davis.

'Everything okay, Phil?'

'Sure.' Davis replied. 'Just getting a little hinky.' He glanced up at the distant window in the depository, hoping for a visual fix on Samartino's position, but the distance was too great and the angle too acute to give him a clear view.

'You know what you have to do?' he asked Donahue.

'Sure. No worries. And Delvecchio is in place.'

Frank Rome was settled on the second floor of the Dallas County records building. He was a small, neat individual, dressed in a conservative suit and tie. He looked harmless, and that was his strength. His view of the sloping Elm Street meant that he would be shooting at the motorcade along an angle that was almost on the horizontal. He was holding an AR-15 high velocity automatic weapon, primed to fire a 5.56mm cartridge at 3200 feet per second. He was a fan of the weapon. The bullet would break up on contact, leaving one heck of a mess.

In the Dal-Tex building situated close to the Texas Book Depository, Eugene Farman, link man to the mob, in Dallas that day as an observer, found an office he could view Dealey Plaza from. He was dressed as a hobo, having been advised this was one of the best possible disguises for such an occasion. Cops might kick him out of the way, might even run him out of town, but they would never suspect him of being involved.

He was nervous, as they all must be, he thought. This had been a long time coming. In a couple of hours it would be business as usual. He looked forward to calling Giancarlo and giving him the good news personally. He looked up; the noise from the crowd increased; the Presidential car was coming.

Between the Depository building and the triple overpass was situated the car park, the back end of which ran into the rail-yards where Tom Boland still watched. It was almost time, Rama thought to himself as he ducked into the rear exit of the depository building, and brought out a bag. Taking off his hard hat, he wiped sweat from his brow, then stalked with an authoritative air back towards the fence, bag in hand.

Donahue, standing between the fence and one of the parked cars, took the bag and squatted down. Taking out the pieces of the rifle, he quickly assembled the weapon, and placed it at his feet. The signal was given; the motorcade was almost invisible. As Rama approached, the man gave a hand sign to indicate that all was well, then moved away to take up his position, midway between the fence and the rail tracks.

The walkie-talkie in Rama's hand crackled into life. '*They are about to turn onto Houston. ETA one minute.*'

Davis lifted the rifle, this was also an Armalite AR-15. He checked the loading and thumbed off the safety. He felt, rather than saw, Rama appear at his side and peer over the fence. 'Still too many people too close to us. Donahue and Delvecchio have fucked up. Look at this . . .' He indicated an elderly man and a young woman standing, some twenty five feet away, atop a concrete abutment to the stone memorial pergola. The man was holding a home movie camera. . . .

'And look at this . . .' Rama was incensed. Only six feet away stood the infantryman Davis had moved on earlier. He too had a movie camera. He fiddled with it, preparing to film the motorcade as it passed. Davis glanced up and recognised the soldier. His nerves were already frayed, now he was close to snapping. 'That son of a bitch. . . .'

'Give me the rifle.' Rama instructed. 'And get rid of him.' Davis glanced beyond the fence, across Dealey. 'What's going on?' he demanded, startled as Rama took the rifle from his hands.

'Last minute change of plan,' came the grim reply. 'Take my place in the running. We haven't got time to get into an argument with anyone, and we don't want to attract attention. Just do as I tell you. Kennedy's almost here, for Christ's sake.' Rama swallowed the intense fury bubbling inside him. 'And do something about that camera. Jesus, if he turned around with that now he could film me pulling the trigger!'

The men were well drilled, Davis no exception. He accepted the order and took up the walkie talkie.

Rama hissed: 'Do it now!' He moved into position, behind the fence. The dense foliage ought to stop him being seen from the plaza.

Davis glanced up. The lead car was about to turn onto Elm Street. 'Too late!' he hissed.

The motorcade slowed to take the corner onto Elm Street. The walkie talkie cracked into life: '*One is sited. Two, are you ready? Three? Four?*'

Davis brought the set to his lips. 'Four sited and ready.' He put down the set.

The lead car was onto Elm. Kennedy's open-top black limo, which he shared with wife Jackie, and Governor and Mrs Connally, was second around the bend. Davis saw the face he knew so well, the man he had served so loyally. That enigmatic smile, bringing back so many bittersweet memories.

Moments, those last fractional moments. All kinds of thoughts flitted through his mind. Sally; he and she reconciled, back together. Making love, laughing, talking of starting a family. Once this was over they would go away. Put all the crud behind them and start again . . .

Rama's concentration was total. The rifle shifting minutely, tracking as the limo rolled down Elm. The sight fixed on Kennedy's face. . . .

'*GO!*'

The Corsican practised plenty with the Mannlicher Carcano. He was familiar, if not comfortable, with the awkward bolt action. In the past few minutes he had steadied himself. His face was impassive, but inside of him was a seething cauldron. Along Houston, in the County jail, prisoners straining for a view through their cell windows were looking at him. Curious stares were directed at him from the ground and he realised the tip of the rifle must be visible. He watched the lead car turn onto

Houston, followed closely by the Presidential limo, which was flanked by two motorcycle outriders. Next came Half-back, the car that carried the nine secret service men making up the Presidential personal guard. The other vehicles, containing the Vice President, other local dignitaries and members of the press were next, forming a chain that snaked back around the corner onto Main. He deliberately drew back; he did not want to risk Kennedy looking up and spotting the rifle.

The lead car slowed, took the turn onto Elm Street, Kennedy's limousine just behind it. The walkie talkie in Carter's hand buzzed, and Halstead's voice, fuzzy through the tiny speaker, cut the air. '*Go!*'

Raoul lifted the rifle and fitted it into his shoulder. He worked the bolt and a cartridge casing from a previously fired shot was ejected. Carter's hand shot out in a nervous reflex and caught the shell in mid-air. Raoul sank into a kneeling position, his right leg tucked beneath him, his left hand steadying the tip of the rifle on the window sill. He wrapped the sling tightly over and under his left arm and concentrated hard, ignoring the telescopic sight, using instead the notch sight on the barrel. He dry swallowed, drew a bead, and squeezed the trigger.

Rama, in position behind the fence, Armalite in place, heard the rifle shot, watched the reaction from the Presidential car, and knew immediately the shot had missed. '*Richochet*,' he muttered.

He saw Kennedy, who had been waving, pause. Slowly his hands came up to his face, and Rama, surprised, immediately thought: 'He's been hit.' Mrs Kennedy was turning to her husband, and Governor Connally, seated in the jump seat in front of the President, started to turn to see where the sound had come from, when a second shot rang out.

Davis confirmed the action with team two. A third shot rang out, and this time Rama knew Kennedy was hit. He tilted forward, and in almost the same instant Governor Connally was hit. His cheeks filled out in a textbook reaction to the shockwave of a bullet bursting through his body. Then he went down in the car. His wife screamed.

'Go,' Rama said, in the same instant taking up the slack on the trigger. The moment he heard Davis give the command on the radio, he completed the motion. The President's head was positioned squarely in the sight. The AR-15 gave very little kickback. He heard the shot from team two explode at virtually the same instant he pulled his trigger, and he knew they had scored a hit. He saw the President's head explode, saw his body hurled backwards and to his left.

But already Rama was moving. He passed the weapon to Delvecchio, who had materialised at his side. For a heavy set man, Delvecchio was surprisingly nimble. He made off with the weapon, walking rapidly along the fence toward the triple railroad overpass that spanned Dealey Plaza. Davis moved fast, rounding the fence he confronted the infantryman, who had dived to the ground on hearing the shot. The home movie camera was still in his hand. Davis reached down and snatched it from him, muttering viciously, voice loaded with pent-up venom. 'You have a film in that? Do you? Give it to me. Give it to me.' When the soldier did not immediately obey, Davis drew a pistol from under his shirt. The man was left clutching at air as the man he thought was a cop stalked off.

The cars were still crawling by. Sirens had not yet started to wail, and Rama guessed that perhaps fifteen seconds had elapsed since he had pulled the trigger. Things were going smoothly. He and Halstead, who was extremely experienced in Black Operations, and knew a great deal about timing of events, had calculated it would be seventy seconds before the crowd reacted with any direction. First would come fear and shock, then confusion, and finally a collective anger and motion. He passed the fence, heading at a sprint for the rear of the depository, where his car waited, engine running. He was pleased. . . .

As he dropped into the rear seat of the Nash Rambler station wagon, behind the heavily perspiring Davis, the car leapt forward on screeching tyres and sped for escape. The action, the dash for the car, left Rama with blurred memories. So intent was he on getting away, he had not bothered to look about him. He was troubled, subconsciously, and ran the final moments over and over in his mind. He sifted the quickly glimpsed images until he had the worrying answer; a child! A child's wide staring eyes peering at him over the top of the fence. Staring in amazement, bewilderment and horror.

He swallowed, and prayed fervently that he hadn't made his first mistake.

In the depository building, Raoul passed the rifle to Carter, who rapidly wiped the weapon clean of finger prints. He ducked down, and placed the empty shell cartridge ejected from the rifle earlier beside the two ejected when Raoul fired. Hiding the rifle behind a stack of boxes, the two men left by the stairs. Within sixty seconds they had reached the rear door and exited. They joined the crowd surging towards the car park; just another two shocked employees among hundreds.

Lee had been waiting for the telephone to ring. He walked to the corridor, heard the distant uproar, and felt a disturbing rumbling in his gut. He walked back into the canteen as the sounds of running feet clattered loudly in the hall. A cop burst into the room followed by one of the building supervisors. The cop had a gun trained on Oswald.

'Do you know this man?' He barked, eyes hard as they bored into Lee. The supervisor stuttered a reply, and the cop turned and raced out of the room and up the stairs. The supervisor followed, yelling back at Lee; 'The President's been shot. . . .'

He felt a strange, eerie feeling crawl over him. Felt something lurking in the dark recesses of his mind. He could sense its presence, he may even have known what it was, but he did not want to expose it to the light and risk knowing his fears were real.

He walked at a deliberately slow stroll to the telephone and dialled the contact number. No reply. He let it ring, and ring, finally replacing the receiver with his heart in his mouth. Pausing to buy a bottle of Coke from a machine on the first floor, his mind blanked out by fear and with a sick feeling in his gut, he walked from the building, pressing against the current as people streamed onto Dealey Plaza.

Ruby got up from his seat and stared out over the scene. Quietly he left the newspaper offices.

The two men in the records building, Frank Rome and his partner, a Cuban named Carlos, made good their escape, but Eugene Farman was stopped by a cop as he left the Dallas Texas building. He had been pointed out to the cop by a secretary working in the building who thought he was acting suspiciously. Farman stumbled out a garbled explanation, claiming he was looking for a telephone to call for help after seeing the attack on the President. Unconvinced, the cop handcuffed him and decided to take him in.

Delvecchio had clambered into a freight car that was part of a stationary train and waited to make his escape in the hobo disguise. Three cops, guns at the ready, ordered him and two others from the freight car and escorted them across the parking lot, past the Depository building and towards the police station. Spotting Farman in a group of people clustered together under the watchful eyes of two armed cops, Delvecchio sidled up to him as the groups merged. Farman was nervous, but Delvecchio, falling into step beside him as they entered the station, tried to calm him. 'Don't worry. The fix is in.'

The Brown House.
Tarrant County. . . .

Within two hours of the shooting, most of the thirty participants in the Dealey Plaza action had gathered at the spacious, vacant and isolated house situated just over the county line. As they entered through the hall they were met by Rama, who directed them down a flight of stairs to a deep, concrete walled basement where refreshments awaited them. Delving into the large selection of drinks, the crew toasted the success of the mission.

Halstead and Carter faced each other over iced bourbon. Carter's eyes glinted with wicked glee, his face was flushed with the elation of ultimate success. He clinked his glass against Halstead's. 'To LBJ, the good "old boy".'

Halstead reciprocated with a broad grin: 'Yeah, it has been some day. You ever think you'd be making history?'

'Hey,' one of the crew members called to Halstead. 'Did we get the announcement yet?'

Halstead nodded. 'Yep, went out like a light at one pee-emm, Central Standard time.' To Carter he added: 'I was going to leave the announcement to Rama, but what the heck.' Draining his glass, he turned to the table for a refill.

A huge metallic clang echoed through the building. The assembled men froze, sharply honed instincts collectively knowing that something had fallen out of place. Worried looks were exchanged as a chill cut through the air like a knife.

Halstead's fingers tightened around his glass until they whitened. In his mind's eye he pictured the heavy steel door at the top of the basement steps. Something told him that door was now closed, and with a sickening lurch in his gut he realised that he and the others were trapped. Carter too smelt a rat. Unease slithered in the space at the base of his belly, began to gnaw at him like a nervous ulcer.

'What the hell —?' a single voice pierced the silence. Flashing a look of intense spite at Halstead, the speaker banged his glass down on the table and broke for the steps. Moments later the others heard the drumming of his fists on the steel, and their spirits slumped even further.

A wide, dusty framed picture – a dramatic reproduction of the killing of Lincoln – dropped from the wall with a heart-jolting crash. As one, the men turned to stare at the space on the wall the picture had occupied, and found themselves staring at a window of dense glass. Rama, and the man they had known as the Executor, stared back at them.

Rama's mouth moved, and his voice, disembodied and much shrunken, squawked from a small speaker set into the wall. 'Congratulations gentlemen. You have done an excellent job.'

Carter, his face pale and drawn, uttered a curse. A voice from the gathering echoed the sentiment. 'Shit. I think our role in this play just changed.'

Halstead stepped forward and demanded to know what was going on. Rama's face hinted at a smile. 'Going on, Ray? Come on.'

The amusement on the face of the Executor was less concealed. He loved toying with people.

'You did well, all of you. Taking the last minute alterations in your stride like professionals. But surely, as professionals, you recognise the need for one last alteration.'

'The pay-off,' Carter sneered, a brittle undertone in his voice. 'You sons of bitches.'

Anxiety rippled through the assembly. 'Forget the money,' someone called out. 'Just let us out of here.'

'Yeah,' called another, backed by a chorus. 'We'll stay away. We'll forget everything.'

'I'm sorry,' Rama replied sombrely, and for a moment Halstead fancied the man's regret was genuine. 'But the stakes are too high. We all just committed not only a capital crime, but a significant and historical act, one that is going to affect the whole world. The more of us there are in the world with that knowledge, the less secure will be those who remain.'

'You mean those at the top,' Halstead spat back, struggling to stall for time while his mind desperately scanned for a way out. Rama did not speak, but his arm moved a lever out of sight. From four grills in the ceiling a fine mist began to descend. Catching the faintest whiff of the odour, Halstead called out: 'Cyanide! get down!' falling dead to the floor as he did so.

In confusion the men fought vainly for their lives. They reeled and collided, falling with a suddenness that was dreadful to watch. Bodies forming limp heaps. A handful made for the corners of the basement. But the gas was inescapable, and in an appallingly rapid succession they succumbed.

Carter had scrambled to the floor, dragging his jacket over his head and pressing his face flat to the concrete. As he went down he snatched a chestful of air, but there was a limit to the length of time he could hold his breath, and he knew he had only seconds left. Already he could feel tiny exhalations bursting from him. He risked taking a shallow breath, and immediately knew it to be a mistake. The cold gas snatched away his breath and froze his lungs.

For long moments he writhed on the floor in spasms of furious agony. Through misted eyes he saw his friend Ray Halstead lying stone still beside him, and beyond, watching dispassionately, as though studying the death throes of an insect, he saw Rama and his master.

Blackness closed about him like an icy blanket. He thought of his wife, and regrets filled his dying heart. . . .

Friday evening.

Rama cocked the gun as he lifted it from under the desk and into view. 'I'm sorry Davis.'

As he stared at the weapon, Davis felt his heart sink beneath the weight of unwelcome knowledge. His worst fears, he knew, were about to become reality. He said quietly: 'Rossi didn't go to a clinic in LA, did he?'

Gaze steady, Rama shook his head.

'And Carter? Halstead?'

'All gone too. You are virtually the last one.'

Davis examined his own emotions, and with some surprise realised he felt calm. He was down to one card, and he knew he had to play it convincingly; Rama was no amateur.

'It's all written down,' he said with bolstered confidence. 'Names, dates, pictures. Pull that trigger and you will be looking at a long stretch.' As he spoke he kept his gaze locked firmly on Rama. He had to be prepared for the slightest flicker, in order to make his move.

But Rama did not flinch. 'I expected that,' he said, icily. 'I don't know whether you are telling the truth or not, but I have to make a judgement.'

'It's true alright,' Davis countered – too quickly, and inwardly he cursed. He had sounded desperate, not like a man in control. He suspected his haste had sealed his fate.

His gaze skittered around the office, searching for a weapon, anything, he could fight back with. His surface control was slipping, he knew he had to take a chance. Spurred by despair, he leapt for the gun.

Rama was waiting. As the straining hands neared he pulled the trigger four times in rapid succession. The force of the shots thrust Davis backwards. He slumped against his chair and slid limply to the floor. Rama rounded the desk and stared down at his victim. Davis peered up at him. His face was drained, and his eyes stared fixedly, as though willing the gun to jam. His fingers clawed uselessly at the air.

'I'm sorry Davis,' Rama repeated, putting the remaining couple of bullets into the man's head.

Lee.
Friday night.

Lee knew. He'd had hours to think this through now, and he had put together all the pieces. Hoover, the bastard, he was letting him drown! For some reason the Director had pulled the plug at the last minute, and left Lee sitting in the spotlight. There was only one thing still puzzling him, as he sat in the barewalled interview room, and that was how on earth Hoover thought he could cut Lee loose and get away with it. Once he got himself a lawyer and prepared for trial, he would spill his guts. The skeletons would come pouring out of the closet then, and the Director of the FBI would really have a problem on his hands.

He glanced up at the redneck cop left to guard him. The man was potbellied, thick necked, with a ruddy complexion, and his eyes gazed vacantly at a spot above Lee's head. His jaw chewed slackly. One hand was draped loosely over the butt of the gun at his hip.

The one thing he had to do now, Lee reminded himself, was remain calm. They would be wheeling him out before the press again, he was sure, and his case would be best served by appearing rational and unworried. He had committed no crime, and there was no evidence he had. There was nothing to fear. The worst they could pin on him was the fake Hidell ID. The parafin test they had used on him might not be conclusive enough to get him convicted. He had fired a gun, sure, but it was in self defense. He had tried to prevent the cop, Tippett, being murdered. Oh yes, once he got to trial it would all come out. At that thought he smiled; he could hardly wait!

At that moment, when his thoughts were not dwelling on the subject, the answer came to him. The Director had stood by and let someone else remove the thorn in his side, and with John Kennedy gone, Bobby would soon be out of the Attorney General's office. . . . Oh, they were so cute!

But nothing had gone right. The plan had been simple enough, but once the shooting of the President had gone ahead, and he realised that he had to go along with the original schedule as plotted by Rama and his people, Lee had gone home to change his shirt and jacket – and to collect the handgun. The signal had come; the police car had drawn up outside his lodgings and tooted the horn as agreed. Lee had met the car a hundred yards away from his lodgings and been driven to the rendezvous point, and it was at that moment things started to go wrong.

He had gotten into a heated discussion with Frank Rome. They became conspicuous, and then the nosey cop, probably jumpy with all the radio buzz after the killing of Kennedy, had pulled up and started to question them. Rome was ruthless, and he had no hesitation in drawing his gun and shooting down the cop. While he was tipping the empty shells from his weapon and reloading, ignoring the groans from the felled cop, Rome saw the look on Lee's face. 'You coming, or do I have to whack you too?'

Lee pulled out his own gun. They argued, but this time Rome knew he did not have time to spare. He lifted his gun. In defense Lee fired a warning shot over his head, and Rome, with a final curse, turned and ran.

And so Lee had run too. He ended up taking cover in the Texas theater, neglecting, as planned, to buy a ticket. As he sat alone in one of the darkened rows, his concentration not on the movie, he sensed events, a larger set of consequences, enclosing him. And when the lights had gone up and police officers brandishing guns had closed in around him, he felt twin emotions; fear that he might be killed by some trigger happy cop too scared shitless to be cautious, and a feeling that at least in police custody he would be relatively safe.

The door opened, and the officer who had questioned him earlier marched in. He directed a warning glance at the guard, then spoke to Lee. 'Come with me.'

Lee stared at him. He had taken a few blows during the arrest, and he was feeling stiff and dishevelled, and disinclined to move unless he had to. The cut over his eye, caused when the ring on a cop's finger had gashed him in the meleé was aching like hell. 'What is it this time, meet the press?'

'Just come with me, wiseguy.'

Lee wearily levered himself upward and walked out into the corridor. Here he found himself surrounded, and, since all the cops were taller than he, felt lost in their midst. He had been dragged before the nation's press and the television cameras earlier. When asked if he had killed President Kennedy, he calmly replied that he had not, and that so far, no one in the police department had mentioned anything about that to him. He respectfully asked for someone to come forward and offer him legal assistance. The cops started to get itchy, began hauling him away. There was a call from the crowd, a final question: 'What happened to your face?'

With a note, almost, of triumph in his voice, he yelled back his reply. 'A policeman hit me.'

Into another room, where an officious looking Sergeant with a ruddy, drinker's face and a vast belly, stared at him across a desk. The other cops stood around and glared. A space was cleared for Lee. Handcuffed before the desk, he listened as, in a dry voice, the sergeant started to read from a sheet of paper.

'Lee Harvey Oswald . . .'

'You've decided who I am then?' Lee chipped in. The sergeant's mouth tightened, then he continued. 'Lee Harvey Oswald, you are formally charged that on the afternoon of November the twenty second, nineteen sixty-three, in the Oak Cliff area of Dallas, Texas, you did murder Officer J. D. Tippett . . .'

Lee glanced at the clock on the wall. It was seven fifteen in the evening. Perhaps they actually believed they could railroad him into jail. They had been clever, so clever, all of them. But not clever enough. If they thought he was going to sit still for this, they were going to be mistaken. He had no intention of being hung out to dry. Once he had himself a lawyer . . .

These same thoughts coursed through his mind on Sunday morning as he was being escorted to the basement of the police building. He had asked for legal assistance, but almost forty-eight hours after his arrest he was still unrepresented. He was being transferred, they told him, as a matter of procedure, to a safer holding facility. But he was nervous; and the more he thought about events, the more nervous he became. If the people behind this thing, behind Rossi, and Halstead and Rama, had gone to this much trouble to set him up, would they risk letting him get to trial?

When told he was being transferred to a safer place he had joked: 'Keep me on ice, you mean?'

Through a final door into an underground parking lot where the press awaited. Cameras, flash bulbs at the ready. More cops. A pair of large plainsclothes officers escorted him into the basement. There were cops in front, cops behind, yet he did not feel safe. There was something odd about the atmosphere; an electricity. A delay occurred, the car was not ready. He waited, impatient and anxious. Thoughts hurtling through his mind . . .

Then they were moving through a final door. Dozens of people were gathered, all eyes on him. From the group to his left there came a disturbance, and a man in a dark suit and pale hat burst to the fore. He charged. There was something bullishly familiar about him . . .

The man rushed forward. In his hand was a gun. There was an explosion, a burst of gut searing pain, and a flash of recognition:

Jack Ruby! Jack Ruby!

The year after the assassination was an eventful one, full of witnesses going missing, vanishing gradually. Seventeen met terrible and violent deaths.

Five women employees of Jack Ruby died within two years of the events in Dallas.

Rose Cherami: 'There is going to be a big disaster in Dallas. They're going to kill the President.' (This, three days before the shooting, while she was recovering from a hit and run incident.)

She was later struck by a car in Big Sandy, Texas, and died.

Had President Kennedy lived until November 24th he would have been present at a conference where the subject of Vietnam was to be discussed. Had he lived it is certain America would not have endured ten years of a war it could not win. Thousands of Americans and Vietnamese citizens would be alive today, and over two hundred billion tax dollars would not have been diverted into the Asian war effort.

'Unless a greater effort is made by the government to win popular support, I don't think the war can be won out there. In the final analysis, it's their war. They are the ones who have to win it or lose it.'

John F. Kennedy,
Sept 2nd 1963

BOOK TWO

'Ghosts stirring us still'

Newbolt was furious.
'Alright man, alright.
Have it your way. But just
answer me this; if Oswald was
acting alone, as the Warren
Commission said he was,
who killed the witnesses?'

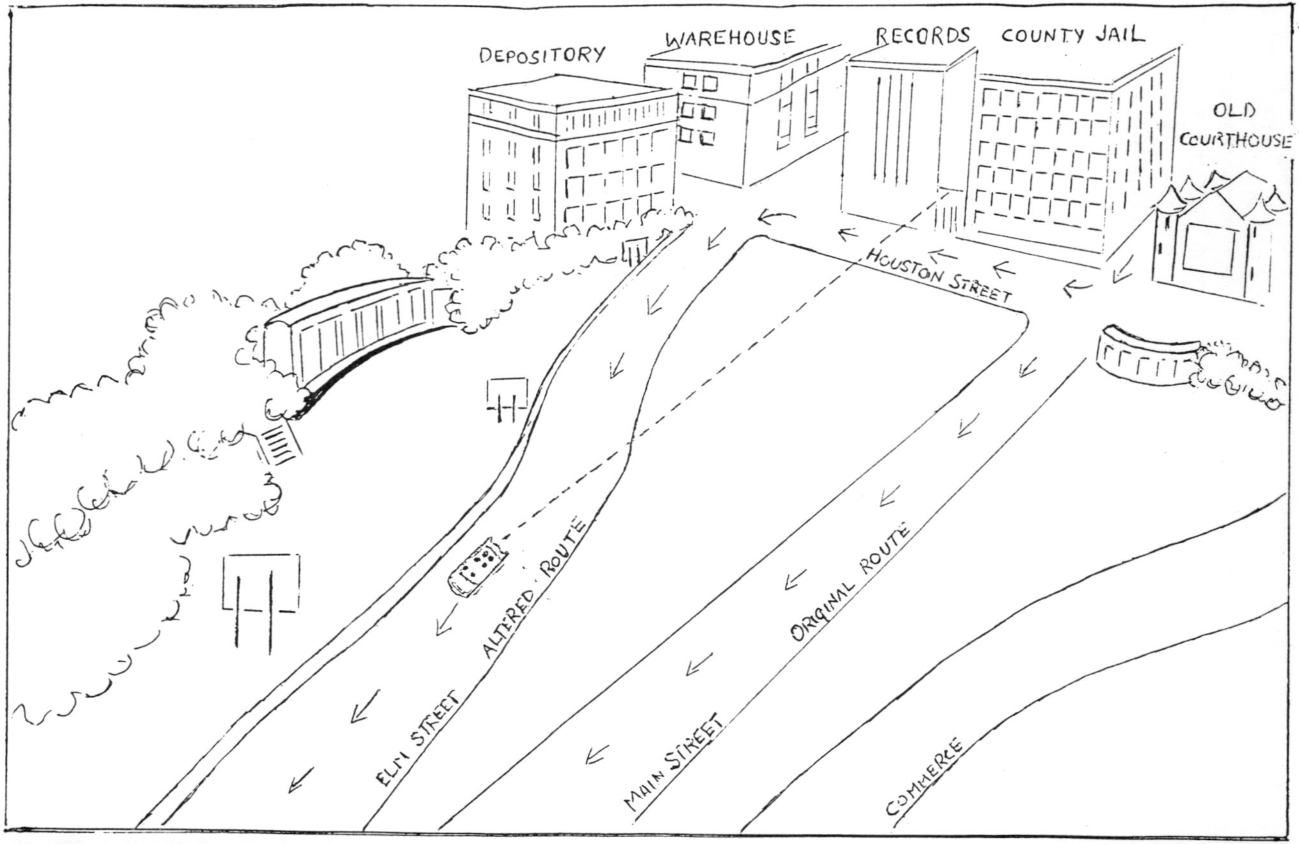
DEPOSITORY
WAREHOUSE
RECORDS
COUNTY JAIL
OLD COURTHOUSE
HOUSTON STREET
ALTERED ROUTE
ELM STREET
ORIGINAL ROUTE
MAIN STREET
COMMERCE

* 10 *

'. . . and in the few short years since the Challenger disaster, NASA has risen, in the great American tradition, like a phoenix from the ashes, and is once more aiming starwards, aiming high.'

The sound of rising applause was cut short and the familiar good-morning form of the anchorman filled the TV screen. 'Senator Galbraith speaking last night in Miami.'

Daniel.
Coco, Florida
some months ago . . .

The wide awake sounds from the TV filtered into his subconscious and nudged him gently towards the new day. Poised dully between slumber and alertness, he absorbed the morning news and shifted restlessly on the bed.

He opened his eyes at last to the sun streaming into the apartment through the partially open curtains. He was covered in sweat. The air conditioner was off, and with the terrace windows shut the atmosphere was muggy. A dull ache throbbed behind his eyes, and he knew that if he didn't get into a cold shower soon he would have one zinger of a headache all day; Wild Turkey always did that to him.

With a groan he worked himself free of the sheet snagged around his legs and swung his feet to the tiled floor. Rising naked to his full six feet, he extended his arms and eased the creaks from his body.

He emerged from the bathroom, some twenty minutes later, feeling invigorated. Still rubbing at his hair he wrapped a towel around his waist, then flung open the windows to the terrace and stepped outside to bask in the recharging warmth of the sun. His head had cleared and he was able to look down, without pain, at the beach below where vacationeers played noisily. He was ravenously hungry and returned indoors to dress, trying as he did so not to notice the mess the place was in. Discarded clothes spread carelessly, empty bottles cluttering every flat surface. Resolving to clear up later, he left for breakfast. There was a Denny's restaurant along A1A. He drove there and over pancakes read a copy of the previous day's issue of *The Sentinel.* The imminent visit by the Senator from the north was the big splash; speculation that he would visit to the rejuvenated NASA program at the Cape. He viewed the article with scorn; Barbara and her agency were handling the Senator's PR, and he tended to view everything connected with her through a jaundiced eye.

He put down his cup with a curse. Dammit! What day did she say she would be arriving at the apartment? He could not recall – He'd been too drunk at the time to take much in. He would have to clean up to avoid a scene.

As was his custom, he spent a couple of hours on the beach, riding his belly board to shore on the crashing Atlantic waves. Then he lunched at a beachside cafeteria run by the Holiday Inn. He chatted idly to a couple of young girls with deep deep tans and cut-away swimsuits.

Late afternoon saw him climbing into his '88 model Camaro for the sixty minute drive to his place of work; a sprawling, L-shaped concrete monstrosity, a hotel on International Drive in Orlando. The sky took on a threatening hue, dark clouds nestled together, and there was a flash of light as forked lightning cut a jagged path across the sky. The Camaro braked to a halt in the hotel lot as the first fat raindrops started to fall. As Daniel ran for the lobby he saw guests fleeing the open air pool.

The bar was his domain. Mirrors and plush-lined walls of a deep burgundy red. Second rate 'sixties glitz. His first task was to make coffee, his second to switch on the TV. Then he settled into his routine; checking ashtrays and wiping tables clean, filling bowls with pretzels and nuts, and bar buckets with uniformly shaped whorls of ice. The soda hose was running slow, and he replaced the CO_2 canister. Outside, beyond the vast windows, rain drummed the ground with force, and he knew he was in for an early start and a busy evening. Preparation finished, he changed into a clean shirt and clipped a bowtie of blue velvet to the collar. He settled onto a stool and munched absently on tortilla chips while watching the local news. Senator Galbraith was once again a major feature. There was footage of him alighting from an aircraft accompanied by a sizeable entourage. Then facing a barrage of microphones, his aides clustered closely around him, he conducted a short press conference.

The man looked most presentable, Daniel had to admit. Enigmatic.

As he watched, Daniel felt a cold chill creep over him. A sudden rush of nausea inexplicably unsettling his stomach. He had no idea why, but he began to feel anxious, almost afraid. He fumbled with glasses, trying, almost obsessively, to keep his hands busy. The news moved on to cover other matters, but he was left feeling agitated, and curiously vacant inside. Unable to shake the feeling of puzzlement.

The evening was busy, as expected. Encouraged by the rain, guests sought entertainment within the hotel. He had spare time enough to do little more than catch a Cagney and Lacey rerun on WOFL.

It was after two in the morning when he parked the Camaro outside the apartment. A Mercedes sports was parked in his space. He cursed; Barbara.

Tension slowly overcame him as he rode the elevator. It had been some time since he'd seen her, and she always made him nervous. He wished he had cleaned the place, but it was too late now.

They had known each other for four years. She was beautiful, a dark eyed Jewish princess with sophisticated manners, striking good looks and a mane of raven-black hair that tumbled in rich tresses to her shoulders. They had first met when she was in Florida on some assignment for her agency and had decided to combine the visit with a search for a second home, preferably an exclusive beachside condominium situated on an upmarket stretch of real estate. She had gone on a foray into a nightclub one Saturday and bumped into Daniel at the bar. He was living in a rundown rented house in outer Orlando. After several bouts of energetic sex, and a frequent number of trysts in motel rooms, she found the apartment she wanted, furnished it, and installed him as a tenant, explaining that she wanted someone to look after the apartment in her absence, adding: 'I hate coming home to an empty apartment.'

They continued to see each other regularly for over two years, a stormy period during which their relationship transitionally attended phases of intense physical attraction and activity, veering towards friendship and rivalry, and progressing to jealousy and possessiveness before deteriorating at last to a bitter state, a virtual war of attrition.

The frequency of her visits south slowed to perhaps two each summer. Daniel was left emotionally confused. Remembering this left him open to the depression that was never far below the surface, and, subconsciously, he tensed as if anticipating an attack.

As he approached the door to the apartment he knew he was

going to resent her talk of the rich and famous people she mixed with. He despised her for her success, and loathed himself for his lack of it. The best he could hope for was that she might be asleep. On opening the door he immediately knew he was going to be disappointed. In the air hung the unmistakable odour of pot. With a frown he quietly closed the door and stalked into the lounge. She was reclining on a chair facing the TV. The cable soft porn channel she subscribed to was on; fuzzy close ups of moving flesh filled the screen. She stared fixedly, eyes glassy.

He was reminded how attractive she was. Her lustrous hair was cut shorter, and her high cheekbones were accentuated by the low light. Her sexy rosebud of a mouth rested in a semi-pout. She was visually stunning, yet the main pull of her attractiveness was not her physical appearance but the way she carried herself. The way she talked, and the direct, challenging way she looked at you when she spoke. There was about her an aura of control. She invited worship.

'Hello Rush.' He greeted her loudly, quietly enjoying her discomfort as, caught unawares, she jerked up in her chair. Anger ignited on her face, and he was reminded that she could look ugly when roused, but the moment passed and she was on her feet. Taking him in a tentative embrace she kissed his cheek.

'Daniel,' she said guardedly. 'You look well.' The words were automatic and untrue. He saw the darting, up and down study she made of him and knew she thought he looked a mess. Hell, he did. It was the crummy life he led, eating junk and drinking too much. Something had to give.

'You startled me,' she went on. 'I didn't hear you come in.'

He felt the burn of a smirk on his face. 'Pot and porn'll do that to you.'

She pouted; a tactic he well recalled. 'Don't be hard on me, Daniel. I think I've picked up some horrid Asian bug.'

'Aw,' he murmured, with exaggerated sympathy. 'I thought you sounded a little punk.'

'I lead a busy life,' she countered. 'Surely you don't begrudge me a little fun?'

He felt increased resentment that she should try her stupid feminine tactics on him; who knew every rotten trick she had in her armoury. 'I'm making coffee,' he snapped. 'You want some?'

In the kitchen he asked how long she would be staying. 'Just until tomorrow,' she replied. 'Strictly speaking, I needn't have come down here personally, but Florida will be increasingly important to us as we run up to the election. I'll be going on to Atlanta next to finalise details for that stage on the tour. I assume you know which tour?'

He snorted. 'The big man from the north.'

A scowl distorted her face. 'It's my job,' she paused, but his expression did not soften. 'What is it with you?'

'Well, what is he going to do for me?'

'Wake up, Daniel. You can't expect to sit back and let the government handle every little detail of your life for you. Get up off your thumb.'

He railed, then relented. 'I'm sorry. I guess I ought to lighten up.' He took a breath. 'So, how are things?'

She managed a taut smile. 'Pretty good. In the past year I've been promoted twice. I'm now Vice President of the political relations department. I got to attend my first international conference in Paris, where I had to make a few diplomatic manoeuvres to avoid offending a powerful colleague who *naturally assumed* we'd be sleeping together. And . . . I scored a plum; we tendered for Galbraith's upcoming Presidential campaign, and he liked my presentation so much I landed the opportunity of a lifetime.'

He handed her a cup, then under her disapproving gaze stirred sugar into his own. He said: 'Especially if he gets into the White House.'

'I'll be seen as a prime mover, instrumental in getting him there.' She almost bleated with glee. 'And he'll do it.'

His face fell again. 'Then he'll do it without my vote.' The smile on her face contracted. 'Yes, he will. You know, Daniel, I will never understand you. You don't know the man. You've never met him or heard him speak. I'll bet you know nothing about his politics, and yet you get all angry at the mention of his name. Why are you like this?'

He swallowed his anger and almost choked on it. He turned away. What *was* the matter with him? Could his resentment really be that great? Couldn't he just . . . ? Swallowing manfully, he forced his tensed and upraised shoulders to relax, then mentally he counted to ten.

The expression on her face was firm. 'You can knock him all you want to, but you won't change a thing. I'm good at my job. I'm happy with myself and what I'm doing, and this campaign can do me nothing but good.'

He was struggling again. 'I need a real drink.' Banging open and shut cupboard doors he took down bottle and glass and poured a hefty measure which he downed in one. He coughed, and when he glanced at her and saw her look of disgust, he felt exposed.

'Quite a few empty liqour bottles in the trash,' she remarked. 'Is that all you do these days?'

He poured another, gulped it defiantly. 'It's as good a way as any to pass the time.' Glass and bottle in hand he swaggered through to the lounge.

'I saw the Senator give his speech at NASA,' he called out. 'What's your angle, planning to be the first public relations woman in space?'

Driven by a surge of anger she overtook him. 'That was cheap and despicable.'

He attempted to meet her stare, but her frigid haughtiness defeated him. Seeing the confusion and exasperation on his face, she softened. She moved closer, laced her arms around his neck. 'Be happy, Dan. Please. We both went through a lot of pain to find the things we wanted —'

The dam burst, bitterness erupting: 'You wanted!'

'Okay, okay,' she ceded with a raised hand gesture. 'I wanted the opportunity to see what I could achieve, but we both have the chance now to make something of our lives.' She moved away. 'You always said you wanted to write. Why don't you give it a try?'

He averted his face. She placed a hand on his cheek and forced him to look at her. 'Separating hurt me too, Dan, but I'm determined something good will come of this. I'm not cut out to be a housewife, cooking and cleaning and raising kids in a little house in the suburbs. I have to see how far I can go. Can't you help me by understanding that?'

He stared at her, his eyes still brimming with resentment. She saw no hint of understanding. He felt choked with anger. 'All I know . . .' he stammered, 'is that I cared for you, very deeply, and you let me believe you felt the same. Then you took off to carve out a new life for yourself, leaving me stranded.'

Her patience strained, she let her hands fall resignedly to her sides. 'Do what I did. Take this chance.'

He turned away to pour himself a fresh drink. She dealt with her anger by clenching her tiny fists until the tension absorbed her fury. She knew that sometimes, to get through to Daniel, it was necessary to hurt him. She had made this discovery the way his father had, many years earlier – through colic experience, a desire to strike out that became a near-physical ache. 'So you hide. You make excuses for yourself, and drink.'

They had always been like this, he recalled; abrasive, whittling sharply away at each other. With a heartfelt pang he realised with regret that she was right; they never would have made it.

After an interval, during which he discovered he could not swallow his drink, he inquired if she was seeing anyone in New York. She replied that she was, adding: 'I met him soon after I was assigned to the Galbraith job.'

The admission seemed to bring home to him with thundering clarity the finality of the separation. In his heart he knew the reason he despised her so was that, in those days before she left, he had begun to depend on her, and their time apart had not helped lessen this feeling. He was hurting, but until now there had been hope . . .

Too abruptly he changed the subject, asking if she really thought Galbraith could win a Presidential election. She was wide-eyed: 'Are you kidding? The man is a political shoo-in. He's the sensation of the century. At last we're going to get a President we not only deserve, but need. He doesn't give a damn for the big interests; he'll be great.'

He gave a doubtful shrug. 'I don't know. I saw him on TV tonight and . . . I can't explain it but, I got this really weird feeling.'

'You're nuts,' she retorted good naturedly. 'This man is something special.'

The effect of this homily was to transmute his scepticism to derision. For this she rounded on him.

'Cut the bullshit, Dan. Name one politician – one – who ever bought fifty acres of innercity ghetto, knocked it flat and built bright modern apartments for poor folk to live in! His money is where his mouth is.'

'And where does his money come from? The sweat of those same poor folk!'

Determined to win, she hesitated only the briefest time. 'He's an industrialist, yes, but he cares deeply. He desperately wants to change things for the better – and he'll do it.'

His eyes twinkled mischievously over the rim of his glass. 'We've seen all this before, Rush. Camelot, the thousand days, all things to all men.'

She glanced up at the ceiling as though invoking divine intervention to her aid in forcing some sense into his skull.

'Why is it,' she asked, 'that whenever we talk politics you drag Kennedy into the discussion? That was a long time ago. Kennedy was a glossy package we bought; people know better now. Galbraith is different. he's a doer.'

He let out a hiss of air. 'It's still the same old sucker punch —'

She cried out: 'Can we just stop this? I didn't travel a thousand miles to argue with you. What do you know anyway? You're just —' She bit down hard to stop herself.

He jerked his head around to face her. He was flushed. 'Oh yeah,' he muttered breathlessly. 'Now we're getting to it. I never was good enough for you.'

She wearily rubbed the back of her neck. 'This is all old ground, Dan, and really I'm much too tired to argue. I think I'll go to bed.'

Alone, he paced the room in a mood of increasing restlessness, until frustration drove him out onto the terrace where a chill night wind gusted in over the Atlantic. The sky was clear, and the stars, toward which the arrows from NASA had aimed so fruitlessly, twinkled amusedly. The ocean, dark and impenetrable, and limitless in visible extent, rumbled warningly. And yet it tempted also. The tranquil lapping of waves on sand a soothing lullaby. An invitation to enter, and forget.

For the millionth time he wondered where he had gone wrong. For years he had trailed along the path to self destruction; drinking too much and paying scant attention to diet. He had done it all wrong, and yet he had no idea how to do things right.

There had been times, many times, when he would have welcomed an end to it all. When sudden and weighty depression took him by surprise and even being alive made him want to scream in despair. Tonight, he thought, heart aching, he could swim out, far enough to be sure he could not make it back. The cure. The cure he hadn't the guts to take.

His body, drained by the exertions of the day and further sapped by the conflict with Barbara, suddenly made clear its demands with a precipitate wave of fatigue. Sighing, he turned indoors, stripped to his shorts and settled full length on the floor.

He slept.

But he was not at rest.

. . . above, the sun glowered down on the plaza from a clear blue sky. It seemed to revolve, first one way, then the other, with a pendulum-like rhythm. He looked about him, saw the foliage, the cool green of the trees, the railroad yards, the fence of thin wooden slats, the white stone of the collonnade. By straining up on tiptoe he could

just see through the bottom row of checkerwork openings in the stone.

He could see his Pa . . . A deep sadness descended upon him. He felt lost, forgotten. He had felt like this ever since his adored mother had gone to heaven.

Looking across the plaza he could see the crowds. A sound like a firecracker snapped the air to his right. He turned and peeped over the fence. The gunmen were there, as they always had been, as they always would be . . . that thought puzzled him.

More shots, from somewhere else! Then one of the gunmen – the one wearing the hardhat, tensed, and aimed the rifle over the fence and through dense foliage. He fired a round, and bucked as the gun recoiled. The air tingled with the electricity of utmost violence. Already the thought was in his mind; he had to get down the slope, to his father. He had to drag him away . . . He wanted to weep with frustration, he knew his father would not listen. He would insist on walking past the depository building as he always did, and the cop would take his name. Danny was numbed with fear, knowing what was coming and yet being still powerless to alter any of it. The gunman half turned, and, for a single instant, Danny felt the man's killer gaze connect with his own, sending down his young spine a shudder he could feel even after all those years. Even at a dream distance. But now, this time, something was different. He knew the face. He knew the face. He knew the killer's face!

Daniel awoke with a scream and sat bolt upright in the darkness. A door opened, and light flooded in, then his father's arms were around him, holding him safe, and a soft voice was whispering into his ear. 'Dan, what is it? What is it?'

The embrace was too gentle to be his father. His mother, his mother . . . Oh, how he loved her. . . . Recollections swamped him, a lifetime of pain and regret landed upon him with heartbreaking force. His face crumpled, just as it had when he was ten years old, and he cried: 'I'm scared Pa, I'm scared!'

She was afraid for him. 'Daniel!' she called urgently, giving his shoulders a shake. He dimly saw her form in silhouette in the pool of light pouring in through the door. 'Daniel!'

Taking a deep breath, he emerged with shaking heart from the horror and slowly resumed control. His pulse drummed, and his chest rose and fell at an alarming rate. Tears coursed salt trails down his cheeks. He looked up at her in the gloom and in a small boy's voice called her name. She hugged his head, kissed his wet eyes, then felt the breath forced out of her as he tightly wound his arms about her waist. Unnerved, and at a loss, she hugged him in return. He was clinging to her like a terrified child. And his voice! Why was he begging her to forgive him? At length his composure returned. He loosened his grip and wiped the tears from his face. He was a grown man again, forty years old and deeply unhappy with life. He'd almost been there, almost seen his mother again, almost found his father. What he wouldn't give to be able to speak to them, tell his Mom he was sorry for not being a good son. Tell his Pa he was sorry for shutting him out. But the shift of history, the men with the guns, got in the way. Pulling the triggers before he could get down the knoll to his Pa. If only he could reach him, he could change things.

His chest heaved in a fresh spasm. His lips quivered, and an unearthly groan burst rustily from the depths of his soul. He shook as he cried, and his chest ached from the spasms.

Barbara held him until the sobs subsided. Then placing her hands one each side of his face, she tilted his head upwards and gently kissed his lips.

'I've missed you a lot,' she said in a comforting, velvet tone. 'Come to bed. I'll make it better.'

Meekly he followed her into the bedroom, and for a while felt safe in her.

He lay staring at the ceiling. Beside him, Barbara ran fingers along his inner thigh. 'No more, Rush,' he giggled. 'Technically speaking, I'm depleted.'

She smiled, and continued the hypnotic stroking. He smoked a cigarette down to the filter, then ground it out in the ashtray on the bedside table. She looped an arm around his waist and nestled her cheek against his chest. 'How do you feel now?'

The gloom was still on him, but weaker. He shucked it off. 'I guess I've been worse.'

The ensuing silence between them was comfortable. So often their differing wavelengths led them into bruising toe-to-toe conflict, the rare moment of accord was to be treasured.

'What was so bad about the dream, Dan? We lived together two years, but I never saw you like that.'

He had known she would ask, and he had decided on a course of honesty. A shared load seemed lighter. He sighed nasally. 'You know where I lived as a child, don't you?'

'Sure, Dallas.'

'What comes to mind when you think of Dallas?'

She blew out her cheeks, and spoke her thoughts. 'Oil. Big money. TV soap. Kennedy died there.'

There was a pause. He wanted to tell her, but his apprehension began to pressure him; keeping the secret had become a habit. He made the effort. 'There is something I never did tell you. In fact, never told anyone except my father. It was our . . .' a lump rose to his throat. '. . . our secret.'

The weight would not allow itself to be shifted without a fight. It had nestled in the back of his mind for thirty years, and it had put down roots. . . .

'I'd like to tell you what happened to my father. How he died.'

It was over. Done. The bad air in his lungs cleared. But the lightness in his conscience was counterpointed by the ache from the opened wound in his soul. Barbara had listened in silence, and when he had finished she lay against him, not knowing what to say. Nothing seemed appropriate. He had opened up entirely new facets of his psyche, but she understood him no better.

Happily he sensed her discomfort and plugged the gap himself. 'You know, Rush, despite our differences I've always felt I could trust you. I'd appreciate you not mentioning this to anyone. What's past is past.'

The promise came easily, but it was no less solemn for the speed of its coming. Impressed by his trust she willingly gave her oath.

'*What's past is past . . .*' His words. But as he lay awake in the darkness, Barbara's slumbering form at his side, he found himself unable to sleep. The past was not past. Something odd was in process. Each time he closed his eyes he saw the gunman on the knoll, saw the cold concentration on the face of the rifleman as he squinted along the barrel. Funny that only that one face stayed with him. Of the other man he had no recollection.

The kick of the rifle as it fired.

He yawned; it was no good, he could not sleep. Sliding out of bed without waking her he went in search of a drink.

The terrace windows were open, and a chilly easterly wind set the flimsy curtains softly dancing. Attired only in shorts, he shivered as he pulled shut the windows. He helped himself to a quarter pint of Canadian Club and sat down to think. The whisky was disposed of in rapid mouthfuls and he rose unsteadily for a refill. He tilted the bottle to pour, then froze. Galbraith had been on his mind; Senator Galbraith.

Daniel had seen him on TV, surrounded by aides and security people. But one face had wedged itself into Daniel's unconsciousness and refused to be dislodged, and now he knew why. The face was fatter, slacker, but that was age. The hair not quite so dark. But the eyes were the same and he was sure, positive in fact, that the man standing on the Senator's right had been on the knoll. One of the snipers. The man who fired the rifle, who had spun, and spotted Danny, before handing the rifle to one of his colleagues and leaping into the station wagon and breaking for escape. One of the men responsible for killing President John F. Kennedy now stood beside the probable next President!

He was brought sharply out of his reverie by the sound of spilling liquid. He glanced down to see the precious whisky running down the sides of the brimming glass to form a pool on the table. Bending low, he drank enough from the glass to halt the overflow, then brought a towel to clean up the mess. When he returned to the chair it was to reason with himself. To persuade himself he had made a mistake. TV pictures were not that good and besides, the man at Galbraith's side was in his late fifties or early sixties. There was a resemblance, he conceded, hurriedly building a wall of comforting logic to cower behind, but surely his imagination – galvanised by the recurrence of the dream, had contributed something?

No. Though he tried hard to deny it, tried his dammedest to direct his thoughts away, the gut instinct only grew in strength. There was more to recognition than mere physical semblance. He knew.

He sat late into the night. The worry of possessing knowledge he had no desire to possess tied his stomach in knots and drove him to nibble a thumbnail to the quick. What was the killer doing? What life was he leading? Was he a legitimate staffer, or did he have some sinister motive? And what could he, Daniel, do? Who could he speak to?

Not Barbara, no. He immediately dismissed that idea. She had indulged him tonight but she would scoff at this revelation. She was more likely to conclude he was making up the whole tale to draw attention to himself. He knew her well enough to predict that. No, he would say nothing to her, not until he knew a lot more.

He was suddenly terrified; how easily that thought came! *Until he knew a lot more!* What was he thinking? Was he actually planning to get involved? Did he actually intend *doing* something?

He had no firm answer, but the fear was as real as the temptation to tell was great. He had not forgotten his father, and the telephone calls in the night. He had not forgotten his father's crushed, shattered appearance those last days. And he had heard of other such 'occurrences'. Others had seen the wrong thing and had the bad judgement to stick to their story.

He would be cautious, he decided at last. Not move too quickly. Secretly he was pleased; he probably would do nothing. He did not want to upset anyone – not after all these years. What good would it do anyway? He just wanted to be left alone.

He wanted to live.

He was awakened by a searingly pleasurable sensation; Barbara's hand scudding lightly across his stomach, travelling lower, electrifying him awake.

'Rush, that's ticklish!' he giggled. His stomach muscles spasmed at her touch and in reflex his hands darted to brush her away.

With a leonine purr she crawled upon him, slipped a hand inside his waistband and slid his shorts along his legs. His head kicked back and he laughed out loudly. 'Okay, okay. I'm all yours!'

In the shower afterwards he smiled as he thought of her and himself in bed. There they had always been good together. It was a pity the physical compatibility did not overlap the more routine aspects of daily life. Fully dressed, they were completely out of synch.

With a deflating surge of pragmatism he resigned himself to her leaving. He was not looking forward to being alone again; for in the back of his mind something had moved. He sensed its faint approach, and he knew he was going to hate and fear it.

Over the next couple of days he managed quite successfully to put the entire business out of mind. He swam with extra enthusiasm, worked with exaggerated cheerfulness, and by sheer effort of will managed to keep the guilt and the worry at bay. But then on the third day, he slipped.

He was out shopping at a mall a mile from the apartment; groceries and fruit from the Publix, toiletries from the Winn-Dixie close by. He was perusing the vast range of goods, from bellyboards to razorblades, when his gaze lit upon an upright wire stand loaded with paperbacks. As if operating independantly of his mind, his hand reached out to take up a particular book; Leek & Sugar's *The Assassination Chain*, and as he thumbed through it he wondered what subconscious control had directed him into the store, to the book stand.

'What's past is past . . .' he reminded himself, fitting the book firmly back into its slot. Yet he knew he was lying to himself. The return of the dream had slipped into gear some dark engine, some unfathomable motor hidden for years in a deeply recessed black corner of his nicely segmented mind. Now it was rolling forward with an impetus all of its own, and he was powerless to stop it. Snatching up the book he hurriedly paid for it and went out to the Camaro. He raced home with elation and a sense of daring in his heart, hardly able to wait to start reading.

He finished it in three hours, then sat down with a drink and read it again, this time jotting down notes on a pad at his side. Nursing a tall drink, and a brooding mood, he took to bed and lay with the light off until dusk bathed the room in red, until night closed his eyes.

All the next day he eyed the telephone. He ought to call, he really ought . . . He was positive now about the ID. He had bought a stack of recent newspapers, and clipped numerous articles and pictures featuring Senator Galbraith. In some of the pictures the killer was visible in the background. Only the name of the man eluded him now. Each time he looked at that face the memories, and the confused emotions, flooded back. The nervous fluttering in his gut made him want to be sick.

He delayed for hours, glad at last when the time arrived to go to work, taking the decision from him. The bar was busy, and he was able to ease his conscience temporarily by forgetting.

He returned home late and, unable to relax, cursed loudly on finding the whisky bottle empty. He retired to bed and fretted until sleep swamped him.

In the morning, guilt was the first thing on his mind. He had barely finished breakfast when his thoughts turned to the bottle. Dashing out to buy a fifth, he sat, staring into space, until noon, when the guilt defeated him. He lifted the receiver and dialled the operator.

'Could you get me a Miami number please? The Federal Bureau of Investigation. FBI.'

He faltered, and the agent's crisp voice filled the void. 'Sir, you'll have to let me have more information before I can take this further. Would you give me your name?'

Daniel licked his lips. A great knot of fear filled him. 'Wha . . .

what kind of information do you need?'

'You said you had fresh revelations concerning the death of President Kennedy. That you saw what happened. Could you describe the circumstances for me? You sound pretty young, how old were you then?' The agent did not try to hide his scepticism.

'I was ten years old.' Daniel's voice was almost a squeak, he was that tense. 'I was on the knoll on Dealey Plaza. I saw what happened. Look . . . could you just tell me who I have to speak to? I can take this further myself.'

'I would like to help you, sir, really I would, but I will need personal details. May I start with your name?' There was a brief pause, then: 'Let me have your name and I'll have someone pay you a visit.'

In all probability the remark was made innocently, he later admitted to himself. But at the time, recalling the visit his father had, Daniel read something sinister into it.

His breathing was rapid and shallow, nervousness threatening to swamp him. 'It doesn't matter,' he stammered. 'It doesn't matter. Forget it.'

The receiver banged down with dull finality. His heartbeat pounded in his ears. His fingers trembled and sweat ran down his brow. He swallowed two glasses of cool water to soothe his dry throat, and felt himself slowly calming.

What the hell was he doing? Why on earth was he getting involved?

Because he had to. He had identified his feelings and he now knew that the unease, with him for as long as he could remember, was guilt – and a feeling of being in debt. Morally he supposed he owed a lot. To many people. Those who died.

His father.

There had to be a better, more subtle way. Some discreet means to probe, for probe he must. He had to go on, there was no use him denying it. But he had to be careful. He was no hero. He wanted to live. He would take no risks but he had to go on. He had to know.

Had to know.

Water was no damm good. For strength he turned to the whisky.

Two nights later he was positive he was followed from the hotel. A pair of headlamps hung like evil, seeking eyes in the rear view mirror, keeping a rock steady distance behind him. It was the weirdest feeling; cold, dead fingers tracing icy paths along his spine. He accelerated as he neared the apartment block, and when the gate loomed he jerked the wheel savagely, forcing the Camaro to take the turn on screeching tyres. He kept his gaze locked on the mirror and saw the car – it looked like a Buick, speed past. He braked, and sat shaking for some minutes before leaving the car and stumbling at last into the building.

The shuddering jangle of the telephone wormed insistently into his head, refusing to stop until he made it. Peering blearily at the bedside clock he let out a groan. Fumbling, he put the receiver to his ear. He muttered.

'This had better be good.'

'Mr Daniel Baker?' He did not recognise the voice. The tone was cultured, scholastic even, but not at ease. Daniel mumbled an affirmative.

'My name is Leon Newbolt, Mr Baker. I'd like to talk to you, today if possible, about something in which we both have an interest.'

Daniel hiked himself up on one elbow. Fatigue pushed aside by gnawing apprehension. 'And what might that be?'

'If I may be ostensive; a call you made to the FBI.'

Daniel felt his stomach lurch, then drop alarmingly. How had they found him? Miraculously keeping his voice even, he asked: 'Are you with the bureau?'

'I'm not with the FBI, no. It really is important we meet, Mr Baker. More important than you can know.'

Anxiety clutched at Daniel's heart. He couldn't do this. 'I made a mistake. The call was a hoax. I don't know anything.'

Newbolt seemed prepared for the denial. He was unperturbed. 'Believe me, I do understand, but you are Daniel Baker aren't you, born June second, nineteen fifty three?'

'I was born on that day, yes . . .' Dan ceded, unnerved by the sudden veering of the conversation. 'But —'

'And you are the son of Harrison Baker, who made a statement to the Dallas police about the assassination of President Kennedy, and later committed suicide?'

'You know a lot,' Dan remarked flatly.

'I merely want to show you, Mr Baker, that this kind of information is freely available. I mean you no harm, but if I can find out so much about you, so can others, those whose intentions toward you might be . . . shall we say, less kindly disposed.'

Threads of fear converged within him, became tangled and knotted until they hurt. The point was not lost on him. He had seen first hand the effects of pressure. He snapped: 'Who are you?'

'Someone concerned with justice. Tell me, have you ever heard of The Assassinations Bureau?' Daniel had not, and said so. Newbolt continued. 'If you agree to meet me I can tell you about it.'

'No!' Dan shrieked as the pressure piled up inside of him. 'How did you get my name and number?'

'Your call was traced, of course. We have friends in the FBI, people who care about injustice as much as we do, but who have to be discreet because of the positions they hold. I'm sure you can appreciate that.'

Daniel was breathing heavily. He was tempted to hang up. Newbolt, sensing the hesitation, pressed further.

'Please, Mr Baker, at least meet with me. If you still don't want to get involved after we have spoken, I give you my word I'll leave you be. Just hear me out.'

'What exactly do you want from me?' Daniel asked as he poured Canadian Club into two glasses and handed one to his guest. Newbolt was black, and slim, with a narrow, intelligent face, sincere eyes and a cultured manner. Yet behind the educated facade, Daniel thought he detected a glimmer of steely obstinacy. Newbolt raised his glass in salute and took a sip. 'Hmmm, that is good. What do we want? The answer is: anything you can let us have. We are still largely an underground organisation. We have to be; there is still risk attached to asking questions about the assassinations, even after all these years. Some of our people have paid the highest price for their idealism.'

Pre-fortified by large swallows of CC, Daniel felt emboldened enough to face the challenge. 'And what exactly is that idealism?'

Newbolt hesitated not an instant. 'We are committed to uncovering the truth behind the killings; JFK, Martin Luther King, Bobby Kennedy.' His gaze was steady, eyes set at an uncomfortable, piercing intensity. 'We have ideas and theories about the why and the how, but we do not know for sure. If we could ever find the men who actually committed the crimes, we'd get the chance to unravel the plots and expose the men behind it all; the big fish. They are the ones we'd like to hurt.'

Daniel was wary. 'It's been a long time. Isn't all this a lost cause?'

'It's still within living memory, Daniel. Any of the proponents might still be alive. It is as important as ever to know the truth.' His tone had lowered to a grave timbre.

'Our tenacity earns us a grudging respect; they employ teams of specialists just to watch us. What we know, and, more importantly, what they think we know, has brought us to a peculiar point of symbiosis, which protects us to a degree from certain powerful people who might otherwise sanction our extermination in an instant. As long as they know we are out here, scraping away the layers of deceit, they are careful.' His mouth twisted into a rueful pout. 'Of course, if we ever find all the answers, and really endanger them, they won't hesitate.'

'So, these people you believe are behind the assassinations, they are alive and still dangerous?'

Newbolt nodded. 'I'm afraid so.' He leaned forward on his seat. 'Tell me your story Daniel, please.'

His hands toyed nervously. 'If I tell you, what then? It's been a long time, why should I risk my life now?'

Newbolt's dark lips flattened into a narrow line. His eyebrows edged closer together. 'Listen mister, you called the FBI. You started all this. So what happened? What made you open up after all this time?'

Dan faltered; of course the man was right, he was owed an explanation, but what might it cost? His glass was empty and he was reaching for the bottle when Newbolt's hand shot out and intercepted. His grip on Daniel's wrist was strong, belying his slightness of frame. 'Talk to me without that stuff inside of you. What woke you up?'

Daniel's mouth was dry, he was tired, he wanted to be left alone. Why didn't Newbolt just walk away? What was so urgent? Racked by indecision, he anxiously licked his lips. He was conscious of standing at an important crossroads in his life. He had a history of impulsiveness, he had never gotten anything right. This time he had to be sure, but could he be? He wanted to unload the secret, yet there lurked the fear of speaking out. A vision of his father loomed large, the back of his skull smeared up the wall. . . .

A tremor rippled his body. His father had seemed invincible, yet he had been scared enough to kill himself. Daniel did not believe himself capable of enduring such pressures, and the vision triggered a decision. 'I was followed last night. Was it you?'

Newbolt's reaction was one of surprise. 'No. Are you sure you were followed? No mistake?'

'At two thirty in the morning, from the hotel where I work in Orlando to here? I was followed.'

The silence was ominous. Newbolt's face had closed into a frown. 'Then someone else knows your secret, and you need our help. What made you call the FBI?'

Daniel ducked the question. 'Who else could have followed me? Who else would be interested?'

Newbolt's simple reply cut through the alcohol haze with a sobering edge. 'The tidy-up squads. The people who still have the job of silencing witnesses and wiping out evidence. You can be pretty certain that whatever information we got from the FBI, they had too.'

Dan exploded. 'That's crap. This is just unbelievable. Get out of here!'

'You're scared, Daniel. I can smell it on you. Y'see, I know about fear. You need our help.'

'Get out of here,' Dan muttered, clamping down his fury. 'The case on JFK was closed a long time ago. It was solved, over, finished.'

Newbolt sneered. 'You trying now to tell me you believe the official version, man?'

'Why not?' Dan railed, the fear suddenly cutting deep. 'The word of the government is good enough for me.'

'Just your saying it won't change a thing, Daniel, but okay . . .' he laughed. 'Okay, so Lee Oswald, acting alone, killed John Kennedy, right?'

'It's in the history books.'

'So what about the witnesses, Daniel? The people like your father who refused to alter their stories about what they saw.'

'What about them?'

'Oswald died, and in the three years following the assassination seventeen witnesses died – violently. What does that tell you?'

When Daniel remained unmoved, Newbolt was roused to fury.

'Alright man, alright. Just answer me this. If Oswald was acting alone, as the Warren report says he was, who killed the witnesses, and why?

'Tell me Daniel, who killed the witnesses?'

The next morning Daniel awoke to a pounding head, and a guilt embedded so deeply that no amount of alcohol could dislodge it. He raised himself, and immediately regretted the movement. Jeezus! His head boomed with pain! Scrambling for the bathroom, he stood beneath the icy, needle-fine shower spray until his head cleared. Then he stood before the bathroom mirror and faced a number of uncomfortable recollections.

He had gone berserk. Fear had imbued him with insane strength and he had forcibly ejected the well-meaning Newbolt. Before the door was slammed in his face, the black thrust a card into Daniel's hand and begged him to reconsider.

'I understand, Daniel. I really do. I know it has to be bad to make you act like this, but we'll be there for you —' The door was slammed, but still his muffled voice rang out: 'If you need help, call me!'

Coffee eased his head. Eyeing the card he halfheartedly firmed a resolve to call and apologise. He wasted the day, pacing the apartment until his nerves could stand no more, then he sat down once more with another of the assassination books he had bought. His eyes, as they scanned the pages, took in little of the bulk. He was absorbing information selectively, focusing on those sections concerning the witnesses; those who disagreed with the official version and were not called to testify, or whose testimony was altered. Those unfortunates who clung doggedly to the fatal lure of the truth. Those who died – violently, more often than not, in a chain of ludicrous coincidences.

His father was not listed. His death certificate had pronounced him a suicide. Murder by mental torture did not qualify.

Still restless, he left for work and somehow made it through the shift. Once again it was after two in the morning when he crossed the hotel lot to his car, his footsteps sounding unnaturally loud as they crunched gravel underfoot. That feeling was with him again, the compulsive urge to look over his shoulder. As if looking alone could keep what it was haunting him at bay.

With a feeling of relief growing in his heart, he gunned the engine and hurled the Camaro onto the road east. He sped one mile, two, three, all the time rejoicing in the blackness reflected in the rear view mirror. He had been nervous about nothing, and he laughed aloud at his stupidity, becoming cheered by the lustiness of the sound. Ahead, the headlamp beams parted the enclosing deep of the night, and behind him was only the blackness, the beautiful, beautiful . . .

His elation drained away. Far behind him a pair of lamps twinkled. Seemingly harmless. Then with predatory speed, they closed in.

He sprinted into the apartment, slammed and locked the door and switched on every light in the place.

‘That’s better.’ He panted, turning on the TV to banish the eerie silence. He had to have noise. Making straight for the bottle, he swore violently on discovering it empty.

‘Damm, Damm!’ he thumped the table top. He shot a glance around the room, then, desperate for something to do, he stalked out onto the terrace. The night was cool and oh, so normal. Just the quiet influence of the wind and the lapping of the ocean. He was tense. He stood with feet apart, body taut with constrained anger and fear.

Realising that in one hand he still held the empty bottle he lashed out, and hurling it far out into the gloom heard it strike the sand with a distant, gritty thud. The action seemed to trigger something in him, and he felt the need for further release. Filling his lungs, he howled at the top of his voice: ‘Shhhiiiitttt!!!!’

He fancied the sound carried far across the Atlantic. He felt better for the expurgation and was calmer when he returned indoors.

Gaze fixed, breath coming in measured draughts, he rummaged in the bottom of one of the wardrobes, seeking an old suitcase. Dragging it into the room by its virtually severed handle he laid the case on the floor. He paused for a moment to reflect, to consider his next move. Just what was it he was on the verge of doing?

With almost reverential care he unzipped the top of the case and flipped it open. Inside, exactly as he remembered it, lay the bundle. Taking it up he hefted the weight. It had always seemed that some charm was attached to the bundle, and that the simple action of opening it could invoke some terrible enchantment. But open it he did, unfolding the layers until the heart was exposed.

The metal was dull. That was his first observation. Lifting the gun, he let the cloth it had been wrapped in fall to the floor. He fitted finger around the trigger, dwelt on the nice balance, the deadly weight. He did not dwell on the fact that this gun had killed his father. The moment he lifted the weapon he felt safer, bolder. With surging excitement began to dismantle it, losing himself in the task and enjoying keeping busy. For the first time in a long time he felt worth something, felt good. After cleaning, he took the weapon to bed with him.

It was not the best night’s sleep he ever had, but the dream did not return to haunt him.

* 11 *

Already he was feeling somehow stronger. It was a peculiar sensation, one he would have been hard pressed to put into words, but he might have described it as an aggressive conceit, a swaggering boldness.

Each time he was jostled accidentally, or imagined he caught someone looking oddly at him, he felt like taking out the gun and snarling a warning.

It was a feeling that would have to be controlled.

He was at a public pool in Orlando. The sun was bright and hot, and the place was crowded. He swam two lengths then clung to the side to observe the other swimmers as they played.

'Hey Mister.' He heard a husky voice by his head. He turned, and as he did so a fat hand was pressed against his face. 'Get another hobby,' the voice growled. Then he was thrust backwards with force, sent sprawling, kicking and splashing into the cool blue water. When he surfaced, sputtering and coughing, he cleared his eyes and lunged for the side. Hauling himself up onto the pool rim, he looked around, catching sight of a conspicuous figure, a stockily built man in a dark suit, ducking rapidly into the changing rooms.

Spitting and snorting, Daniel hauled himself out of the pool and set off determinedly in pursuit. The man would be easy to spot, he ruminated angrily; he had been totally bald – bullet headed!

He hesitated on the threshold. Coming in from the intense sunlight, the interior of the changing room seemed dark and slightly forbidding. Taking a step, and taking care not to slip on the wet and slimy tiles, he entered the gloom. The air inside was thickly humid. Ahead could be heard the spraying of a shower. Wending his way between rows of lockers he rounded a corner that brought him before the communal showers.

He halted with a gasp.

. . . a naked man stood under the spray, his head upturned, his back flat against the tiled wall. Before him stood another, hands working busily. The first man groaned. His back arched . . .

Spinning away in disgust, Daniel returned to his allocated locker where a second shock awaited. The door had been forced open, his clothes strewn across the wet floor.

'Oh shit,' he muttered, bending to pick the dripping garments from the floor. Anger tightening his grip, he wrung the water from them. When he straightened it was to see the pool and the mens room in a different light. Suddenly it was a seedy place, a dangerous place. The two homos, the bullet-headed thug. He had caught a glimpse of society's soiled underbelly, and he felt tainted by it.

As he struggled into the wet clothes, his mind was filled with an imagined vision of the bullet-head's face. He guessed at vicious eyes, and row upon row of tiny, shark's teeth, and he shuddered at the apparition. Suddenly he was thankful he hadn't been forced to confront the man, thankful for what he was sure was a close escape.

His keys were missing, and he returned to the apartment fearing the worst. The door was ajar, the keys hanging in the lock, but the apartment appeared untouched. As he stood in the centre of the lounge, gazing perplexedly about him, something on the coffee table caught his eye; tiny cut up squares of paper. He crouched beside it and lifted a handful, letting the pieces filter between his fingers like confetti. The assassinations book.

'Find another hobby.' Bullethead had said. He felt sick. Was that it?

'My God,' he muttered. 'My God they know. . . .' He swallowed the lump in his throat. Told himself it was impossible, that he was being unreasonable. He tried to shake the fear but it would not go.

A sudden impulse galvanised him into frightened motion. Flinging open the closet door he dragged out the suitcase and in a panic rummaged for the bundle. He heaved a huge sigh; it was there. They'd missed it. He had not dared risk being spotted with it in the changing room. He hugged the weapon close to his chest. Next time he'd be ready for them!

It was that night he began to think about the book. The book. What was it Barbara said? '*You always said you wanted to write – why don't you?*'

Why didn't he? He certainly had a story to tell. But could he do it? And would anyone read it? He had nothing to lose. Or did he?

Newbolt had called them the tidy-up squads. Men given the job of removing evidence – even after all these years. He had also claimed that the information *he* had about Daniel would be equally available to others. Was Bullethead one of a team waiting for Daniel to trip up? He shivered. When he thought about what he had, what he knew, his blood ran cold. Of all the people on earth, only he – apart from the killers themselves, knew what had really gone down on Dealey that day, and he guessed they would kill to keep him quiet.

Producing a book intended to expose them might not be the best way to maintain a low profile. He would be an easy target. So he agonised. He spent an hour doodling, putting down what he had and adding snippets remembered from the assassinations book. He left for work a little later that night and was kept busy until the end. Not one minute passed when the gun was not to hand. When he returned, keyed up, to the Camaro, all was quiet, and he was not shadowed.

The following day he was off, but instead of spending the day in bed, as was often his custom, he rose mid-morning and restlessly moved about the apartment, tidying, treading water while he made up his mind. He lunched in Orlando – at the Red Lobster on International Drive, then drove slowly into the centre of town. He needed to lay a fear. He needed to swim.

The gun was in the tote bag he left by the poolside. He swam two lengths, then, as if expecting a repetition of history, he trod water at the side. But of bullet-head there was no sign, and he soon began to feel foolish for being worried. During the late afternoon he indulged himself, reclining on a lounger, a tall drink at his side. Idly he watched the swimmers, and for no particular reason found himself studying a tall, lithe girl in a cutaway swimsuit. When she dived she cut the surface of the water cleanly, and she stroked the length of the pool with powerful ease. He found himself admiring her strength and poise in the water.

When at last she climbed out of the water, and peeled away her bathing cap, he saw that her hair was a light reddish colour, cut stylishly short. As she passed him, on the way to the ladies changing room, he admired her figure. She was slender, but shapely, with a musculature that was powerful and attractive. She had a pretty face, with a pert, upturned nose and a clear direct gaze. As she vanished into the changing room he smiled wistfully to himself, saddened slightly by the thought he would probably never see her again.

At length he showered and changed. Dusk was settling when he emerged. There was a chilly edge to the breeze that blew across the parking lot as he made for the Camaro. He was preoccupied, and did not immediately notice the hubbub taking place some one hundred metres away. But a shrill cry brought him to a halt. He turned to look, and, with his stomach churning, realised that someone was being assaulted. His first reaction was to turn away, and he was on the point of doing so when he recognised the victim – it was the sandy haired girl from the pool.

He watched in horror as she struggled with her attacker, a tall stringy black man wearing a full length leather coat. He had hold of her handbag and was trying to wrest it from her, but because she was physically strong she fought furiously and gave as good as she got.

'It won't last . . .' Daniel thought to himself. 'He'll hurt her . . .'

He could hear her panting, and then, almost without his realising it, he broke into a trot, then a run. As he drew nearer he saw the black's arm lash out like a whip, and he winced at the sound of the blow as it struck her face. Faster he ran, dimly aware that other bystanders were doing nothing. If he had not been running he might have cursed them, but in truth it was his own reaction that was the surprise. He heard a crack as a second blow connected with her face. She fell to the ground, but her hand remained firmly enclasped on the bag. Not really knowing what he intended doing, Daniel hurtled in. He collided with the mugger and the two of them crashed to the ground. The black was stringy and streetwise and powerful, but Daniel was on top and he lashed out wildly with his fists, grunting as he bounced blows off the man's face. The black tore free an arm, and suddenly a knife glittered in his hand. Daniel was powerless to do anything more than watch in cold fear as the blade was jabbed into his belly. He felt the prick of the needle point, felt the flesh give. When the blade emerged again his frightened gaze noted the ruddy smears, and he felt nausea sweep over him. The knife went in again, and once more, and he felt himself going. He toppled sideways and came to rest with his face pressed to the road surface. He felt the attacker slither free from under him, and heard the sound of footsteps retreating.

His mouth was dry, and in a daze he gently probed the wounds with his fingertips. Through misting vision he stared up as people closed in a ring around him. But in the sea of faces he saw only one face clearly – hers. A wash of babbling voices enveloped him, but he heard only her voice. He felt her hands gently framing his cheeks, saw her concerned eyes staring directly into his. Then his vision blurred and he felt cold. His thoughts rambled, and he chided himself for being dumb enough to tackle the mugger. But then, he told himself, if he had not, *she* would not be leaning over him now, worrying about him, thanking him.

He strained to keep her face in focus but the effort was beyond him. Something wet struck his cheek, and he knew it was a tear just as instinctively he knew they were no longer strangers. Not caring he was hurt, not caring he might be dying, he sank into unconsciousness. He felt proud.

His nose twitched as the chlorinic hospital odour stung his nostrils, and he knew he was awake. His opened eyes blinked under the soft glare from the lights above, but, before he could adjust, a dark shadow parted the glare and, after a further readjustment he realised it was the sandy haired girl. The utter whiteness of the background lent her features a soft-focus aspect. She looked stunning, and when she asked how he was, in a voice that set strange emotions fluttering in his belly, he replied that he felt fine, but dry.

She vanished from view, to return moments later bearing a tumbler of water. Raising his head gently she touched the rim of the glass to his lips and tenderly urged him to drink. The water was lukewarm, but he felt better for having taken it, and he thanked her.

The smile was still on her face, but now his vision had cleared he could see it did not sit comfortably. He felt compelled to ask what was wrong. The smile vanished:

'I just feel so bad about what happened to you. I know I should have given in, but . . . well, thank you anyway. I couldn't have held on much longer.'

He found the strength to smile. 'What did you have in there, the family jewels?'

She gave a disconsolate shrug. 'Family trait. I couldn't just give in.' This last was said with a feeble smile.

'I think I know the feeling.'

'I really am sorry for the pain you've been caused. I truly am. I wish I'd given him the bag.'

'No you don't,' he assured her, 'Not really, and neither do I. You gave that guy the shock of his life, and I wouldn't have missed it for the world.'

Her smile told him he had said the right thing. The formal tension between them evaporated. Thanking him for his understanding, she told him it was time for her to leave. When she reached the door he called out: 'Will you come visit me again?'

She considered the barest instant. 'If you like.'

'I'd like,' he replied, too quickly. He knew his desperation was showing but he didn't care; the only thing that mattered was that he see her again.

'Okay then, I'll see you tomorrow.' She opened the door, the action further intensifying his feeling of urgency. He wanted so badly to delay her. He called out: '. . . what's your name?'

Her smile was contained to a pert curve, and there was a knowing amusement in her eyes; she was toying with him. 'Pamela.'

'I'm Daniel,' he told her.

'I know. See you tomorrow.' With a wave of her fingers she was gone, the door slowly swinging shut behind her.

Cursing his over-eagerness, but mindful of his wounds, he slowly eased himself up in the bed. She'd think he was a jerk, coming on like that. At the thought he was struck by an uncomfortable revelation. Was he really that lonely? So lonely he would snatch at, and cling for dear life to, the first sign of unforced human concern and kindness? The embarrassing truth was that he was. Still, she was coming to see him again . . .

His face relaxed into an expression of satisfaction. The vision of her smile stayed with him, and he was content to lie back and dream on it.

As she helped him into the apartment he once more felt embarrassment. He had been gone eight days, and the place had been a mess when he left it. The air was thick with the stink of fermenting garbage, but Pamela appeared not to notice. Opening the windows, she settled him into a chair on the terrace, and, while the fresh sea wind scoured the room, she tidied up. She had brought groceries, and at length she produced a bottle of white wine which she served over ice.

She sat beside him, and overlooking the beach and the blue wastes of the Atlantic they drank in silence for a while until she announced she was going to prepare dinner. He protested feebly that she ought to let him help her, but she would not listen, and secretly he was glad. He was still weary.

He enjoyed the feel of the wind on his face. All was good, and he knew he ought to feel contentment, but there was a gnawing unease in the pit of his belly. Galbraith, and the killer at his side. The images taunted him.

Over dinner Pam noted his restlessness and tried hard to

break through, but when he remained ill at ease, she misunderstood: 'Dan, am I doing something wrong? You seem so withdrawn. Be honest, would you rather be alone?'

'No,' he was quick to reassure her. It was nothing. While she concentrated on her meal, he struggled to come up with a line of conversation. 'Did you speak to Mr Bailey at the hotel?'

She had. 'Everyone there is very proud of you. There are newspaper clippings pinned up in the bar, and they're calling you *The Champ*. Mr Bailey said to take your time; your job will be waiting.'

He was pleased. 'That's a relief.' There was a pause, and then, on impulse, and without any prior thought he heard himself saying: 'I have to go to Miami. I know it's a lot to ask, but, I don't think I can manage it yet. Would you drive me there?'

She faltered. 'Sure. When?'

'As soon as possible. I have things to get done before I return to work. Do you mind?'

'No, I'll be glad to help. I have a few personal days coming. I'll just call my boss.'

He breathed relief. 'Thanks.'

'Do you mind if I ask why you want to go there?'

He hesitated only a moment. 'It sounds crazy, I know, but I have to visit the library.'

The long drive, to Miami, and then back to the apartment three days later, left them both tired, and upon his insistence she took the bed while he slumbered fitfully on the couch. In the Miami city library he had photocopied what seemed like a mountain of pages from reference books, then he and Pamela visited the largest bookshop in the city and bought a few he wanted to take with him, ordering three more.

As they loaded the back seat of the Camaro, Pamela eyed the book covers. 'You've been busy,' she mused running a hand along the spine of a book she read aloud some of the titles; '*Rush to Judgement. Oswald – the truth. Should we now believe the Warren Report . . . ?*' Do you mind if I ask what all this is about?'

He licked his lips. He could not talk about it. Not yet.

In the middle of the night he was awoken by sounds from the kitchen. Shifting his feet to the floor, he yawned, and stretched the tension from his cramped shoulders. As he walked through the lounge he spotted a shaft of light slanting under the kitchen door. He pushed the door open to find Pam seated at the table, coffee cup at her elbow. She was intent upon his photocopied sheets, and when she glanced up he saw in her eyes an odd emotion, an amalgam of anger and sadness and concern.

'This is incredible,' she said in a monotone. Moving to her side and viewing the page over her shoulder, he was forced to agree. 'It is, isn't it? I've been astonished myself, reading about it.'

'But all this physical evidence, all these coincidences and inconsistencies, and yet the history books still tell the wrong story.'

Pulling up a chair, he sat beside her. Taking up a sheet he gazed at it. 'The more I discover, the more frightened I become. How could all this happen, in this country?'

'I never gave it much thought before,' she admitted. 'I mean, I wasn't even born when JFK died. But if all this is true, and I do mean IF, the lies and the suppressing of evidence . . . the way everything seems to have been worked out in advance . . . if it could be proven, we'd have a cover up story that would make Watergate look like something out of Sesame Street.'

He ruefully agreed with her. 'It's a big if, and that's the problem. No one knows.'

She looked at him. 'Why are you researching into this?' He stared into her eyes and saw a friend. The urge to tell was strong, and the time was right. He told her.

His story shocked her. She looked at him in awe for long minutes, incredulity and disbelief vying for dominance. But when he showed her a page that actually mentioned his father she placed her arms around him and hugged him close. 'Oh Dan, I'm so sorry.'

Moving back, she held him at arm's length. 'I have to admire your strength. To come through all that and still be so . . . . unaffected. I know I couldn't do it.'

He flushed modestly, for the first time he could ever recall. 'I've been affected alright. . . .' He was tempted to confess the drinking, the suicidal depressions. But with her there, all these seemed like parts of some long-forgotten nightmare. With her beside him he felt strong.

'Can I help?' she asked. Her grip on his hand was tight, and he felt buoyed by her energy. He muttered warningly, about it being dangerous, but she brushed his words aside.

'If you don't want me interfering, Dan, I will understand. But speaking personally, I'd love to help.'

Those were, he thought, the loveliest words he had heard in years. He wanted to reach out his arms and embrace her. 'You mean it?'

She gasped, then delivered her broadest smile. 'What kind of question is that? Of course I mean it!'

The following day they sat down, books and papers to hand, and began to scrap out notes. Each time he looked at her, his heart felt so full of joy he was afraid it might burst. He felt so good, having her there to share a burden, that occasionally he would stop to just gaze at her, and to secretly hope that she might be his forever. He had a feeling that he might achieve with her a kind of relationship he had never experienced before; friends as well as, hopefully, lovers.

For a long while she said nothing, though she could not avoid being aware of his scrutiny. Eventually she felt driven to ask if something was wrong.

He blushed, and shrugged sheepishly. 'Nothing's wrong. I just . . . I'm just glad you're here. That's all.'

She beamed shyly. 'I'm glad to be here.'

His breath caught in his chest. She meant it! It felt so good not to be alone!

They ate on the terrace, a takeout of light salad and chicken from Fat Boy's along A1A. Over dessert he began to pry. So far she had revealed little about herself. He hoped that, once relaxed, she might open up. He did so want to know her better.

He had guessed correctly about her age. He had pegged her at twenty nine and he was right. She hailed from San Francisco, he learned, and had been adopted.

'My natural father died at sea. Went overboard in a storm. My mom took it hard. She couldn't bear to raise me, so she placed me in safe hands and went her own way.' She halted, her eyes gazing vacantly out to sea, and with her teeth tugged on her lower lip.

'I had a nice upbringing, a wealthy caring family who gave me everything I ever wanted and more than I needed. After my graduation I worked in oceanography for a while. I love to be around the sea.' Her face lit up. 'I spent some time on the reefs off Australia with an underwater film unit. That was wonderful. It's an entirely different world down there. There's a kind of natural balance, a harmony . . .' she chuckled. 'I don't really have the words.'

'Don't you feel strange about that?' he asked, adding, in response to her look of puzzlement. 'Your father dying at sea and you having such a love of it.'

'I never really thought about it.' Her manner became elusive. She played with a forkful of fruit, her eyes once more staring seaward.

He decided on a change of subject. 'What are you working at now?'

'I have a friend at Seaworld. He got me some part-time work with the whales, just for the busy season. I work three days a week. I don't need the money, so I can afford the time off, if that's what's worrying you.'

He sipped at his wine. 'You know, I can't tell you how much it means to have your help. To be able to share the secret with someone who understands is . . . wonderful.' He put down his glass. 'I'd just like you to know I'm really happy you're here.'

Her cheeks flushed pink. She joked as she gestured with her glass: 'I can't take this stuff.' She fanned herself with a hand. 'Phew, am I hot!'

He reached across the table, his fingers stroking the back of her hand. She recoiled, fractionally, her face reddening deeper.

'What is it?' he asked, stunned by her reaction. He had been so sure she liked him enough, so sure the moment was right. He apologised hurriedly, but she got to her feet and hastened indoors. He followed her. 'I'm sorry. Pam?'

He touched her shoulder but she gently removed his hand. 'No, Dan, I'm the one who's sorry.'

'No . . . I'm such a meathead. I didn't mean to . . . it was just the sun and the wine . . .' Her head was still averted. Desperation gripped him. 'I'll understand if you want to leave.'

'Why would I want to leave?' She dabbed at her eyes with a handkerchief. 'I'm not upset. Excuse me . . .' she brushed past him and took refuge in the bathroom.

He walked out onto the terrace. His fingers gripped the rail with their full force as he fought to contain his pain.

What had he done? Why did he always have to spoil everything?

A lump rose to his throat, and he struggled to down it.

She appeared on the terrace behind him. 'Daniel?'

When he turned there was fear in his eyes. Fear of rejection, of being hurt.

'Still friends?' she asked. Her eyes were red rimmed, but she was composed. He heaved a sigh, and nodded. 'Let me get you a drink.'

When dusk fell she prepared to leave. The silences between them had become lengthy and uncomfortable, and he feared he had lost her. When she asked if she might use the Camaro to drive home, he readily agreed, saying: 'At least you'll have to come back to return the car.'

'Daniel . . .' she began, but he interrupted with a hand gesture. 'It's okay,' he insisted. 'Really, it's okay.'

'No, let me explain. I do like you, it's just I'm not sure I'm ready for anything more than friendship right now. I had a bad experience recently, and, well, I'm sure you can guess . . .' She shrugged. 'I'd still like to come around to visit.'

Weak laughter trickled from him. 'I'm glad about that. Here . . .' He held out the car keys. 'See you tomorrow?'

At the door he stalled her, placed his hands on her shoulders and lightly kissed her forehead. 'Thanks.'

She looked puzzled, and slightly embarrassed. 'For what?'

'For not walking out on me. I can't tell you what that means.'

After she had gone, he turned to the whisky bottle and went onto the terrace to pour. Something was odd; he had poured a smaller than usual measure. He searched deep within himself and was surprised to find no trace of the destructive urge that normally drove him to drunkenness. As he mulled over the whisky he delighted not on its effect, but on its taste – something he had not done for a long time. He delighted too in the touch of the breeze on his face. Contentment sated him; life was good.

Another week passed. His wounds had healed well and he had regained a pleasing amount of mobility. Pamela visited him each afternoon and together they worked through the piles of information he had gathered, outlining passages that might be useful.

'What form do you intend this book to take?' She asked him one evening. He paused to think.

'I'm not really sure. Something factual, my experience backed up by cataloging the evidence that was ignored by the Warren Commission. I'd like to make people think, perhaps ask a few questions of their own. When I read these books, and think about what happened to my Pa, I get so damm angry. What ever happened to the ideal of justice?'

'Maybe you ought to reconsider contacting the guy from The Assassination Bureau.'

As he had before when she had voiced this idea, Daniel expressed doubts. She sat up straighter in her seat, appealed directly to him.

'Come on Dan, be positive. They have more experience than you when it comes to dealing with this stuff. They must have contacts. Didn't you ever hear the phrase, *strength in numbers?* What can hurt?'

He brooded for a while, then reluctantly agreed.

It was dusk when he found the address. The hallway in which he stood was submerged in gloom, and Newbolt, little more than a shadow in the darkness, apologised for the lack of light. 'I have to be careful. I'm sure you understand.'

He led the way along a narrow passage to a study walled with crammed bookshelves. Masses of paper besieged a typewriter on a beaten desk, thick curtains hid the windows, and atop a filing cabinet a portable television collected dust.

Newbolt bade Daniel sit, and Dan, taking the opportunity to cast a glance around the room, commented: 'This is some collection.'

Newbolt shrugged. 'It's getting there.' His tone was friendly, but on hearing Daniel's next question, he became wary.

'Who runs the bureau?'

Newbolt studied him intently. 'Just a few concerned citizens. We act within our constitutional rights.'

'Concerned about what, exactly?'

Newbolt's expression teetered towards scorn. 'The deceits practised by our democratically elected dictators.' He spread wide his arms. 'All this you see around you is evidence that our governments repeatedly lie to us to protect their own interests, and the vested interests of others, the multi-nationals and the military. They're all in these books; the killers, the cheats, the heroes: Kennedys, Martin Luther King, Nixon, Onassis, Hughes, Coniston, Vincent. The saints and the robber barons. Many of the lesser known are here too, and the victims, most of them. Some we missed.'

Daniel's face showed his scepticism. He wanted no indoctrination. 'Are you ever followed the way I was?'

Newbolt remained impassive, his eyes betraying nothing. 'When you do what we do, being a subject of surveillance becomes a condition of life. Tell me, what brought you around?'

'I've been doing some thinking.'

'Glad to hear it. I'm ready whenever you are.'

'You know about my father?'

An odd expression flitted across Newbolt's face. He directed a lengthy smouldering stare at his guest. 'Yeah, I know about your father. He was a fool, blowing his brains out that way.'

Dan felt the swift rush of blood as anger suffused his face. 'What are you talking about?' he shrieked. 'They drove him to it!'

Newbolt yielded before the intensity of Daniel's stare. 'Maybe I spoke out of turn. I'm sorry. I wasn't there.'

'Damned right you weren't! I felt the fear in the house. I saw what it did to him. Who the hell are you to moralise?'

Newbolt held up his hands. 'I'm sorry. I guess I had that coming. It's just that no matter how many deceits we uncover, they don't mean squat without the reliable testimony of people who were on the scene.'

His heartrate increased; Daniel felt charged. Placing his hands on his thighs, he leaned forward to lend emphasis to his words.

'That's all about to change.'

Newbolt listened in rapt silence as Daniel related his history. When he was done, Newbolt went into the adjacent kitchen without a word and made coffee. He needed to think. At length he returned, and studied Daniel over the rim of his cup. So intent was he, his eyebrows were almost knitted together.

'Daniel, I'm stunned. I don't know what to say.'

'I need you to tell me what to do next. Where do I go, who do I see?'

Newbolt put down his cup. He took a deep breath as he composed himself. 'You are the most important single piece of evidence ever to emerge. You have to be protected. Unfortunately that is beyond my immediate resources.'

'What are you saying, I'm alone?'

'Patience. What I am saying is that you need specialist help. The bureau has connections, but the level at which I operate is not part of all that. I have to pass you on to someone who can help.'

'Who?'

'There is a man. I've never met him, but I know of him. As far as the bureau is concerned he's right at the top. The problem is, he knows so much he is dangerous. That makes him vulnerable, so he keeps a low profile.'

'What's his name?'

Another shrug. 'I know him only by a code name. They call him the Zealot. TAB is supported by several wealthy people with consciences; they pay to keep him in safe locations, they make sure he has whatever he needs. He's the one I have to get you to.'

'Can you contact him?'

'It's going to take time. I pass on a message, it goes through numerous intermediaries and eventually arrives at his door. Give me a few days.'

Heightened perhaps by the shades of intrigue, the drawn drapes, Daniel's nervousness returned. 'Leon, I may not have a few days. I've been followed, you know that.'

Newbolt's expression became earnest. 'So stay safe. You have to be careful from now on, Daniel. You're going to be important, and dangerous, and many people a whole lot less dangerous than you have been removed.'

All the way home he kept an eye on the rear view mirror, anxiety clutching his stomach in a sharp-toothed vice. And the headlamps were benind him all the way, closing in when he accelerated, falling back when he slowed. Toying.

His mouth was dry, a lump he could not swallow blocked his throat. *God! Could they be so close? Could they really be so near?*

He had never been so glad to see anyone. He almost fell into Pamela's arms. She gasped at his blanched face, led him to a seat. 'What is it?'

'I was followed,' he croaked. 'All the way from Tampa.' Her eyes widened, and he saw that for the first time the reality of the fear had struck her. He gripped her shoulders, willed his strength into her. 'We'll be okay. Newbolt is going to help us.'

They talked far into the night, but the fears would not recede. If anything, talk only seemed to churn up their anxieties afresh. Pamela tried her best to soothe him, and though he was not completely convinced, he was glad she had made the effort. Beyond the window, dawn was beginning to tint the horizon when she brought him yet another mug of sweet coffee. 'Drink this,' she said, 'It will make you feel better.'

He sipped. Grimaced. 'It doesn't.'

She sat beside him. 'I was thinking. Could we be getting just a little paranoid about all this?'

He looked to her. 'I'm not imagining all this.'

'See,' she darted back. 'How easily you fly off the handle. Let's try to look at this rationally. There have been no threats, no attacks, not even a scary telephone call. We read books, we talk, our imaginations become inflamed. We frighten ourselves.'

'What about the guy at the pool?'

'There's a creep at every pool,' she returned. 'All I'm saying is, we could be wrong. If you are such a danger and they are onto you, why haven't they silenced you once and for all?'

'They have their reasons . . .' he started to say, then dried up. 'You sure know how to cheer up a guy.'

She smiled, and taking his arm led him to the window. Dawn light fanned up over the distant horizon, color-washing the sky with bold brushstrokes, while below it the ocean remained immutably dark. 'This is reality,' she said. 'Look at that view.' He smiled at her.

'Let's get out of here,' she proposed. 'Feel like a walk?'

They walked north, towards the cape. The sand was soft underfoot and the sound of the surf crashing inshore had a soothing effect on strained nerves. 'I really love this coast,' she said. He murmured agreement. 'It really is a nice place to live. I envy you.' She paused, and turned to him, and in the soft light he saw, and was warmed by, the brilliance of her smile.

'Well it is Barbara's apartment. I suppose one day she'll want it back. Jeeez . . .' He pointed ahead, to where a lone jogger pounded the sand some half a mile distant. 'Will you look at that guy? At this time of the morning.'

She continued. 'You never talk about Barbara. How do you feel about her now?'

He shrugged. 'Nothing much to say. We just weren't suited.' He whistled in admiration; the jogger was nearer. 'That man must have some stamina.'

'And yet she let you stay on in the apartment?'

'I pay a small rent, and she has someone looking after the place.' Seeing the look of uncertainty on her face, he added: 'We were never going to make it.'

'Do you still think about her?'

'It's been known. Why?'

'I just wondered. Any . . . phantom feelings?'

He threw back his head and laughed. When he stopped, his

face wore a vast smile. 'Aahh, that's great. Really great. I needed that.'

'Don't mock,' she said, digging him with her elbow. She was finding it hard not to laugh.

'I'm sorry,' he said, chuckling, "The only phantom feeling I have for Barbara is . . .'

'Is what?' He did not reply. Sensing his disquiet, she decided to venture an opinion. 'Let me get a little out of line here. I have this feeling, from the few things you have said about her, that you resent Barbara, and the success she's had. Am I right? Is that why you're so sour? Be honest.'

He heaved a sigh. 'It's complicated. I'm not even sure I know how to answer you. I was a wreck in those days. This last couple of weeks, since meeting you, I've started to feel like a new man.'

The jogger was very close. His breathing was audible. Daniel halted, turned to face Pam.

'She and I, we —' His words were cut off as something heavy struck his nose. Stunned, he fell back and was delivered a sickening blow to the groin. He felt blood at the back of his throat, and confusion swirling in his mind. As he collapsed to the sand he heard Pamela scream. He moved to help her, but when he tried to open his eyes he was savagely kicked in the head. His entire body pounded with pain, sand filled his eyes, his mouth, and he coughed and gagged violently.

As he lay, helpless in the sand, he felt hands hurriedly rummaging through his pockets. He attempted to get up, but another kick, this time to his midriff, drove the air from his lungs. Then all was quiet, save the dull sound of running feet.

The insulating mist of confusion that surrounded him started to clear as he felt himself being hoisted up. He hurt everywhere, and more than that he felt humiliated by the ease with which he'd been caught. He wanted to scream with frustration. He wiped sand from his eyes, and, hearing Pam sob, peered through half opened eyelids to view the cold reality of his position. He had been mugged. That was all. Nothing more. He had dared walk without thought of what might happen. He told himself he ought to have known better.

He tried to say: 'This is getting to be a habit,' but his mouth was full, and when he spat, his saliva was dark with blood. Pamela shrieked, and folded to the ground. He crouched before her, and disregarding his own pain he wiped away her tears. A sudden upsurging of pain in his ribs forced a wince from him, and he tenderly explored the bruised area with a hand.

'Some new man, eh?' he spat through swollen lips. 'Same old shit after all.' With an effort he rose to his feet and wearily brushed the sand from his clothes. He stared along the beach. The mugger was a good half mile away, little more than an indistinct figure receding into the distance. Now the assault was over, Daniel found himself in reaction, clenching his fists and glowering around impotently, demanding a measure of satisfaction, revenge. . . . He growled helplessly, a mixture of despair and fury. Then helping Pamela to her feet, he wrapped an arm around her shoulders and they struggled back to the apartment.

He called the police. Within the hour a patrol car arrived and a uniformed officer was taking down details in a detached manner. When asked for a description of the attacker, Pam was infuriatingly vague, and Daniel said so. The officers left at last offering little hope.

Dan stamped out onto the terrace. It was early morning, the first vacationeers were already on the beach and the dark Atlantic was dotted with swimmers.

'Dan?' she spoke from behind him. He turned, and though he knew he was being unfair, he glowered at her. 'Pam, I can't believe you didn't see the guy.'

Her lips quivered. Her eyes shimmered with tears. 'I did see him,' she admitted in a frail voice.

'What????' he screamed. 'So why didn't you tell the cop? What the fuck do you think you're doing?'

She shook as if mustering her strength for some great effort. 'I didn't say anything, because . . . because . . . he was bald, he was completely bald!'

His jaw dropped. Her reserve broke, she ran indoors and collapsed onto the couch. He followed. Her head was wrapped in her arms and her entire body tremored as she sobbed. 'He . . . had on a cap. When he tore it off I saw . . . I saw . . . his eyes!'

He embraced her, murmured into her ear, but she seemed inconsolable. For a while they remained like that, locked in pain, until she was too drained to cry any longer. He spoke to her in a low voice, talked of his fears for her. When she glanced up, her face was lined and ravaged by red blotches.

'He looked so vicious, Daniel. He waited until you tried to move, then he kicked you with everything he had. I couldn't stand that. I took a step . . . one step . . . to help you, but he saw me and . . . Oh, Dan, *the look in his eyes!* I froze on the spot. He would have killed me. . . .' She sounded wretched. 'You needed me and I couldn't do it. I'm sorry.'

He held her close, kissed her wet eyes, assured her she had

done the right thing. 'I'd never forgive myself if anything happened to you.'

Little by little he salved her terror. Then, stumbling over the words, he gently suggested she leave and not return. 'I don't want you mixed up in all this.'

In reaction she clutched at him tightly. She nestled desperately close to him and whispered into his ear.

'Make love to me, Dan.' The grip tightened. 'Do that for me. Let me feel safe.'

He studied her intently. Wondering if she meant it, wondering if he ought. Sensing his hesitation, she placed a hand on him, and tentatively, inexpertly, began to rub and knead. Lifting her face she hungrily pressed her lips to his. The fervour gripped him too and he moved over her, his fingers trembling as they unbuttoned her blouse. Then she was bared, and he was urgently kissing her breasts. His hand travelled, and in a voice rich with arousal she groaned: 'Not here. The bedroom. Quick!'

Hoisting her up, he carried her to his room. They undressed and then he was upon her. She was moist, and with tiny angling movements he positioned himself and advanced. She stiffened, but relaxed under his coaching. Then he was deeper in, feeling the closeness, and he knew he would be finished long before her. But he persevered until his movement was fluid and even, and discovered to his surprise that he was in control. He would not have to disappoint her.

He felt her begin to respond. Her spine arched like a bow as she began to climb that long first peak. She embraced the feeling, and gasped as it slipped away just before attainment. Then it was back, stronger this time, and she knew she had it for sure. Her fingernails raked the length of his back . . . The intensity between them increased. Nothing else existed. Being one, moving together, revelling in the sensations as they raced for the top. Then it was upon them; he moaning as he dove further in, she screaming in response.

The movement slowed, and slowed. The tempo downwaving until they relaxed against each other, hearts racing, and slipped back into reality.

He was first to ask how it had been. 'Beautiful,' she replied breathlessly, brushing away a tear.

'I'm a believer.'

He laughed, kissed the tip of her nose. Her face altered, her expression became more urgent, and she hugged him tightly.

'Whatever happens Daniel, remember this moment. Remember I love you.'

Nothing more was said, and soon they slept.

* 12 *

Pamela was in the shower when he awoke. From the waning angle of the sunlight coming in through the window, he guessed it was late afternoon. He was on the edge of the bed, listening to the sound of running water from the bathroom, when the door opened and in walked Barbara.

She eyed him with a vaguely interested, slightly cynical half smile. 'Daniel. How are you?'

He gave an embarrassed shrug and drew the sheet up to cover his body. 'Shy boy,' she joked, peeling off her coat. The bathroom door opened and Pam emerged, a towel wrapped tightly about her. She halted abruptly. She and Barbara eyed each other, and to Daniel it seemed Barbara's eyes hinted at malicious amusement. 'Very nice, Daniel,' she smirked.

Snatching up her clothes, Pam retreated to the bathroom. Barbara's smile remained the same. 'I'm assuming you met her before you got that face. What the hell happened?'

'I was mugged, okay? What are you doing here, Rush?'

'I'm sorry I didn't have time to call, but you'll be pleased to know this is only a flying visit. I can be out of here in less than an hour. We're here for three days of gladhanding. The organisers have us booked into the Ramada, and courtesy demands I accept their hospitality.

'I just came by to pick up a scarf and a few items of jewelry I'll need when I fly north, so I'll be —'

She broke off as Pamela stepped into the room. 'Excuse me,' Pam said frigidly, adding: 'I'll see you later Dan.'

She swept from the apartment, leaving behind her a disturbing silence.

Irritably he toyed with his swollen lip. The stare he directed at Barbara could have melted ice, but she was unperturbed. She patrolled the room, touching an item here, an object there, the arcane expression never leaving her face.

'You can be very infuriating at times, Rush.'

'But Daniel . . .' she protested with mocking innocence.

'I have come bearing gifts. I was planning to ask you to escort me tomorrow evening to a dinner being held in the Senator's honor.' With a flourish she produced two tickets. 'But now I see you are busy.'

'I'll leave these —' Sauntering to a bookshelf, she tucked the tickets into the space between two books, 'in case you decide to come along with your friend. I expect I'll be able to find someone else to escort me.'

Pulling his robe around him, he jerked tight the drawstring.

'Thank you Rush. Don't let me keep you.'

She crossed the room and stood close enough for her perfume to reach him. Half smiling, she let her hands play on his shoulders, palms pressing against his chest. Gathering his wits, he pulled away. 'Damm you, get out of here.'

'This is my apartment. I'll leave when I am ready,' she replied, cheekily stroking the underside of his chin with her finger. 'What's the matter honey? Did I spoil something? Are you all pent up and frustrated?' Her tone was heavy with a sickly, devilish charm.

He spun away, then changing his mind he rounded on her, the expression of savage anger on his face startling her into taking a backward step. 'You whore! How could I ever have been in love with you?'

Stung, she recoiled. Then regaining her composure she edged provocatively nearer. 'You still are.'

He lunged for her, gripped her shoulders tightly. 'You love to bait me, don't you?' He felt his throat seize up, dry out. There was no direction for his anger. He was speechless.

'My darling, you are so easily baited.' She moved closer, and her hips pressed against his navel. The subtle friction drained his willpower, as artfully she slipped open his robe and began to work on him with her hands, drawing her fingernails down his chest. His head bowed as he felt his being start to yield. Then she was kissing his face, her breezy auburn hair brushing against him.

Inhaling the perfume he knew so well, he felt himself going. She was in control – she had always been in control, for she alone knew the thing that could purchase him.

He threw back his head and groaned as she enslaved him again.

'You know, Rush, there are times when I almost like you,' he said with a dry smile. They were sprawled, naked, on the bed, her head on his chest. She chuckled warmly. 'Good.'

'And . . .' he went on. 'There are other times when I could cheerfully choke the life out of you.'

'I'm in a tough business. It pays to be a bitch.' Looking askance at the bedside clock, she shifted. 'I better make a move.'

'Must you?' he said, reaching to stall her. But they both knew his reluctance was a sham.

She gave a wistful sigh. 'You don't want me here, Dan.'

'Stay a little longer.'

She ran the tip of a sharp fingernail in a provocative curve down his belly. 'There are limits, even to my altruism,' she replied, reproachfully lifting an eyebrow. Without a sound, he eased down and lay beside her.

'This one's for you.'

After she had left, and he had showered and dressed, he noticed the two tickets, corners jutting between book covers. He picked them up and wondered if he ought to go. Then his thoughts turned to Pamela, and the guilt drove a pike into his gut. He knew the most difficult moment had yet to be faced.

Pamela returned to the apartment that evening. He was alone in the kitchen. At first, neither spoke. She opened a bottle of Napa Valley red and poured two glasses before taking the seat opposite him.

Morosely, he took a hefty swallow. He smacked his lips slowly, then looking at her, he said: 'I guess I owe you an explanation.'

She looked flustered. 'Not really. You don't owe me a thing.' She was feeling uncomfortable, both of them aware of the invisible barrier that had been erected by Barbara's intrusion into their tight little world.

He was staring intently at her, as if seeing her for the first time. Gauging, measuring and, she guessed, comparing. Uncomfortable with his scrutiny, she stood. Taking her glass she walked to the window. She sipped nervously as she stared out across the glassy ocean, flitting a glance over her shoulder at one point to find his gaze still upon her. She turned to face him, upraised glass lightly pressed against her cheek. 'You hungry?'

The intensity of his stare lessened. His eyebrows shrugged. 'I ought to be.'

'But you're not.'

Slowly he turned his head, striving to find something else upon which to lock his attention.

'I can't hold this in,' he said abruptly. 'I can't lie to you. I slept with her.'

The hurt visible in her eyes lanced him deeply. He felt no better for coming clean, and he loathed the weakness that made him want to confess when lying could have come so easily.

With an effort she turned her back to him. Her eyes, glistening moistly, stared out unseeing at the coming night.

The wine in her glass sloshed gently from side to side as her hand trembled. Taking a deep breath she tried to force the hurt downwards, towards the pit of her belly, tried to bury it deep within. But the corners of her mouth began to quiver, and she had to put down her glass and hug herself as the first sob burst to the surface.

In an instant he was out of his chair and hovering uncertainly behind her, wanting to hold her but dreading a rebuff. 'Listen . . . Pam, I . . .' His voice sounded weak. He hated the sound of it.

Her lowered head shook from side to side. She hugged herself tighter, as if to contain an explosion, or bind together her fractured spirit.

Deciding to take the plunge, he placed his arms around her and drew her stiff body towards him. At first she seemed to shrink further within herself, but then she turned within his embrace and it was as if a dam had burst. She hugged him with a strength that was alarming, her face pressed close to his chest as she wept bitterly, body heaving, tormented groans pouring from her soul.

They lay in bed. She in his arms like some small and frightened child. Nothing sexual had occurred between them; he had felt too guilt-ridden to try, and he sensed that any attempt would have met with resistance. She had wept long, and his shirt was damp from her tears. Idly running fingers through her hair, and deriving from that simple action some comfort for himself, he puzzled over the intense desire he had to confess, to talk. Always, with him, there had to be discussion and analysis, to the point, more often than not, where he made things worse. He had never learned the art of leaving well alone. Now as he began to talk about his life, about the burden of futility that haunted him, he recognised that, typically, he was using her to assuage his guilt. She was hurt, but he was the one baring his soul. Instead of seeking to console her, he was fishing for solace, as if that might make things better, banish the guilt and the weakness that made him a user.

'You know, in my entire life I never won a fight. Since I flunked out of school I never once tested myself. For years I've wasted my life. But now I feel I'm beginning to know why. This book I want to write, the whole issue of the assassination, somehow I feel it's all been for this. I've been waiting for it, or it's been waiting for me. I've been treading water until fate decided the moment was right.'

This brought no response, but undaunted, he continued.

'I kind of feel my life hasn't begun yet. That I have to get this out of the way first. Once it's over, I'll be able to start living.'

He felt her head move against his chest as she peered up at him in the gloom. 'Do you think you feel guilt about your father?'

His answer did not come readily. He half clenched a fist in frustration at not being able to voice his true feelings.

'I can't really define it. I feel that I've been waiting . . . to put things right.'

Her next question struck like a blow. 'What's the story on you and Barbara?'

'Aw, you know most of it. We were good together in the sack, but out of it we were on different planets. I was always a drifter, she's a strong person who knows what she wants and goes all out to get it. Intellectually we were worlds apart. I'm a realist, she suffers from delusions of grandeur. She buys all the right books for the coffee table, reads the right articles, eats in the right places. She thinks that appearing cultured and current buys her credibility with her bosses and her clients.' A note of pique crept into his tone. 'She doesn't see that the only reason she's gotten so far is that she's attractive and they like having her around to enhance their own image.'

Pam raised her head. 'You are jealous!' she exclaimed. 'You resent that she's gotten ahead on her own terms.'

He looked uncomfortable. 'Let's face it, she's beautiful. The clients are tripping over their tongues and the bosses exchange sly winks. Believe me, I know.'

Pam laughed out loud, and when he asked in a wounded voice what was so funny, she poked a finger into his ribs. 'You are. You're a male chauvinistic dinosaur. Don't you see how petty you are being? If she's as strong as you say, there's no way she would take the casting couch route. For her it would have to be advancement on merit or nothing.'

He looked bemused. Smiling, she shook her head. 'Women have pride too, Daniel. Your jealousy is totally wasted.'

She laughed again, and squeezed him tightly. 'After that, Daniel, I could forgive you just about anything.'

He was perplexed; unsure whether he'd been paid a compliment or insulted.

* 13 *

So it begins . . .

The auditorium was packed, the noise from the crowd quite deafening as Daniel surveyed the scene from the rear of the hall. Huge photographs of Senator Galbraith lined the walls, and still larger blow-ups of his smiling countenance were suspended from the ceiling. Colored bunting, arrayed in vast crescents, brightened the atmosphere, and everywhere badges and placards proclaimed the message: Galbraith for President!

The laminated photopass clipped to Daniel's lapel had bought him access, but he still felt very much the outsider as he picked his way down the sloping aisle to his seat in the third row.

He had barely settled when a voice boomed from the loudspeakers. 'Ladies and gentlemen, we are ready to begin. Would you please take your seats.'

He scanned the stage, where a podium had been draped in the Stars and Stripes. He scanned the aisles, the exits, in search of a particular face, *that* face.

On stage last minute checks were being carried out. The lights dimmed and a spotlight hissed into life, bathing the podium in a bright circlet of light. The loudspeakers boomed once more:

'Ladies and Gentlemen, Senator Cyrus Galbraith.'

The audience were on their feet, applauding as a figure in a dark suit stepped energetically up to the podium.

Backstage, security personnel hovered nervously in the wings. Chief of security Mather himself stood before a bank of TV monitors, watching his employer pound his fist as the speech gathered momentum. He was always nervous when Galbraith made a public appearance; none knew better than he how vulnerable such a position was.

Someone called his name. Reluctantly taking his gaze from the monitors, he registered the approach of a trusted aide. The man had a slim folder in hand. Knowing the matter he was coming to discuss would be a confidential one, Mather steered him to one side. Taking the file, he opened it and slowly read the first page.

'There's no mistake about this?' he demanded with a piercing stare, thanking God he'd given the job to a man he could trust.

'No sir. It all checks out.' The aide hesitated, then wondered aloud if he might ask a question.

'No,' Mather responded curtly. 'Your job is to follow orders. One thing I don't need right now is questions.'

The man accepted the rebuke without rancour. 'On the surface he seems harmless. Of course, if there was something beneath the surface, something I was not asked to look for . . .' He let the statement hang.

Mather chose his next words with care. 'Suppose the possibility existed that this man could seriously harm the campaign, completely compromise the Senator's position. What actions might you recommend; speaking from a purely hypothetical standpoint?'

The aide considered his reply. A former CIA asset, he knew he was being tested. He knew too that there might be much in it for him if he made the right noises. 'If there was the slightest danger to the campaign, sir, I would recommend corrective action.'

'To what degree?'

'I would not rule out a non-attributable removal. We both know the White House needs Galbraith.'

Satisfied with the response, and glad he had an idea how far the man might go, Mather closed and returned the file. 'Increase the level of surveillance. Have the apartment listened to, and transcripts delivered to me daily. For now we shall contain the problem.'

With a nod, the aide turned and vanished into the crowd.

Pain drove deep into Mather's chest like a long needle, reminding him that his angina pills were back in his hotel room. He had to ease a deep breath. Catching sight of himself in a grand mirror nearby, he was surprised how healthy and strong-looking he still looked. His face, though flabby, was relatively unlined, his hair barely tinged with grey. Little enough trace of the sixty-one hard years he had endured showed on the outside. No one would ever believe he was not a totally healthy man. And yet, there were days – like this one – when he felt oh, so tired of it all, and it was an effort to maintain the tough facade. He grimaced as the tightness in his chest intensified. He could not resist massaging the spot.

As he watched the Senator on one of the monitors, his gaze sustained a fatigue with worldly concerns. Yet the look of inherent cunning never really left his face. He was a man honed to be always ready. And as he watched, his thoughts drifted back – as they often did these days, to that morning in Dallas, and he smiled.

That had been his moment. His time. And what a job he had done; no one had even come close to netting him. The masses of contradictory evidence he left behind, exacerbated by the fervour of conspiracy theorists, had fooled them all, and the best of them. Confusion? That had not been the half of it. He had left leads in every direction, layers of deceit; Oswald, the communists, the mob, the CIA the Cubans, the Russians. The rest had been down to efficient tidying up, and in some respects that had been the greatest achievement of all. Keeping the secrets. Staying on top of the situation and tying up loose ends as they appeared. It had required constant watchfulness, and it had been a strain.

A burst of thunderous applause snagged his attention. The speech had ended, and Mather was instantly all business, issuing orders, mobilising the crew. Daniel Baker was relegated to a spot well down the list of priorities.

Threading the crowds, Daniel picked his way backstage, his gaze all the while rapidly examining faces. He was wondering how he would react if he actually *saw* . . . He halted, dead in his tracks, to stare rigidly at one particular face. A face belonging to a tall, heavily built man standing to one side. As he stared, Daniel tried to refine the facial features, strip away the years, iron away the creases, imagine that face thirty years younger. Then he was sure, and his heart leapt to his mouth. In the midst of an organisation committed to getting Cyrus Galbraith elected to the Presidency of the United States, stood the killer of JFK.

A uniformed guard brushed past. Daniel grasped his arm and drew him near. 'I'm sorry to bother you . . .' he said in a low voice. 'But could you tell me who that man is, the one over by the monitors?'

The guard looked where directed and nonchalantly replied: 'That's Mr Mather. Senator Galbraith's Head of Security.'

Daniel thanked him. He stood in a daze, at once exhilarated and afraid. At last! At last he had a name!

A man in a neat dark suit approached Daniel. He addressed him politely. 'May I see your pass, sir?'

Daniel obligingly angled his shoulder to afford the other a clearer look. The man regarded him coolly. 'I'm sorry, but this does not permit you up here. Please follow me.' Guiding Daniel firmly by the elbow, he steered him toward an exit.

'I'm waiting for Ms Rush . . .' Dan protested vainly. Barbara appeared at that moment, entering through a nearby door on the arm of a young and very handsome man dressed in an expensive tuxedo. The new man in her life, no doubt. Though he felt a momentary pang of hurt, he could not deny they made a perfect looking couple. He called to her. Excusing herself, she hurried across to him and Daniel was duly released.

'I thought I was going to miss you,' he said. She seemed in good spirits. After looking him up and down in an appraising fashion, she said: 'You don't look in too bad a shape. How are you?'

Flattered by her interest, he beamed. 'I'm fine.'

'What did you think of Galbraith?' she asked him.

He shrugged. 'He seems a . . . positive individual.' He laughed, then commented. 'You look pleased.'

She giggled, then held up her left hand to show him the ring glistening on the third finger. The size of the diamond caused his eyes to bulge. He whistled enviously. 'I suppose congratulations are in order.' He felt near to tears, and she sensed this. She kissed him on the cheek, and whispered: 'Be happy for me, please.'

He sniffed. 'Of course I am. Well, aren't you going to introduce me to the lucky man?'

The young man she had entered with had joined the group clustered around Mather, and she led Daniel towards them. He felt his heartrate increase, and a cold wave of anxiety sweep over him. Could he face the killer? What would he say if he had to speak to him? Then he was standing within the group, Barbara radiant at his side as she effected introductions.

'Daniel Baker,' she said in a proud voice. 'I'd like you to meet my fiancé Barry Mather.'

Dan was unable to keep the shock from his face as the bigger man took his hand.

It was all too much! Too much! How was it possible? Could it all be part of the plot? Must he expose Mather and destroy Barbara in the process? Unbalanced by fear he blindly walked the streets until a falling drizzle drove him into a bar. Ordering whisky, he drained the glass in one shot and ordered another. Hours had passed, yet he was still unable to string more than two thoughts together. How he had managed to stumble out his congratulations and retire discreetly from the scene without screaming, he would never know. He was sure the sly glimmer in Mather's eyes had conveyed some subtle message.

'Oh my God,' he whispered, his trembling hand spilling whisky from the glass as the shockwave hit. 'Are they coming for me?'

He tried to leave the bar, but his legs were reluctant to carry him and he swayed dopily. He had to start thinking, had to find a way to protect himself. A sudden thought dove into his brain with the force of a blade; *Was he being watched?* He glanced shiftily around only to find that, to his despair, every single person in the place looked suspect. He ordered another drink, but his hand shook so violently he could barely hold the glass, and it took a special effort to raise it to his lips.

'Write it down,' he told himself. 'Write everything down and place it in safekeeping.' That way, he reasoned, if anything were to happen to him . . . no, that thought was too horrible to contemplate.

His breathing was rapid and shallow. His mouth chewed air and his eyes stared fixedly ahead. Managing to down the whisky, he was on the point of ordering another when he remembered Pamela. She had to be protected. He could not allow anything to happen to her. For a moment the despair, the fear, overpowered him. He wanted nothing more than to end the suicidal quest and go back to being a nonentity. But it was a vain wish and he knew it. It had begun. He was a loose end, and as long as he breathed he would be a danger to Mather. To have any hope of reaching safety he would have to continue.

The conscious realisation of his own commitment had a sobering effect. Finding a stool, he sat, and thought, and as he thought he drank, the whisky going down at an incautious rate.

Finally he found determination enough to move. But he had taken on too much drink, too quickly, and as he turned from the stool he stumbled headlong, thudding heavily to the carpet. Climbing groggily to his feet he lurched to a payphone and with clumsy fingers dialled the apartment.

'It's going to be alright,' he repeatedly murmured to himself. The ring tone trilled reassuringly, but as the ringing went on unbroken a dreadful vision loomed large; had they taken her?

'It's going to be alright . . .' he whispered once more, then he almost collapsed with relief as the telephone was answered by her cheery voice.

'Pamela?'

'Daniel is that you? You sound odd.'

'Yeah. Listen honey, can you come get me? I'm a little drunk.' His tongue seemed to fill his mouth, mashing his words to a blur. But she understood enough.

'Sure. Where are you? I'll drive over —'

'NO!' he cried out, and felt her recoil. He forced himself to stay calm. 'Don't travel alone. Take a cab. I'm at a bar called Plato's.'

'I've seen it,' she said. 'Why are you drunk? Whatever happened?'

His voice contracted to a taut murmur. 'I've seen him again, Pam. I've spoken to him. *Him.*'

There was a pause. 'Are you sure?' She sounded strange; suddenly fearful.

'I'm sure. Come get me, huh?' He hung up. Reeling back to the bar he thought about another drink, but fought the temptation. He had to be awake. Fear gave him the strength for abnegation.

On tottering legs he ascended the stairs to the exit. The air outside was chilly, but the drizzle had stopped and the sidewalk was dry. The chill and the wind combined to annul the insulating effect of the scotch. He pulled tight his coat. Impatience turned to agitation as he waited. His fretting hands wrung each other and he transferred his weight from foot to foot as the waiting grew unbearable. She was taking too long. What if they had her already. What if a sinister note awaited him at the apartment; come, or the girl gets it. What then?

The wind chill cut him to the bone. His jacket was no protection, and it was with joy and relief he heard the blast from a car horn. A cab glided to a halt by the kerb, tyres whispering audibly, then the rear door was open and she was there, beckoning him.

He clambered in. 'You're frozen,' she exclaimed, rubbing his hands between her own.

'I know,' he replied through chattering teeth.

'The alcohol brought down your body temperature,' she rebuked him.

Once back at the apartment, she started a fire in the ornamental grate and made fresh coffee.

'That's good. Thanks,' he muttered after the first sip. 'For the fire as well as the coffee. This is the first time it's ever been used. It's an inspiration. The place will never look the same without it.'

Settling onto the arm of his chair she eyed him with a gentle scowl. 'You're in a fine state. You want to talk about it?'

He looked sidelong at her, in some odd way feeling reassured by her presence. When he needed her, he knew, she would be there for him. Slowly he told her of his meeting with Barry Mather.

There was a pause when he finished. She was gazing thoughtfully at the grate, at the flames curling lazily around the logs she had produced from who-knew-where.

He said: 'I think, maybe, you should leave town.' He laughed. 'I'm sorry, that sounds melodramatic, but I do mean it. I want you safe.'

She admonished him with a raised eyebrow. 'I thought we'd settled that.'

'This is serious. The killer, the man on the knoll, is head of Galbraith's security. He is in a position of power and he is dangerous.'

'You're positive he's the same man?'

He nodded wearily. 'I'm sure. I wish to God I wasn't, but there is no doubt in my mind. And we're in danger. I think he wanted me there, to get a look at me, and to let me see him. He knows.'

'Daniel, that's not reasonable. How could he possibly know? Even if he is the man from the knoll, how could he know you were the child that saw him.'

'For God's sake, he's engaged to Barbara!'

Her astonishment was total. 'Your Barbara?'

He winced. 'Yes, my Barbara. She has no idea Mather was there, but she knows what I saw that day.'

All of her aplomb had vanished. The implication had sunk home. She shrank back on her chair and, in an unconscious display of nervousness, drew up her legs. 'Did you give anything away?'

He looked down in shame at his clasped hands. 'I'm sorry, Pam. The shock . . . I just wasn't in control.'

She swallowed, hard. 'What do we do now?'

'I have to tell Newbolt. And you – you have to get out of here.'

She was obstinate. 'I'm not leaving you to face this alone.'

'This is for real!' he persisted. They argued, he pleading, she digging in her heels, until at last he pressed her hands between his own and urged her: 'Please, Pam. While you still can.'

She fought to keep the hurt from showing on her face.

Abruptly breaking free, she strode out onto the terrace and

stood with head lowered, hands clasped before her. Joining her, he placed an arm gently around her shoulders. 'Pam.'

She shifted her head to look at him, and there were tears in her eyes. 'Ever since we argued . . . over Barbara, I've known I can't leave you. I've never been as happy as I have these past weeks. Don't send me away.'

He felt the resolve in his heart melt away; how could he hurt her so? A storm of mixed emotions gathering in his breast, he rocked her gently, relenting at last. 'Okay. If that's what you want, we'll face this together.'

They lay in bed and held each other – nothing more. Not yet. The time was not right. Yet the air was alive, sizzling with the electricity of anticipation. As if they had agreed upon something undefined by words, and awaited only the correct opportunity. When he spoke, there was gloom in his tone. 'I'm truly sorry about all this.'

'Daniel, do you really think there's danger?'

He gazed at her naive, open face, into those trusting eyes, and was tempted to lie. He wanted to tell her that everything was going to be fine, but because she was a grown woman, he told her the truth. The hurt and the fear on her face pained him. He could have spared her. He could have lied. If she had been a child . . .

He suddenly felt a new awareness, an understanding of the anguish his father had suffered. The fear for a young dependant. He realised he was prepared to die, if doing so meant he could save Pamela, and he now realised his father had killed himself to save his ten year old son. With this awareness came a new respect; one bordering on reverence. His father had not been a coward, deserting his son in a funk. He had decided what must be done to save the boy, and he had done it. No one imagined the child knew anything. If the father was gone the kid would be left alone.

He shuddered. What courage. . . .

His head was aching from the intensity of concentration. Lifting a hand, he massaged his brow. He pictured his father as he never had previously. What courage! He felt as though he knew him, understood him, better than ever before. It was as if he could slip back in time and stand inside his father's mind and see things as he saw them. He felt the decision being reached, saw the deliberate lifting of the gun. Felt the cold metal upon his tongue, tasted the blood-tang of iron. . . .

He awoke with a jolt. It was the middle of the night, and in the next room the telephone was ringing. Pamela was breathing sonorously at his side, and as he rose from the bed without waking her he felt something new awakening within him. Some new spirit. The guilt had gone, and the bold spirit, for so long pinioned by the weight of the guilt, sprang upwards with impatient force. He felt strong. Alive and tingling and ready to take on the world. His father had been a hero, not a coward! He lifted the receiver.

'Dan?' a panicked voice shouted into his ear. Raw fear poured along the telephone line, and with trepidation Daniel unconsciously raised a hand to his throat. 'Who is this?'

'Leon Newbolt. Listen, they've come to the house.'

'Who? Who's come?'

'You know! They know you've been here. Did you tell anyone?'

'No. No.' Daniel frowned, confused. What was Newbolt talking about?

'Check your apartment. Maybe it's bugged.' There was a pause, the black's laboured breathing echoed down the line. In the background something heavy crashed. Newbolt's voice was strained. 'Listen Dan, I'm finished. They're coming for me now.'

Daniel shouted in alarm: 'Call the cops!'

'No good! I'm finished! Listen, I've sent —'

'YOU LISTEN!' Dan screamed. 'Stall them, anything, just get the cops!' His voice cracked. He knew it was too late.

Leon cried out: '*THEY ARE THE COPS!*' He yelped, as if in pain, then came the sounds of a fierce struggle. Daniel felt a warm tear on his cheek as he heard Newbolt panting as he fought for his life. His voice rang out clearly one last time, pleading, the words and the terrorised tone etched indelibly onto Daniel's memory.

'RUN DAN! RUN DA —'

The cry ended abruptly. The struggle was over. Someone quietly hung up the telephone.

The longest of long nights. The terrace windows were bared, curtains drawn back to admit moonlight that dusted everything in a spectral glow.

Daniel was prostrate on the couch, his head on Pamela's lap, tears drying unseen on his cheeks. Inconsolable, he blamed himself for Newbolt's death. He had cried for a full hour, mourning the death of a good man who dared only to want to tell the truth.

She, smiling wanly in the moonlit gloom, tried bravely to comfort him. He had been tempted to seek solace in lovemaking, however briefly, but could not find within himself the strength to make the effort. Too, there lurked the guilt that to do so would be somehow disrespectful to the memory of a lost friend. Eyes gazing without seeing, and refusing to be drawn by her gentle insistence, he stared into the gloom. When at last he disrupted the silence it was in a tone as vacant as his stare.

'What do we do? We have no one to turn to. No way of going on . . .' a despondent sigh escaped him.

She asked him: 'What about the man he mentioned. What was he called . . . the Zealot?'

He shrugged. 'Where do I start looking?' Then, as a thought occurred to him, he sat up abruptly. 'The sons of bitches!' He leapt from the couch and in a maniacal frenzy began to search the room. He ran his hands around picture frames and furniture.

'Aha!' He announced in mad triumph, ripping something from under the coffee table. 'The sons of bitches!'

'What is it?' she asked in alarm. Flicking on the light, he tossed a tiny object onto her lap. She held it up between thumb and forefinger to examine it.

'The place is bugged,' he snarled. 'Who knows how many more of those things there are. Every word. They've heard every word.'

She got up, saying: 'I'll help you look.' But he waved her back to her seat. 'Why bother? They can hear us. They know we won't spill any more secrets in here.' His mouth was pursed tightly in anger, his eyes darted warily and his hands rubbed against each other. A decisive, defiant glimmer illuminated his face. 'Pam, you stay here.'

'What are you going to do?' she sounded worried.

He struggled into a jacket. 'You stay here with *that*. I'm going out and I'm going to bring back the cops. We'll throw this crock of shit right back at them.'

'Be careful!' she cried out as he hurried for the door.

Fear suppressed by self righteous anger, he rode the elevator to the ground floor and stalked across the lot to the Camaro. As he reached the driver's door he heard a dull thud, quickly followed by a rush of escaping air. There came a second soft retort, and a third, and he realised that the tyres on the car were being punctured. He stared into the night, wondering how?

A bullet richochetted off the gravel. Someone was shooting at him! Grasped by panic he launched himself for the entrance to the building.

His mind screeched hysterically. '*GET IN. GET INSIDE. GET INDOORS!*'

He fumbled with the key – it just would not fit the lock! Then a loud crack made him wince as a neat hole, ringed with veins of fractured glass, appeared in the panelled window only inches from his head. The sudden rush of unused adrenalin left him faint and nauseous, and his heart was pounding, but fear pushed him to his feet and propelled him towards the elevator.

Dishevelled and breathless he burst into the apartment and gasped at the incredible sanity and quiet of the place. The wonderful appearance of normality. He could hear Pam bustling about, and the aroma of freshly made coffee filtered from the kitchen.

She smiled on seeing him, but her look quickly changed to one of concern as he sagged into her arms. She dragged him to a chair and settled him, then fetched him a cup. His chest rose and fell at an excited rate. He felt insanity swelling like a balloon inside of him, and he was afraid he might not be able to hold it. The horrible, unpalatable truth had seeped in. Now he saw its macabre significance in entirety, he felt close to collapse. This had been no friendly warning, no harmless push into a pool, no mugging. This had been a serious attempt to quieten him. The gun had been silenced; obviously they were using professionals.

That brought him up with a start. He was outfaced by his own logic. If they were using professionals, men good enough to shoot out his tyres in near total darkness, surely they could have hit him – had they wanted to. He had been a much larger target. Maybe it was a friendly warning after all – perhaps the last.

Afraid, he wondered why he was being treated with such respect. Newbolt had been erased.

Why was *he* still breathing?

* 14 *

No sleep for either of them that night. As the reality of being shot at sank in, Daniel had to rush to the bathroom to retch dryly over the lavatory bowl. Pamela, appearing in the doorway, looked sympathetic. He was uncomfortable, letting her see him that way.

Standing up, he splashed water on his face at the basin, and eyed himself critically in the mirror. He looked bad; unshaven, haggard and hollow-cheeked. Fear haunted his eyes.

'We have to stop,' he gasped. His voice was tilted at an odd pitch; verging on hysterical. 'We can't go on.'

She placed an arm around him. 'We can't stop now, Dan. You know that. We've come too far. We are close to Mather. We can do it.'

He lowered his head. 'Maybe I was wrong, and it wasn't him.' This was said sheepishly.

'Come on,' she snapped. 'That's crap. Don't let them scare you.'

His eyes darted. He could not meet her challenging look. He shrugged, an expression of hopelessness, and she exploded. 'Damm you! You suck me into this, and now you want to leave me out on a limb!'

His head jerked up. 'Four shots, Pamela. Fired at me. Now I am scared. Not just for me but for you too!' He brushed past her and went into the lounge.

'I know that!' she screamed, following him. 'And I'm as scared as you. But we're in too far to pull out now, and even if we did, do you think they'd leave us alone? We're noticeable now. We either commit ourselves to going on, or we sit here waiting to be taken care of.'

He was by the table. Fear had broken out, like a rash, on his skin, distorting his features, lathing away the years. He was a scared little boy, lips trembling as he fought for control.

'They could force me to stop. All they'd have to do is threaten you.'

Reaching out for him, she gently squeezed his hand. 'Then we'll make a pact. We won't be deflected. If either one of us vanishes, or has an accident, the other will carry on. That way, threatening me won't stop you and you won't have to feel any guilt about possible consequences. We each know where we stand. Is that okay?'

He leaned forward, hand tightly gripping the edge of the table as he fought to stabilize. He seemed distant. His lazily roaming the room. 'They could have easily killed me . . .' he murmured. 'Why didn't they?'

'I want your word on it, Daniel,' she said. She was steely, bravely adamant. As he looked at her he knew that for the first time in his life he had not only found true love, but was aware of it. His fingers closed around her hand. He said: 'My word on it. We'll see this through to the end.'

She brought in the morning's mail while he was lingering over coffee and toast in the kitchen. Sluggish with fatigue he stared blank-eyed at the wall. Intent on nothing. Casting a speculative glance at him she placed the mail by his elbow.

'They're all for you.'

Pulling back from the haze, he managed a wry smile. 'Surprise me.' He tore open the first envelope and eyed the contents. 'Late payment warning . . .' he muttered. He tore open the second. 'Disconnection notice . . . I'm gonna have to get back to work.'

She smiled. 'Just hang onto your sense of humour and you'll be fine. You know, if you need money, I could help.'

He dismissed her offer, assuring her he was financially sound. She persisted. 'Really, I have money saved, and I have been spending a lot of time here recently.'

He paused. 'Well, I guess if you want to please me you could consider moving in here. You spend hardly any time at your own apartment these days.'

She nodded, blushed slightly. 'Are you asking me to live with you?'

He shrugged. 'Just a thought.'

'Thanks,' she replied, looking pleased. 'I will consider it.'

Draining his cup he turned to the remaining envelopes with a will. The contents of the final one, a letter, stole his good humour and rocked him to a standstill. His fingers shook as they tightened on the paper. 'It's from Newbolt. It's an address. The Zealot. Leon must have posted it before he . . .'

He looked distressed. Leaning back on his chair, he trapped his head between his folded arms.

Pamela looked fearful. 'What are you going to do?'

He looked up at, blankly at first, then blurted out: 'Go see him of course. What else can I do?'

* 15 *

It took a night and two days. Not pushing the Camaro, but keeping halts to a minimum they made good progress. It was dusk on the second day when they crossed the limits of the industrial suburb where the Zealot kept his base.

They asked directions of a beat cop, marking, as they drew nearer their destination, the subtle changes in the neighbourhoods. Wide streets of attractive colonial style residences gave way to narrow, double and triple deckered brownstones, crammed together and decaying as if infected with some contagious wasting disease.

'Not such a small town after all.' Daniel commented. 'It's big enough to have a ghetto.'

'Yeah,' she agreed in a slightly apprehensive tone. 'And it's beginning to look as if our guy lives smack in the middle of it.'

As they cruised the increasingly poorly lit streets, the knot in Daniel's gut, an irritating niggle when he opened Newbolt's letter two days earlier, had conflagrated into a gnawing storm. The fear caught in his throat.

The Zealot. The man had been on his mind ever since they left Coco. He had been building up a mental image of the man.

Now he wondered; what would he be like, this man who shrouded himself in mystery, this man who knew it all. In his fatigued state he was easily propelled by fear into a lightheaded state of high expectation. The Zealot would put everything right.

She broke into his thoughts. 'This is the street.'

He slowed the Camaro to a crawl, and braked. Dimmed the lights and cut the engine. They climbed out and studied the ramshackle house where the Zealot lived. The paintwork was blistered and flaking, the wood rotting, and the windows were barred. The house stood alone, and the expanse of garden that surrounded it was wildly overgrown. But what caught and held their attention was the tall fence of thick chain-link that surrounded the property.

'Jeeezus,' whispered Pam, eyeing a sign that boldly proclaimed: *Trespassers will be shot!* 'Will you look at this?'

They approached the gate. An intercom was fixed to the frame, and Daniel jabbed the call button. An eerie, reedy voice piped from the single small speaker: 'Who is it?'

Daniel announced himself, and Pam, adding: 'Leon Newbolt sent us.'

There came a loud buzzing as the electronic lock was switched off, and the gate yielded to Daniel's thrust with a rusty whine. He was careful to close it, and he and Pam advanced to the darkened front porch. Before they reached the door, lights linked to sensors burned into life, bathing them in white glare. Shielding their eyes they walked the final few yards.

The door opened, but the gloom beyond was so dense they could see no further than the threshold. Then an arm beckoned them in, and they found themselves closeted in total blackness, standing uncomfortably while their host frisked them. At length he stood back.

'I've been expecting you,' he said in a hoarse voice. A flash-lamp in his hand beamed into life, and he gestured with it. 'Follow me, please.'

He led them down steps to a cellar that had been converted into a spacious office. Shelves that extended from floor to ceiling were packed with books. Filing cabinets stood in an organised row against one wall. TV and VCR stood on a shelf. There was a cluttered desk, upon which the cursor on a PC screen blinked contentedly. The place reeked organisation, and already Daniel was feeling more confident.

There were three chairs, and the man bade them sit. 'So,' he began, 'How is friend Newbolt?'

Daniel had been making a rapid assessment of the man. In appearance he was something of a disappointment, being small and wiry, with eyes that glinted and darted with ferret swiftness in a face gaunt and pale. His thinning light brown hair cut short. A guess would have placed him in his early to mid-fifties. Daniel felt apprehension; was this the man he had all his hopes pinned on?

'Newbolt's dead,' he replied flatly, quickly going on to enlarge the statement.

The change in the Zealot as he absorbed the news about Leon was alarming to behold. His hands flitted nervously with each other, and when Daniel had finished, he darted questions at him. On hearing of the bugged apartment, he let out a groan.

'You were followed, the apartment was bugged, and yet you still came here? Don't you know what you've done, coming here?'

Daniel, taken aback, could only stare back at him dumbly. Incredulously he watched the Zealot rise from his chair to remonstrate with emphatic hand gestures.

'You've put all of us at risk. All the years of work. Coming here you've left me, and all this priceless information vulnerable.'

Seeing Dan's face redden as anger surged, Pamela intervened to apologise, but the Zealot cut her short. 'You have to go. You have to leave. Come on, come on . . .' He herded them to their feet and into the corridor. He had unlocked and opened the door before Dan could speak out, but when the Zealot forcibly tried to push him outside, he resisted.

'What's happened? What the hell is going on? You can't just push us out onto the street!'

'Can't I . . . ?' The Zealot turned and groped in the darkness. When he faced them again it was with a shotgun in his hands. He jabbed at Daniel with the barrel. 'You watch me. Come on mister, out.'

'But we've come so far.' Pamela pleaded. 'There's no one else we can turn to.'

He pushed them onto the porch. 'I'm sorry. I really do sympathise. But the bureau's information has to be protected. God knows what damage has already been done. They could close in on me any second!'

Daniel stared at him, frigid in his contempt for the man's stupid fear. Had he really put all his faith in this little shit? This cowardly runt . . . ? At that moment an automobile cruised past the house, appearing to slow momentarily before accelerating away. Suspicion fraught with fear made this more than enough for the Zealot. He pushed them down the path and out through the gate. He hurried back indoors and shut the door. They heard the scraping home of bolts.

Daniel glared in glassy anger at the closed door. At last his chest stopped heaving, his fury abated and he turned and snatched open the gate. At a furious pace he returned to the Camaro and paused by the driver's door.

'That son of a bitch,' he muttered bitterly. Facing him across the roof of the car, Pam shrugged; 'What now?'

He drove with a fierceness owed totally to the ire smouldering within him. His gaze was locked on the road ahead, hands tight on the wheel.

'Please Dan, slow down,' she said in a worried tone. 'I know you're angry, but —'

'That bastard! We came all this way – for what?'

She winced as he wrenched the wheel and the Camaro took a corner at a sickening tilt. He swore: 'Jesus Christ, if I'd —

The rest of his words were lost in the loud blaring of a horn from behind. He glanced right as a heavy sedan drew level.

'What . . . ?'

'*Daniel!!*' She screamed as the sedan struck with a metallic crunch they felt bruise the Camaro. The car swerved under the blow, barely recovering before the sedan swung to the attack again, connecting with a force that nudged them towards the dangerously uneven roadside.

'*Hold tight!*' he bawled, and jammed down the throttle. The Camaro surged ahead of the sedan and hugged the centre of the road. The heavier car responded by accelerating until it sat upon their tail, and the glare from its headlamps flooded the interior of the Camaro with blinding light.

'What's he doing?!' Pam shrieked hysterically. 'What's he doing???'

There was a sickening jolt as the sedan thudded into them once more, and through the corner of his eye Daniel saw Pam's head whiplash with the violence of the crash.

His fingers wound grimly around the wheel. He felt his self control slipping. A lump caught in his throat, and he wondered what on earth he ought to do, what he *could* do. He longed to push the car faster to try and escape, but the night was deep black, the road ahead poorly lit, and he feared he might be forced into losing control. Another jolt shook every bone in his body and he cursed in impotent anger. He caught a glimpse of Pamela's face, pale and vulnerable-looking in the light, and the sight seemed to force some measure of determination upon him. For her sake, he had to get them out of this!

Ahead, he saw another set of headlamps approaching fast. Then a sudden change in the light from behind made him glance back in the mirror. The sedan had braked dramatically, the headlamps shrinking fast, and when he looked ahead once more he saw why. A huge truck was bearing down on them at high speed, it was perhaps two or three hundred metres away, and as it neared it seemed to grow to fill the entire road. It would crush them, flatten the Camaro without breaking stride!

Inside his head a terrified voice screamed, and as the final moments approached he perceived in a glance many things; the enormous, brutal front-end of the rig as it charged, snorting and roaring like some enraged beast; Pamela, rigid with fright, hands curled into tiny white fists. He winced, headlamp beams clashed as they neared collision point and then, at the last possible moment, he decided on an action. With a scream he hurled the

Camaro left, his foot hard down in terror, expecting at any instant to hear the crushing of tortured metal, feel the hot breath of the iron beast as it trampled them. . . .

The Camaro mounted the high embankment and ran along at speed, and at a perilous angle, until the truck had passed. Then he hauled the wheel around and powered back onto the road, crossing it at desperate speed, caromming wildly. He was about to lose it. At the last desperate moment he spied a dark turning and aimed for it. Seconds later they were bouncing uncontrollably along an unlit and badly pitted dirt track barely wide enough to allow passage. The truck had missed them by a whisker, he realised vaguely as, mesmerised and unable to react, he watched the twists and turns in the track hurtle towards him, the narrow sides naturally guiding the Camaro downhill until it burst out of the trees and skidded sidelong down a dusty slope that banked a broad, dark river.

But now he was regaining control, wrenching and jerking the wheel until, on protesting wheels, he had the car established on a track that snaked parallel with the river.

One of the headlamps burst as it struck a rock a glancing blow, and the sudden encroaching rush of blackness scared him enough to apply the brakes. The battered auto slithered to a halt and he fell over the wheel, gasping for breath, his heart pounding fit to burst open his chest.

The silence was total. An insulating haze seemed to gather around him. He felt dull, and strangely comfortable, a feeling he did not want to fight. For long moments he sat, while his heart steadied, quietly revelling in the silence, the lack of motion. Small sounds began to seep through the haze; metallic, ticking sounds from the engine. Then a shrill, strangled cry from Pamela shattered the haze, jerked him out of it completely. He glanced at her, and what he saw scared the hell out of him. Her face was a mask of terror; eyes bulged starkly, her mouth gaped. Tiny whimpering sounds grew in strength until they completely overcame her and she was screaming, shaking her head and clawing at her hair.

Heart close to breaking, he wrapped his arms tightly around her, rocking her gently for long minutes until the panic exhausted itself and she was able to collapse limply into his embrace. Tears streamed from her, and her lips, drawn into a sad crescent, trembled violently. Her screams gradually were reduced to sobs that tremored her entire body.

He had no idea how long they sat like that, but it seemed an infinity. When at last she had stopped crying, and he had wiped dry her face with his hankerchief, she gently freed herself from his arms and sat with hands clasped tightly between her knees. Her eyes still brimming, peering blankly ahead, she resisted his efforts to make her talk, and at length he too lapsed into silence.

At further length he decided to get out. Opening the door with difficulty, every movement sending shards of pain darting through him, he stood upright at last. The muscles in his shoulders ached from the strain of fighting the steering wheel, and he felt bruised all over. An inspection of the exterior sent another pang arrowing into his heart. His pride and joy would never be the same again. The entire driver's side resembled a jagged moonscape. The rear was crumpled, with the trunk twisted open at one corner. The rear suspension on the offside had gone, leaving the vehicle listing pathetically. The front end was comparatively unscathed, though the busted lamp gave the Camaro the look of a beaten prize fighter with a blacked eye.

Weary with despair, he leaned back against the hood. His mental processes were operating on some automatic level, sifting, wondering, looking for answers. Suddenly his body grew taut, his eyes glinted angrily, and returning to the driver's side door he leaned inside and began frantically to search the interior. He cursed as he rummaged:

'Where is it? Where is it? I know it's here somewhere. Sons of bitches.'

'Daniel?' Her speech was sluggish, expressionless. At the sound he looked up. Her face still looked numbed. 'What are you doing?'

Reining in his anger, he forced a rigid smile. 'I was wondering how they knew where we were.'

She frowned in puzzlement, then awareness flooded upon her. 'You think the car might be bugged too?' He nodded. She began to come alive. Moving stiffly, she offered to help: 'What can I do?'

He considered for a moment, then, deciding it might be good for her to be active, handed her the keys. 'Thanks. Check the trunk will you?'

'Sure.' On quaking legs she hoisted herself out. Holding onto the roof for support she made her way to the rear. Daniel probed beneath the dash, anger growing with each passing minute. When at last he heard her call his name he snapped to attention. She was faint with exhaustion. Her eyelids hovered just above closing and her voice was still heavily torpored. 'Is this the . . . the thing?'

He took the small object from her and examined it in the poor light. 'Bastards . . .' he breathed. Then closing tight his fist he spun, and hurled the bug far across the river. He was panting furiously, working himself into a frenzy, when she grasped his arm weakly. 'Would you help me into the car. I don't think I can make it . . .'

Seating her as comfortably as he could, and placing his jacket around her to stave off the cold, he watched as she sank into a thick stupor. Her eyes closed, and in minutes came the reassuring purr of gentle snoring. He found a pack of cigarettes in the dash and lit one. Finding himself rediscovering the joy of inhaling, and wondering how he had managed without it. When only the butt remained, he screwed it flat in the ashtray and let exhaustion take him. He was too tired, and too scared, dammit, to risk driving up that track at night after what had happened earlier. Who knew what awaited on the freeway? In minutes he was sleeping too, the rest-needs of his body too powerful to resist.

Morning saw him waking with a groan as the stiffness in his body bit. When he moved, one arm started to buzz as blood surged afresh. His mouth tasted vile, and uncomfortably he ran a hand over patchy stubble on his cheeks. Pushing out his chest and extending his arms, he tweaked the stiffness from his shoulders.

'Morning,' he heard her say. The torpor had gone. She was bright eyed. 'You look well,' he commented, glad he was able to say so.

'I don't feel too bad at all,' she admitted. 'I slept like a log. Must have been the shock.'

'Wish I could say the same,' he muttered ruefully, massaging the back of his neck. He ran his tongue around the inside of his mouth to ease the dryness and dispel the acrid taste.

'What are we going to do?' she asked. 'Surely we can't risk going home?'

He considered for a few moments, then, lips set in a determined line, he said: 'We go back to see our friend the Zealot. We're going to make him help us.'

She did not argue. Just sat quietly while the engine churned rustily into life, and they crawled back up the slope.

* 16 *

'Why the hell have you come back?' the Zealot demanded, eyeing them with a mixture of suspicion, and concern for their obviously distressed state. Closing and bolting the front door, he led the way to a first floor lounge and poured each of them a drink. He listened in stunned silence as Daniel quickly told him of the assault the previous night. As he listened, the Zealot nodded, as if the story had confirmed his worst fears.

'Can we stay a while?' Pamela asked him, her desperation plain.

He studied them, and there was something shifty, an elusive shadow, some lurking dread, just behind his eyes. With a resigned tilt of his head, he agreed. 'It's too late now anyway,' he said. 'They obviously know you've been here. I'm no safer than you now.'

He hesitated a few moments, then held out a hand to Daniel. 'David Turner. I'm sorry about last night. I get a little crazy sometimes. Really, I'm on your side.'

Daniel was glad to accept the hand; right then he needed all the friends he could get. He re-introduced himself, and Pamela, and then asked if there was any coffee.

Pam sprang up, offering to prepare breakfast, and the two men signalled appreciation. Dan asked: 'Are you sure you don't mind?'

'Of course not,' she replied. 'You two have a lot of ground to cover.'

After a few stilted attempts at conversation, Turner asked Dan what he knew about events in Dallas 'On November twenty second, nineteen sixty three?'

'I know the basics. I've read a few books. I'm no expert.'

'Well I am.' Turner said without bombast. 'Do you mind if I ask what made you interested in the assassination?'

Daniel baulked; it was too early to just open up. He knew that when the time came he would happily spill the contents of his tortured psyche, but he did not yet trust Turner. Traces of resentment at the behaviour meted out the previous night still remained. 'Can we get to that later?'

After a pause, Turner agreed. Over breakfast they talked, about Kennedy, about Oswald, about the links to David Ferrie, the mob, Clay Shaw. 'The morning of the killing, Oswald took a parcel – containing what he said were curtain rods, into the depository building with him. It is around this point that Oswald starts to look guilty as hell . . .'

'Hmmm,' Daniel spoke around a mouthful of bread. 'It's hard to know what to believe. I've read about the inconsistencies; Oswald was said to be not much of a marksman by men who were with him in the marines. The type of rifle he is supposed to have used, which was fitted with a poor quality, left-handed telescopic sight, was so badly made that no one using it has ever managed to equal the feat the Warren Commission attributed to Oswald. Firing three shots at an extreme angle, at a moving target, in less than five-point-six seconds. There are just too many inconsistencies.'

'Okay,' Turner said quietly. 'Let's start by running through the facts used by the Warren Commission to inform the American public of Oswald's guilt.

One: He had a poor upbringing; no father, and a mother who allegedly fraternised with mobsters. He grew up a lonely, introspective kid with a chip on his shoulder.

Two: He joined the marines. He was something less than a model soldier. He was stationed at a top secret base in Atsugi in Japan. He had access to secret information, including some about the U2 super spy plane. He learned Russian. In September 1959 he was given a discharge on compassionate grounds, claiming his mother was sick. He flew home, stayed there three days, then took off to Russia, via England, where he announced his intention to defect and make available to the Soviets all and any information he had about the US military.

Three: He lived well in the Russian city of Minsk. He had a job in a radio factory, and his pay was supplemented by an allowance from the Soviet Red Cross. In Russia at that time, Red Cross was another name for the secret service. The KGB.

In February, 'sixty one, after fifteen months in Russia, Lee applied at the US embassy for permission to return to the US. In March of 1961 he met a Russian girl, Marina Prusakova. In April they were married. A few months later she had a daughter. He took his family to the US, financing the trip with a loan from the US State department. He and his family returned here. He had a succession of jobs, and wrote to the *Fair Play for Cuba Committee*, offering to fund a chapter of their organisation in New Orleans.

Four: He was seen on three occasions on a street in New

Orleans, passing out leaflets advertising the policies of the *Fair Play for Cuba Committee*. FPCC was a pro-Castro organisation. On one occasion he got into a fight on the street with a Cuban member of an anti-Castro group. The man, Carlos Bringuier, later said he had been approached by Lee a few days earlier. Oswald had introduced himself as a marine vet with guerrilla experience, and offered to train Cuban exiles.

Five: In March 1963, Oswald purchased a Mannlicher-Carcano rifle by mail order. The rifle was despatched to a post office box in Dallas. The box number, 2915, was in the name of A Hidell. Oswald allegedly used this rifle to take a shot at General Walker in Dallas in April 1963. Walker was a controversial right-wing figure.

'When arrested on the afternoon of November 22nd, Oswald was carrying a fake ID card in the name Alex J Hidell. In his rented room there was a certificate of vaccination signed in the name of Doctor A. J. Hidell, Post Office Box 30016, New Orleans. The box number, 30016, had been taken in the name of Lee Harvey Oswald. He had listed Marina Oswald and A. J. Hidell as other people authorised to receive mail at that box.

By this time Lee and Marina were living separately. He had a succession of addresses in rooming houses in New Orleans.

Six: The Mannlicher Carcano was found on the sixth floor of the depository building, soon after the assassination. A palm print on the rifle was identified as being that of Lee Harvey Oswald. And fibers, found trapped in the wooden stock of the rifle, were identified as being from the jacket Oswald was wearing when arrested.

Seven: Photographs were found showing Oswald holding a rifle, identified as the rifle found in the depository.

Eight: Oswald was identified as being the man seen running away from the scene of the shooting of police officer, J D Tippett, for which Oswald was originally detained.

Nine: Evidence was introduced to indicate that he showed strong communist tendencies. He was doomed from the start.'

'The case for the prosecution,' Daniel muttered dryly.

'It fooled millions of people, Dan. If the critics had not existed, the government would have gotten clean away with it. Like you said, there are just too many inconsistencies. I don't believe that any thinking human can look at the evidence and convict Oswald.'

'If he hadn't died, Oswald I mean, if he had gone to trial, would he have been convicted?'

'No,' replied Turner. 'No way. And the people behind the whole thing knew that. In open court there was no way Oswald would swing the right way. He was never destined to reach the courtroom.'

'So,' Daniel asked. 'You're the expert. What do you think his role was?'

Turner sat back on his chair. 'I won't answer that. What I will do though is present you with a few facts and let you make up your own mind.' He stood and beckoned Daniel from his seat. 'Here, take a look at this.'

The wall at one end of the cellar was hidden behind a thick curtain that extended from floor to ceiling. Turner tugged on a drawstring, and the curtain slid cleanly aside on smooth runners. The wall behind it was white, but sketched upon it was a mass, a veritable map, of lines and scribbled names. As Daniel stared in awe he slowly realised what it was he was staring at.

'These names . . .' he muttered. 'They're all people involved in the assassination.'

'Correct, my friend.' Turner moved to Daniel's side and beamed proudly at his handiwork. 'What you see before you is the result of over twenty-five years' work. As complete a charting of the assassination of JFK as you will ever see. Every name is here, and with each name there are clearly defined links to other names involved.' He stepped nearer to the wall and ran a hand over the smooth surface. Every name and circumstance that has ever surfaced is on here somewhere. . . .'

'My Pa . . .' Dan whispered. Turner hesitated the barest moment before placing a finger under a name on the periphery of the vast chart. 'Here you go . . . Harrison Baker.' Beneath it was written a short notation and file reference. He read aloud: 'On Elm. Statement to Dallas police read that shots came from behind picket fence. Brother killed, shot through the head, on December fourteenth, 1963. Harrison Baker died same day. Coroner's verdict: suicide.'

'Uncle Tom.' Dan whispered. 'Pa . . .' He felt the weight of sudden recollection descend upon him.

Turner was watching for Daniel's reaction. 'Why do you think your father killed himself, Dan?'

'It was the telephone calls – and the visit. But mostly the calls. . . .' He related what he knew. Turner listened eagerly, but did not judge. Instead he seemed to agree. When Daniel had finished his tale, Turner nodded. 'I can tell you now, Dan, that you are absolutely right. It was the pressure killed your daddy.'

Daniel felt emotions surge from him. Felt tears burn at his eyes. He swallowed. He felt gratitude, an almost gushing gratitude, to the Zealot. The man knew the truth.

'Okay,' Turner muttered. He glanced away, deliberately allowing Daniel time to compose himself. 'Let's get back to answering the charges laid by the Warren report.'

He paused at the wall. 'One: he joined the marines. When you consider that almost the entire basis of the evidence against Oswald was that he was a lone malcontent, a communist with near-rabid tendencies it is surprising that his army buddies did not notice.' He stepped up to a bookshelf and lifted down a fat file. He turned to a page and prepared to read. 'Let me give you a few examples:

'Nelson Delgado roomed with Oswald. Here is an extract from the Warren report. Warren Commission attorney Liebeler is asking the questions; '*You told the FBI that in your opinion Oswald was not a good shot; is that correct?*'

DELGADO '*Yes.*'

LIEBELER: '*And that he did not show any unusual interest in his rifle, and in fact appeared less interested in weapons than the average marine?*'

DELGADO: '*Yes. He was mostly a thinker, a reader. He read quite a bit.*'

'Daniel Powers served with Oswald. He was questioned by Warren Counsel Jenner: '*Did he ever express any sympathy towards the communist party?*'

POWERS: '*None that I can recall.*'

'There were other comments from others who knew him. Donald Camarata, Peter Connor, Allen D. Graf, John Heindel, Mack Osborne, Richard Dennis Call. All of them knew Oswald, none of them ever heard Oswald make any pro-communist statements. The only man who *did* make any statement indicating Oswald had communist leanings was Kerry Thornley. He had not served with Oswald for as long as the others, and had not lived on the same part of the base. But his testimony was heard directly by the Warren Commission, whereas the testimony of the others was not.'

Dan interrupted. 'So the Warren people only heard evidence designed to make Oswald look bad?'

'Exactly. Nelson Delgado testified that on the rifle range Oswald often missed the target altogether. He always had to be reminded to clean his gun. He was not interested in guns.

'While in the marine corps he learned Russian. Well, how

many marines have any need to learn Russian? In September 1959 he was given compassionate leave. He went home, briefly, to see his mother, then he took a boat to England. The through ticket to Russia cost fifteen hundred dollars, yet we know from bank records that Oswald had only two hundred dollars saved. He arrived in England on October 9th 1959. The Warren people claimed that he left for Helsinki the same day for the next stage of his journey to Russia. However, the immigration stamp in Oswald's passport showed that he left England on October 10th. We know he checked into his hotel in Helsinki on October 10th, but there were no commercial flights to Helsinki from England that day. He had to have travelled on a military flight.'

'Let's move forward a little. He returned to the US with his new wife and baby daughter. He was given a loan by the State Department to travel back to the US. I want you to bear in mind that this man was a traitor! He had defected, claiming that he was going to make available to the Russians all he knew about the military, including information about the U2! Anybody else would have been arrested on arrival in New York and put on trial!

Ordinary people in Russia at that time found it next to impossible to get out. But he had no difficulty in getting Marina and the child out, and this at the height of the cold war!'

'So you think he was involved in some kind of secret mission?'

'Absolutely.' Turner was emphatic. 'Here are a few other strange coincidences for you. On January 20th, 1961, three months before the Bay of Pigs incident, two men claiming to represent the *Friends of Democratic Cuba* turned up at a Ford dealership, Bolton Ford Inc, on Canal Street in New Orleans. One of the men was a Latin, powerfully built, the other was a thin white man. They claimed they wanted to buy ten Ford pickups, and asked for a bid on the price. The Latin man called himself Joe Moore, but said the bid had to be in the name Oswald. The white man confirmed that Oswald was his name, and that he was the man with the money. Now, if you remember what I said earlier, Lee Oswald was in Russia at that time, and would be there for another year. But they were using his name!'

'But how could that be . . .' Dan gasped. 'How could that be . . . ? Another Oswald, perhaps . . . Someone else?'

Turner made a hand gesture, bade Daniel to be patient.

'J Edgar Hoover, head of the FBI, wrote a memo warning agents to be on the alert for someone using the name Lee Oswald and fake ID.'

'In a file somewhere here I have a copy of the articles of incorporation of *The Democratic Friends of Cuba*. Among the organisation's incorporators is the name Guy Bannister.'

Daniel brightened. 'Him I have heard of.'

Turner snapped fingers, pleased that Dan was staying with him. 'Oswald was seen on three occasions on a New Orleans Street passing out leaflets for the *Fair Play for Cuba Committee.* The address stamped on the leaflets was 544 Camp St, New Orleans. That address is a corner building with two entrances. Each entrance is on a different street, the second entrance being 531 Lafayette Street. If you walked inside 544 Camp Street in 1963, and walked up the stairs, you would arrive at the office of Guy Bannister and Associates, address 531 Lafayette Street. Bannister was a former FBI man who set up his own agency while maintaining links to FBI and the Office of Naval Intelligence, where he started. He was a frenetic anti-Castro activist, involved in all kinds of activities; CIA, Operation Mongoose. Training Cubans for a second major strike on Cuba. A second Bay of Pigs.

'Jack Martin was a private eye employed by the Bannister agency in the summer of nineteen sixty three. He later told District Attorney Jim Garrison that he had witnessed a great many strange things happening in Bannister's office that summer. He had seen many Cubans passing through. There was training going on at Lake Pontchartrain. Armaments stolen from a munitions factory were stored at Bannister's. Martin had seen a man called David Ferrie there. He had seen Lee Harvey Oswald there.'

'Wait a minute,' Dan cut in. 'If Oswald was meant to be a communist, and pro-Castro, he wouldn't be mixing with all these anti-Castro factions.'

Turner smiled approval. 'Exactly. Now you're getting it. The whole thing; his public persona, was faked. Either he was being set up on some kind of long term plan, or he was deliberately wearing a communist mask for some other reason.'

Daniel shook his head. 'Will we ever know the truth?'

Turner shrugged. 'In its entirety, probably not. But here's something for you to chew on. After Oswald's arrest for fighting with Carlos Bringuier, he called the local FBI and was visited in jail by special agent Quigley. Now this was not an arrest for a major crime, why would the FBI rush an agent down there to see Oswald unless he had some connection to them? Agent Quigley later destroyed his notes, in complete contravention of

FBI policy. Lee was also in frequent contact with other agents, Hosty and Savage. In fact when Oswald moved to Dallas, Hosty and Savage were transfered temporarily there too.

'On returning from Russia he was debriefed by the FBI and engaged as an informant. He was given the number S179 and put on a monthly stipend of $200 a month. This is a matter of public record.

The social circles that became his habitat in the Dallas area also are worth a look. One man who became Lee's friend and mentor was George de Mohrenschildt. He was a Russian aristocrat with ties to the intelligence community. He was ostensibly engaged in the oil business, but he did travel on special duties linked to the CIA. The others with whom Lee socialised also tended to be what are known as *White Russians*. That is, they were people who had been driven from Russia, or whose ancestors had been forced to flee the country. They were anti-communist. It does seem odd that Lee, such an ardent communist, or Marxist-Leninist, as he liked to be described, would spend so much time with those whom he was so idealogically at odds with.

'De Mohrenschildt introduced Lee and Marina to Ruth and Michael Paine. They were both Russian speaking. Michael was an engineering designer engaged on classified work for a major defense contractor. Ruth's father was employed by the Agency for International Development, regarded by many as a source of cover for the CIA. Michael was away from home much of the time, and Ruth invited Marina to stay with her at her home in Irving. Lee was then staying for short periods at rooming houses, and of course travelling between Dallas and New Orleans. Incidentally, the newspapers and the authorities in November '63 made much of the fact that Oswald had chosen the depository building, the so-called *assassin's lair*, with great care. In fact Lee never did apply for a job there. Ruth Paine contacted Depository Supervisor Roy Truly and persuaded him to give Oswald the job. A message was left at Mrs Paine's, offering Lee a better paid job at the airport, but Lee was never told!' Turner was warming to his subject. Holding fingers to each side of his head, he moved away from the wall, pacing as he marshalled his thoughts.

Daniel chipped in: 'There's just so much to take in.'

Turner grinned at him. 'You got that right. I'll try to keep it simple for you; just skim the surface.'

'Okay,' he took a sip from his cup and continued. 'As a matter of interest, in '67–'68, when Jim Garrison, the New Orleans District Attorney, was building his case, he was refused permission to examine the tax records of Michael and Ruth Paine. They were classified, secret. A designer and a housewife? Why? There were also Warren Commission documents relating to the Paines and their relatives that were unavailable for the same reason. Why?

'I'll move on to the evidence. In the depository building, immediately after the assassination, Oswald was found on the first floor by a police officer who dashed in there. This was, according to the policeman, no more than ninety seconds after the shooting. In that ninety seconds Lee was supposed to have left the sixth floor window, arranging the three spent shell casings from the rifle in a nice neat line on the floor. He had to hide the rifle behind boxes at the opposite end of the sixth floor and then had to run down five flights of stairs, passing two secretaries who were running down the stairs at that time, and who never saw him, and arrive at the first floor, not out of breath, and looking relaxed by the time the police officer arrived.

Then instead of making good his escape, Oswald buys a Coke from a machine in the lunchroom before slowly leaving the building by the front door. Four witnesses saw a man matching Oswald's description get into a Nash Rambler station wagon that contained three other men. Other witnesses had earlier seen two men run from the back of the depository and get into the Rambler. The car then drove away, returning minutes later, almost as though it had driven around the block, and come back to pick up Oswald. Interestingly, Jack Ruby, a man we will talk about later, was seen earlier that morning getting *out* of a Rambler. Mrs Paine, who you'll remember was Marina's landlady, also owned a Nash Rambler station wagon, and when, later that day in the police station, Captain Will Fritz challenged Oswald that he had been seen getting into the car, by Dallas police deputy Roger Craig, Oswald protested, quote: '*That station wagon belongs to Mrs Paine. Don't tie her into this!*'

The Warren Commission said that Oswald returned to his rooming house on a bus, but on the issue of identification, the bus driver could not say it was Oswald on the bus. He testified: quote: '*I could not do it. I could not do it at the line-up, and I could not do it now.*'

Once back at his rooming house, which happened, according to his landlady, at about five minutes to one pm, Oswald changed his shirt, put on a jacket, tucked his handgun into his waistband and set off. Before he left, however, the landlady testified that a police car drew up outside her house and the horn was pressed twice. It sounded, she said, like a signal. She last saw Lee standing at a nearby bus stop.

Daniel was shaking his head. 'You're a mine of information, a walking encyclopaedia!'

Turner laughed. 'I know. I'm sorry to go on so. It's just, I spend so much time in here, working on this, the thing builds up inside of me, like steam pressure. Talking to you . . . I'm just letting off steam.'

Pamela was watching and listening from the doorway. She stepped inside the room and sat on the floor beside Daniel's chair. He draped a hand over her shoulder. She lifted her hand and grasped his fingers.

Turner smiled at her, then picked up the thread of his tale. 'So, we arrive at the Tippett shooting. The Warren Commission relied on the testimony of Helen Markham, who said Oswald killed Tippett, and that she sat comforting the dying police officer for twenty minutes. This despite the medical evidence that Tippett died immediately, that Markham was unable to pick Lee out in a lineup, and that other witnesses could not place Helen Markham herself at the scene!

'A taxi driver identified Oswald as the killer, but later admitted he did not actually see the shooting, but ducked down onto the floor of his car when he heard shots. He saw Oswald run past, gun in hand, muttering something that sounded like 'poor dumb cop.'

'But there were other witnesses, who did not place Oswald at the scene, and who were never called before the Warren Commission. Mrs Acquilla Clemons, who was sitting on her porch when Tippett was shot, told attorney Mark Lane that she saw two men, and that the man who killed Tippett was kind of chunky, heavy. Not Oswald. Domingo Benevides, who was closest to the scene of the shooting, didn't place Oswald at the scene, nor did Warren Reynolds, who did not change his story until he was shot in the head two months later. When he recovered he was able to place Oswald at the scene.

'Frank Wright saw the shooting of Tippett, saw the police officer fall, roll over and lie still. He saw the gunman get into an automobile, a 1951 gray Plymouth and hare out of there.

'Johnny Brewer worked in a shoeshop. He saw Lee acting suspiciously, and watched him enter the Texas theater. He spoke to the cashier in the theater, and the police were called.

'Once Lee was in custody, the vultures descended. The information released to the press was coming in spurts. At first the buzz was that a parafin test, a nitrate test, would prove Lee had fired a rifle and would convict him.

'But the test came up negative. Captain Fritz told the press that the test proved he had fired a gun, and under repeated urging from the press to say that Oswald had fired a rifle, Fritz would only say that he had fired a gun. Ten months later, in the Warren Report, the nitrate test, proclaimed after the assassination as the factor that would trap Oswald, was called, and I quote: "Totally unreliable."

'Then we come to the gun, and the bullets. The Warren report said that the shells found at the scene of Tippett's slaying were fired from the revolver in Oswald's possession when he was arrested. This immediately caused problems. The first cop on the scene, officer Hill, radioed in that the shells at the scene indicated that the gun used was an automatic. Of course, Oswald was carrying a revolver, so the answer simply became that the experienced officer, Hill, had made a mistake. Witness Benevides gave two shells to officer J M Poe. Poe scratched his initials onto the shells, a standard procedure for marking evidence, but those marks were not on the shells the Warren Commission asked him to identify. Then we come to the type of shells. The slugs removed from Tippett's body were three Winchester-Westerns, and one Remington Peters, whereas the shells found at the scene were two of each. The Warren report postulated that to save money. Oswald might have placed one make of bullet into another case. This assumes that Lee owned loading equipment, and of course there is no evidence that he did.

'When he was arrested, Lee was carrying the revolver, and had five live Winchester-Western shells in a pocket. No tests were done to see if the gun had been fired recently. There are other examples, but I don't want to go over the top. Suffice to say, there is no proof that Oswald's gun was used to kill Tippett. There are all kinds of problems with identifying Oswald, and yet the Warren people just went ahead anyway.'

Daniel offered a comment. 'This is pretty much what I've read. All these coincidences just disregarded.'

Turner spoke again. 'Lastly, we come to timing. Warren Commission tried to place the time of Tippett's death at 1.15pm. As his landlady said he left her house a little after one o'clock, that leaves Lee with twelve minutes, to cover over one mile, kill Tippett and escape. Yet no one saw him running, or even walking quickly during that period. The problem increases when you consider that even Helen Markham, remember her, said she was sure of the time Tippet died because she was waiting for a bus due at 1.12pm.

'T F Bowley, the witness who used the radio in Tippett's squad car to call for help, looked at his watch. It was 1.10pm. Could Oswald, without help, have covered that distance in that time? Not unless he ran – and quickly. You have to admit, it is a puzzle.

'Just two more interesting anecdotes, then I'll move on. A man named Burroughs who became assistant manager of the Texas Theater where Oswald was arrested, said Oswald entered the theater just after 1pm, and not twenty minutes later, as Johnny Brewer said. His story is backed up by another man in the theater at the time, Jack Davis, who I last heard of hosting a Christian music show on radio. If Oswald was in the theater when Tippett died, who killed him?

'All this, positively pleading for investigation, and yet two hours after the assassination J Edgar Hoover called Bobby Kennedy and told him they had the man who killed the President.'

Pamela had rustled up dinner, and watched in silence as the two men continued the conversation. Turner apologised for what he called 'getting onto his hobby-horse.'

'Then there were the witnesses coming forward after Oswald was taken. On Saturday, one day after the assassination and one day *before* Jack Ruby killed Oswald, Julie Ann Mercer told the FBI that on November 22nd, at about one hour before the assassination, she had been parked in a line of traffic on the off side of the triple overpass. While parked there, she glanced to her right, where a pickup was parked, on the kerb. She saw a young man take from a car a bundle, shaped like a rifle wrapped in a cloth, and carry it up the grassy slope. Inside the cab of the pickup was a middleaged man. On the Saturday, after hearing her description, the FBI showed her a number of photographs. She identified Jack Ruby as the man she saw in the pickup.

The FBI told her she must be mistaken. Later, she told New Orleans DA Jim Garrison that the statement in her name in the Warren Commission Report had been altered, her signature faked.

Dallas police officer, Tom Tilson, driving with his daughter towards Dealey Plaza from the other side of the overpass, immediately *after* the assassination, testified that he saw a man who looked incredibly like Jack Ruby, whom he had known since 1957, run down the grassy slope and thow an object into the rear of a waiting car. The man drove off, and Tilson, having heard the buzz about the shooting on the police radio, followed. He had his daughter take down the licence number of the car. They followed for some distance, then Tilson decided that if the man in the car was armed, he ought not to put his daughter at risk. He turned around and returned to Dallas where he contacted the homicide department and passed on the information about the man, and the licence plate. Tilson though, is one I discount. I have a home movie shot from the other side of the triple overpass about twenty seconds after the shooting, and I cannot spot the car that Tilson says was there.

'On the triple overpass were two police officers and a group of railroad workers. Two of the workers testified that there was a fourth shot and that they saw a puff of smoke from the knoll. On the top of a building across Dealey Plaza sat J C Price. He testified that the shots came from the knoll and that he saw a man running behind the picket fence towards the railroad. The man was carrying something, but Price could not say exactly what it was.

James Tague was standing by the overpass when he was struck by a fragment, his face cut. He and a police officer found a clear mark on a kerbstone where a bullet had richochetted. Abraham Zapruder, who took the most famous film of the assassination, was standing on a small concrete wall close to the knoll. He was sure the shots came from there. Billy Lovelady was having lunch on the steps of the depository building. He recalled the shots coming from: quote: '*There around that concrete little deal on that knoll . . . between the underpass and the building right on that knoll.*'

There were dozens of witnesses who thought the shots came from the knoll. Scores of them ran across Dealey and up onto the railroad yards.

Police officers who ran up the knoll, guns at the ready, were met by a man flashing Secret Service credentials. The man told them the area was clear, but to keep looking.

One woman, filming from the centre of Dealey Plaza, had possibly the best view of the killing. But her camera was taken from her by a man she later claimed resembled FBI agent Savage.

Three hoboes were pulled off freight cars and marched to the sheriff's office for questioning. No record of their names, or what questions they were asked, exists. But they were photographed as they were escorted to the police station. Here . . .' he flipped open another file and drew out three black and white prints.

'Here they are . . .' he passed them to Daniel and Pam.

She mused . . . 'They vanished without trace?'

Turner smiled. 'There have been numerous theories about who two of the tramps were. Later, I'll show you something that will interest you.' He rubbed his hands together. 'Okay, did you know that Oswald was questioned for over twelve hours, and yet there is no record of anything that was said? An experienced police officer like Will Fritz would have known that without a record being taken, nothing Lee said would have been admissible in court.

Now we're getting to the end. Jack Ruby. He had underworld connections going back to the forties. There is evidence he ran guns to Cuba. And in the weeks prior to the assassination he made telephone calls to a great many interesting numbers in New Orleans and Chicago. He was under pressure. He was in debt – over forty thousand dollars worth. The IRS were after him. He was too small to break free, and too small to say no when he was given the order to kill Lee.'

Daniel shook his head. 'All this makes my head spin. I know from the little I've read that you really are just skimming the surface here.'

'You are right. There are just so many layers, so many unexplained connections; Oswald to Ruby, to Ferrie, to Clay Shaw and back to Oswald. Witnesses who saw them together, witnesses who were on the inside and who warned about the assassination. Richard Cason was a federal agent who was assigned by his superiors in the summer of '63 to investigate a group who were acting suspiciously. Cason spent time establishing relationships and making observations, and by September 1963 it had become apparent to him that a very large operation was underway to kill President Kennedy. He wrote FBI Director Hoover a letter, sent registered with a return receipt requested, outlining all he had heard. When there came no reply, he began to wonder about the extent of the plot. He found himself being frozen out by the agency. As time went on, and Hoover did nothing, Cason became more desperate. He started to wonder about himself. He had mixed with the plotters, had listened to their plans. He knew they had decided that one man, probably a Cuban, would have to be sacrificed. Now, in the shadow of a terrible silence from the Director of the FBI, he started to think that *he* might be the one who was being set up.' Turner paused.

Pamela was the next to speak. 'I wasn't born when JFK died, and frankly I never gave any of this a thought until I met Daniel. But what I have read shocks me. Do you have a copy of the Zapruder film we could watch? – it might give me a clearer picture.'

Turner smiled, indulging her. 'I have the Zapruder film. I have several films.'

She was surprised. 'Were there others?'

'Oh yes, quite a number. If you add up all the films and still photographs taken in Dealey Plaza that day they come to over five hundred pictures. The Zapruder film was not seen by the American public until the nineteen seventies, but it is the best known of the films taken. Zapruder had the best view, after all. Other significant films were the Nix and Muchmore films. Most of the other films showed very little – except one.' He paused dramatically. 'One very special film. Because Oswald was arrested and named the killer so quickly, and then just as quickly murdered, the man who took the film, a former private investigator, smelt a rat. He held on to the film, waited until he could afford to develop it himself, then jealously guarded the negative. Few people have seen it. Even fewer copies exist. But I have one.'

'Can we see it?' Daniel was intrigued.

Turner glanced at him. 'You ready to tell me yet?'

Dan shot back: 'You ready to run those films?'

Sensing that a show of trust was required, Turner grinned. Touché. He did not quite know what it was about Daniel Baker that gave him this odd, almost precognitive feeling; Baker had something. 'Okay.'

Unlocking a wall safe, he took out three video cassettes, and set the VCR to play the first of them.

'What happened to that man you were talking about . . .' Pam asked. 'What was his name . . . Cason?'

Turner inserted the cassette, took up the remote control and returned to his chair. 'Cason decided that his best chance for safety lay in being inside a federal institution when the killing took place. He did not have a date for the assassination, so in late October he walked into a bank and fired his gun at the ceiling. Then he went outside and sat on the kerb. When the bank guard ran out, he sprinted past Cason. Cason had to call him over to arrest him! His intention was to get himself charged with malicious mischief, and do maybe six months. Instead he was charged with armed robbery and sentenced to *ten years!*' He pressed play on the remote. The tape ran.

Pam moved to Daniel's side and gave his hand a squeeze. Dan had moved to the edge of his seat. His throat was dry, clamped tight around a lump that had developed there as the screen flickered. Then as if from some nightmare, a familiar scene struck Daniel a thundering blow.

Dealey Plaza that day. God, it all looked so achingly familiar. He felt he could reach out and be there. The colors were ill-defined, slightly washed out with too much emphasis on duller shades, but to him the images were real. Real. He swallowed; somewhere out there, just beyond camera range, infuriatingly just beyond the edge of the screen, was his father. He willed the camera to move, but it did not. Not yet.

'This is the Presidential limo,' Turner commented. 'Two outriders to the rear. This here is JFK . . .' He indicated with a finger. 'Beside him is the First Lady, and seated just before them is Governor and Mrs Connally. A shot is fired just before the limo reaches the road sign. Now the limo is behind the road sign and JFK starts to react to being hit. Now he's visible and his hands are up around his neck and face.

Governor Connally begins to turn to his right. He has heard the first shot, and is looking around. Now he is shot, and falls left into his wife's arms. Here comes the head shot . . . THERE!' He cried out as JFK's head exploded in a vivid splash of red.

'Oh my God,' Pam said weakly, a hand raised to her face in horror. 'I can't believe I saw that. Oh my God.'

The film ran out in a blaze of white. Turner rewound the tape then set it to play once more. They reviewed the horrific scene. As Jackie Kennedy clambered up onto the trunk in a panicked attempt to retrieve the scattered fragments of her husband's destroyed skull, the film ended. Pamela covered her face with her hands.

Turner looked at Daniel, saw and misinterpreted the look on his face. 'Pretty horrific isn't it?'

When Daniel did not reply, Turner rewound the tape once more. 'A railroad man, Tom Boland, was ideally sited to see what happened behind the picket fence at the top of the grassy knoll. He was standing in the railroad supervisor's tower, approximately one hundred metres from the fence. He described three cars entering the yards in the hour before the assassination.

The cars had out of state plates, political stickers, and were dusty, as if having come in from a hard drive. The driver in one of the cars had what looked like a walkie-talkie held to his face. Boland described four men behind the fence just before the shooting. Two wore police uniforms, and the other two, well, one was dressed like a construction worker, complete with hard hat. The fourth man was dressed casually in sports jacket and slacks. At the time of the shooting, Boland could only describe what he felt; that something out of the ordinary, a flash of light, occurred at the fence. Now I'm going to run the Zapruder film again. This time, after JFK is hit in the head, watch the foreground.'

The tape ran. Once more Daniel stared, fixedly at the screen. The instant Kennedy's head was blasted open, Daniel winced – but kept staring. He watched the foreground, studied the foreground as a blur of foliage streaked across the screen. And then . . . 'I saw, something,' he said, feeling puzzled.

'What?' Pam exclaimed. Turner smiled warmly. 'Good man.' With the remote he rewound the tape, the picture moving rapidly backwards, a blur of motion. 'Now, watch carefully. JFK has been hit. Jackie has climbed up onto the trunk and back again . . .'

'THERE!' Daniel shouted. Beside him Pamela jumped with fright. 'There!' Dan cried again. He left his seat and jabbed a finger at the screen. Turner had pressed the pause button. The picture, a mass of mottled green foliage filled the lower half of the now stilled screen. And in the lower right hand corner was what looked like a construction worker's hard hat. Round and white.

'Look just in front of the hat.' Turner prompted. 'You don't see it? I'll take out the color.' Using the remote, Turner drained the color from the picture.

'A straight line . . .' Dan mused. 'A rod of some kind . . .' he went on.

'How about a rifle?' Pam finished. 'This is incredible. Incredible.'

'I know this . . .' Dan muttered. Beads of sweat had blossomed on his brow. He felt his heart flutter. 'I know this.' Turner flashed a quizzical glance at him, but Daniel ignored him.

Turner felt something shift in his gut. The oddest feeling. He felt like a man who knew he was on the brink of cracking some great mystery – and who feared what he might find. A shiver ran over him, and he could not work out why.

Removing the cassette from the machine, he slotted in another. 'This is an extract,' he said, 'The important extract, from what is known as the Hughes film.' The tape began.

'Two things to watch for. The depository building will be visible, and also, for a second or so, will be the sixth floor window Oswald is supposed to have fired from. There *is* someone at the window. The question is – who?'

Daniel strained, and for an instant it seemed he did see a figure at the window. Then the point of view changed. The camera was now aimed across the plaza, towards the knoll. Scores of people were running, not away from the knoll, but towards it. Turner commented. 'People there all seem to think the shots came from the knoll.'

Daniel spoke up. 'What was the special film you mentioned?'

'The Parker film. In my mind it is the most significant of the films taken on Dealey that day. I knew Parker briefly. He was terrified the film might become famous. Scared rigid about what might happen to him. He's dead now anyway. They can't hurt him.'

'If the film is so important why haven't you made it public?'

'Firstly, because as you'll see it would not wholly exonerate Oswald in the public eye, and secondly, when I do present it, I want us to have an airtight case in support. It's too good a shot to waste. Everything, evidence, testimony, timing, has to be exactly right. We can risk no more accidents, coincidences, no more freak-fires or legal technicalities. And, as of yet, we still do not have anyone to prosecute.'

He pushed the play button. 'Incidentally, the original is very safely stored. As you'll see, Parker knew his stuff. He did not waste a single frame.'

The film began. The quality was eight millimetre and fairly grainy, but to Daniel, remembering, it all seemed so vivid. The view across the plaza as seen from a spot along the southside of the grassy area in the centre of Dealey. Looking at the depository. Looking at the stone memorial, the Pergola, looking at the knoll.

Daniel gasped as his vision scanned the crowd trailing along the kerb on the opposite side of Elm Streeet. One of those people standing there was his beloved father, and he himself was there somewhere too. It was hard, so hard to see, but he hoped he would catch a glimpse of his Pa. Then he was able to precisely locate the spot where his father had been standing, and he almost cried out. To anyone else the figure might have appeared to be little more than an indistinct blur, but to Daniel there was no mistaking the familiar, so familiar, figure of his father. Standing relaxed, shoulders slightly angled, head craning as the motorcade approached.

Time had obviously passed. The next shot was of the depository building, panning across it and pausing to focus on the south western corner, then moving slightly before settling. There was a figure there!

Turner interjected a comment. 'Parker told me his wife had seen the man at the window with a rifle. Thinking him to be a secret service agent, she mentioned his presence to her husband.'

The shot altered again, focusing on the corner of Houston and Elm. The lead car, a pale colored open top, rounded the corner and approached the camera. The figures in it unrecognisable. Parker was preparing for the main shot, a close up of JFK and his wife. The Presidential limousine neared, and Dan seemed almost transported back in time. He could hear the crowd noise, the cheering. Then the spitting crackle of a firecracker split the air. Parker filmed the limousine as it approached, panning left as it drew level until it was only feet away. The First Lady was close, and beyond her the President was visible. He was leaning forward, his hands held up to his face. *And his face was clear!*

An expression of bewilderment, and pain, was on John Kennedy's face, and watching, Daniel felt himself near to tears.

Then the limousine was close enough almost to touch, and, inexplicably, the zoom lever on the camera was moved. The shot became wider, encompassing both Elm Street and the grassy slope. The trees that topped the slope and the fence that fringed it.

The figure of the President was seen to lurch, then the limousine was haring away down the slope of Elm Street and towards the overpass. The camera moved back, to concentrate once more on the knoll, and all three watchers in the room strained to study the screen.

Many members of the crowd had dropped flat to the ground. Others were standing in numbed shock. For Daniel the mood was invoked with terrible clarity. He felt the hush descend.

Then as the film ended in numbered trailer he felt cold envelope him. He knew the timing of the dreadful events of that day. He had seen something . . .

An instant before the film ended, a small, indistinct figure appeared in the shade of a tree on the top of the knoll and stood there, rock still.

Daniel blinked back the tears. So much of that day was brought back to him, so much sadness. Turner saw his expression, and a look of concern creased his brow. He asked Daniel if he wanted to see it once more, adding: 'You ought to. There were probably a few things you missed.'

So the film ran again. This time, when the camera shot pulled dramatically back, Turner directed them to study the foliage at the top of the knoll. There was a movement of some sort, a fuzziness. 'Was that smoke?' Pam voiced the question. No one answered.

Then the film was ending and that tiny figure, as indistinct as a finger smudge, appeared again.

Turner sat back. 'Well, what do you think?'

It was Pamela who answered. 'Incredible. That was the gunshot from the knoll?'

Turner nodded. 'The final, irrefutable proof. The best we are ever going to get. What Sam Holland and the others on the overpass saw, we just saw. When the time to go public comes, that will be the clincher.'

'I see what you mean about not clearing Oswald. There was definitely someone at the window.'

Turner shrugged. Daniel was sitting quietly, face rigid with intense concentration. He spoke at last. 'Did you notice that blur on the knoll, right at the end?'

Turner frowned. He had not. He ran the tape once more, this time pausing the tape to study the blur, and confessed himself baffled. 'All the dozens of times I've watched this film. I never saw that before.'

'It was pretty dark in that spot.'

Turner was still aghast. 'It looked like . . . someone coming from behind the fence. Coming from behind the fence. JESUS!'

He exclaimed. 'It may even have been one of the killers trying to lose himself in the crowd!'

'The figure was too small to be a man.' Daniel corrected him. 'It was not one of the killers.' He paused. The timing was right, now, and he was relishing the prospect.

'I was ten years old when John Kennedy died, Mr Turner, and as you know I lived in Dallas. You know my Pa was on Dealey that day, but what you don't know is that I was there too.' He faltered, realising it would take an effort to prise out the secret.

'I guess what I am trying to say is . . . I was on the knoll that day. I was behind the fence. The blur on the film was me.'

Turner's jaw dropped.

* 17 *

The words flooded out. Gushed out. At times both men grew so excited they chatted simultaneously and at cross purposes while Pamela, watching over them, smiled indulgently.

The mistrust had been banished. Already they were friends, huddling closely, swapping information, each marvelling at the other's revelations. At last Turner sat back on his seat and rubbed at the back of his neck with a tired hand. A look of utter satisfaction illuminated his face.

'So, we get back to my original question. What brought you around?'

This time Daniel did not hesitate. 'I got a good look at one of the assassins. A couple of weeks ago I saw him again. Ever hear of Barry Mather?'

Turner blew out his cheeks. 'Him? Jeez, are you positive? I mean, really positive?' Daniel insisted he was. Turner leapt from his chair and raised a fist in triumph. 'YES!!!' He danced.

But when the elation subsided he began to fret again. Was Daniel sure? It had been years, the man would have changed. He paced the room, his head framed by his tensed, raised shoulders. Then again, how could they prove it?

He halted, body frozen into a comical half-stride stance, head cocked to one side, palms pressed together, then in a fever he searched the shelves and took down a book, flicked through it and handed it, open, to Daniel.

'Is that the man you saw in sixty-three?' Confirmation came instantly and Turner looked pleased. 'That picture was taken in sixty-one. It's about as accurate a shot as we'll ever get. He's not the kind of man who takes kindly to being snapped.'

Daniel lapsed into thought. He began to feel cold, started absently to rub slowly at his upper arms. Tilting his head he looked to Turner in a gloomy cast. 'What do you know about him?'

'Mather?' Turner asked with a raised eyebrow. 'From the beginning?' Daniel nodded. Turner took a breath. 'Okay, the pocket history. He was born in 1930. His folks ran a small general store, the usual Mom and Pop setup. They wanted him to grow up to be a lawyer, and he was smart enough to do it, but there was a dangerous, slightly reckless streak in him. While still young he joined the FBI and rapidly became an excellent Special Agent, highly thought of for his abilities. After five years of advancement and cosying up to people in the know, he quit the bureau to go into business for himself.

'He founded a company called Metrotel. It still exists; you'll find it listed in the Management Consultancy columns in the yellow pages. He sold out his share in sixty one. It's been something of a moot point whether or not the Metrotel was genuine, or a front for renegade CIA operations. Certainly it handled a large number of activities the CIA could not touch because of its charter. In order to make Metrotel a success he exploited to the fullest every contact he had ever made. The result was that in the nineteen fifties, Metrotel came to represent state-of-the-art private intelligence.

'There was no shortage of demand for its services. Corporations looking for an edge over competitors queued up to get Metro on their side. The big clientele list brought Mather greater influence and that, in turn, brought in more clients, more money. Until all the work Metrotel could handle began to be monopolised by one client; Beresford Coniston.

'The billionaire?' Daniel expressed surprise. 'Wasn't he the richest man in the world? What did Mather do for him?'

'For the first couple of years the work was fairly standard, which for Coniston meant only slightly wacky. In depth background probes of prospective high-level employees. Same sort of thing on key men in Congress and the civil service. Basic espionage against business rivals. Old man Coniston had dreadful possessive urges about women; each time he courted one he would become convinced, he would convince himself, that he was being cuckolded. So Metrotel would be engaged to keep her under constant, and I mean constant, surveillance.'

'And Mather didn't object?'

The man was putting millions of dollars each year into the Metrotel coffers. Mather was only human. He had his price. But when the work for Coniston began to veer beyond the bizarre, to the just plain dangerous, kidnapping women for the old man's parties, plotting military coups for business ends, there was some adverse publicity and the supply of clients dried up. Metrotel suffered a cash crisis and Mather was forced out to keep his hide intact. 'Hey Pamela . . .' He cried out. 'How about some more coffee?'

Grimacing selfishly – she didn't want to miss anything, she got up and hurried out to the kitchen.

Turner went on with his story. 'He went out to Hong Kong in an attempt to recreate Metrotel, but could not break the stranglehold of the powerful Triads out there. He went to Thailand, and then on to Laos, where he started to run with old friends working for the CIA. In early '63, he vanished. Because of you, I now know why. Until now the general run of opinion was that he went deep undercover in Vietnam, and that's a rumour he's reluctant to dispel.

'He did not re-emerge until sixty-seven, when he became head of security for the rapidly expanding Vincent Industries. Cyrus Galbraith headed the company then as he does now, and he personally chose Mather for the job. He's been with the V.I. ever since, and to all intents and purposes has become a model citizen.' He paused. 'But, you know, in light of what you've said, I wonder. . . .'

Getting to his feet he took another video cassette from a shelf and slotted it into the VCR. A blurred scene lit up the TV screen.

'This was taken at the Ambassador Hotel the night Bobby Kennedy received the wounds that eventually proved fatal. I got this film from a freelance named Sutton. Watch.'

A montage of shots. Bobby Kennedy at the rostrum, addressing a wildly cheering crowd. Bobby amongst a group of aides, being shepherded from the stage. Bobby moving towards the camera.

'Sutton scraped dredged up snippets of film and tape from all kinds of places to put this together. It's the most complete record of the RFK attack I've ever seen.'

The picture was fuzzy as the cameraman was jostled. 'It's not all in color. This is the hotel pantry.' Crowds, figures crammed together, jostling. Bobby Kennedy barely held in shot. Shots rang out, and the cacophony of sounds rose to a distorted pitch. Screams, rapid movement, blurred colors. Hysteria ruled, charging the atmosphere around the three watchers with cold electricity. The camera struggled to hold focus.

Bobby Kennedy lay on his back, a glazed look on his face. His head moved slowly. Someone loosened his shirt collar. Daniel became aware of the shouts, and his skin rippled cold. Above the screeching, voices could be clearly heard.'

'Get the gun!' a man cried. 'Hold him Rafer, hold him! Get the gun. GET THE GUN!!!!' The voice roared to the accompaniment of a stamping foot.

'Senator Kennedy has been shot,' a distressed newsman droned. 'Is that possible? Oh my God. Senator Kennedy has been shot. Rafer Johnson has a hold of the man . . . who apparently . . . has fired the shots.'

'Get the gun. Get the gun.'

'His hand is frozen. Take a hold of his thumb and break it if you have to! GET THE GUN!'

'Hold him. Hold him. We don't want another Oswald!'

The horror in the air when Turner stopped the tape was palpable. Their nerves, reeling from the combined assault of uncontrolled emotions, hung in ragged shreds. The element of sound, missing from the other films, added a nightmarish dimension; the full horror of the moment had been unleashed.

Pamela loosed a gasp. Turner looked at her. 'Harrowing, wasn't it? Even after all this time it still sends a chill down my spine.' To Daniel he said: 'What do you think?'

Daniel too looked breathless. 'Pretty scary stuff. Fairly straightforward though. None of the confusion you find in the JFK shooting.'

Turner's mouth tightened. 'You missed it. You didn't see what happened.'

Daniel swallowed. He looked apologetic. Turner pressed the rewind. 'Try it again. This time look beyond the screams and the horror. Use your eyes and your ears.'

The tape re-ran, and this time Daniel studied it with a heightened sense of awareness. As he watched Bobby leave the stage, hurrying to his appointment with the gunman, Dan felt a terrible feeling of foreboding douse him. Among the figures pressed together he thought he saw the stocky figure of the gunman, Sirhan, and the gun. . . .

The dreadful moment in history was repeated. His mind was filtering at high speed; counting the shots, watching the faces. Just to the rear of Kennedy a uniformed security guard raised an arm as if warding off a blow, then came the first in a series of shots, and Daniel gasped aloud.

Bobby Kennedy's head bucked forward! The Senator half turned and crumpled to the floor as the shots continued to rain. The gunfire ceased, the shouting and screaming reached a new pitch, and Turner cut dead the tape. He knew from the expression on Dan's face that the point had been made. 'Now you know.' He said.

Daniel shook his head in disbelief. 'It can't be true. How can it happen twice?'

'What? What?' A mystified Pamela broke in. Daniel and Turner exchanged a look. 'You tell her,' said the Zealot.

'Kennedy's head jerked forward when he was shot, but the gunman was in front of him.'

'But —' Words failed her, momentarily. 'But I saw the gunman.'

'So did everybody.' Turner replied, that is what you were supposed to think. But the coroner's report supports what Daniel saw; that Bobby was shot in the back of the head, at a point just behind his right ear, from a distance of about one inch. There were powder burns on his scalp. Sirhan, the gunman, by the best estimate, never got closer than six feet. He stepped right into Oswald's shoes.' Turning to Daniel, he asked him if he had counted the shots.

He had: 'There were twelve or thirteen.'

Turner appeared satisfied. 'Good. Would it surprise you to hear that Sirhan's gun would not hold thirteen bullets? No? What may surprise you is the ballistics evidence presented at trial to prove that Sirhan's gun did the killing. There was precisely none; his gun was inadvertently destroyed in some police screw-up. There was no evidence. The autopsy report was bypassed, and Sirhan was certified crazy and put away for the rest of his life.'

Daniel remarked: 'So once again we have the perfect murder carried out, with a patsy at hand to take the fall.'

Turner nodded agreement. 'And this time, to make sure there was the minimum hint of conspiracy, they gave the patsy a gun and put him in front of an audience.'

'So who did kill him?' Pamela voiced the question. Turner switched on the VCR and the screen once more flickered into life.

'The security guard standing behind Kennedy when his head jerked forward, watch for him now.'

The tape ran, and this time the guard was unmissable. Weaving a path between the crowded figures, his face impassive as he relentlessly made his way towards the Senator.

'That face . . .' Pamela whispered. 'So cold and so very determined.'

Turner shrugged. 'He's been there, on the videotapes, for years now. But no one in power has ever bothered trying to locate him. There is a fascinating sidebar to all this. Sirhan did not really become interesting until he was psycho-analysed in custody. Under intensive hypnotic debriefing it was discovered that he had at least four different personalities in his mind. One of his personnae described being in Vietnam. Another would hold an imaginary gun to his head and pull the trigger after a series of letters were spoken. He had been programmed to have four separate identities. It seems certain he was a courier for one of the intelligence agencies, a graduate of one of the mind-conditioning programs run by the CIA, or perhaps the National Security Agency. They make the CIA look like kid-scouts.'

'It's frightening to think those people are still out there,' Dan murmured. Pam echoed the sentiment.

In a businesslike manner Turner reached for the VCR once more. 'Okay, let's complete your education.' He set the tape in motion. Using a long pointer, he paused the tape at a particular moment and asked if there were any familiar faces in the crowd. Both Daniel and Pamela peered hard at the assembled faces, the ranged expressions of horror and distress, frozen in time. But one face stood out. And Daniel exploded: 'Mather! Oh my God, there too!'

'Jeeesusss,' Pam whispered.

'I've often wondered about his presence there that night. He was no fan of the Kennedys. In the light of your story, Dan, I can only conclude he had a hand in the killing of Bobby Kennedy too. And like that day in Dallas, he wanted to be in at the end.'

Daniel managed a smile. His face was flushed. 'You look seriously surprised.'

'I am, and the reason for that is this; over the years we've managed to tie many names to the JFK assassination. We've done this through statements of witnesses, circumstantial evidence, and a process of elimination. For example, on November 21st, 1963, the men who killed JFK and a small number of middle level organisers met in a motel outside Dallas. Some of them, including the three gunmen, travelled into Texas in two cars. I can tell you the names of five of the eight people in those cars, yet Mather was a name that never came up. He's covered his tracks brilliantly.'

'Which could mean he operated on some higher level, do you think?'

'Yes, or he was smarter than everybody else when it came to covering his tracks.'

'What about his current employer, Senator Galbraith? What's his background?'

Turner shrugged. 'Nothing especially exciting. Successful businessman. Took over the ailing Vincent Company in 'sixty three when the company was on the brink of collapse. In 'sixty five he managed to persuade the shareholders to swing with him and oust Nathaniel Vincent, the founder, from the board. In a decade the Vincent Company grew one thousandfold and became Vincent Industries, the collosus it is today. Do you have any idea what the VI manufactures?'

'Sure,' Dan answered with a slanting grin. 'The Vincent patent masterchoppa food processor and the VINKAN electronic can opener.'

Turner's reply was dryly caustic. 'You're forgetting mortars, grenades, flame-throwers, automatic weapons and sidearms under licence. Helicopters, combat clothing, water canteens, radio equipment, military combat simulators at thirty mill a throw. In short, every single item a country the size of the USA needs for its defense forces. Vincent's R&D is virtually unrivalled. In the 'sixties a man like Mather would have been useful; he had all the contacts an aspirant defense multinational could use. . . .'

'But the Senator, Galbraith. He's political now. He's a man with a big reputation. If he's as spotless as you say, what's he doing hiring a professional killer like Mather? Surely a link of that kind could harm his career?'

Turner rewarded him with a patient smile. 'First of all, Galbraith does not have the benefit of your knowledge. In all probability, all he knows about Mather is that he's ex-FBI, ex-Metrotel, and that he's performed superbly as head of security at the VI for over twenty-five years. As for hiring Mather at all, well, the man was no saint, but if you were talking expertise in intelligence and security in the 'sixties, he was as good as they came. The same goes today. Any politician with White House ambitions needs a good line of intelligence.'

'And Galbraith, can he be trusted?'

Turner shrugged. 'As far as I know, he's as clean as a hound's tooth. There can be few politicians with as spotless and productive a record.'

A wry smile twitched Daniel's lips as he toyed with a thought. 'What do you think Galbraith would do if he were suddenly to learn the truth about Mather?'

Turner looked at Daniel with a glint of respect in his eyes. 'You thinking of telling him?'

'Just a wild thought. He seems a straightforward sort of man. What do you think we ought to do? I'm new at this. Guide me.'

Turner's lips pursed. 'For now we stop. Take time out to think. When we do make our move, we really have to know we're doing the right thing. But for sure; with your story to back up the Parker and Sutton films, our chances are better than ever.'

Frustration flickered on Daniel's face. 'There has to be some way we can turn the law on him.'

Turner sympathised. 'What we need is an ear in a high place, someone with weight. Someone with clout enough to get us heard by the justice department. Now I grant you, Galbraith could well be our man. Our problem will be getting by Mather. Head of Security is a filter. Everyone who sees the Senator has to be checked by him first.'

'There has to be a way.'

'Ideally of course,' Turner mused, 'Once we've pinned Mather down we would use him to nail the men who stood behind him. If we just put him away for the killing of JFK we'll have failed; the big fish will have escaped.'

'Do you really think he'll roll over?' Daniel asked. Turner thought not.

'So, we can't win?' Pamela chipped in gloomily. 'We have virtually no chance of hurting Mather, and not the slightest hope of even bruising the men behind him. 'It's useless.'

Elation dissipated quickly, leaving them shivering. Gloom descended with the speed of night.

Daniel was roused from sleep by Turner gently tapping his shoulder. 'What is it?' he answered sleepily.

'Come with me.' Turner whispered. He nodded at Pamela and placed a finger to his lips. 'She's tired. Let her sleep.'

Dan crawled from under the sheet and pulled on his clothes. He followed Turner down into the office and watched in astonishment as Turner lifted a rug and raised a trapdoor beneath it.

'What is this?' Daniel wondered aloud as Turner vanished through the trap. 'Come on,' his voice echoed back.

Dan clambered down a narrow ladder and stepped into the glare from a bare bulb. He blinked in the harsh light, stared around at the hidden room. The walls, like those in the room above, were lined with shelves, and on a desk sat a computer terminal.

'Secrets . . .' Daniel muttered. Turner flashed him a sly grin. 'Watch.'

Stepping up to one of the bookshelves, Turner removed a book and reached into the space between those that remained. A motor gently hummed, and the entire bookshelf started to move to one side along cleverly concealed runners. The space behind the bookshelf was barely wide enough to admit a man, but the two of them squeezed inside.

'What is this?' Daniel repeated the question. Turner groped around in the darkness until he found a lamp switch. The lamp clicked on, and they were left blinking until eyes adjusted.

'This,' Turner said in a quiet voice, 'is where I do my real work.' Stepping up to a filing cabinet, he opened a drawer and took out a bottle and two glasses. 'How about a little snort?'

'Sure. Fine.' Daniel stared around him. This room, in contrast, was small and functional. One tiny desk upon which sat another computer terminal. A substantial looking filing cabinet stood in a corner. The room was small enough to make Daniel feel slightly claustrophobic. Accepting the drink, he remarked: 'This is a bit odd, isn't it? A room within a room within a room.'

Turner took a pair of stacked stools from a corner and separated them. He bade Daniel sit, then sat looking at him, an odd expression on his face. Daniel felt uncomfortable under the scrutiny. He squirmed. 'What's wrong?'

Turner leaned forward slightly. 'What was it like, Dan, to be there on that day, and see what you saw? How did it feel?'

Daniel managed a feeble smile. He had never been comfortable opening up to others, even those he was close to. But he found he did not feel that way with Turner. He *wanted* to talk. After an initial hesitation he began, haltingly, to let the feelings pour out. He recounted the events of that day in detail, surprising himself, for he was recalling things he thought he had forgotten years ago.

When he began describing the events on the knoll he started to feel detached – a witness instead of a participant. He revealed things he had not told Barbara. Feelings and fears – things a man might find hard to admit to a woman. The man in the police uniform, the man with the hard hat and the rifle. The retort as hardhat fired the rifle, and the peculiar trace-odor of gunfire that hung in the air. Then the men running. Hardhat racing past the small boy, sparing him a glance that seemed tinged with . . . with what? Guilt? Shame? Pride? Somewhere between those three. Then Daniel told how he walked onto the top of the knoll and stared down at the scene below. . . .

'I just stood there. I couldn't believe the silence. No, not really silence, just this terrible stillness. There was this sense of numbness all over the Plaza. Everybody shocked to a standstill. I remember, thinking later, that it was odd, because of course the cars in the motorcade were still coming.

The people in the cars were looking around. They must have known something was wrong, how could they think otherwise – there were people cowering on the ground, but they had no real idea. Then I watched, stunned, as dozens of adults ran towards me. It was scary for a child, I can tell you. Then my Pa had his arms around me, and we were walking away from the Plaza. We stopped by the depository to talk to that cop, and the rest you know.'

Turner seemed steeped in thought. His face was drawn and gaunt in the light from the lamp. He stared long into his glass, then looked across the small room at Daniel.

'Something wrong?' Daniel asked him. Turner slowly pulled a face; he was not sure. 'It's just . . . erm . . .' he stumbled. 'I'm not sure how to tell you this. You are pretty sure that the man on the knoll, hardhat you called him, was Barry Mather, right?'

'Sure.'

'And you saw him fire the rifle?'

'I told you I did. What is all this?'

'Do you think he shot JFK?'

'I didn't see the bullet hit, but I saw him fire, I heard the gun-blast, and we watched the Zapruder film earlier and saw Kennedy lurch backwards as the bullet blew open the right side of his head.' He paused. 'Are you going to tell me what you are trying to say?'

'I'm trying to tell you that neither Mather, nor hardhat, nor anyone on the knoll shot John Kennedy. All of the bullets came from the rear.'

Dan peered hard at him, face puzzled and slightly suspicious. 'What, are you kidding?'

'No, I'm not kidding. All the bullets came from the rear.'

'Wait a minute, there's something weird here. I thought this whole set-up, the assassination bureau, the years of research, that damm wall upstairs charting every person and incident involved in the killing of Kennedy, I thought all this was supposed to prove that Oswald did not do the shooting, that there was a conspiracy!'

Turner sighed wearily. 'The answer to that is, that there is no simple answer.'

'Well then what the hell am I doing here?'

Turner held up his hands. 'Look, stay calm will you. I want to explain a few things to you, but I need you to sit there with an open mind and to be prepared to listen. Can you do that?'

When he did reply, Daniel's tone was cold. 'I'll do my best.'

'Okay, thanks for that. Do you know much about high powered rifles?'

Dan replied no, of course he did not. Turner nodded, then went on. 'Well, as you might expect of someone who has spent twenty-five years studying the assassinations, I have done some research. One of the things I have learned is that different types of bullets, fired from different rifles, behave differently. Now, I expect you've heard of the Magic Bullet?'

'Of course. The crazy bullet that the Warren Commission Report says inflicted at least seven wounds on Kennedy and Connally and emerged virtually pristine.'

Turner noodded. 'Very good. What do you think of the theory?'

Daniel almost laughed. 'It's bullshit. No bullet could do all that without being seriously mangled.'

'Okay. Next, the Warren people claimed that Lee Oswald, with his cheap Mannlicher Carcano, fired three shots in around 5.6 seconds. The time-frame based around the Zapruder film and the approximate speed of the Presidential limo, which was known to be moving at eleven miles per hour. Any thoughts on that?'

'Of course. It's impossible. The FBI had three master marksmen try, they all failed. No one could do it.'

Turner was nodding. 'Well, you have absorbed the main prejudices.'

Outrage ballooned onto Daniel's face. 'Just what are you doing?'

'I'll tell you. The basic premise that underpinned the Warren Report was that Oswald owned the rifle found in the depository, and was a communist with pro-Castro leanings. Likewise, on the side of the critics of the Warren report, the so-called conspiracy buffs, their case is underpinned by tales of Oswald being a poor shot, of being an FBI informer, that the rifle was too poor to do the job, and that the shots came too fast to come from a single bolt action rifle. Both sides have weaknesses. What I am about to do is make you aware of them.

'The Mannlicher bullet is perfectly capable of passing through two men and emerging relatively complete. A slight flattening at the base of the bullet is often the only sign that the bullet has been fired. The bullet taken from the stretcher in Parkland hospital was slightly flattened at the base. It may surprise you to know that in 1967 the CBS network commissioned a test to see if the Oswald feat of marksmanship could be equalled or bettered.

They set up a platform on scaffolding, at the same height as the depository window. An electric car, with targets on it to represent Kennedy and Connally, was set to run along a track at eleven miles per hour. Of the dozen or so men chosen to fire the Mannlicher, one of them, Howard Donahue of Maryland, did it in 4.8 seconds, and hit the targets accurately too. So it can be done.'

Daniel interrupted. 'Yeah, but one guy out of a dozen marksmen? Those are pretty long odds. Don't forget that Oswald was a poor shot.'

'Well, Oswald did qualify for marksman status. In his last months in the corps he was lazy about accuracy, and careless about looking after his weapon, but he had initially achieved the score he needed for a marksman rating.

'I have been to Dallas and done what Oswald is supposed to have done. That is, hidden the weapon and made it down to the first floor in less than ninety seconds. So that can be done too.

Daniel snarled. 'Sounds to me like you are saying Oswald *did* do it.'

Turner opened his mouth to speak, then seemed to think better of it. Instead he reached into the breast pocket of his shirt and took out a computer disk. 'Okay, I can see I'm going to have to show you the proof.'

Daniel's temper was fired now. 'What proof? What are you up to?'

'Proof that the killing shot did not come from the knoll. From Mather.' He inserted the disc into the base of the computer and entered a code on the keyboard.

Daniel reached across and grasped Turner's wrist, staying him. 'I saw him fire the rifle.'

Turner grimly returned the stare. 'I don't doubt that. Will you release my arm now please?' From nowhere, Daniel realised, hostility had materialised. Suddenly regretful, he snatched back his hand. He mumbled an apology, adding: 'I'm just a little freaked out.'

'It's okay. I understand.' Turner paused for a moment, then swivelled on his stool. Behind him on the nearest wall a small TV and VCR were balanced upon wall brackets. Producing a cassette from a drawer, Turner slotted the tape into the machine and jabbed at buttons.

'I'd like you to watch this before I show you what is on the computer.'

The TV screen lightened to show a peculiar scene, one Daniel could not quite make out. 'What are those things?' he asked.

Turner settled onto his stool. 'Melons,' he explained. 'Wrapped with duct tape to simulate the texture of a human skull. Four of them are impaled on rods fixed to the ground, and four of them are suspended from wires.'

'Representing what?'

'Human heads. When you see John Kennedy's head explode, what do you think did that to him?'

'A high velocity bullet. I've read it was thought to be frangible – a type of bullet that breaks up on impact to inflict severe damage.'

'Correct. Do you have any idea how an object behaves when struck by a high velocity bullet?'

'Are we talking about a human head?' Daniel asked. When Turner replied that they were, he continued:

'I suppose the . . . head, is thrown away from the area of impact and breaks up.'

Turner leaned forward, and said in a near whisper that cut the air with its intensity. 'Wrong. Watch.' He released the play button. There came the sound of a gunshot, and one of the melons exploded and fell from the rod upon which it was fixed. The view on screen altered, widened. Now it was possible to see a rifle set up on a tripod. It fired, and the nearest melon burst open and fell backwards. Daniel stared, not quite sure what it was he was supposed to be observing.

'You see,' Turner said quietly, 'the rifle, an AR-15, fires a bullet at high velocity, some 3,200 feet per second. It fires a small round, which tumbles and disintegrates explosively upon impact with semi-liquid material. When it strikes it behaves like a soft point or hollow-tipped bullet. A dumdum.'

The rifle fired again, this time striking one of the melons suspended from wire. The entire front side of the melon blew open, sending the melon spinning in a crazy arc, free of the wire, to land with a splatter on the floor. Another shot rang out, and another melon on a rod blew open, falling from its place.

'Still don't see it, do you?' Turner said. Daniel shook his head.

'Let me explain. Imagine that the next melon on a stick is a man's head. The AR-15 fires, the high velocity bullet strikes the head, leaving a small wound of entry. As it passes through the melon, or a man's brain, or any semi-liquid material, the bullet tumbles, breaks up, becomes almost liquified and bursts into dozens of pieces, exiting explosively, leaving massive damage to the skull. You got that?'

'Yes, so?'

Turner sighed. 'The bullet enters the rear of the head. It breaks up and explodes through the front of the skull and the force of the exit pushes the head backwards. Watch.'

He released the pause, and in horror Daniel saw what he meant. The rifle fired at the rear of the melon, the explosion came from the front as the bullet exited in a mass of broken melon flesh, *And the melon flew backwards!!!*

'My God.'

Turner leaned back, triumph on his face. 'Now you've got it. Now you see. Now you have more understanding than many people who have covered this subject for years. If Kennedy had been struck from the front by a high velocity bullet, it would have left a small entry wound on the right side of his head, and a massive exit wound on the left rear of his skull. We know that didn't happen because we saw the Zapruder film. We saw the front right portion of his head burst open. Skull X-rays show that there was a small wound of entry on the back of Kennedy's skull, and a massive exit wound on the frontal right side.'

Daniel stared in awe at Turner. 'But I saw Mather fire . . .'

'And I told you I don't doubt that. But there is no evidence he hit him. He missed.'

Daniel had a fist over his mouth as he took this in. Everything he had believed, everything he had read, had just been overturned. 'You managed to hide a rifle and get down to the first floor of the depository building. So it was Oswald after all?'

Turner smiled. Now he was toying. 'No. I'll put you out of your misery. Let me show you what the computer has in store.' Tapping in a series of digits, he sat back while the VDU buzzed into life. The words, DEALEY MODEL, flashed onto the screen. Daniel sat up with a jolt. Turner started his explanation.

'In here I have a complete computer mock-up of Dealey Plaza. It is a scale model accurate down to the last detail. We have run the Zapruder film through it, and have been able, by sophisticated techniques, to place the motorcade onto the model.'

'Why? To what purpose?'

'To create a true three-dimensional ballistic model. Do you know much about ballistics, Dan?' He did not wait for an answer, but sped on. 'Basically it is the study of moving projectiles. Imagine this. If a man is shot through the head and does not move, it ought to be possible to look back along the line of the wound and trace a path to the origin of the shot. In the case of JFK, if we could halt the film at the instant he was struck in the head, and somehow step into the picture, we could theoretically place a piece of dowelling through his wounds, in through the exit and out through the entry. By taking note of the angle of entry, the slope of Dealey, the angle of JFK's head, we could track the path of the bullet to its source.'

'Nice theory, but not possible.'

'With this baby,' Turner tapped the terminal. 'It is possible. We can revisit the assassination from any angle. We can stand on Dealey Plaza, at any spot we choose, and we can watch the killing. We can also step into JFK's limo at the moment of the shot, and we can look back through his wound and track the shot to its source.'

'You can really do this?'

In response, Turner struck a key. The screen was filled with motion. An animated line-drawing of Dealey Plaza, and the movement of the motorcade. The figures in the car were sketches, moving exactly as they had in the Zapruder film. The President jerked as the bullet struck his head.

'Alright,' Turner said. 'Let's move in. The action rolled back, to the instant Governor Connally was struck. 'Now here, there is a moment, a fraction of a second, when both Governor Connally and John Kennedy are lined up in a position that allows for the magic bullet theory to work. See here . . . the bullet strikes Kennedy in the back and exits through his throat. It then hits Connally in the back, exits through his chest, shatters his right wrist and ends up in his left thigh. See, the position of Connally's body – his right hand is holding his stetson in front of his chest, perfectly placed for the bullet to inflict the wounds.

'Now . . .' He tapped in a command. 'We ask the computer for a trajectory.'

The picture remained still, then a line appeared, cutting across the picture, lancing the two figures. 'We now follow the line . . . and we arrive at the sixth floor of the depository building, approximately the sixth floor corner window. Now move ahead a little, to the headshot, and again ask for a trajectory . . . and . . . we arrive at the County Records building.

'Yes. A different building, a third sniper with a high powered rifle.'

Daniel shook his head. His expression showed he was not convinced. He blew out his cheeks. 'I . . . I don't know.'

'Now perhaps you can understand why I have refrained from exploding this theory in public; you are a recent convert to this cause, you ought to be fairly receptive to new ideas. The people who have spent three decades delving into this are steeped in rigid theories. They will take a lot of convincing. I need an air-tight case before I let this one out.' He tapped the keyboard and the graphics shifted rapidly, changing the view to an aerial shot.

'Okay,' he began again. 'Let's see if I can persuade you. One of the other benefits of a three dimension computer model is that I can try the what-if scenario. We know where Kennedy was positioned, both in the limo and in relation to Dealey Plaza, when the head shot hit. I can ask the computer to give me a view of what events would look like if the depository sniper *had* fired that shot. Now, bear in mind that the depository window is behind JFK, and to his right. See the track of the bullet? Explain what you see.'

Daniel peered hard at the screen, straining to pick out detail. 'Is it possible to zoom in on the limo so I can see the strike closer up?'

Turner did as bid, and the view changed. Now it was possible to see the line of the bullet as it would have passed, from right to left, through the head of John Kennedy. 'Daniel, where does the bullet go?'

Daniel inhaled. He saw the flaw in his thinking. 'The depository is behind JFK and to his right. The bullet travels from right to left, entering the rear of his head and exiting above his left eye. I see what you mean.'

Turner was pleased, and it showed. 'The bullet is also travelling downwards at an angle of about eighteen degrees, if you take into account the slope of Elm Street. Travelling downwards, it would have struck Mrs Connally, or at the very least landed in the limousine.

Now forget the hypothetical, if you watch the Zapruder film and study the head X-rays you will see that the bullet, to exit the right side of JFK's head, had to travel from left to right. To exit the upper right frontal side of JFK's head, the bullet had to move along an almost horizontal trajectory, which indicates that it was coming in from a position quite low. If it had been fired from higher up, it again would have come down at a more extreme angle.'

'And this shot came from the other building?'

'The County Records building. Or, more approximately, the ledge between it and the next building. The County Jail.' He paused to sip from his glass. 'Do you remember what I said earlier, about the way different bullets behave?' Daniel replied that he did.

'Well, one thing the Warren people never did ask was why the bullets supposedly fired from the same Mannlicher rifle behaved so differently. Why one moment the magic bullet, the type that would be fired by the Mannlicher, could pass through Kennedy and Connally and emerge relatively undamaged, while the head shot broke up into over forty tiny fragments. There are some arguments that the bone of the skull caused the heavy Mannlicher bullet to break up, but I have questioned over thirty pathologists, experts in gunshot wounds, and I have been unable to find a single one who would tell me that a heavy full-jacketed bullet like that would fragment. The most common answer to my question was that the jacket would be pared back by the hard edge of the wound. The bullet would have broken up into three or four largish pieces. Not over forty tiny, exploded fragments. Then there is the question of wound size. The entry wound in the back of JFK's skull measured 6 millimetres. The Mannlicher bullet was 6.5 millimetres wide. A bullet generally leaves a hole a fraction larger than itself, but we are asked to believe that the 6.5 millimetre bullet from Oswald's rifle could pass through a hole smaller than its own diameter. The smaller 5.6 millimetre AR-15 bullet leaves a 6 millimetre hole.

'Lastly, I have this.' From a pocket he drew a bullet. He passed it to Daniel. 'A friend of mine found this in nineteen sixty four. He was a private investigator who thought something was not right. He went to Dallas to do some work of his own. He ran a metal detector over the grassy central area in Dealey Plaza and found this, a slug from an AR-15 high powered rifle, buried in the earth directly opposite the grassy knoll. It had rained in Dallas the day of the assassination. The ground was soft. The bullet just plunged right in.' He hesitated. 'This, Daniel, is the bullet you saw Barry Mather fire.'

Dan swallowed dryly. Tears burned the corners of his eyes as a wave of mixed emotions broke over him. 'Dave, I really don't know what to say.'

Turner felt a lump form in his throat. He had shared a secret, *his* secret, and the effect was a purging.

* 18 *

The following day they discussed their next moves, deciding finally that they must try to enlist the aid of the Senator. Daniel promised to speak to Barbara.

Turner offered a warning. 'Don't forget she's involved with Mather. She will not help us destroy him.'

'Then I won't tell her the full story. Just enough to get us through. Don't worry . . .' he said to their dubious faces. 'I'm sure she'll want to help.'

He called her later that day. She seemed genuinely pleased to hear from him, and was surprised to learn that he was so close to New York. At length he broached the difficult subject. 'I've decided I want to speak to someone about what I saw in Dallas,' he said. 'It's been on my mind ever since we spoke.'

'I'm glad to hear it,' she said. 'What can I do?'

'I've been watching Galbraith. After what you said about him, I've been thinking he might be the man to approach.'

Immediately she became guarded. 'Dan, he has an awful lot on his plate right now . . .'

'I understand that, Barbara. But he could be just the man we need to bring this into the open. You said yourself he has a strong social conscience. He's interested in justice, and he has enough clout to make everyone sit up and listen.'

'Dan . . .' She remonstrated patiently. 'I'm sure that at any other time he'd leap at the opportunity. But right now. . . . He has a primary on the horizon.'

He tried the weapon he had been holding back. 'You're his public relations guru, Barbara. Can't you make him see what a boost this could give him in the run-up to the election? Eighty five percent of Americans do not believe the conclusions of the Warren report. If he were to come out on this issue, and not hedge like every other politician in the country, the voters would see that he really does give a damm. He'd buy my vote at least.'

There was a pause. He could sense her trying to formulate a way to say no without provoking a bitter argument. 'Daniel, it's more complicated than that. More complicated than you know. Politics, and getting into power, is about alliances, checks and balances. Carrying a torch for a lone campaign is still too off the wall for a man who wants to be President. He has to think taxation, budget deficit, the wider picture.'

'Barbara give me a break. Give him a chance to put his money where his mouth is. Please. This is really important to me. Just put the idea to him. If he says no, then I'll accept what you say, but let him decide.'

She sighed; it was easier to agree. 'What do you want me to say?'

He wanted to yell in triumph, but he took a breath and steadied himself. 'Just have a quiet word. Find out if he's willing to see me alone. It has to be alone. No one else must know about this yet. No one.'

'I'll speak to Barry —' she began. He caught his tongue on the point of screaming. 'No, please, I've had a hard enough time getting you to agree. If I have to give a repeat performance for every staff member between you and the Senator, I'll never get through.'

'But absolutely everything goes through Barry. Surely you can understand that?'

'Please,' he insisted. 'Trust me on this.'

After a further interval for thought, she reluctantly agreed to try.

Hitching up her skirt, Barbara sank onto the bed beside Barry Mather. She nudged him playfully with her elbow, and followed this by nuzzling against his ear. 'I love you.'

He growled, that affectionate deep rumbling of his, and turned his head to meet her kiss. 'Don't change the subject. Where do you want to eat?'

She glanced at the bedside clock. 'Barry it's late.'

He chuckled. 'So we'll eat breakfast out. We have time to get down to the shore. Champagne breakfast on the terrace of a private and very select hotel I know.'

She straightened up to look at him. 'You are not only incorrigible, you are incredible. You were up at five in the morning, put in a fourteen hour day, ate a hearty dinner, made love twice, and here you are at 2 a.m. as wide awake as I've ever seen you, raring to go through it all again.'

He gave her a broad smile. 'Life is for living, young lady, and I'm not the kid I used to be. A minute wasted is a minute lost, and I don't intend to lose a single second when I could be with you.'

She kissed him again. 'Well, as you're in such a generous mood, I have a favor to ask.'

'Oh?' Briefly there was on his face a measure of calculation. It was the only expression of his she did not like. It gave her the willies, she admitted privately, but pressed on, asking her favor and awaiting his response.

Silence. He lay back on the pillows, his hands behind his head, his jaw working slowly as he ruminated. Nervously Barbara lit a cigarette. She studied him, reminding herself how fortunate she had been this time in her choice of partner. Barry was the strongest, most self-secure man she had ever met, and though he cared deeply for her she knew he would not pine if she left him. In that, he was different from every other man she had ever known, and she wondered if that was the lure that attracted her to him. The other men in her life had all been variations of the same theme; moths to her flame. Like Daniel, pretending to be in control when in fact frailty was never far beneath the surface. It was always her that did the dumping, the men being the ones to cry and plead for a second chance. But with Barry, she was sure, that would not be the case. It wasn't that he didn't give a damm, he just knew life was too short to spend time crying over things he could not have. He did not need anybody. Existing in his shadow had made her aware just how close to the edge she had been living since moving into New York. It was an effort to keep up with the fast paced crowd she worked and socialised with, but Barry was a help, he was a rock, there for her to cling to when the current threatened to suck her in. A shadow she could hide in when things got hard to bear. So very, very different.

She compared him with Daniel, so beset with sexual hang-ups and guilt over just about everything in his life.

When at last he turned to her his smile was not like any other she had seen on his face. His lips were flexed as wide as ever, but his expression was cold, and she realised it was his eyes that were not smiling. They bored coldly into her, and she suddenly felt uneasy about what she had done.

'Leave it with me,' he commanded with finality. Then the frigidity was banished and he was back with her, adoration beaming from him. 'What about that champagne breakfast?'

She hugged him tightly, and felt safe in his shadow. 'Oh yes, Barry. Yes, yes, yes!'

* 19 *

The limousine cruised toward Daniel at a graceful speed and braked smoothly. Sleek and black, it had the look of a glossy predator, dark tinted windows lending it a sinister appearance. The rear door kicked slightly as an electronic lock sprang, and he was invited to enter. The interior was dimly lit, and it took a moment for his eyes to adjust.

A glass partition separated him from the driver, but he could see the man's outline. The experience might have been unnerving had the driver not turned, presenting a friendly smile.

'Sit back and enjoy the ride, Mr Baker. It'll take about a half hour to get to the Senator's residence.'

Daniel thanked him, feeling himself start to relax. 'Help yourself to a drink,' the driver continued. 'There's always an excellent scotch in the bar just in front of you.'

Daniel was happy to partake. The small bar, illuminated upon opening, contained a small but selective stock of superior quality liquor. There was ice in a frosted container, and he helped himself to a cube. Glass in hand, he settled back once more, visibly unwinding as the scotch banished his anxieties.

At length he caught a glimpse of heavy iron gates swinging open. Then the limo was streaking smoothly along a floodlit avenue neatly corridored with trees. He glimpsed a uniformed guard patrolling with a dog.

The limo reached the end of the avenue and pursued a gentle arc, gliding smoothly to a halt before a large, colonial style house. The building was bathed white in the bleaching, upward glare from floodlights positioned discreetly amongst the landscaped gardens.

Immediately upon stepping out he was surrounded by a group of stern faced men in sober suits. No common or garden heavies these, their movements were economical, and their gazes moved constantly in a state of preparedness. He was escorted into a reception hall he would have described as opulent, complete with bejewelled chandelier suspended from a high domed ceiling, and a vast sweeping staircase.

He loosed a low whistle. 'The man certainly knows how to live,' he joked, but no one laughed.

A ramrod-erect butler, with impeccable English manners and a disdainful way of peering along his nose, took charge of Daniel, leading him away from the group and towards the study.

A set of huge, oak panelled doors closed behind him and he was facing the great man himself. Senator Cyrus Galbraith, a little shorter than imagined, and thinner, but as vital in life as his television image. His grip when they shook hands was firm, but on becoming aware of Daniel's bruised features his face registered alarm. 'What happened?'

Daniel smiled, he gave a small shrug. 'Unrelated incident.' His natural suspicion was ignited momentarily; was it his imagination, or did Galbraith look relieved?

A drink was offered, and accepted, and both men retired to chairs by the fireside. The flames had been allowed to diminish, but the heat from the glowing coals had a lulling effect.

'Very cosy.' Daniel remarked.

The Senator nodded. 'The fire is not really necessary this time of year, but when the nights close in it can be a comfort.'

While the Senator was settling into his chair, Daniel subjected him to a brief scrutiny. There was about him some enigmatic force that charged the atmosphere. At present that force was directed towards relaxation, but Daniel could imagine it being utilised to awesome effect in a serious confrontation. The Senator would be a hard man to stare down.

Galbraith rolled his brandy glass slowly between cupped palms. He smiled kindly, and that simple action seemed to drain away all of Daniel's anxieties. The effect was almost hypnotic. This was a man of unimpeachable integrity. A man he could trust. He cleared his throat. 'I'd like to thank you for agreeing to meet with me, sir. I know you must be busy.'

'You are most welcome. Miss Rush hinted that the matter you wish to discuss is of national importance. I have learned to respect her judgement, and so feel duty bound to listen.'

'I hope you continue to feel that way, sir. Because I believe both our lives may be in danger.'

Another reassuring smile. 'That, as they say, comes with the territory.'

Daniel attempted a smile. 'I know that, sir. It's hard to know where exactly to start. Sometimes lately I've wondered if the whole world is going crazy. All I know is that I can't stop the madness, and that is why I've come to you. If anyone in this country can do anything, you can.'

Galbraith smiled urbanely. 'I'm flattered to hear you think so.' He replied, and Daniel was reminded of Barbara's words. What was it she had called him? A man without vanity. A man who put others first.

'I really don't know where to start.'

'You mentioned madness.' Galbraith prompted him. 'Why not start at the beginning. What madness?'

Faced with the moment, Daniel felt haggard. He wanted to drink – God, he wanted to drink! But he had to make a start, before fear seized his tongue. He swallowed, and his throat hurt from the dry movement.

'The madness that began the day John F. Kennedy died.'

The telling was done. Galbraith had listened politely, even at moments when he wanted to break in with a question. Now, at the conclusion, and nursing his second cognac, he looked uncomfortable. Then came the bombshell. The remark that almost floored Daniel.

'An interesting tale, Mr Baker, but tell me: what is it you expect from me?'

Daniel could not believe his ears. He wanted to scream: '*You're the big shot, you tell me!*' but he held his tongue, instead saying calmly: 'I was hoping that you would help me close the case once and for all. What I've told you is the complete truth. You have influence. People will listen to you. The case could be reopened.'

Galbraith shook his head. 'I'm rather surprised at your naiveté Mr Baker. Persuading the Justice Department to reopen the investigation after all these years, especially in light of the lack lustre and incomplete work done by the Select Committee on Assassinations in 1978, would take nothing short of a Presidential initiative, and as you know, I'm not in the White House yet.'

'But people will listen to you . . .'

'Let me ask *you* a question. I hope you will forgive my directness, but I have to know; what is in all this for you?' There was an odd twinkle in the Senator's eyes; amusement?

'I should have thought that was obvious,' came the blurted reply. 'I want to be safe. I want to sleep nights.'

'Nothing more?' The keen gaze darted with laser precision. 'No book deal, perhaps?' The gaze settled upon Daniel and bored into him. He quailed under the effect.

'I certainly would not welcome commercial exploitation of any efforts I may make,' declared the Senator.

When Daniel offered no defense, Galbraith rose to his feet and stood erect, his hands linked behind his back.

'You ask me to believe that Barry Mather, a man in my employ for over twenty-five years, a man whom I trust implicitly, and to whom I betrust my personal safety every day, is or was, a hired killer? That is the morsel that sticks in my craw. Quite frankly, I'm tempted to have you tossed out of here, but, because I believe in always knowing the true facts myself, I will take your accusations at face value. I shall have a thorough investigation conducted.'

'And if it comes up the way I said?'

Galbraith swallowed his ire. 'If that is found to be the case, you have my word that every single resource I can bring to bear will be with you. And I guarantee a result.'

Daniel heaved a sigh of relief. 'That's good enough for me.' He stood. 'Shall I wait to hear from you?'

'Please.' Galbraith replied. He held out his hand. His grip was warm and dry. 'Thank you for coming to see me, Mr Baker. I'm a man who usually relies on his instincts, and I can tell you I have a good feeling about this. The driver will be waiting. I wish you a good night.'

The limo left him at the airport in time for a late flight to Greensboro. The trip back to the house passing in a timeless haze. Turner and Pam greeted him at the terminal, and, swollen with elation, he told them his news. His enthusiasm was infectious, and Turner let out a screech of joy: 'I told you he'd help! I told you!'

Days passed in a blur of impatience. Hours spent locked in debate and conjecture. Each time the telephone rang there was a hushed silence, then a scrambling for the instrument in haste to hear the good news. But none came. Within a week, Daniel and Turner had talked each other dry, and cabin fever set in. Tempers became frayed. Tiny disagreements became debating articles of monumental proportions which were picked over for hours, laid to rest on a handshake and then disinterred at the next outbreak of hostilities.

On the ninth day, Daniel announced he could take no more. Turner urged patience; the investigations, the resistance from the government, had lasted thirty years, things were bound to move slowly. Unpersuaded, Daniel went out to the telephone. The others followed.

Galbraith was not available. Home, but not available. Daniel persisted to the point of annoyance, and when the Senator's personal assistant could take no more she left him on hold. He waited, fuming, muttering determined asides to Turner who anxiously transferred his weight from one foot to the other.

The line clicked open, and an irritable, husky voice spoke to Daniel. 'Mr Baker, the Senator sends his most sincere apologies, but he cannot speak to you at the moment.'

Daniel forced tolerance into his tone. 'I understand that he is a busy man, but I need an answer. Surely he can let me have a yes or no. His people have had time to produce some kind of a result.'

He heard a sharp intake of breath at the other end of the line. 'Well, I guess I could give you that. I happen to know the results of the rapid, but fairly stringent appraisal that has been carried out.'

Daniel's mouth was dry. He swallowed. 'Well?'

'I'm afraid it is N. G., Mr Baker. No go. Nothing turned up to alter the original conclusions, certainly nothing spectacular enough to warrant any prolonged focus.

'The Senator offers you his apologies, but feels sure you will understand he did his best, given the limited resources at his disposal. He hopes that another occasion might present itself, perhaps after the election, and promises then to review the evidence once more.'

Daniel's jaw dropped. His mind reeled with disbelief. 'That's crap . . .' he muttered, 'I don't believe it.' At his side, Turner's anxious state worsened.

'I'm afraid there are insufficient grounds for further investigation.'

'I don't believe you.'

'I assure you, it is true.'

The voice sounded smug. Daniel could not be sure but, he felt the owner of it was laughing at him. 'Let me hear it from him,' he snapped. He felt himself losing control. The waiting had been hard, the pressure telling. He was faintly surprised at his own reaction, the tumbling into anger, but found himself powerless to alter it. 'Let me speak to him, you son of a bitch.'

The other man mentally counted to ten. 'Temper.' Again that gloating tone.

'Don't preach to me . . . !'

'WISE UP, BAKER!' the man interrupted. 'You're not that important. Don't step too far outa line!'

'Who the hell is this? What's your name?'

The gloating voice had been waiting. The reply came in a tone that was sickly sweet. 'My name is Barry Mather. I head the Senator's security – you turkey!'

Mind in a whirl, body trembling, Daniel let the receiver fall. 'Oh my God . . .' he whispered.

The day ahead was stormy. Prophetically, dark clouds jostled for position overhead, and when Daniel and Turner walked out in a mood of deep gloom to fetch beer and wine with which to drown their sorrows, the bottom fell out of the sky and they were deluged. They ran laughing, arms full, back to the house.

'Is it raining?' Pam asked innocently as they burst in. The two men collapsed into a paroxysm of hysterical hooting.

Drinking, heads becoming heavy, their thoughts fogged with dashed hopes, and tongues thickening until words became hard to form. But nothing productive emerged, only an outpouring of bitterness, recrimination, and self pity in abundance.

They drank until the last drop was drained, then they sat, slumped and mumbling incoherently about eternal friendship until dawn began to caress away the night sky. Turner slept half out of his chair. Daniel snored on the rug, Pamela supine across his lap.

They slept virtually all of the following day. Once awake, and despite dull heads, the talk soon centred on Mather and Galbraith. As Turner remarked; it was time to plan.

Numerous courses of action were debated. Going to the newspapers, to the television stations, picketing the White House. But there was nothing they could agree on, nothing seemed the correct course. The wind had been taken out of their sails, and it would take enormous effort to re-install the drive.

Afternoon drained away and it was night again, and they could barely swallow the food Pamela, looking feverish from the effort of cooking, had managed to rustle up.

As night deepened, they decided to cut their losses for the day and retire to bed. Turner's security arrangements were elaborate. After a lengthy program of turning on and testing sensors, locking doors and setting alarms, they slept. Daniel and Pamela bedded down on the inflatable mattress in one of the bare upstairs rooms.

They were deeply asleep when Turner crept into the room and shook Daniel by the shoulder.

'It's me,' he hissed. Daniel worked life into a numbed arm. 'What is it?'

'I have an idea,' whispered Turner. 'Come on, coffee's ready.'

Daniel slid from under the covers and shivered in the chill. Turner nodded towards Pamela's sleeping form. 'Shall we wake her?'

'No, let her sleep,' Daniel muttered, then grinned. They were behaving like a pair of naughty schoolboys, trying not to be caught by teacher. He followed Turner down to the cellar.

'I hope this is good,' Dan murmured as he was handed a mug of steaming coffee. Turner settled on the seat opposite. An enthusiastic gleam lit up his face. 'So good I couldn't sleep. I want to run a few ideas past you. I've been thinking about what we need, and about who has what we need.'

'I don't understand.'

'Add it up; we want to nail Mather. Now, even with your evidence, and the films, and even if we can sweat him, we still might fail. He's a pro, and after all these years the odds are on his side.' He got up from his seat and started to pace. 'Really we want to hurt the people beyond Mather. No matter how dangerous he was and is, he has only ever been a pawn. Tell me, have you ever heard the term, The Octad?'

'Can't say I have.'

'I want you to hear something . . .' He fished in a desk drawer.

'It's an interview we taped, with a professional killer. A man who claimed to know who was behind the assassinations. We were trying to negotiate a safe passage for him when he vanished.'

He produced a tape cassette and slotted it into a player on the desk. He thumbed the play button. The tiny speaker squawked into life.

'*. . . the guy who shot Wallace was a kook, but the man who had the Kennedys taken care of, and King, he musta got a secret medal. I've fired the kind of rifle Oswald is supposed to have used. You can't rapid fire it like he's supposed to have done. No, what you have is pretty much what Ike, President Eisenhower, focused on in his farewell address to the nation; the military-industrial complex. A group of individuals tied together, military, industrial, intelligence, who actually run most of the country for their own benefit. They are not elected. The elected politicians are figureheads for those behind the* *scenes who hold more power, day to day, than the President.'*

'You mean the President is powerless?' The questioner sounded sceptical.

'Not exactly powerless. He makes decisions based on information presented to him. But they don't have to tell him everything. There are all kinds of power. They control the sources of information – just like they did with the Warren Commission. America is effectively controlled by these individuals. Many major policy strategies originate from them.'

The interviewer cut in. 'But who are they?'

'They are high ranking military men, bred in a climate where the machinery of defense, that huge, money-consuming beast, needs more each year. They are mandarins in intelligence, who run secret wars and make secret pacts the way they always have. They are media barons, with power over what we see, hear and read.

'You have to wonder at the gullibility of the public. How long will it take before they wake up to what's happening? It's a matter of record the CIA has lied to Presidents, all the way down from the Bay of Pigs to the Pentagon Papers.'

Turner cut short the tape. Daniel looked at him, unconvinced. 'That man may have his own reasons for saying all of that. How can you know if he's telling the truth?'

Turner locked the tape back in the drawer. 'That recording was made in the early 'seventies. It was he brought our attention to the security guard on the film I showed you when you came here. He *was* the security guard. He killed Bobby Kennedy. Once he realised the organisation that hired him was the one that killed JFK, he decided to go to ground. He told us that most of the men involved in Dallas were eliminated the same day to protect those higher up the ladder. He wanted to live. As things turned out, he vanished before we could help him. No trace.'

Daniel slowly nodded his head. The gravity of Turner's words seeped in. 'What was his name?'

Turner shook his head. 'You have enough worries without that burden. All that matters is that this group of eight men, this Octad, exists today as it did in the 'forties, 'fifties and 'sixties. There are people involved in TAB who have researched it, and everything they have learned bears out what that man said on the tape.'

'So what's your point?'

Turner paused to refill his cup. 'Two points really. One, given the stranglehold on intelligence in this country held by the FBI, and the CIA with its Mafia links, would it really be possible, or even feasible, for any group to assassinate the President of the United States, without the Octad knowing something about it? I don't think so.'

'Maybe they were just good at keeping secrets.'

Turner treated Daniel to a patronising smirk. 'You know that's not the case, Dan. You've read the books. A lot of people seemed to know in advance; the waitress lying in hospital, pleading with the doctors to warn somebody. The mobsters, the small time criminals, the memos flashing between police departments and the FBI. The teletype that was distributed to every FBI office on the 17th of November, warning that an attempt was to be made on JFK's life in Dallas.

'Remember the police informer who taped a conversation with John Rossi, the hoodlum, a few days before the assassination? Rossi described the upcoming events, including the fact that someone would be blamed quickly.'

Daniel conceded the point, but added: 'I still don't know where this is leading.'

'Okay, I'll lead you to it. Was there ever a group of any kind that didn't have one member who thought he wasn't getting his share of the limelight, or the responsibility, or the money? Or who thought he wasn't given credit for the work he'd put in? Again, I don't know of any. A team can be balanced for a while, but it has been my experience that eventually the human factor kicks in, through jealousy, perhaps, and the resulting imbalance undermines the team.'

He drained his cup. The coffee had awakened him. As he spoke he gesticulated with his hands, working himself up to an enthusiastic peak. 'I believe the answer may lie in a power struggle at Vincent Industries.'

Daniel's interest was immediately lifted. 'Galbraith's company?'

Turner nodded. 'Galbraith's company. The Octad started as some kind of social group. A gladhanding operation dedicated to oiling the wheels between members. One or two of them were charitably motivated, committed to building hospital wings, that kind of thing. In the earliest days, up to the mid-fifties, they raised money for veterans of the Korean war. But the potential for power brokering was always there.

Nathaniel Vincent was one of the original group, but he was a bully. He'd built up his steel business by bulldozing over those who got in his way. More than anyone, he was responsible for the way the group developed. He was a manipulative animal, and he used the others for his own ends. As the membership of the group fluctuated he would introduce people he thought he could use.'

'Was Galbraith in the group?'

'Not then. Not until much later. In the early sixties a number of crises struck the group. On the industrial front, labor troubles brought Vincent Steel to its knees. The military members of the group were being squeezed. President Eisenhower saw the danger in a rampant military, intelligence and industrial force and warned against it in his final address before handing over to JFK. And on the intelligence front, the CIA had been waging private wars in South America, and the Caribbean. The agency was running a full scale unauthorised operation against Cuba. Over three thousand contract agents were employed, training camps were set up, and over fifty businesses set up to front operations. A force of Cuban exiles was trained, and a series of night attacks on the island took place.

After the Bay of Pigs, when Kennedy was forced to publicly take responsibility for the mess, he threatened to smash the CIA, and in 'sixty-three he signed a document that placed responsibility for covert operations in the hands of the army. This placed JFK in an adversarial position to the forces he was Commander-in-Chief of.

'Vincent blamed Kennedy's administration for many of his problems. His stock suffered. He was teetering towards Chapter Eleven bankruptcy protection when Galbraith hove into view. He was representing a private Lebanese bank, and he had the cash to bail Vincent out, on the condition the old man stepped aside. Galbraith became Chief Executive, and later ousted Vincent from the board, literally snatching the company from under the old man. Vincent demanded help from the Octad, but he was vulnerable, and the group took the opportunity to ditch him.'

'And you think that if the Octad did know something, Vincent might also know, and be inclined to tell us?' Daniel's tone betrayed his feelings. He was disappointed. All he saw was another dead-end.

'He retired bitter. Forced to watch from the sidelines as Galbraith took the company to new heights; in a single decade it expanded one hundredfold.'

'The tie up with Galbraith, just coincidence, you think? Do you still believe he's clean?'

Turner was adamant. 'Absolutely. I know nothing to the man's detriment.'

Dan was feeling in urgent need of a drink. He absently wiped his mouth with the back of his hand. 'You think Vincent would actually help us?'

'Yes,' Turner replied as confidently as he could. 'He's a bully. A natural spoiler. If he did know about the plot, and if his grudge against Galbraith is big enough to make him want to tell us, then I think he might.'

'Isn't that a little slim?'

Turner smiled lamely. 'Very, but what other route can we follow? What we have now, no matter how convincing it seems to us, will not break the case.'

Daniel rubbed at his eyes. He was tired. 'So first thing tomorrow we set out to find the old man – if he's still alive.'

Turner held up a hand. Two fingers were crossed. 'If he's still alive.' He started to pack up for the night.

Daniel strolled across to the wall and stared at Turner's map, his family tree of the assassination. He gazed at the names and the neatly inscribed footnotes. 'Here's something I always wondered about. The tramps they took off the freight train in Dallas.'

'Hmmm.' Turner opened a filing cabinet, withdrew a file and joined Daniel at the wall. 'I know what you mean.' He opened the file and extracted a half dozen six-by-eight black and white photographs. 'Take a look at these. Here we have pictures of three men taken from a train only yards away from the grassy knoll, only minutes after the assassination. They were taken to the police station and released. No record of their names or what they said was ever kept. This is what is so frustrating and unbelievable about the entire thing, the succession of coincidences and the constant incompetence of the police, all of which went unheeded by the Warren Commission. If I shot you dead in the street, the police would want all your details, all mine, they would take statements from witnesses and neighbors. They would investigate fully, and you are not as important as the President of the United States.'

Daniel was nodding. 'But wouldn't you think that someone, somewhere, could put names to these faces.'

Turner agreed. 'You'd think. There have been theories of course. My choice for this one here . . .' He pulled out a second black and white print and held it side by side with the picture of the three hoboes. 'Would be this man, Emilio Delvecchio.

Daniel was awake again, staring at the photograph. 'Who is he?'

'He is of Cuban extraction, one of the diehards who masterminded the Bay of Pigs invasion. He took place in the raid on the Stermstein armaments plant in Louisiana, where all kinds of weapons, from small sidearms to heavy artillery, were stolen in a daring midnight raid. The weapons were carried away in a convoy of trucks. It's been alleged that some of the stolen cache was stored at the address at Camp Street, New Orleans, where Lee Oswald was seen in Guy Bannister's office. When the Bay of Pigs invasion failed, Delvecchio was in a boat off the coast, watching. He was one of the more forceful critics of John Kennedy. It was he published the letter in a propaganda paper about a Texan being put into the White House within weeks, about burying Kennedy and retaking Cuba.' He held out the prints for Daniel to study. 'What do you think?'

Dan frowned. 'They do look alike.'

'I had some work done on these,' Turner continued. 'I ran a computer program to compare physical characteristics between the two men in the pictures. The hobo picture was taken in 'sixty-three, the picture of Delvecchio in 'sixty-five. The result of the computer analysis was a better than eighty percent chance that they are the same man.'

'This may be a stupid question, but, has anybody ever thought to ask him where he was on November 22nd?'

'Oh yes. That question has been put to him many times. He claims he was in Washington that day. He has told three or four stories about his whereabouts, but has never been able to produce a single witness to corroborate his story.'

Daniel asked if Delvecchio was still alive. Turner replied that he was, 'To the best of my knowledge. He must be pretty old now. He was in his early forties then.'

'You know I sometimes wonder about the size of all this. When I think about all the influence and manpower it must have taken to cover up everything, I have to ask myself; could a secret that big really be kept? Surely someone would talk.'

'Well, by definition, if a conspiracy or a secret that big was kept, we wouldn't know about it because it would still be secret. It is only because people made mistakes, or others in the wrong place at the right time saw things and reported them, that we know anything at all. But one thing we do know is that each time someone leaks information, or an investigator gets too close, witnesses vanish, or die. In the late 'sixties, when the

Garrison prosecution of Clay Shaw locked onto David Ferrie, the conspirators were faced with exposure. Ferrie was a former pilot, fired from his job with a major airline for his involvement in an alleged homosexual incident. He was famed for his ability to fly into or out of any field, he had run guns and trained Cuban exiles in the run up to the Bay of Pigs. He was placed in Guy Bannister's office by a couple of Bannister's employees. He was placed in the town of Clinton with Shaw and Lee Oswald, by a cop, no less, and one hour after the assassination he left Dallas for Houston with two young friends. They went to an ice rink in Houston. The two young friends later said that Ferrie did not skate. He spent the entire time on the payphone. Ferrie was good at keeping secrets unless he had been drinking. To numerous people between '63 and '68 he confessed while drunk to having knowledge of the assassination. He was supposed to rendezvous in Houston with one of the gunmen, he said, a man named Raoul. Ferrie was then supposed to fly Raoul to Canada in a twin engined aircraft. But Raoul did not show, and Ferrie felt stranded out there.

'Ferrie was Garrison's best lead, but he turned up dead. Natural causes, the coroners reported, though an empty medication bottle was found in his apartment. The medication was of a type used for a low thyroid condition – it speeds up the metabolism. But if taken in great quantity, say perhaps by the bottle full, it can kill, and is impossible to detect in the course of a normal autopsy.

'Ferrie's Cuban paymaster was found dead in Miami, two days after Ferrie's own death. He had been hacked to death with a machete.' Turner paused. 'You see Dan, even three years after the assassination, whoever was behind the plot felt threatened enough to want to silence anyone thought capable of being dangerous. They took measures. They had people out there, taking care of business.

'There are other examples; Marie Soper, a waitress who told doctors that Kennedy was going to die in Dallas. Rose Cheramie did the same. Johnny Rossi, who was a made guy, and incidentally the right hand man of mob boss Giancarlo Giometri, was recorded on tape talking about the imminent assassination. He vanished just before the 22nd November. In January '64 his body was found crammed into an oildrum floating in the bay. He had been garrotted, and his legs cut off.' Turner was pacing the room now as once more the juices started to flow. 'Four journalists met in a motel in Miami in May '64. Three of them had been working the JFK story and promised the fourth man a story that would quote: *crack Washington wide open.* Three days later those three journalists were dead.'

'Look at Jack Ruby, pleading to be taken from Dallas to Washington where he said he could talk freely. Time and time again people who have claimed some special knowledge have died, and that has always been the problem.' He paused, to look at Daniel. 'You know, my friend, we have chosen a dangerous hobby.'

The following morning, while Pam prepared breakfast, Turner made telephone calls. When he finally joined them at the table he gave a fatalistic shrug.' They'll let me know. Probably later today.'

Pamela bounced a glance of each of them. 'Now will you tell me what you two are cooking up?'

Daniel explained the plan to locate and contact Nathaniel Vincent. She looked doubtful. 'Are you sure about this? Sometimes ideas which sound brilliant in the middle of the night don't look so bright in the daytime. What could possibly persuade Vincent to want to help us?'

Turner answered. 'Revenge, Pam. He was a man known for harbouring grudges. He never let a slight go forgotten. I think if we put our case well, he'll see his chance.'

During the afternoon, as had become habit, they chatted about the assassination, and some of the peripheral characters who reappeared time and time again at crucial moments in American political history. 'What astonished me,' Pam was saying, 'was how the same names kept cropping up. It is quite maddening trying to work out exactly how they all tie in, if they do.'

Turner smiled indulgently. 'I know what you mean. What names do you have?'

'Well there are all these social circles that overlap. Showbusiness personalities who were friendly with the Kennedy family and also friendly with Mafia figures, who in turn were tied up with the CIA. A couple of actresses claiming affairs with the President. Here is a woman who had an affair with JFK, while at the same time having an affair with a Mafia boss. Then there are showbusiness figures who mixed with the mob; Max Valentino, the jazz singer. And Todd Fletcher, the English actor who married

Hollywood actress Julie Starr. She had been the lover of the underworld Tsar, Giancarlo Giometri, and reputedly JFK himself.'

Turner chipped in: 'Add to those some of the names from the CIA's Cuban operations who surfaced around Dallas at the time of the JFK assassination, and again when Bobby Kennedy and Martin Luther King were killed. A number of these same people surfaced during a bugging scandal in the 'seventies that led to prison for some of them, and the resignation of a number of eminent politicians.' He ruefully shook his head. 'The whole affair is a snakepit.'

The telephone rang, and Turner excused himself and left the room. He returned with an optimistic smile in place. He gave a thumbs up.

'He's still alive?' Daniel asked. He was slightly incredulous.

'He's in a clinic in Minneapolis.'

'He's sick?' Dan rose from his chair. Turner nodded. 'If you can call being ninety years old a sickness. I think I'd be more surprised if he was healthy. My contact said he's deteriorating rapidly. If we want to see him alive, we better be moving. There's a flight to St Paul in two hours.'

They travelled light, only a single bag between them. They were not planning to stay longer than overnight. The aircraft left the ground in a downpour, powering steeply upward as lightning cut a jagged path across the sky. As they attained height, turbulence buffeted the aircraft. Turner nervously clutched at the arm of his seat.

'You okay?' Daniel asked him. 'You look a little green.'

'I feel a little green. Can't you say something to take my mind off the flight?'

Daniel obliged by telling a couple of weak jokes. Turner was unimpressed, but managed a feeble smile. 'Thanks for the effort, but if you have any more like that, just stow 'em.' Hostesses brought around drinks and assurances. Daniel fought the urge to order whiskey to steady his nerves, asking for club soda instead. Inexplicably, he was making an effort not to drink, it was becoming important that he not lose face in front of Turner. And Pamela. Turner was gripping his glass so tightly his knuckles shone. 'God, I hate flying.' He swallowed, hard. His skin was clammy and he looked feverish.

Daniel peered out through the window. Beyond the great wing, which was quivering violently in the wind, there was nothing to be seen save mountains of massed black cloud. He dozed, his thoughts drifting loosely, far and wide. Relaxed, he tried to think of a question to ask Turner. Then he had one. 'Do you mind if I ask a question?'

Still trembling, Turner sipped from his glass. 'Sure, go ahead.'

'How did you get into all this? We know about me, but why do you have such an interest in the assassinations?'

Turner pursed his lips. 'College days. It was about the time students started to protest against the Vietnam war. I attended a lecture given by Mark Lane. He was one of the early investigators into the JFK killing. As I listened, something inside of me just ignited. I went out and bought a couple of books; *Rush to Judgement*, and two about Oswald. I felt outrage, and for the first time in my life I had a sense of direction. I've stayed with it ever since.'

Daniel settled into his seat and tilted back his head. He sighed. 'I wish my involvement was that simple.'

It was early afternoon the following day when they approached the clinic in the Oldsmobile they had rented at the airport. Turner had his foot down, and there was a worried set to his face.

'What's the hurry?' Daniel wanted to know. Turner, hunched intently over the wheel, grimaced. 'Just a feeling I have.' He muttered, forcing the words through gritted teeth. He squeezed the throttle harder against the floor. 'Just a feeling. Come on.'

The clinic was not easy to find. Privacy was of paramount importance to many of the patients. The gate was neither well lit, or signposted. Once through the gate and parked, reception was the next obstacle. It was late, and despite their polite remonstrations there was no by-passing the secretary at the desk.

'Miss, you don't understand.' Daniel chipped in over Turner's shoulder. Though he would be unable to explain it, he had been infected by his friend's urgency. 'This is a matter of life and death.'

'Oh, but I do understand.' The receptionist, a smartly uniformed slim black woman in her late thirties, was firm but polite. 'It is you who do not. We are responsible for the wellbeing of our clients. You can do only harm, bursting in on old Mr Vincent so late. I don't even know he'll want to see you.'

'Would you do one thing for me?' Turner pleaded. 'One favor. I'm begging you.'

She eyed him sternly. 'Do I have to call security to haul you out of here?'

'No, no, you do not,' insisted Turner. 'We will go. We are willing to leave, but we are worried, extremely worried, about Mr Vincent's health. Please, go to his room. If he's awake tell him that David Turner from . . . from Octad Enterprises, would like to see him. Ask him if he'll speak to us. If he won't, or if he's asleep, just come and tell us and we'll leave. I give you my word.' He paused, his eyes implored her.

She drew a deep breath that swelled her constricted chest. 'Alright,' she muttered warningly, coming around the desk. 'You stay right there. I'll be back, and you better be as good as your word.'

'We will. We will.' Turner called after her. He sank limply against the counter. 'Oh man, I'm shot.'

Daniel reached out and gave his friend's shoulder a friendly squeeze. 'Just hang on. We're almost there.'

Turner looked up at him. His face hangdog. 'I just hope we're in time,' he whispered. 'I just hope we're in time.'

He had battled cancer for twenty years, but it had him now and he knew it. His aged heart strained in his chest. Almost strangled by pain it fought on, maintaining its slender hold on life.

Sleep was beyond reach. The drugs kept most of the pain away, but they could not entirely remove it. It was always there, lapping at the edges. His breathing was rusty and laboured, and his eyes, huge in sunken sockets, stared up at the ceiling.

In the gloom surrounding him, something moved. A shadow over to his right. With an effort that left him sapped he turned his head. A huge anthropoid shape closed in.

Vincent chuckled to himself. His lips drew back, airing his loosened teeth. A gust of his own fetid breath offended his nose. So, death was here at last, the son of a bitch! Took his time! These last years, most of his lucid moments had been squandered in contemplation of this moment. The moment when he would learn the truth about life, about God, about death. Now he knew.

The angel of death lifted broad hands, as if to cast a spell. Vincent exhaled rustily, welcoming the imminent release. It was good to know he was close to the end of the pain. Then Cutter's grinning, feral features loomed from the darkness, and the bald dome of his head shimmered in the pale light seeping in through the blinds. He swooped, and Vincent recoiled from a gust of breath more fetid, more repulsively vile and rotten than his own. With fiendish glee Cutter clamped a pillow over Vincent's face – and pressed down. The old man's hands lifted, and the fingers flexed without strength, dying claws clutching hopelessly at life. Then they fell limply to the sheet and lay still.

Cutter shuddered at the kill. Drew a deep relaxed breath as if after climax. His gargoyle expression softened, and as he lifted the pillow and viewed the old man's features he had a sad, almost tender, glimmer in his eyes. Then stepping back, he left the room as he had found it.

The receptionist ran, sprinted back to the desk. Hurtling a hostile, wary glance at Turner she picked up the telephone and spoke rapidly into it. An alarm chimed, and nurses and two white coated doctors raced past the desk and along the corridor.

The receptionist faced Daniel and Turner. 'I'm sorry gentlemen,' she said, trapping the telephone receiver under her chin. 'Mr Vincent has passed away.'

They had known. The instant she had reappeared, running along the corridor, they had known. It was as if they shared one consciousness. Supporting each other they reeled out into the night air and stood by the car, sucking in great draughts of cold air.

Daniel grew heated. It was the heat of frustration, fed by fear until it threatened to engulf him. Burn him up. 'Damm!' he growled, banging a fist down upon the roof of the Oldsmobile. 'How did they know? How did they get here first? How?'

Turner was almost doubled up with fear. One hand was clutched to his brow. 'Christ, this is all getting a little too real for me.'

Daniel glowered at him. 'What?'

'Can't you feel it?' Turner held out his hands, clutching at air. 'Can't you feel it all closing in around us? Jesus, I am scared.'

There was silence. Daniel paced a full circuit around the car. 'There will be an investigation in there.' He nodded towards the Clinic. 'We better get out of here. We don't want to be answering questions just yet.'

'What do we do?' Turner cried. He had not heard. He had been brushed by the terror Daniel had known, and it had shocked him. 'What do we do now?'

Daniel grasped him firmly by the elbow. 'Come on. I'll drive.'

As they journeyed, Turner rambled. 'It could have been natural. He was old, we don't know they got to him.'

'Yeah, right,' Dan breathed. 'Another coincidence? Come on Dave, you know that's bullshit. No more. No more.'

Desolate, and with heavy hearts, they endured the seemingly endless journey to Turner's house. Daniel's mind was a warren of unsolved mysteries, catacombs echoing with questions. How? How?

Pamela saw from their faces the news was bad. She took Daniel in her arms and held him close. The emotions pent up during the journey brimmed to the surface. He was close to tears.

'We can't win, Pam. They know. Somehow . . . they know.'

That night as they lay in bed, she with an arm looped around his bare chest, he murmured a question. She sat up. 'What did you say?'

'I asked if you would take a trip with me?'

'Sure. Anywhere in particular?'

'I've been thinking about something Dave told me. I asked him how the killers got away so easily after the assassination. He said some of the higher ranking Dallas cops might have known beforehand that something was going on and been primed. A couple of men from the assassination team were rumoured to have been among the tramps arrested on Dealey Plaza. They were released without questioning. I had an uncle on the Dallas force. He's retired now, but he might know something . . . Come to Dallas with me?'

She sat up straighter. 'Do you think you'll find the answer there?'

'I don't know for sure, but I have a feeling.'

'Then we'll go,' she said. 'Together.' He hugged her close, kissed her eyes, her forehead, her lips. 'Pamela, I love you.'

* 20 *

Cyrus Galbraith's face was purple with rage. 'What I want to know is how did this get published? How did it even get written?' He hurled the magazine – a renowned international periodical, on to a coffee table in the hotel room. His own face smiled up at him from the cover.

Spector, deputy to Barry Mather, and Cutter, the dome headed thug with the eager, canine mouth and the weasel eyes, watched bemusedly as Barbara Rush, in her role as PR consultant, pleaded with the Senator in an attempt to calm him. But he refused to be calmed.

'Don't you realise the damage this could do? Get onto the Editor in Chief, get the dammed publisher! Who owns this rag? I want it retracted!'

Barbara swallowed uncomfortably. 'You cannot make them retract the truth, Senator. It's a matter of public record.'

'I don't give a fuck!' Galbraith screeched. 'I will not be hurt. Not after coming so far!'

'Senator,' Spector cut in, soothingly. 'It's one sentence. It won't even be noticed.'

Barbara granted Spector a look of gratitude. She hated this part of the job, smoothing the ruffled feathers of a prima donna out of control. She had to remind herself of all the good Galbraith had done, and could continue to do.

'We can live with it,' she said. 'Believe me. Right now we have to concentrate on the present. We have to get to this dinner and meet a few people.'

The Senator breathed heavily through his nose. The eruption had released the pressure, he was back at the helm. 'Okay . . .' he panted, the flush on his face starting to fade, 'but it goes no further. I want it fixed.'

'Leave it to me,' Spector replied. 'I will make sure any subsequent issues are amended. I have friends in the networks who will watch out for signs of it surfacing.'

Galbraith stopped before a mirror and adjusted his appearance. Then, with Cutter loping at his heels like some large and dangerous dog, and with Spector wearing his professional frown, he left the hotel room and headed for the elevator down.

'Uncle Ray!' exclaimed Daniel. He ran from the car to the old man and they embraced affectionately. They stood back to look at each other. Their smiles were bright, and genuine, and watching them Pamela felt warmed.

'How ya bin, boy?' Uncle Ray growled. He was as large as Daniel remembered, though flesh formerly muscular now hung slackly on his great frame. His hair, still cut short in a regulation crew cut, was blond silvered with grey, and it shone in the light from the dusk sun. The old man turned a pair of bright blue eyes upon Pamela, saying: 'Danny boy, aren't you going to introduce me to this lovely young lady?'

Laughing, Daniel did just that.

Ray was a generous host. The moment he had heard they were coming he had begun to prepare a meal. They feasted royally on prime Texas steaks, then collapsed with full bellies onto the huge and comfortable armchairs in the lounge. Ray had them in stitches throughout dinner, spinning tales that had grown longer and funnier during the years since Daniel had last heard them. Afterwards, even as they sat in good natured quiet, the odd spontaneous chuckle would ripple.

Holding a hand to her belly, Pam got to her feet and toured the room. On the bureau were arrayed numerous framed citations and photographs; Ray in uniform, erect, square-jawed and tough looking. Ray on his wedding day. She remarked on the beauty of his wife. In a gentle voice he thanked her.

'She was the best, if I say so myself. Best day's work I ever did, marrying Norma. You remember, Danny? Could she cook?'

Daniel smiled at the memory. 'I'll say she could.' The room was suffused with happiness and Daniel was glad he'd made the trip, even if nothing resulted. It was good to see Ray. The man was old. They might never meet again.

Midnight was long past. The air was cooler, the lights dimmed, and with good rye inside of them the three had mellowed.

Ray gave Daniel a shrewd look and said at last: 'It's been good to see you, Danny. Damm good. And I'm glad we had the chance to chew the fat again. But we both know you didn't come clear across the country to drink Wild Turkey. What's ailing you?'

Daniel and Pamela exchanged glances. 'Well, Uncle Ray, it's kinda hard to know where to start. I'm thinking of writing a book about something that happened in Dallas, and I was hoping you'd be able to tell me something.'

'You're writing a book? That's quite a turnaround, son.' Ray's eyes narrowed. 'Just what is this *something* that happened?'

Dan paused. 'November twenty second, nineteen sixty three.'

Ray was visibly disturbed. His face slowly blenched, and there was an uncomfortable interval before he spoke. 'Kennedy. Why you gettin' involved, Danny?'

Striving to remain casual, Dan shrugged. 'It's the greatest mystery of the twentieth century. I have to admit I'm interested.'

Ray looked pained. 'It was the most shameful event in the history of Dallas. It ought to be buried and forgotten. In this town people don't talk about it.'

'The killers were never brought to trial. Maybe it's time people did talk about it.'

Ray grimaced. 'Oswald did it and he's dead. The Warren people wrote that page in history and it's time we closed the book.'

'Uncle Ray . . .' Daniel peered into the old man's eyes, golden bright in the light from a nearby lamp, and held the stare. 'Tell me, in your heart of hearts, do you really believe that?'

The old man knew he was trapped. His eyes flickered and gave him away. He averted his head.

'You were a cop.' Daniel challenged him. 'The straightest man I ever met. You must have some ideas of your own. Would you share them with me?'

Face still averted, Ray shook his head. 'That's all past, Danny. No sense raking it up. For the life of me I can't think of one sensible reason you should want to dig into all that.'

Dan said abruptly. 'They killed my father.'

The effect on Ray was startling. He jerked, and his eyes, when he looked back at Daniel, radiated fear. 'Your Daddy killed himself, son,' he said gently. 'You found the body. I know it was hard on you, I know it made your upbringing especially tough, but if you've spent all these years convincing yourself that something else happened, well, I'm sorry to have to disabuse you of the notion.'

'Uncle Ray, where were you when JFK was shot?'

Ray cleared his throat. 'I was on the intersection at Commerce and Houston. Looking across Dealey.'

'And you heard the shots?'

Ray was slow to nod his head. Daniel went on. 'Tell me, do you think they came from, the depository or the knoll?'

'Impossible to say from where I was standing. You know Dealey, it's wide open. And rifleshots in an open space often sound as though they are coming from a point other than the source. With all the crowd noise it was hard enough to hear the shots at all.'

'An opinion then?'

'I can't say for sure.'

Daniel shifted on his seat. He was building up to tell his story, and he was nervous; the telling got no easier. 'Uncle Ray, me and my daddy were there that day. He was standing with the people strung along the base of the knoll. Kennedy's limo passed within spitting distance, and my daddy was sure the shots, at least two of the shots, came from the knoll behind him.'

Ray cut in: 'Sure, other people said the same. But the shots were over before anyone realised what was happening. It would be the simplest thing in the world to make a mistake.'

'I was on the knoll too, Uncle Ray, but I was at the top, playing behind that white stone structure, y'know, the one the bums sleep in on hot days?'

Ray nodded. His face was ashen. He had the look of a man who sees his fate hurtling unavoidably towards him.

'I saw four men behind that picket fence overlooking Dealey. One of them had a rifle. I watched him fire a shot over the fence. He handed the rifle to one of the other men, and they split up. In seconds they were gone. But I saw them. My daddy refused to change the statement he gave to the police and the FBI. He had visits from men who appeared to represent the authorities, and he was threatened, but he would not lie about what he saw. So they hounded him until he snapped, and killed himself. He was scared for me. With attention on him there was the chance my story might come out. He knew once he was gone, I'd be safe.'

Ray was studying his nephew with a different, an awed expression. At last he spoke. 'You tellin' the truth, boy?'

Daniel nodded solemnly. Ray sank into deep thought. The pause extended, and Pamela moved to speak, but Daniel motioned her to be quiet. He wanted Ray to be the one to break the silence.

Ray's voice was a whisper. 'We all knew there was somethin' gonna happen. It was in the air. I was there too when Ruby blew away Oswald. That stank too. We all knew it.'

Pamela cut in. 'Why didn't any of you speak up?'

Ray threw her a sharp glance. 'Most of us were family men, with time in the job, needing the money, the job security. A couple of the guys tried to bring some of the inconsistencies to the attention of superior officers, but the pressure came down. When all was said and done, what could one or two cops hope to achieve when all that official weight wanted to conclude Oswald killed JFK? The line was that Ruby killed Oswald to prevent Jackie Kennedy the pain of testifying. We were discouraged from thinking otherwise. This has always been a cops' town. The law is strong here, but it's still a tool for the rich. You learn to know when to look the other way.'

'Did you know Ruby?' Dan asked eagerly. He wanted the old man to spill it out.

Ray nodded. 'I've been known to have a drink with him, in the Carousel Club, and before that in the Silver Spur. The man was a bum, with money problems and a history of being used by the mob, but I kinda liked him. A lot of us did. He'd do the occasional favor, and we'd do the same. Over the years he was arrested twice for carrying a concealed gun, three times for breaking the licensing laws, once for a traffic violation and once for assault. He was only ever punished for the traffic violation.' Ray shifted on his seat. 'But I'll tell you this. Whoever sent him to kill Oswald must have had him in a real headlock. There was no way Jack would risk a death sentence voluntarily. He had a temper, and he liked to solve problems with his fists, but I never saw him as a killer.

Ray got to his feet and poured them all another drink. He sat, he was looking weary. 'I knew Jack, I knew the man who let him into the station too.'

'So Ruby's story that he decided to go into there on an impulse wasn't right?' This came from Pamela. Her face wore a slightly amused expression.

Ray mustered a wasted smile. 'Oswald was supposed to be brought down at ten in the morning. Why didn't Jack appear then? How did he know to come down one hour and fifteen minutes later? Here's a scenario for you: One guy on the Oswald security detail that morning hears about the time change. He goes to buy a pack of smokes. He stops by a payphone situated next to the cigarette machine and calls the diner where Jack eats breakfast. Jack's impulse stays on hold for another hour. The same cop lets him in through a side door, shelters him until Lee is brought out, then bam; Oswald is put away.'

'You know this for a fact?' Dan posed the question. Ray paused, then rose slowly to his feet. 'Danny, I'm tired, and really I'd just like to have all this put behind me. The things I know, I'll take them to the grave with me. I still have kids, you know that, even if they are grown up. Then there are the grandchildren. We all deserve some peace.'

Daniel knew better than to push too hard. Nothing would induce him to put the old man at risk. 'I understand, Ray. Thanks for giving me this much.'

The following morning, after a sumptuous breakfast, Ray walked them out to their rental car. 'When you leaving Dallas?'

'Probably tomorrow afternoon,' Daniel replied. The old man nodded his head, then held out his hand. 'You take care now.'

Daniel took the firm, warm grip. At the thought he might never see his uncle again, a lump rose to his throat. 'You too Ray.'

'He didn't give us much,' Pamela remarked as they turned east, onto Jefferson, and headed into downtown Dallas. She had her window wound down and one arm resting along the window frame. The sun was warm, but promised torrid heat, and a balmy breeze flooded the interior of the car.

'He gave as much as he dared,' Daniel rebuked her. 'He's a gutsy old man. When you add up all the people who paid the price for speaking out, you can understand his not wanting to talk. He does still have family to consider.'

She stared out of the open window. 'I still think he could have given us more.'

They checked into the Holiday Inn. Pam showered first while he unpacked. When she emerged from the bathroom, he asked her what she wanted to do with the day. She suggested finding a nice place to have lunch. 'Then you could take me sightseeing. Is there anything in particular you would like to see?'

It had been poised on the tip of his tongue all morning, waiting to spring free, he let it out. 'If it's all the same to you, I'd like to walk to Dealey Plaza. It's not far from here.'

She agreed it sounded a good idea. She too was interested in walking the ground where shocking history had been made.

'Well?' she asked him. 'Has it changed?' They were standing before the old courthouse, on the stretch of Houston between Commerce and Elm. The Plaza was a triangle, and they were standing on the base, the sides angling away from them, converging at the triple railroad overpass some two hundred metres distant.

Daniel looked around. 'It's hard to say. The buildings this side are the same.' They crossed the road, to the ornamental ponds, two of them, each about twenty metres wide, and rectangular. Small plumes of water, miniature fountains, broke the surface of the water. There were trees on this side of Houston, and in the shade the growing heat from the sun was not so cruel.

'That wasn't built back then.' He pointed ahead, where to the left and beyond the overpass, gleamed the mirrored walls of the buildings that made up the Reunion complex. The glassy walls glistened brilliantly.

Pamela recognised the building immediately, 'From the opening titles of the TV program. This is a nice spot.' She eyed a nearby memorial collannade of gleaming white stone, set up to commemorate the founding of the city, and her gaze lit upon a plaque, set atop a stone pillar. She began to read aloud: 'John Neely Bryant, 1810 to 1877 . . .'

Her voice faded as he walked away from her, his gaze fixed on a solitary building across Elm. A flat topped structure built of orange brick, from where a man named Lee Harvey Oswald supposedly fired three shots.

Back at the memorial, Pamela was still reading aloud. '. . . lived to age 94, and saw Dallas attain a population of 150,000.' She turned and saw with surprise that he was some distance away, standing on the corner, head tilted as he looked up at a building. She hurried to his side. 'Is that what I think it is?'

There was a rapt expression on his face. He nodded. 'The Texas School Book Depository.'

In silence they crossed Elm. Daniel deliberately avoided looking down the slope, towards the knoll. One thing at a time. They stood at the base of the steps, the entrance to the building. Pamela glanced at him. He looked odd – almost in a trance. She asked if he was alright, but he did not reply.

He was hearing voices, faint echoes. It was almost as if he was back there, standing alongside his father. As if he could, by sheer effort of will, summon up the past.

'What the hell's going on?' His father's voice, sounding hollow and distant. He recalled the huge bulk of the cop on the steps, replying:

'Some son-of-a-bitch took a shot at Kennedy from up there.'

His father's fatal response. 'That's not right. I was over there, near where the President was hit. The shots came from behind me.'

He was jolted back to reality when Pamela shook his arm. 'Hey, are you okay?' The echoes faded, he smiled weakly. 'I'm alright.'

There was a plaque on the wall beside the entrance. They read it together.

'Look at that,' he said, pointing to the last three lines.

'. . . national notoriety when Lee Harvey Oswald allegedly shot and killed President John F Kennedy from a sixth floor window as the presidential motorcade passed this site.'

Beneath the word *allegedly*, someone had taken a sharp object and etched a deep line. Looking up, Daniel pointed out the window, then Pamela asked where he had been standing. Swallowing his trepidation, he re-trod the ground he had walked that day. He led her to the rear of the knoll, showed her the car park that was bordered by the railway yards. He showed where his father had stood, showed her where Abraham Zapruder had positioned himself, camera in hand, recording on twenty-two feet of color film the crime of the century. The stone collonnade, he showed her how he had peered over the fence, saw the place where the two men, the gunman in the hardhat and his partner in the police uniform had stood.

'After the shooting, the gunman handed the rifle to one of the others, a man dressed like a . . .' He gasped. 'Like a tramp. My God, it's all coming back. He moved away with the rifle. The man in the hardhat, the gunman, sprinted past me. He looked at me, saw me, I know he saw me, but he could not stop. He couldn't risk being caught. He vanished around the back of the depository. His partner walked to the far side of the car met the cops and the crowd as they ran up into the car park. Dressed like a cop he just melted in. The man in the plaid jacket, he took out a wallet and waved it around. I guess he was the man with the secret service ID. By this time I had walked to the top of the knoll. That was what I saw before I ran down to join my Pa.'

He put a hand on the top of the fence. The wood was old and dry, rotted. 'He held the rifle up like this . . .' He aped the gunman's stance. He peered along an imaginary barrel, and as he did this a shudder ran through him. He could see the gunman, feel the recoil, hear that dreadful burst of gunfire. The shots that signalled the ending for so many people. 'I saw him fire. That's why I find it hard to believe . . .'

She looked to him. 'To believe what?'

He thought back, recalled Turner's secret, and said: 'Nothing.' Emotion snowballed, swamped him, and he had to shut his eyes and clench his fist to hold it off.

They walked the top of the knoll; the Dealey side. As he trod the ground, Daniel was intoxicated by the surging of released memories. He felt at once sad and despairing; so much of promise had died on this sunny spot so many years ago. He looked back up the gentle slope towards Houston, he envisaged the limo rounding the corner . . .

'I've seen enough,' he said abruptly. 'Do you mind if we leave?'

The day grew hotter as noon approached. They ate at a nearby Burgerking, then strolled along a circuitous route with the intention of returning to the hotel. By chance they came upon the JFK memorial. A simple engraved slab of black marble, placed in the centre of a large square paved area, bordered by four walls of dull concrete. There were openings on each side to permit the traffic of onlookers. Someone had left a wreath of pale flowers, and attached to this was a note on which the words: PRAY PLAY USA AS JFK LOVED FOR US ALL TO DO were scrawled in a childish hand.

Despite her best efforts to cheer him, his black mood only deepened. On returning to the hotel, he stayed in the bar while Pamela went to the room to shower. As he nursed a large whiskey, he looked around for something to do, and his gaze lit upon a copy of a magazine lying on a table. The smiling face of Cyrus Galbraith beamed at him from the cover. The cliché headline: *Man behind the myth*, was emblazoned across the cover in bold black. Picking up the magazine, he flipped it open and began to read.

As he became involved in the text, his eyebrows crept closer together in a scowl. His glass was refilled, but it sat ignored. Finally he looked up, threw back the drink in a single gulp, and returning to the room made straight for the telephone.

It was early evening, and in Greensboro, Turner was surprised to hear Daniel's voice. No contact was planned until after the trip. He started by asking how the visit had gone, but Daniel brushed aside the inquiry.

'Turner, I've been doing some reading. Did you know that in 1962 Cyrus Galbraith's business affairs were investigated by the SEC?'

There was a pause before Turner admitted that he did know. Daniel challenged him: 'So why did you tell me he was clean?'

'He was exonerated!' Turner flared back.

'It doesn't say that here. It just says the investigation died for lack of evidence. That's not the same as being exonerated.'

'Daniel . . .' Turner sounded exasperated. 'What is all this?'

Dan's anger grew with each word he uttered. 'There's something else I've learned, something very interesting. Let me quote: 'He was instrumental in the setting up of the Senate Assassinations Committee to investigate the assassination of President Kennedy . . .' Here Daniel paused, but Turner did not fill the space. 'And . . . because of his deep-rooted concern for justice, both social and legal, he has provided funding for one of the numerous assassinations bureau that have flourished since the late 'sixties. End quote.'

He could sense Turner almost swooning from the shock. 'How . . . how did they find out?'

'I don't have to ask which bureau he's funding, do I?' There was no answer. 'Do I, Turner?' Daniel was breathing heavily now. 'Remember Vincent? How I wondered about them getting to him before we did? It was you, wasn't it? You.'

'No,' Turner's voice was choked. 'No.'

'Why?' Dan felt impelled to ask. He was on the brink of tears; another betrayal. A lifetime of betrayals! 'Why deceive me like that? Now I know why every time I tried to link Galbraith to Mather you sprang to his defense. Don't you see how clever he's been? The witnesses killed, clues lost? He's —'

'STOP THAT!!!' Turner screamed. 'He's a good man. He's genuine. He wants to help, godammit!'

Daniel decided to let it all go. There was no changing things, he had run head first into a wall. He was too small a part to change the scheme. The men at the top had truly demonstrated their power. They were even capable of controlling so-called independent investigations into their dealings. They could not be stopped.

For him, it was time to get off the wagon. In a tone of bitter exasperation he snapped: 'Turner, I'm out of it. I've had enough. Tell your master I'm through. I'm going back to living my life!'

He slammed down the receiver to find Pam staring at him, dumbstruck. She did not have to speak. Her eyes asked the question with an eloquence beyond mere words.

'Turner sold us out,' he said gruffly, words clipped by anger.

'Every step we took, every decision we made, they knew.' Drained by the effort of concentration, he flopped onto the bed and lay with his palms over his eyes.

'What are you going to do?' she asked him much later. He had spent hours engrossed in a contemplative sulk. Now his scowl softened; he ought not take his anger out on her. Steepling his hands beneath his nose, he stared at her. He looked weary.

'I'm going back to Florida. I'll get back my old job and mind my own business.'

She was perplexed. 'But what about me? What about us?'

He smiled feebly. 'You are a great girl, Pam, but I've nothing to offer you. You deserve better than the life you'd have with me.'

Her expression hardened. 'Where do you get off, telling me what I deserve? Answer me one question; do you love me? I mean, really?'

He swallowed, and a great and mysterious sadness descended upon him. 'I do. Very much.'

'Then that is enough,' she said. He would not meet her gaze. He felt undeserving of her loyalty. She gently grasped his chin and turned his head, forcing him to look at her. 'Maybe in the long term we won't make it, Dan. But for now I feel good around you, and I'm coming with you.'

'But your work!' he blurted. 'You're smart, you could have a good career. What will you do?'

She was not worried. 'Right now, I can do anything except quit on you. I'll sell popcorn in Disneyworld if I have to. Who needs a high-powered career?'

He was filled with elation. What a woman! The real thing at last! Loving him enough to give her all. Taking her in his arms he hugged her tightly, and a tear strayed from one eye. 'I love you!'

The wind over Fort Worth airport was typically hot and dry, but he did not care; he was going home. He and Pamela were made to feel welcome aboard the aircraft, and settled into their seats with drinks and newspapers. In a cheerful aside he whispered to her: 'This has to be our last extravagance for a while. I'm running up one spectacular tab on my card.' She joined him in laughter.

The aircraft taxied, then under the powerful thrust of the

engines it thundered along the runway. Daniel was glad to see the city of his boyhood fall away beneath him, and he silently vowed never to return. The seat belt lights went out, and an air of relaxation descended. He reclined his seat and unfolded a newspaper. As he started to read, his gaze tripped over a small item, a half column inch at the bottom of the front page, and he froze. Sensing his tension Pamela glanced sidelong.

She registered the horror etched on his face, and in a rush of panic asked what was wrong.

He was too choked to speak immediately, but he gathered his wits, and, his face white with dismay, began to read aloud: 'Retired Dallas police sergeant Ray Hollis, sixty-eight, died last night in a fire at his home on Ross Avenue. A gas explosion is believed to have been the cause of the fire.' He looked to her, and on her face found his own horror mirrored.

'Many Dallas policemen were admirers of Kennedy. Many others were cowards. The plot did not extend beyond the hierarchy. The rank of a Dallas policeman was in direct proportion to his degree of corruption.

It may be assumed that all of the Dallas police realized afterwards what had happened. Few protested, but a handful muttered their disapproval. Three of them were murdered, and the others were obliged to flee from Dallas. The Warren Commission even refused to hear their testimony.'

quote from: Farewell America.

BOOK THREE

Payback

* 21 *

Idyll.

The moon was high, a brilliant beacon shining through a tear in the clouds. Daniel smiled. Ahead of him on the silvery sand Pamela ran lightly toward the sea. Pausing to strip she ran naked, with arms held high, into the surf, her shrieks of delight carried far by the breeze.

He followed at a stroll, halting beside the bundle of discarded clothes. He wriggled his toes, enjoying the gritty feel of sand between them. He watched her swim, thrusting forward with dolphin grace, arms cutting the water like blades, and he admired her power, her ease in the water. He wondered idly what it was about strong women that attracted him. Perhaps he harboured a deeply buried inferiority complex and sought security. He had been without a mother figure for most of his life, perhaps that was the reason he felt safer being led.

Pamela strode out of the water. Body erect and lithe, movements fluid and supple. An alluring silhouette set against a glistening backdrop. Slowing her pace for the barest moment she pushed back her hair with her hands, then strode on at a renewed pace, provocatively heedless of any reaction her nudity might arouse in him.

'Hi,' she bent to sort her towel from the bundle. In a hoarse voice he returned the greeting while eyeing keenly her cultured physique; the long legs and narrow hips, the breasts that pendulummed tautly as she bent in her search. The urge within him grew until he felt himself reaching out to touch her wet hair. She halted at the contact, then straightened, and gazed into his eyes. Tiny seawater droplets lent her countenance a fresh, virginal look, but her eyes were knowing and expectant. His heart raced and a lump rose to his throat.

'I don't want to go back to the apartment just yet.' She said, breathlessly. Staring in fixed wonder at her beauty, he nodded, voice swept away by a storm of emotion and want.

She licked salt from the corners of her mouth. 'I've never made love on a beach. Have you?' Still not trusting his voice, he nodded again.

'Where would be the best spot?' The innocence of her tone set his senses reeling. Running his tongue around his dry mouth he glanced about, settling at last on a patch of shade beneath a slatted boardwalk of roughly hewn wood. Taking her hand he led her into the shadows and before her fascinated gaze undressed himself. He felt the desperate squeeze of want, the need to lose himself in her, if only for the briefest time. Then thought was interrupted as she drew him down onto the sand.

Days passed in harmony, and, obligingly, time slowed to accommodate their loving. Long hours were spent walking hand in hand and talking late into the night, and making love of a quality neither had experienced before. For Daniel, it seemed life had delivered at last.

Over a number of afternoons they converted thoughts and suspicions, facts and theories, into a boxfile full of notes. Daniel talked about the book he would hew from the massed scribblings, and they would laugh together when he talked of how they would spend the fortune he would earn from it. But he was careful to hold the conversation on a notional, rather romantic level, for the truth was that within him there no longer burned the guilt-spurred driving urge to fight back. For the moment at least, circumspection suited him. Commitment was the last thing on his mind.

Then in the still of the night, as the wind that ran before the dawn blew in through the open terrace window, and the lovers slept entwined on the bed, the sweat from their exertions already cooled on skin, the jarring note of the telephone shattered the peace.

Daniel was first to stir. His eyes refused to open, and in order to silence the ringing he was forced to grope blindly for the receiver.

'Mr Baker?' a voice barked into his ear. 'Mr Daniel Baker?'

Dan snuffed a yawn and answered sleepily. 'Yeah, who is this?'

'Detective Henry Turkel, NYPD.'

Tightlipped, Daniel steeled himself as the draw rumbled out on well oiled rollers. He glanced down. The form beneath the sheet, though undeniably human, was still without identity, and thus far he could take it. With unease, he gave the signal to uncover.

First impressions, oh God, help him! He drew a quick nasal breath to tighten his gut. Thoughts streaked through his mind at reckless speed. Impressions. Still and white and dead. How she must have suffered!

Nausea rose like a spume of gas to the back of his throat. He covered his mouth with his hand and began to turn away, but Turkel grasped his elbow. 'Can you identify please, Mr Baker?'

Knowing that this would be the last sight of those beloved features he would ever have, he looked again, and his eyes glistened with brimming tears. Suppressing a gut spasm, he forced his affirmation through gritted teeth and fled the room, anxious only to leave the horror and the clinging smell of death behind.

Trailing out into the corridor, Turkel found Daniel sitting doubled up on the edge of a bench. His arms were wrapped defensively around his middle. He began to rock back and forth as if in a fit of pain, then he uncoiled his arms and trapped his clasped hands between his thighs.

Turkel stood over him, sucking on his teeth as he studied the other's anguish. 'I appreciate your making the journey up here. Among her effects we found documents listing you as next of kin. Were you related?'

Daniel shook his head. 'We lived together for a couple of years. We remained friends.'

Turkel moved nearer, and placed a hand on Daniel's shoulder. 'I know it was hard on you. I'm sorry, but there was no other way.'

Daniel slowly raised his head. His face had paled to a deathly, greenish hue. He looked at Turkel. The cop was middle-aged, plump and world weary, balding and unshaven. He wore a crumpled gaberdine mac over a wrinkled off-the-peg suit, and he looked down at Daniel with kindly, but knowing, eyes.

'Why . . . ?' Daniel whimpered, breaking off as vomit threatened to gusher. He controlled himself. 'How did she . . . ? What happened to her?'

Turkel hesitated. He was not convinced Baker could handle the details. 'It does not make pleasant hearing. . . .'

Daniel's expression hardened; he wanted to know, so Turkel took the plunge. 'She was gutted, and dumped in the river.'

Engulfed by distress, Daniel shut his eyes tightly and let his head loll back until it touched the wall. Biting down on his lower lip until it bled, he shook as a heart-quaking spasm shocked his body. His head flopped forward and he covered his face with his hands. 'Barbara. Barbara.'

Finding it hard to watch, Turkel turned away. To Daniel, vision blurred by stinging tears, it seemed the whole of his life had been brutally amputated, ripped away from him wholesale. His mother, father, even old Ray. Now Barbara. They seemed determined to leave him nothing but bitter memories. Determined to put him through as much pain as possible.

'Why?' He desperately wanted to cry out. 'Why not just kill me?' It was his fault she was dead; a challenge had been thrown down, and to lure him back into play they had sacrificed her. His thoughts turned to Mather, and the sudden focusing of his hatred for the man was frighteningly intense. What kind of monster was the man? Willing to let his woman be butchered in order to play a gambit and bait a trap?

Sanguinely, Turkel decided that Baker would be of little use for hours. He could not blame the man – the slaying had been particularly brutal. It was the worst that he personally had seen, and only the sheer calloused weight of attendances at murder scenes had provided him with a stomach lining sturdy enough to save him from embarassment. He wandered away in search of a coffee machine.

Daniel uncovered his face. Tears coursed the anguished contours of his face, and his lips, drawn into a taut downward curve, quivered uncontrollably. His heart rocked, and rocked. What now? What now?

Somewhere deep within him echoed the voice of a small boy.

'I'm scared, Pa. I'm scared!'

The police allowed him the use of Barbara's apartment, but once indoors he found himself haunted by the ghosts of her presence; the faint fragrant residue of her favorite perfume — particularly strong in the bedroom, favorite items of clothing, the tiny jewellery casket he had given her one Christmas — the one good Christmas they had had. It was all too much. It made the fact of her death impossible to confront, and, as if hounded by some dark and malignant spirit, he felt impelled to leave.

He wandered the streets, eyeing nervously the towering buildings that seemed almost to close in above him. To him New York was an alien place, forbidding and gloomy after the ocean-side environment he was used to. The city throbbed with a dark energy he feared, and with its streets aglow with peep-shows and nudie revues, sidewalk hustlers on the make and pestering hookers liable to turn offensive no matter how polite the refusal, New York seemed to embody all the seediness, all of the evil in the world.

After walking for hours he blundered, in a haze, into a bar and exchanged a dollar bill for telephone change. He had to call Pam.

The words they spoke to each other were too personal, too intimate to report as he, struggling against the massive wave of grief bearing down upon him, cried out in anguish at his inability to project, and thus release, the pain. They both cried, and she poured out words, mere words, of comfort. But whatever she said, it had all been said before and the lines sounded rehearsed, clichéd, dimly remembered from some half-forgotten movie. And none of them helped.

After his call she lay awake for hours, too disturbed to sleep. He had sounded so low, so depressed. Identifying the body must have been a nightmare. The apartment around her was silent, save for the distant lapping of the Atlantic on the shore. She tossed and turned but sleep remained impossible. Then, as the earliest hues of daylight beaded the horizon, she slept at last, but the nightmares that flooded her mind with vivid images prevented her from resting.

Daylight hurt no less than the night. In a fog of aimlessness, mind still reeling, he stood in the centre of Barbara's apartment, surrounded by reminders of her, and knew the true nature of desolation. He was unsteady, as if drunk, but not a drop of alcohol had passed his lips in days. The fear had marooned him, delirious, in a fog of terror, left him with not a single focused thought in his head.

Recurrently his mind switched back to that final image of Barbara lying in that mortuary drawer, the sheet mercifully drawn up to cover the fearful mutilation enacted upon her body. A casual observer might have remarked how much at peace she looked; she did indeed appear to be sleeping. But he, who knew her every feature so well, could easily detect the signs – the scars terror had indelibly glazed on her porcelain fine skin. He could not shake the image, nor did he want to. How she must have suffered!

The onset of dawn and the filtering into the room of a pale but strengthening light sent a chill over him. He glanced at his watch, and in his first lucid moment for hours, recorded the time. 'My God,' he muttered. He had been up all night! The last residues of fear waned, and weariness draped over him like a seductively warm and comfortable blanket. He wanted to close his eyes and sleep.

Yielding unconsciously to the need, he stirred toward the bed, but even as he moved guilt set in; how could he even contemplate sleep when Barbara's killer was out there, waiting for him? For her sake, if no one else's he had to hit back. They had gotten away with too much for too long. It was time they were stopped once and for all. With leaden movements he made coffee, massaging his shoulders and stretching the tautness from his arms while the cona burbled quietly. His eyelids rasped, as if lined with sand, and fatigue blurred his vision, but he dared not close them. Seated at the kitchen table, coffee warming inside of him, he let his thoughts circle the thirty year history of the conspiracy. The myth had become self-perpetuating, until its subtleties pervaded every aspect of life in America. The shield erected by the plotters for defense, was itself in need of protection. To achieve this the men behind the plot were forced to hire men of a certain breed; faceless professional killers, vicious sadists, some of them, men who enjoyed their grisly work. But even these needed protection. And so the secret manipulators levered where necessary, letting these men and their dreadful deeds be masked, and in the process granting them, quite literally, a licence to terrorise and butcher.

'Round she goes . . .' he whispered, '. . . and where she stops, nobody knows.'

The ache in his gut suddenly intensified, pressed to bursting point. He had to talk – had to share the pain. In a fever of fumbling he reached for the telephone and jabbed at the keys. The receiver lay cool against his ear. He needed her more than he had ever needed anyone, and he longed to be soothed by the sound of her voice. He never wanted to lose her, and this admission took him by surprise, for he was unaccustomed to thinking of the future. But with Pam at his side life had become more than just treading water, more than just waiting to die.

The ring tone purred. It was early. He imagined her asleep, stirring at the sound and drowsily reaching for the telephone. But the ringing went on for too long, and in his imagination he moved her to the shower, not hearing the sound initially because of the rushing water. He pictured her hurriedly wrapping a towel around herself and dashing to the bedroom.

The ring tone continued unbroken. Unease slithered alive just under his heart and he held his breath and waited, waited until there was no doubt. She was not in the apartment.

'She must be out shopping,' he muttered aloud, knowing it was too early, knowing she had promised to wait for his next call. She had promised! At last he slammed down the receiver, but his fist stayed locked around it, locked so tight that ivory colored bone shone through. He had to talk. There had to be someone he could call on.

There was. As the fear sown in his gut began to blossom, he set his jaw and dialled a second number. Turner, the Zealot, he would help. He had to help. Daniel would make him!

Pam was out walking the shore. The morning was bright, though blustery, and she had the strip of beach to herself. She was glad of that. She wanted to be alone.

A sudden rumbling, pitched higher than the sound of the ocean, made her glance up. Flying in from over the Atlantic at a height of about five hundred feet, was a NASA 747 jet, with a space shuttle perched squarely on its back. The craft followed a landing trajectory towards the cape just a few miles north. Pamela turned as it passed her, and followed the jet's progress as it descended below the horizon. She turned again, and a pang of fear cut into her. God, the man was still there!

He wore what looked like a grey suit, and appeared ill at ease on the Florida beachside. He was perhaps a half mile distant, little more than a small and rather indistinct figure, standing on the jetty tied to the nearby Holiday Inn. She could see that his hands were raised to his face, and she knew she was being studied through binoculars. She swallowed her nervousness. She wanted to march up to him, challenge him, but she dare not face what it was that was happening here. Turning away was the easiest option, she decided, and walked with heavy heart back to the apartment.

Turner did not reply immediately. A guilty pause stifled the impulse to speak without some consideration. 'I'm sorry,' he said at last. 'Do you think there could be . . . Do you think . . . ?'

'Do I think what?' Sensing that Turner was on the brink of copping out again, Daniel felt his anger begin to surface. The anger was transmitted, and Turner faltered. 'Do you think her death has anything to do with . . . you know?'

'Of course. Don't you?'

A silence, then: 'Murder is common in New York.'

'BULLSHIT!!!' The bitter force of the explosion took even Daniel by surprise. 'Will you quit that? You know I'm right. You know this was done for a reason!'

'So why are you calling me?' Turner shouted back. 'After our last conversation I had the impression I came pretty low in your estimation.'

'I was angry because I was taken in by you. Because I let myself be deceived. That won't happen again. I thought you were sincere about solving the assassinations. . . .'

'I was sincere. I am.'

'Then why the whitewashing of Galbraith? Isn't that the kind of thing TAB is supposed to be against?'

'Dammit, I was grateful to the man. Maybe he did do nothing to help you, but I owe him. Do you have any idea how much it cost to set up TAB? How much it all costs to run? Nobody wanted to know. Oh, yeah, everyone was interested, there was no shortage of goodwill, but no one was willing to put a hand into pocket to help out. No one, until Galbraith. Me and the other volunteers had just about busted ourselves when he came along. I wouldn't have a roof over my head today if he hadn't cleared the mortgage. So he takes an interest, so what? He wants to get at the truth, but he does not want to exploit the connection for personal gain. Mather working for him is a coincidence. Galbraith is a good man, and I owe him.'

Daniel decided to concede the point. 'I hear what you are saying, Turner, but I'm here to tell you I think he's tied up in all this somehow. Don't ask how I know, it's just a feeling. But I'm going after him.'

'Impossible!' blurted Turner. 'You are talking about a man with an impeccable record.'

'Then why didn't he do something? I gave him everything we had and he did nothing. Now Barbara is dead.'

The pause before Turner responded this time was longer, and his protest when it came was weak. 'You expect me to help crucify the one person who has helped me more than any other . . .'

'Are you scared? Is that it?'

'Dammit, yes I am scared if you want the truth! I don't want to end up on a slab.'

'You've been running that risk ever since TAB started. Can't you see? You've been doing his spade work for years!

'He calls you up, you are flattered by his interest, and you want him to think all the expenditure is justified, so you tell him about the new leads, the latest clues, the fresh witnesses. Then suddenly your lead goes up in smoke. There's a strange fire, a coincidental accident, and the new information gets lost or destroyed. Or killed.'

Silence. Daniel could almost hear Turner agonising over his fears, his conflicting interests. Gritting his teeth, he willed himself to be patient. 'I have to know where you stand. If the evidence leads to the Galbraith camp, or even to the man himself, I have to know you are willing to stand beside me. Decide now, because with or without you I intend to act.'

The pause extended to a frustrating length. Daniel felt the sands of his patience running out. He wanted to hang up, fuck 'em all, and do it himself, but he knew he needed Turner and his contacts, his abilities. Finally, in a spasm of anger, he went for Turner's jugular – his pride:

'If you're not with me, maybe you ought to give up your work at TAB. You could wind up embarrassing your friends.'

In the ensuing silence he could feel Turner wavering. He was almost ready to fall in line. Just one more little push . . .

'Chew on this; they know I can identify Mather, and for that I must be scheduled to die. But you know it too, and you know how they hate loose ends. It's him or us.'

The line tingled. Turner's dread almost palpable. At last he drew a deep breath and reluctantly said: 'What do you want me to do?'

The scent of victory buoyed Daniel to a smile. 'What you're best at; dig into Galbraith's background and get some answers. He's either in this thing or he isn't. You remember we talked about the Octad, and old man Vincent being a member?'

'Rumoured member.'

'Whatever. Can it just be coincidence that Galbraith went on to become head of Vincent's company?'

'I'll find out,' Turner declared, and abruptly hung up. Daniel replaced the receiver with care and turned his thoughts to his next move. Mather!

The day passed in a fever of inactivity, ideas brooding in his mind. He paced the morning away, snatching mouthfuls of coffee while in the background the television blared – for he could not bear the silence. Pam was still not home. A dreadful thought occurred; if they had done anything to her . . . !

He had made a dozen wasted calls to Florida, anger fermenting all the while, bubbling and seething until he was ready to blow. What he needed was a direction for his furies; a road to the answer. He wanted full and complete vengeance, but on who?

Mather. If he wasn't behind all this, he was at least a good place to start. He must be holding the leash attached to that bald-headed berserker. Of one thing he was sure; the next move was his to make. The sacrificing of Barbara had been their gambit, now it was his turn, and offense was the best defense – especially when the opposition employed professionals.

Pulling his holdall from under the bed, he rummaged and drew out his father's gun. All those years he had maintained it, lovingly and religiously cleaning and oiling and now, as he hefted its solid weight, his mind flitted backwards in time, and an image of spattered brains danced before his mind's eye. The recollection was a reflex that occurred each time he handled the weapon. The instant passed, and after a moment's further reflection he took the gun onto his lap and began expertly to strip it. The cleaning was probably unnecessary, but the action, the fact that he was engaged on the task, brought some comfort. Steadfastly ignoring the flitting images, knowing they would fade, he tipped the bullets onto his palm. Out came the small pack of cleaning materials . . .

. . . red veined globules of grey matter . . . drying rivulets of blood . . . thrusting gashes of appalling vividness up the wall . . .

He shuddered, took a great gulp of air to compress the nausea, and picking up a soft cloth began to clean the gun.

He worked, and when dusk came he worked on, ignoring the deepening gloom and pausing only to massage his burning eyes. He was lightheaded with fatigue, and though he tried to hold on, he fell asleep at last, on his seat, head tilting forwards, chin resting on his breast.

* 22 *

An insistent knocking on the door woke him. He sat up – too quickly, wincing audibly as his neck stiffened in protest. His eyes cowered behind their lids at the sudden rush of bright sunlight, and he guessed it must be at least mid-afternoon. Taking the gun, he crept to the door and demanded to know who was there.

'It's me, Turner,' came the muffled reply. Cocking the weapon, for he had not yet regained a trust of the man, Daniel eased open the door and admitted him.

Turner looked agitated. He was unshaven, hangdog and jittery. A battered leather briefcase was tucked under one arm. Daniel looked him up and down. 'You look awful,' he said.

Then it was Turner's time to make a quick up-down appraisal. His face creaked into a credulous half smile. 'You obviously haven't looked at a mirror this morning.' Putting down the briefcase, he asked if there was any coffee.

Daniel made fresh, and they drank in the kitchen. They filled the vacuum with small talk. Turner asked about Barbara, the funeral arrangements. Daniel's tone, when he replied, was grave, plainly he was still very distressed. 'She has a father, but he's in Europe. Nothing will happen until he's been traced and flown back.'

'Do the cops have a line yet on the . . . the killer?'

Dan shook his head. Tears welled.

Draining his cup, Turner sighed, then hoisted the case onto the table. 'Okay, to business,' he muttered, pulling a thick clutch of papers into view.

Grateful for something to focus on, Daniel eyed the stack. 'You found something then?'

Turner nodded, and pushed the pile towards him. 'Could be something, or it could be nothing. There's more back at the house, but this will do for now.'

Daniel leafed through the sheets. There were photographs; Senator Galbraith caught through a powerful lens and at a distance, shaking hands with an unidentified man on the steps of a palatial house. The pictures were of a grainy quality, yet clear enough to enable recognition. Mather featured in some of them, but he was always in the background. The personification of the loyal, discreet retainer.

After the pictures came masses of typed reports. Diary pages. Dates, places. He asked, 'What is all this?'

Turner dug in a shirt pocket and unearthed a crumpled pack of Camels. He lit one and inhaled before replying. 'I think I told you that TAB attracts all kinds of people; hell, they are volunteers, and beggars can't be choosers. They all have their own reasons for being involved, and the majority will never come across a good lead, but they collect data, and send it in to us. It trickles in daily, and it's part of my job to evaluate this information, to either dump it, or file it and submit a basic summary to our running log. In this way, over a long period, we are able to construct an overview from the masses of minutiae.

'Now, inevitably, many of the people involved in TAB will have a bee in their bonnet about a particular subject, be it the JFK assassination, or the killing of Bobby Kennedy, or Martin Luther King. Others study the manipulations by the military and intelligence agencies, the supranational corporations, and the Octad. These . . .' he indicated the pile of papers, 'are some of the fruits of those researches.

'The diary schedules are probable Octad meetings. The pictures show Galbraith with suspected Octad members. Suspected is the best we can do, as nothing about this group is official.'

'But this is proof.' Daniel's voice rang with triumph.

Turner raised a cautionary hand. 'None of this is proof,' he said sternly, but then, on seeing the disappointment on Daniel's face, he added: 'Patience. Our people have been watching for years. They have seen Octad members come and go, they've seen the group evolve and they have built up a picture of the way the unit works, the type of men invited to join and the events they influence.

'Think of the Octad as a secret government, existing for the benefit of a secret nation, a sort of parallel America, that hides itself on acres of private land, behind tall electrified fences patrolled by armed guards. Being at the same time both loosely knitted and tightly meshed, this organisation leads the business community by the nose. They make billions out of currency transactions, running down the wealth of entire nations for profit. They hold enormous blocks of stock in the Blue Chip industrials, and wield influence to mold the markets to their advantage. And this tiny group, this microcosm of America, is the fourth richest nation on Earth.'

He sighed. 'And . . . we have to accept, Daniel, that they are untouchable. We might get to Mather, nail the assassin, find the reasons and break the codes, but you can be sure there will be no traceable links to the men ultimately responsible.'

'It must be possible to at least hurt them. . . .'

Turner shook his head. 'It isn't. What do we do – go to the papers? They *own* the papers! We have to set our sights lower, aim at Mather. At best we may throw a scare into Galbraith, but we won't be allowed to hurt him.'

'Why not?'

'Are you listening to me? Because he has the power! One thing our watchers have ascertained about Octad meetings is the pecking order; time of arrival is definitely linked to seniority, and the head honcho is always last to arrive. The others, all greatly powerful in their own spheres, wait on him. Since 1978, Galbraith has been last to show for every meeting.'

But, that means he is . . .' Daniel dried up. He looked confused. He ran his fingers over his scalp and around the back of his neck.

'He's already the single most powerful man in the country. Presidents are elected at the forbearance of the Octad, and they can be removed. You remember Nixon? Watergate? Well we have a theory —'

'Wait a minute.' Daniel cut in. 'Not so fast. If he's already that powerful, why does he need to be President?'

Turner shrugged. 'Who can understand the needs of the rich? The people who have it all but want more?

'Old Joe Kennedy craved political power. High office would have given him a legitimacy his millions could not buy him. But true political power stayed beyond him; reckless remarks made during his time as the Ambassador to Great Britain wrecked his ambitions. He desperately wanted to succeed through his oldest son, Joe junior, so imagine how intense his private desperation must have been when Joe junior was killed in World War Two. All his hopes were then transferred to John. . . .' He sat back on his chair. 'It may be that Galbraith has the same cravings. Perhaps he wants to come out, allow his influence to be recognised publicly.' A thoughtful grimace flitted across his face. 'There's a magazine at the bottom of the stack. I've opened it at the right page. Take a look.'

Daniel sifted heatedly through the mass, found the publication and read aloud the bold headline: 'Strategies for corporate conflict, and guidelines for the subsequent consolidation.' He paused. 'What does this mean?'

'That article is based on a speech Galbraith gave to a select number of powerful men at a dinner in Washington fifteen years ago. He sees the day coming when governments become so enmeshed in bureaucracy they become impotent. When globalisation of corporations is the order of the day, when multinational companies cease to have national identities, and when they own everything and employ everyone. He envisages power struggles, with the corporations resorting to hardware to settle matters.'

'Is he crazy?'

'Not as crazy as you might think. There is a logic to his argument. Already there are embarrassing overlaps between government and industry. Many multinationals have too much influence in political matters. Galbraith envisions social pressures splintering the Soviet block; the oppressed masses, sick of having nothing while the wealth of the West beckons, will force out the old guard. He sees us stumbling into an age where the computer is king, and where everything known about every man is on file. In other words – today, almost. Crazy or not, he wants to consolidate his private and public ambitions by becoming President. Who can say how far his megalomania, for want of a better word, extends? Perhaps he sees himself as the world's first Chief Executive.'

Daniel was moved almost to scorn. 'But there is more to the world than the industrialised West —'

Turner, seeing the objection coming, cut in. 'Read the article. It is politely put, but the underlying message is clear: The lesser developed nations will be bled into submission, starved into conformation and bankrupted into compliance. Powerful members of the eastern cultures, Japan and Singaporean, will be integrated into the power structure; remember, corporations will no longer have national identities. They will become global entities, and anything that stands in the way will be removed. Kennedy was just one of the earliest casualties. He didn't need them, and that was what hurt. With Joe's fortune behind him he did not have to make the compromises a politician normally has to accept as the price to pay for power.

'Howard Hughes was powerful. They called him the Stockholder, and he went a long way toward achieving his ideal. Cyrus Galbraith calls himself The Executor, and his ambitions extend much further.'

Daniel stared fixedly, as if concentrating on some distant object. When he looked again at Turner, his gaze was fiery. 'Then we'll have to find a way to put a stop to it. Bring him down.'

'Great.' Turner exclaimed cynically. 'Not content with solving the crime of the century, you want to save the world too. Get real, Daniel.'

'No, listen to me. I've thought about this. I know how we have to go about it. Galbraith is tied up with Mather, he's also linked to you and the other investigators, keeping his finger on the pulse at TAB so he can see trouble coming. A fact he did not disclose to me at our meeting. If he is that powerful he must know something about the assassination, must have had some level of involvement, however small.'

Turner remained sardonic. 'Okay, I'll buy it; how do we go about bringing him down?'

Fired by the burning desire to fight back, Daniel grew tense. He could almost smell the imminence of the conflict and he was at once excited and afraid at the prospect. It was so close now.

Gone was the fear, forgotten the gnawing anxieties; this was more important than any of them. He swallowed, and as he spoke he gathered the energies generated by the fear and channelled them into a growing stridency.

'We'll take things one step at a time, and our first step will be Mather. He was there. He is the key. We'll take him on, head to head, and we'll break him.' He paused. Then said, 'I am glad you're here, Dave. You don't have to travel back to Greensboro, you can stay here.'

'I'll think about it.' Turner said, his already pale face had drained to the ashen color of stone as he thought about what they were about to do.

Daniel was on hold, the telephone receiver cradled between shoulder and cheek. The secretary had crisply informed him that Mr Mather was in a meeting, but Daniel doggedly insisted on waiting until he was free to speak to him. At last a rough baritone voice barked into his ear:

'Baker? I'm busy, what do you want?'

'This won't take long. I want us to meet, tonight. Just you and me, no one else. We'll settle this once and for all.'

'Settle what? I don't have any idea what you are talking about.'

'*Dealey Plaza!*' Daniel hissed vehemently; there was no more containing it. 'November twenty second, nineteen sixty three! You know I was there. I saw you, and I know you saw me. We talk tonight, or I walk straight into the offices of *The New York Times.*'

The pause was brief. Daniel could sense that beneath the bluff exterior, the sneering arrogance, Mather was uneasy. 'What can you tell them, really?'

Daniel smiled to himself but said nothing. He was starting to enjoy himself – he could play this game too! Mather was in trouble and they both knew it. Let him squirm!

Mather tried disdain. 'No one will believe it,' he sneered. 'Who'll even print it? You're a joke, Baker. Get back behind your bar.'

Dan's smile widened; it had been a good try at bravado. Now it was time to pull tight the noose. 'The end result won't matter. The noise I make, and your close links to him, will be enough to keep Galbraith out of the White House. That will be enough for me, but how do you think he and his seven friends will take it?'

Mather's intake of breath was audible, and the pause was longer this time. Daniel held on, knowing that he could only win if he had the strength to remain quiet. He had to let Mather's own anxieties do the persuading. 'Okay,' the gruff assent came at last. 'Where, and what time?'

Daniel felt a deep and warming satisfaction. They *could* be played at their own game! 'Barbara once told me you owned an apartment overlooking Central Park.'

'So?'

'So that's convenient for what I have in mind. You go there and wait until nightfall, when you enter the park by the 72nd Street entrance. Turn right along West Drive and left towards Bethesda fountain. When you reach the fountain area, you wait. I'll find you.'

'And what time do I take this . . . stroll?'

'Ten o'clock you walk into the park.'

'Are you crazy? You want me to walk into Central Park alone at night?'

'Yes, and one more thing.'

'What?'

'Come unarmed.' Daniel severed the connection and sat with his chin balanced on his hand. His gaze drifted to the gun on the table. It gleamed dully, and the clean, oily smell from it infiltrated his nostrils. Mather might try for an ambush. He would have to be prepared.

Mather stood by the telephone for some moments, a disturbed frown creasing his brow. Things were coming to a head too soon for his liking, but he remained confident that Baker could be contained until the time came to finish him off.

Bolstered by that thought, he turned and was faced by Galbraith, approaching from the dining room with Cutter at his side like some faithful killer hound, his bald dome sheeny, thick arms swinging, large calloused hands half-clenched and eyes darting with the piercing, atavistic intensity of a beast honed to survival.

'Barry,' the Senator greeted him with a guarded smile. The charm was brittle, and he sensed Mather was aware of this. They knew each other too well.

'Anything wrong?' Cutter asked with unwelcome familiarity. His mouth hung open in a grin that was almost canine in its eagerness. Mather would not have been surprised to see his tongue come lopping out.

'Nothing I can't handle,' he responded, adopting a blank aloofness calculated to infuriate the bald hoodlum. In his ignorance, Cutter spent much of his time feeling slighted. His eyes glinted venally as he tried to decipher the expression he had observed on Mather's face.

As Mather stalked away, Galbraith said: 'I have this feeling, there is something Mr Mather is not telling us.' He and Cutter exchanged a look.

'Me too,' the thug replied. 'You want him followed?'

The Senator gently inclined his head. He had learnt years ago that on occasion, and for the sake of future deniability, it was better to avoid specific verbal commitment. But Cutter took the hint, and, bowing in an almost obsequious manner, departed in Mather's wake.

Galbraith watched him go, then took up the train of thought he had set aside earlier. The friction between himself and Mather – never inconsiderable, had increased manyfold in recent months. He had begun to suspect that the once seemingly invincible Rama was starting to question his prospects, to show doubts. Perhaps begun to view himself as a man with a limited future. That and age, and the fact that they both knew he was not as able as he had once been. His quota of personal dilemmas had increased too, ever since Barbara Rush appeared on the scene. His attitudes had softened. He was no longer a team player. He had become expendable.

But Rama knew too much, and that was the simple truth at the heart of Galbraith's problem. The nearer they grew to the election, the more acutely aware the Senator became of the vulnerability of his position. Mather knew too much to be allowed to live, yet repeatedly he had insisted it was all written down, the entire multi-layered plot, waiting like some unstable explosive in a lawyer's safekeeping; life insurance, Mather called it, and so far it had worked. But what if an accident were to occur? Something genuinely beyond control, and the information were to get out, what then? It would all be over.

Some compromise would have to be reached, some arrangement arrived at, for if the much respected Senator ordered Mather's liquidation without safeguards, who knew what brand of scandal would adorn the nation's newsstands? There were so many skeletons in that particular cupboard, the foreign press especially would have a field day. He considered, and quickly discarded, the idea that Mather might be bluffing; he was exactly the type of man to have a fallback plan.

There existed another difficulty. Whomever he hired to kill Mather might suddenly decide to turn blackmailer, and that would never do, not if he were to actually become President of the United States. The only answer would be to kill Mather himself, then find some way to neutralise the information. The killing would have to be done quietly, with subtlety, preferably appearing to have been due to natural causes.

He put aside the plan for future refinement. There was still Baker to be taken care of. The ploy with the girl had worked well, but she was out of the game now. Baker had to go too. And Turner.

He glanced at his watch, realised he was late for an appointment, and hastened upstairs to change.

Turner glanced at the time, and hurriedly began to wind up the researching. If he did not leave soon he would be late for the rendezvous in the park, and that must not happen. He dare not let Daniel face Mather alone. The man was just too goddamm dangerous. How Dan had ever gotten him to agree to the meeting in the first place . . . He blew out his cheeks, partly in admiration, partly through fear. Facing that hardfaced sonofabitch was not his idea of a relaxing night out.

Putting aside the papers he had selected to show Daniel, he ducked to open the lowest drawer in the desk and lifted out the fourth and final bulging file TAB had compiled on Galbraith. Just one quick last look, he told himself.

As he opened the file a rush of musty air swam up to meet him. With an oral sigh he tipped the contents onto the desktop and began to sift the tangled mess of flimsy cuttings and magazine pages.

He froze, a single page gripped manically tight in his hand, gazed locked on the magazine picture. Senator Galbraith, immaculate in stylish tuxedo, snapped arriving at a swish benefit dinner. His smile was brilliant, wide and assured. At his side, the beautiful young woman with her arm looped through his smiled brilliantly too. It was plain from the way they leaned against each other that they were close.

He read the caption, and felt his heart accelerate until it pounded in his chest. The pulsing behind his eyes blotted out all senses but one; danger. The dreadful peril that awaited Daniel at the park. He swallowed nervously, re-read the words, and felt his heart sink under the weight of dread.

'Senator Cyrus Galbraith arriving at the Ambassador Hotel accompanied by his ward, Miss Pamela Davis.'

His heart skipped beats as he fumbled for the telephone, dialled at panic speed, and stood, cursing as Daniel's number rang unanswered. Too late. He had left.

Stomach fluttering, he hurriedly donned his jacket. He had to get to Daniel, warn him, before it was too late. Before *she* destroyed him. How clever they'd been, how fucking clever!

'SHIT!' He cried out, wishing he owned a handgun.

Folding the picture, he slipped it into a pocket and dashed out to the car.

* 23 *

Central Park . . .

Mather swung his car onto Central Park West at a paced crawl, braked close to the 72nd Street gate, and cut the engine. He stared through the open gateway into the gloom beyond; the infamous Central Park night. Taking a grip on his indecision, he opened the door. He had one foot on the ground when the cold bore of a gun muzzle lightly touched his temple, freezing him in his seat.

'I'm getting into the back seat,' Daniel said. The night was not cold, yet his teeth were chattering. 'Don't make any sudden moves . . .' he warned.

'Or you'll blow my brains out.' Mather was sanguine. 'It's okay, I saw the movie.'

Daniel clambered into the rear, slammed shut the door and fitted the tip of the muzzle into the hollow at the base of Mather's skull. He pressed too hard; he was nervous, and showing it.

'Where to?' Mather prompted him.

Daniel hated him for his aplomb. Indecisively he sucked at his lower lip. The planning, the rehearsals, had gone so well, but now his nerves were in shreds. 'Just drive,' he snapped abruptly. 'I'll direct you.' Mather calmly started the engine and they drew away from the kerb.

Turner was two hundred yards away when he saw Daniel getting into the black Buick he assumed was driven by Mather. He had run from Columbus Circle and his heart was pounding, chest aching as if stretched. Breath rasped in his lungs. As the Buick moved away he groaned, and collapsed against the park fence to recover.

Once he realised he might lose the Buick if he did not move, he cast his gaze about and located the rental car Dan was using while in the city. They had agreed the keys would be under the dash for Turner to find if he did not arrive in time. Sprinting across the road he snatched open the driver's side door and fumbled for the keys, letting out a gasp of relief on finding them.

'C'mon . . .' he muttered, firing the engine. Swinging the wheel wildly, he made a perilous and illegal turn and pressed his foot to the floor to set off in pursuit.

A mellifluous smile spread slowly athwart Cutter's mean countenance. He watched Turner set off after Mather, then nudged his own car into gear and followed at a more sedate pace, keeping the prey just in view.

They were on an unlit stretch of turnpike, the throbbing of the engine a comforting rumble. Without turning his head Mather asked how much further they were going.

'We are almost there,' Daniel replied. 'There's a bridge coming up in a mile or so. Once we cross it I want you to slow down. The turning I want you to take is narrow and I don't want to miss it.'

Mather gave the smallest of nods, then lapsed into silence. His gaze casually drifted to the rearview mirror, where the headlamps of the car following them still hung in sight. Good. He suspected that Cutter was on his tail, and was glad; for once, the bald-headed jerk might prove useful. He had not anticipated being trapped in his car, and cursed his lack of foresight. He wondered what his people waiting in the park had made of his non-appearance. Never would he have guessed that Baker's fear would send him onto the offensive. For the first time that night he began to feel uneasy; perhaps Baker really was crazy enough to pull the trigger.

Half a mile behind, Cutter smiled bleakly as he recognised the location. He had to hand it to Baker; the guy had a sense of humor!

In between the two cars, Turner was hunched over the wheel, squinting ahead. His eyes ached from peering at the tiny red tail lights. They flared brighter as the car braked, then they appeared to slide closer together as the Buick turned into a hidden side lane. They vanished. He braked to locate and take the turn, and for a fleeting instant harboured the wild idea that the car behind him, the car that had remained at a constant distance, might be following. But then he was into the turn, driving into solid blackness, and the lights behind him were forgotten as he fought to pilot the car down the narrow, bumpy lane.

Cutter let his engine die, doused his lights and coasted into the turn. Once placed, he braked, then took from the glove box his favorite weapon; the SEAL knife he always kept near. He loved the feel of the razor's edge along his thumb. Fitting a comfortable grip around the handle of the knife, he left the car and vanished with expert ease into the nearest patch of undergrowth.

They were cruising along the uneven river bank, rolling at an angle that would have been perilous had the ground been wet.

The powerful lamp beams probed far ahead before dissipating into the blackness.

'Cut the engine,' Daniel ordered, grinding the muzzle against flesh when Mather was slow to react.

'Take it easy.' Mather growled impatiently. The engine died, and the acrid, poisonous odour from the exhaust wafted in through the partially opened window.

'We'll get out here. Leave the lights on.' Pushing open the door, Daniel eased himself out. Mather followed slowly, pushing his door shut with a click. 'Where the hell are we, and why are we here?'

'We're here because it's just about the most isolated spot I know of. I've been here before – but you know that already.'

'How would I know if you've been here before?'

Moving cautiously, and keeping the gun trained, Daniel placed the hood of the Buick between himself and Mather. He snarled his reply. 'Because this is the place your bald-headed friend tried to run me off the road.'

'Bald . . .' Mather's surprise was plainly genuine. He frowned, and in the pause the breeze picked up. A few fat raindrops splatted flat on the hood, and from some distance away came the low rumbling of thunder. Mather's face cleared. 'Cutter. You've been having trouble with Cutter?'

'If that's his name, yes.'

Mather exhaled loudly, as if wearily contemplating some sudden and disturbing news item, and his brow furled. He should have guessed; Galbraith had agreed much too readily to his request to be allowed to handle Baker alone. The son-of-a-bitch just HAD to interfere! When he got back to New York, he and the Senator were venued for one hell of a row. To Daniel he said: 'Do you want to talk about it?'

'No,' Dan snapped. He swallowed – still afraid, and the fingers holding the gun butt shifted uncomfortably.

'Okay then,' Mather responded, just as curtly. 'Let's hear what you have to say.'

'I saw you on Dealey Plaza the day Kennedy was shot. You fired a rifle.'

After a brief consideration, Mather conceded the point with a tilt of his head. Daniel's mouth curled in triumph. At last! At last!

'You son of a bitch,' his voice was fraught with released venom. With the enemy helpless in his sights, he felt the urge to hit back grow strongly. 'Killing Kennedy wasn't enough for you.

You had to wipe out all those others. Why?'

Mather was momentarily uncomfortable. He gave the tiniest shrug. Dan went on: 'Why so many . . . ?' he faltered, the words snagging in his throat. '. . . why my father?'

'My information is that your father committed suicide.'

'NO!!!' Dan screamed, banging the hood with his free hand and startling the bigger man. 'You pushed him until he went out of his mind! He knew what I'd seen, he knew that if he broke he'd give me away. He killed himself to take the pressure off me, but it was you drove him to it.'

'You were just a kid then, Daniel. You have no idea what the times were like. Tensions were high; industry, the military, the CIA, the Cuban opposition to Castro. Kennedy sanctioned actions against Cuba, then backed out at the last minute. He knew about the operations they were running all over the world. After the missile crisis he made a deal with Kruschev that left many of the Generals in the Pentagon feeling emasculated, and then when he signed a document taking authority for covert operations away from the CIA, sacking the Director of the CIA, Allen Dulles, and threatening to splinter the agency into a thousand pieces, he placed himself on a collision course with forces he could not possibly hope to contain. We were on a virtual war footing against our own President! There was a strong feeling in our community that if he hauled us out of Vietnam, following embarassments over Cuba and Laos, the US would have lost just a little too much face. Add to that the anger of the mob, traditional allies of American intelligence, and the pressure they were exerting to have the pressure from the Attorney General reduced, and you gain some idea of the cauldron of hatred for Kennedy that was boiling. Admittedly, the ripples after the assassination spread further than anticipated — we had to tidy up more than planned, but that was due to a fuck-up by the Dallas police. There should have been no one allowed onto Dealey Plaza.

'It was sad, I know that, but we were just protecting ourselves.' His tone was placatory.

Daniel swallowed, hard. 'You know I have to kill you, don't you?'

Mather gave a confident half smile. 'I understand you feel you have to try.' Experimentally he took a step, halting as Daniel tightened his finger on the trigger. 'Don't doubt me!' Dan warned, voice wavering. 'I'm a dead shot with this thing! I've had thousands of hours of practice.'

Mather's smile filled out. 'That's odd. I had some pretty extensive research on you carried out. There was no mention of you ever handling a weapon.'

He sounded so smug, Daniel wished he had the nerve to blast him right then. In truth, he was not positive he could pull the trigger, but there were things he had to know, and it was vital Mather believe he possessed the will to kill. Squeezing the trigger he sent a bullet past Mather's shoulder. The reverberation quickly died, and, as if on cue, the wind picked up another notch.

Cutter, moving stealthily through dense foliage, ducked instinctively at the sound. Absently fondling the handle of his beloved SEAL knife tucked into his belt, he drew comfort from its touch.

Turner halted at the blast, then, trembling in the cold and from fear, he pulled his coat about him. Driven by fears for Daniel he had been crashing blindly through the undergrowth, unheeding the noise he was making and the many tiny smarting cuts the jagged branches had made on his face. His breath came in loud shallow gasps, and, despite the coat, the cold incised deeply.

Mather had tightened reflexively at the shot. Now he relaxed. Baker had made his point. Perhaps he had miscalculated. . . . 'Killing isn't easy. Is there some other arrangement we can come to?'

Secretly pleased to hear Mather offer what might be a way out, Daniel snatched at the opportunity. 'There might be, if we can talk.'

Mather felt burgeoning triumph, but kept his face still. He had bought time for himself, but when the moment came, as it surely would, he would grasp the chance and punish Baker for his weakness. He smiled. 'Sure, what do you want to talk about?'

'Tell me about Oswald. What was he, really?'

Mather smirked. 'Lee was born to be a sucker, but he was Hoover's mistake, not ours. He'd been playing the role of *agent provocateur* for the FBI ever since coming back from Russia. But he was obvious, playing the pro-Castro role while associating with the anti-Castro lobby at Guy Bannister's office on Camp

Street. He stumbled onto Dave Ferrie, his old pal from the Civil Air Patrol, and was as intrigued as ever by him. Ferrie took him down to one of the camps where the CIA were still training the anti-Castro cadres. Once Lee got wind of the scheme, he went to the FBI and presented Hoover with a dilemma; by giving the Director of the FBI knowledge of the plot, he unwittingly made him an accomplice. It was no secret Hoover hated the Kennedys, and they were waiting to get rid of him. He had a handle on them; he had warned JFK off seeing Judith Exner and Julie Starr, and he knew all about the links to the mob, Sam Giancana and Gioncarlo Giometri, who Bobby Kennedy had deported. He had a grip on them through the links to Monroe, and her death. There was a lot going on.

'Lee faithfully kept Hoover's office informed, believing that Hoover was serious about averting a threat. Don't forget that all the things I just told you about were not public knowledge in 1963. Oswald, like every other member of the public, thought Hoover had the best interests of the nation at heart. Promises were made to him, he thought he would be rewarded for saving the President's life with a fully fledged FBI Special Agent's job. But they kept stringing him along. The agency job was always one crummy assignment away.

'On the day itself, well, when the shooting occurred he must have realised what happened. He may even have guessed he'd been left exposed – he had brought the so-called untraceable rifle to the depository, ostensibly for one of the gunmen to use. He travelled with us to his rooming house. We had a police car pick him up outside his lodgings and set him down near the rendezvous point where he was to meet Savage, his FBI contact. He saw the killing of Tippett, recognised the man who pulled the trigger, and knew he was in deep. He took refuge in the Texas Theater, and the rest is history.'

Daniel said: 'Then he wasn't one of the killers?'

'He wasn't even near the window.'

'Then who was?'

'He's dead now. His name can mean nothing to you. His family were told a tale about his death, they would be the only casualties if the story broke after all these years.'

'You're becoming quite the humanitarian.' Daniel remarked, acidly. Mather shrugged, and, unnoticed by Daniel, edged a few inches nearer. 'Perhaps some of my ideas have changed.'

'Perhaps. I am surprised Hoover didn't close you down. He could have, couldn't he?'

'He could. Once we'd seen through Lee we knew the FBI could wrap us up at any moment. Lee had us fooled at first; with his contacts in the Cuban groups he was just one of those expendable little people we decided to make use of. It was almost too late when we discovered his infiltration into the group had been deliberate. We knew that to keep Hoover off our backs we had to compromise the bureau. To achieve this, we decided to go for Hoover's jugular – his pride in his image as the guardian of American morals. He valued the reputation of the FBI more than anything, certainly more than he valued the life of JFK. So Oswald became Hoover's part of the deal. The meat in the sandwich. The sacrificial lamb. To appear genuine, Lee was so gung-ho he didn't question the way events were woven about him. He drove away from the depository in a car with myself and three others, and he was numbed. He could hardly speak. It must have been terrible for him; pretending to be one of us while knowing that something had gone wrong with the FBI. Until the very last minute he actually believed Hoover's agents would step in and scoop us up.' Mather smiled as he described this scene.

'Couldn't Hoover have arrested you all, anyway, and announced that Lee was an agent put in place to uncover the plot?'

'He could have done that – if Kennedy lived. Otherwise that story wouldn't wash. Lee had kept him well informed — we made sure of that. His problem, as I said, was that he wanted JFK off the scene as much as we did. John and Bobby were major pains in his ass. He knew that if pushed to trial we could prove the FBI, through its inaction, had colluded in the assassination. He dare not take that chance. In the end the temptation was just too great. He left us alone.'

The darkness and the need for stealth aroused animalistic instincts in Cutter. Brow furled in concentration, senses stung alive by the feeling of anticipation, he crossed the damp earth, and its carpet of leaves, with the minimum of sound. In his head, no conscious thought. Some instinctive survival relay had taken control of his actions. He might have been back in 'Nam. The feeling was the same; the tingling nerves, the sick-gut sensation and the sprung crouch, the readiness.

To his right, he heard the sound of someone trampling the undergrowth with no attempt at stealth. As the crashing stopped, Cutter sank lower, senses divining sounds from the air, picking up the noise of strained breathing. His eyes narrowed, and reaching out a fat hand he gently parted the curtain of branches. There before him, mere feet away and clearly outlined in the light from the moon as it slipped from behind a cloud, sat Turner. He had a hand pressed to his aching chest. He lunged forward once more and vanished noisily into a thicket.

A cruel smile spread slowly across Cutter's face. Choosing a deliberately circuitous route, he set off in pursuit.

Thunder rolled, and the clouds frowned threateningly. The moon slid behind a mass of cloud so dense even the vapourlight disappeared. Rain was falling steadily, and Mather had twice asked if they might get back inside the car.

Daniel was still probing. 'What about Ruby? Why did he kill Oswald?' He was getting wetter. He would have liked to have been inside the Buick, but he dared not risk being trapped with a man as deadly as Mather in an enclosed space.

Mather sighed. Raindrops in his hair glistened like cheap jewelery in the reflected lamplight. 'It had to be Ruby. You need a lot of leverage to force a man to commit murder. But with Jack there was leverage to spare. He was into our Italian friends for a heck of a lot of money, and the IRS were after a piece of him. We managed to persuade him to take the lesser of two evils. When he heard what happened to Johnny Rossi he decided to do the right thing. He did what he could to wreck things — he called the police station the night before and told the duty officer that Oswald was going to be shot, but the fix was in, and ultimately he had no choice.'

With his free hand, Daniel wiped rain from his face. Then as Mather's words struck him, his jaw dropped. 'Rossi was found dismembered, crammed into an oil drum fished out of the harbor.' He dwelt on the image, and a cold chill fingered his spine. 'Jesus. Were you involved in that?'

Mather's hair was flattened by the rain, and his face, illuminated but pale in the weak light, looked menacing. Suddenly Daniel knew it was Mather who butchered Rossi.

'Right there . . .' he said quickly, in a surge of fear. 'Not another step.' His thoughts churned, and he felt close to helplessness. To tears. He could not pull the trigger, he was not a killer, and only feet away stood a very dangerous man who knew, with greater certainty every passing second, that he could not pull the trigger.

Oh God, what was he going to do?

Breathing through his mouth, Cutter sank into a predatory crouch, slipped the SEAL knife from his belt and wound his fat fingers around the handle. The situation was perfect. Ahead of him, within easy leaping distance, stood Turner. He was peering through a gap in the branches at the scene below him; Mather and Baker.

The growing frenzy, the strengthening urge in him struck a vital pitch, and Cutter sprang. In a single fluid movement he clapped a hand over Turner's mouth and rammed the knife into his lower back, angling the blade up under the ribs and thrusting with all his brutal might. . . .

To Turner it was a cold shock, a total incomprehension of what was happening. He felt a scream burst silently inside him, then every ounce of strength seemed to flood out of his body and he sank to his knees.

Cutter withdrew the knife and let Turner crumple. The injured man's hands clawed weakly at the earth, his breath coming in pitiful snatches. Cutter wiped the blade clean on the grass, then studied the dying man's feeble attempts to get up with a wry amusement. He was getting ideas. . . .

Suddenly voices from below drew his attention. Parting the branches, he peered down at the two men below.

'Tell me about Sirhan,' Daniel demanded. He was more nervous than ever. Their roles seemed to have reversed; the gun in Daniel's hand might not have existed. Mather had crept closer. 'I know you were at the Ambassador Hotel the night Bobby Kennedy was shot.'

'That's another story,' Mather replied. His tone implied stubbornness. He would say nothing further.

Dan eyed him with a mixture of fear and awe. 'How could you do it? Just kill him like that? Didn't you know what you were doing? Don't you have any scruples at all?'

The rain was falling heavily, gusting in slanting sheets as the wind rose and diminished. Mather haughtily drew himself up to his full imposing height. It was no consolation that Mather looked uncomfortable. 'We knew what we were doing,' Mather snapped. 'Kennedy was fucking the country. We did what we had to do and America got the benefit.'

'You didn't do us any favors. You led us into Vietnam.'

Mather's reply was stolid. 'Defense is a vital part of the economy. America benefited.'

Daniel was fast approaching eruption point. He had held onto his trump play long enough. 'Oh yeah?' he snarled, feeling the reins fall loose. 'So who benefited by the death of Barbara Rush? Will you tell me that?'

Mather stalled. Not even numbed – it was too early for that. Puzzlement shone on his face, as though he was sure he had heard incorrectly. He stared, open-mouthed, at Daniel, and when he mustered his energies to speak his voice came out small, and vulnerable. 'Barbara . . . ?'

'Yes, Barbara.' Daniel's voice was harshly cynical. 'You remember Barbara, the woman you were engaged to —'

'I KNOW WHO SHE IS!!!' Mather hollered. He looked strained. Panic danced across his face, and propelled by powerful emotion he rounded the Buick, stopping only when the gun was raised, trained on his face. He stared directly into the muzzle. His chest rose and fell as he fought to understand. 'You're lying,' he said, breathlessly. 'She's fine. I spoke to her a few days ago and she was . . .' His voice failed him. He looked lost. His head slumped forward and a mad fix glimmered in his eyes. 'It's not true. It's not true.'

He did not know. Mather had not known she was dead, and the awful truth began to dawn on Daniel. He felt guilt, inexplicably, felt shame and a fresh wave of despair.

Someone else had killed her!

In panic he wondered if he had miscalculated. He had been so sure! Now when he looked at Mather, saw him wracked with pain, his arms slowly rising, wrapping around his head, he felt a strange kinship. If his own heart had not been so burdened with grief he might have whooped in jubilation to see the butcher in torment.

'The police called me . . .' he said in a low voice. 'I flew up from Florida to identify the body.' He paused. 'You really didn't know?'

Mather appeared not to have heard. He was standing rock still, one hand caressing his brow. 'Oh God. Oh God.' The words were said quietly. There was no great show of emotion. Not yet. But inside . . . inside, the pain, he would not have believed the pain. He stood there and felt the life draining from him. He tilted his head far back, and through a mist of gathering tears peered skywards. His gaze panned the vast heavens as though searching for some answer.

All of his professional life he had been able to view death with the necessary detachment. This ought to be no different, but it was. For years he had parried the pain, but it had found a way under his guard and thrust savagely for his heart.

The rain poured unseen from the deep of the night, unnoticed by the two men sharing their grief. Both were soaked, hair plastered to their scalps, yet they cared not. Mather had retreated into some unholy inner sanctum, where worship of death and conspiracy paid dividends, but he glanced up when Daniel spoke. He said: 'What was that? What did you say?'

Daniel repeated patiently. 'I said: do you have any idea who might have killed her?'

The question seemed to do something to Mather. Until that moment he had not looked further than dealing with the reality, struggling to accept the awful. Pain had swamped him, and all he could see was her beautiful face, smiling at him. Now his thoughts turned to the who, and the why, and his eyes blazed with sudden knowledge and the desire for vengeance.

His voice was guttural. 'Oh, I know. I know alright.' His mind swung back in time, to the journey to this place, and the headlamps of the car following them. In his gut, with every instinct, he knew that Cutter had been the one to put out Barbara's light. And he knew that he was out there, in the woods, watching. In his heart he resolved to make Cutter pay, and pay.

His fist was clenched so tightly the knuckle joints cracked. The violent beast that lurked within him, that had been his strength in every dangerous situation he had ever encountered now raged, but he knew he must control it, hold it down, until the right time.

Control, he found control, and Daniel, watching the change that overcame Mather, had the feeling they had, through some peculiar trick of fate, become allies. 'Why was she killed?' he asked. 'Who could gain by her death?'

Mather turned away to peer into the impenetrable gloom. When he faced Daniel again the anguish had vanished from his face to be replaced by an eerie calm. Not a flicker of emotion remained.

Daniel marvelled at his control.

'It has to be . . .' Mather said softly. 'Well, she gave us you. She told me about you being on Dealey. It wasn't intentional . . .' he added hurriedly, on seeing the hurt on Daniel's face. 'She had too much to drink and I encouraged her to talk. You came up in the conversation. I guess I was jealous that she'd seen you, so she decided to explain. That same day I ordered your telephone tapped. When you called the FBI you gave me the opportunity I needed; I passed the word to the Assassination Bureau. They were ignorant of the source, but I hinted I was FBI and had traced the call. Newbolt was a blowhard, I knew he'd rush to get in touch. All we had to do was watch.'

Daniel lowered the gun. 'Why would you want Newbolt to help me? We might hurt you.'

Mather shook his head. 'We never would have let you become that dangerous. Once you knew too much . . .' the pause conveyed much. 'We are always alert to the possibility that some fragmentary lead we overlooked might surface. It was our intention to let you get as far as you could, then close you down and bury your disclosures with you.'

He stopped, yielded to the irresistible urge that gnawed at him, and turned once more to the woods. He scanned the darkness. His shoulders rose as the tension in him mounted, and at his sides his hands were bunched into fists.

'But why Barbara?' Daniel persisted. The rainfall was heavier, coming down in great slanting sheets. He wiped his face.

Mather reluctantly tore his gaze from the search; his senses warned of danger and he wanted to see it coming.

'You'd given up,' he said. 'I guess they wanted to lure you back into the game. If damaging evidence does exist, they reckon you'll be motivated enough to find it. They can clean up later.'

Daniel looked in despair at the gun in his hand. Clean up! Was that all it was? Was that all Barbara had been to them – a piece in the game? His mind reeled beneath the weight of guilt and confusion.

'There was nothing personal in all of this,' Mather said mechanically, 'they're just taking care of business.'

'Business,' Daniel echoed dully. Then he froze. 'They. You keep saying they. Who are you talking about?'

Mather appeared subdued; mouth clamped tight. He had been hurt, immeasurably so, yet the grip they had on him was still so strong it was hard to speak. Then the storm gathering within him broke. Barbara was dead; what the hell did he owe them?

'The vested interests. The Octad,' he muttered. 'Since the twenty second of November, 1963, I've been in charge of the tidying up. It was my task to have you watched, and eventually remove you.' As he spoke, Mather's attention wandered; his senses probing the night air, patiently awaiting the tell-tale sign he was sure would come.

Cutter was jubilant. What a stroke of luck! If Mather was involved, then Galbraith was too! He had always suspected the two men must share a dark secret – how else could they work together in an atmosphere of mutual loathing?

His cruel heart brimmed with wicked glee; he would be going back to New York with some pretty powerful leverage. He could *be* somebody. If his nerve held, he could be right hand man to the next President of the United States!

But in his elation he grew careless. As his concentration veered his weight shifted, and as he moved to correct his balance a branch snapped loudly underfoot. The sound cut the air like a rifleshot, and he cursed, knowing that the error had betrayed him. Mather was no fool.

The cold and the rain, the fear, and the realisation that it was his fault Barbara had died had bled the spirit from Daniel. Had he wanted to, Mather could have taken him with ease, but his attention was elsewhere.

At the sound of the snapping branch, Mather had sunk into a combat stance. He seemed oblivious to Daniel's presence. Moving away with sure steps he made his way up the incline and halted before the ranked trees. His mind was focused. Cutter was a borderline psychopath, a man who enjoyed inflicting pain. It could only be he that killed Barbara, the only woman Mather had ever loved, the woman he had hoped to build the rest of his life around. And Cutter was Galbraith's man.

All his emotions converged, centring into a cold, loathing fury. He would kill!

'Cutter!' His voice was guttural with hatred. 'Come on out you son of a bitch. Let me see your ugly face. Cutter!'

Cutter had been in Vietnam. He was big and strong, but Mather was big and angry, and Cutter knew that to be sure of winning he would have to take and sustain the initiative; strike first and make it count. Licking his lips in heightened anticipation, he let Mather draw nearer until he reached a small clearing, then he lunged from his crouch in the undergrowth, knife poised in raised hand to strike the killing blow.

The two men collided. Mather deflected the knife strike with a sweep of his arm, and Cutter retaliated with a head butt to the body that sent them both sprawling, Cutter on top. He plunged with the knife, but Mather's reflexes were equal to the attack and he clamped fingers tightly around the descending wrist, halting the diving blade mere inches from his throat. With a savage wrench he twisted the knife aside and punched Cutter under the nose. The bald man reared back, and Mather snatched the opportunity to struggle free and regain his feet.

Upright, but skidding on the slimy mud, the men exchanged blows. They fell against each other and wrestled in the shifting watery mud. Cutter lost his knife and found himself without an advantage, brawling chin to chin with a man whose sole intent was to kill him. The rain drummed down, drenching them as they wrestled. They stood, slid and fell, only to clamber up again to trade punches before falling again. Panting fiercely, they stumbled over a ridge and rolled, locked in a frenzied embrace, down the slope, coming to a halt on the flat treadpath above the river.

Sinking to a crouch at the side of the car, Daniel watched the battle in transfixed silence. He watched Mather, weakened by the fall, struggle to his feet. He saw Cutter, bounding animal-like from the clutching mud, easily deflect Mather's punch and counter with a gut blow that doubled up the bigger man. Seizing the chance, Cutter beat him to the floor with a series of viciously powerful blows. Mather raised his arms to protect his face, only to have them smashed aside by the sheer fury of the onslaught. Finally, when he was too weak to defend his head any longer, his hands dropped, and Cutter set about a systematic and sadistic destruction of his face. He built up a rhythm, hitting until his knuckles bled, until Mather's face was a blur. Then with the last great effort in him, Cutter hoisted the bigger man to his feet and thrust him over the edge and down towards the crashing waters. The body tumbled, struck earth and cartwheeled, landing at last face down in the fast-flowing river. The black waters were quick to claim the body, and in moments it had vanished.

Daniel cowered behind the car. Nerve gone, mind echoing with recurring images; Cutter's bald dome glistening in the pale moonlight as he pummelled Mather's unresisting head with his great fat fists. Pummelled until only fatigue could halt him . . . Daniel shuddered. He had to get away. He could not face Cutter. The man was too strong, too dreadful. He was inhuman. Fumbling in a pocket he reloaded the gun.

Cutter sank to the earth and sucked in great gulps of air. Though soaked to the skin he felt warmed inside; Mather hadn't been so tough. He grinned, shark's teeth glistening, and looked about him. Baker was next on the agenda. He was going to enjoy killing him. Grunting with effort he shuffled to his feet. He had to get moving before cold set in, before he lost his edge.

As he watched Cutter approach the car Daniel shrank further

into the shadow. His knees felt weak, and nausea churned his stomach. He gulped back the first welling of vomit as it neared his throat. Panic engulfed him. He had to get away. Cutter would butcher him if he stayed where he was.

A shadow fell across him and he glanced up to see Cutter's apelike form looming. Mere sight was enough; forcing himself up onto his feet he ran for the woods. His feet skidded on the greasy slope, and twice he sprawled headlong, but fear spurred him, and attaining the top he plunged into the trees, the sound of Cutter's laughter ringing in his ears.

'Come on back, Danny boy. I got somethin' to tell ya. Come on back!' Peals of maniacal laughter flooded the air.

Daniel broke his sprint to pause. He leaned against a tree and clutched a hand to his straining chest. He felt emptied of strength, but managed to urge himself on. 'C'mon, come on . . .' The sound of laughter was nearer. He turned, and on palsied knees launched himself forward.

Cutter remembered something. Went back down the slope. He lifted the knife from the mud and lovingly brushed it clean.

'Almost forgot you, didn't I?' he muttered softly, stroking the blade with his fingers. 'What say we go cut some meat?'

Turner stirred weakly, a feeble moan wheezing from him. Gently he pressed a hand to the wound in his back and smarted at the touch. Thickening blood smeared his fingers. Wincing in pain he laboriously hauled himself upright and clutched at a tree for support. Then he heard the laughter, and his blood was chilled as the significance of the sound seeped through to him. When a figure came crashing through the undergrowth and into the clearing, he turned his head sharply and gasped in relief. 'Daniel!' His voice sounded alarmingly frail. He lurched forward, falling into the arms of his friend.

Daniel was shocked at the paleness of Turner's face, deathly white in the moonlit gloom. 'You're hurt?' Turner nodded. He made a half turn to let Daniel see the black gaping wound. 'Jeezus,' Daniel hissed. 'We have to get out of here. Do you feel up to moving?'

Turner coughed, and a trickle of black liquid ran from a corner of his mouth. 'How much choice do I have?' He winced, then added: 'Let's go.' Leaning heavily against Daniel, he let himself be ferried from the clearing.

Cutter viewed the terrain and calculated the path the slope

would force Baker to take. He set off along an oblique, intercepting course. He was a man who enjoyed the chase, and as he powered his bulk into the undergrowth he started to laugh.

Daniel was following a narrow path that wound gradually upwards. He hurried the injured Turner along the path as quickly as he dared. Turner was mumbling deliriously. Daniel was gasping, every breath an effort, and finally exhaustion forced him to stop. Gently setting his friend down with his back against a tree, he paused to catch his breath.

'We'll move on in just a minute,' he panted. 'Just give me a few seconds to catch up.'

Though frightened, Turner was glad of the respite. He relaxed against the tree and his gaze darted about. Sensing a furtive movement beyond the bushes to his right, he frowned, and peered harder. Then he saw Cutter's evil bulk sidling in, and the cold shock jolted him. Swallowing hard, too scared even to yell a warning, he started to clamber upwards.

Cutter lurched murderously into the clearing, and his form emanated a raw, subhuman virulence. Plastered in mud he charged with unnerving animal confidence. Unstoppable.

In the sudden knowledge that his funk had endangered his friend, Turner found strength to squeal a warning. Daniel spun with less than a moment to spare and the plunging knife whisked past his shoulder. Untrained to react to such a situation, Daniel was welded to the spot, no idea what he should do. When Cutter grasped his lapel with a huge fist and raised the knife, he knew it was the end . . .

Turner lunged in desperation. One hand closed on Cutter's throat, the other scratched and clawed wildly in an attempt to contain the hand holding the knife. He screamed: '*RUN DAN RUN!!!*'

Cutter growled, and swung Turner around in an attempt to throw him off, but the wounded man held on with panicked strength. It took Daniel only a second to realise that if he stayed they would both be lost, so with barely a pause, he ran. He ran until the sounds of the struggle were left behind and he could no longer hear the desperate gurgling noise Turner made as he bravely fought to pinion the beast. He plunged through the undergrowth, and all sounds were blotted out by the noise of his blind rushing through the tangle of jagged branches.

Turner swung a clumsy, ineffectual punch at Cutter's gargoyle head. He missed, then found himself being forced to the ground, forced onto his belly, until he lay helpless, gasping and whimpering. Cutter sat astride him, grasped a handful of hair and jerked back Turner's head. Arching his spine until he cried out. His breath came fast and shallow, and tears brimmed in his eyes. Adjusting his grip on the knife, Cutter made a deep cut across the neck of his prey. The taut skin split easily and Turner started to spurt. Panting in excitement, a low, menacing giggle teetering just below the surface, Cutter made a second deep cut, and a third, meeting resistance from bone and gristle. He wrenched at the head to help the knife through, and a spasm of crazed laughter rocked him. Spittle sprayed from his mouth as he gave a last savage jerk. Muscle and vertebrae yielded, and head was parted from shoulders.

Cutter held his trophy aloft, and was transported into a rapturous state by the sight of blood dripping from the jagged neck to a pool at his feet. His eyes glistened madly, and he threw back his head and loosed a paroxysm of insane laughter. Between his feet, Turner's body jiggled convulsively, then fell flat and still. Cutter laughed again and then, possessed totally by the killing rage, he tilted his face skywards and howled at the moon.

Daniel's headlong dash through the undergrowth was brought to a halt by the bloodcurdling cry of a beast triumphant, ecstatic in the grip of the killing spell. Cutter! What had he done? His anxiety raged inwardly. Poor Turner!

He was still breathing heavily, but to his surprise the discomfort had passed. He had gotten some kind of second wind.

He started to think; it was pointless to run without direction. He either had to know where he was headed – or he had to stay and face Cutter.

Face Cutter! The very thought weakened his sphincter, but sooner or later it had to happen. He was not fool enough to believe Cutter would leave him be. No, if he had to face the brute he better get it over as soon as possible, while his anger over Turner was still fresh enough to spur him, and while Cutter, still in the throes of killing ecstasy, might get careless. He breathed hard through his nose. He had to do it – but not without some preparation.

Once the decision was made he felt better in himself. The price Turner had paid, and the blood-lust baying of the beast had brought home the terrible reality of the situation. He had no choice.

He heard him coming, heard the brutish rasp of his breathing, felt the approach of his menacing presence. He heard him tramping with unnerving confidence through the undergrowth. Then the voice, disembodied and subhumanly gleeful, seemed to melt in from all sides. 'Hey Danny boy!' Daniel darted his gaze from spot to spot. Each individual sound seemed threateningly near.

'I got somethin' to tell yoooo!' No mistaking the joy in the voice.

Daniel took out the revolver, tightened his fingers around the butt, and with his thumb stroked the dead contours of the chamber.

A devilish chuckle rippled the night air. 'It's about Barbara. Your good friend Barbara. You wanna hear what I did?'

Daniel swallowed, steeled himself, and fervently wished the horror he sensed was coming could be avoided. But Cutter's voice rang out:

'I killed her Danny. Just like I'm gonna kill you.'

Daniel shut his eyes and clamped his trembling lips together. Stop it . . .

'I fucked her first though . . .' again came the chuckle, spiced with unearthly evil, rising in pitch until it jangled the nerves. 'Then . . . then you know what I did next . . . eh? I took her to pieces . . . a little at a time, yeah. Fucked her every which way there is and then let my lovely knife have some fun. Opened her up and took out the pieces one by one. Did she scream??'

Daniel had to tighten every muscle to suppress the swell of nausea that doused him. In vain he shut his eyes to blot out the power of the image Cutter's words conjured up. The voice and the trampling sounds were unbearably close. He could sense Cutter breathlessly winding up to taunt him further.

'Then guess what? Guess what?' he snorted, piglike. 'When there was only her little bitty heart left, beatin' away like shit, and she was a screamin' and a hollerin' beggin' me to kill her, guess what? Hell, I did her again! I'll say she screamed!'

Daniel drew his elbows tightly in toward his body; an involuntary spasm, and clamped a fist over his mouth. He shuddered as peals of maniacal gaiety echoed around him. A tear coursed down his face and settled upon his upper lip. Even with the gun in hand he felt weak, his resolve bleeding away as the image of Barbara in pain hung dammingly before his mind's eye. His knees were beginning to jelly when something hurtled through the gloom at him. He snapped to panicked attention and lifted the gun – one sight of the grimacing countenance was enough to set him blasting. The face fell to the ground, and for one blissful moment he believed he had downed the beast. He let fly another shot at the face and then halted, frozen in a rigid posture, locked tight with terror. The gunshot had kicked the head into a spin, and it was only when it came to rest that he recognised Turner's face. His dead friend stared directly back at him. Seeing the neat hole his bullet had drilled in Turner's forehead, Daniel felt despair swamp him. His heart sank to unimagined depths, he was caught in a whirlwind of horror. Turner's face seemed to be glaring accusingly at him, dark blood trickling from the neat round puncture.

The image of Cutter standing over Barbara's ravaged body, gloating as he tortured her, filled his mind. It was too much. It was too much. Too much to bear! All he wanted was to die too, end the nightmare. Let him die and find peace from the torture his imagination insisted upon.

Then the wind stopped, and all about him seemed still. Beyond his control or understanding he felt a change occur within him. Fear and terror – there were limits, and he had passed saturation point. The prolonged dread and the repeated surges of adrenalin had a cathartic effect. A fresh lucidity flooded his mind, and the frightening images receded. He envisaged his father, standing tall and proud and afraid of no man, reduced to putting a gun into his mouth to protect his son. He saw Newbolt, silenced in a bout of savagery because he sought the truth. And Barbara, caught in the fallout simply because she had known him. Surely that was the most appalling atrocity, the most meaningless of all. Cutter, and those like him, were responsible for many such dreadful acts, and it was time the worm turned – whatever the cost. All this he knew in a fraction of a second.

He sank into a half-crouch, and as he turned on the balls of his feet he had about him the look of the hunter. The haunted look had vanished, and he was suddenly predator. His breath rattled in the back of his throat and a snarl rumbled as he prepared to fight back.

Cutter crashed towards him, and he knew the moment had arrived. The gun was in his hand and ready; it had always been ready. He knew with fatalistic certainty that the years of keeping the weapon primed had been for just this one moment. Bolstered by the thought that he was strong, he stood poised for the challenge.

Cutter burst into the clearing and landed flat-footed, knees sprung, eyes scanning warily. In his right hand the SEAL knife glinted hungrily. He peered in mild amusement at the gun, and a guttural vibration rattled in his throat. 'No way, shithead. You ain't got the balls for that I know.'

Holding the look, Dan flexed his thumb and drew back the hammer. It set with a loud click.

Something in Daniel's calm demeanour pierced Cutter's animal frenzy. A flicker of uncertainty crossed his face before belief in his brutish invulnerability reasserted itself, and a lop-sided grin divided his face. The rumble in his throat grew louder as he wound up to pounce. He advanced.

Faced with the beast, Daniel felt his resolve start to slip. Cutter moved in a cautious arc, the knife turning in his hand. Determination flooded out of Daniel as his gaze settled on the blade. But as if to spur him, a vision of Barbara sprang to mind. He pictured that same blade sinking into her flesh, travelling in a long cutting stroke from navel to throat. He imagined her face, contorted with pain, and he imagined how she must have screamed: '*Daniel help me! Help me!*'

It was an image potent enough to freeze the blood, to churn the stomach. More real than reality. He felt a great burst of nausea and disgust and loathing, and as Cutter launched himself forward with rabid ferocity, knife poised for a killing thrust, Daniel fired twice.

But Cutter's forward momentum was too great. He crashed into Daniel, knocking him flat on his back, then sprawled atop him, struggling to pinion the gun hand beneath his knee while forcing the knife downwards . . .

In a desperate, reflex action, Daniel grasped the wrist of the knife hand, resisting with a strength he did not know he possessed. But though he held on grimly, the knife slowly descended, and he could sense the demonic hunger of the blade as it strained. Cutter grasped Daniel's throat with his free hand and leaned all his weight behind the push. The corrupting reach of his foul breath flooded Daniel's nose and mouth, his tongue swam in mud, and he gagged at the taste of rank water. Blinking away the mist of rainwater he focused on Cutter's murderously intent countenance, saw close-up the narrowed killer eyes and the gaping open mouth, tongue lopping in canine fashion between slack lips. Long moments passed, the two men locked in a fierce battle of wills, a battle Daniel knew he dare not lose. The only sounds the whimpering and snorting of men caught up in extreme physical effort. When a pear-shaped globule of saliva escaped Cutter's mouth and fell in a sickening strand onto Daniel's lip he almost vomited. He prayed for the strength to survive, and as the saliva trickled into his mouth he forced himself to one last mighty effort. Fiercely twisting his hand, he aimed the gun and pulled the trigger.

The force of the blast shook them both. Cutter paused to glower in stupefaction at the burning hole in his shoulder. His arm dangled uselessly at his side, and both men had the same thought at the same moment . . .

Daniel had seen the hand fall limply and knew he would not have a better chance to take the advantage. With a roar he strained upwards, almost cheering as Cutter gave way, but with a sudden furious surge the beast fought back, until it seemed he must force Daniel to the ground again. But the gun was between them, and Dan pressed the muzzle to Cutter's chest and let blast. This time the effect was awesome. Cutter was hurled backwards. He rolled over as Daniel hurried to stand.

Cutter sat where he was, bellowing more in anger than pain. With a hand he explored the wound in his chest, then glancing up, a base grin spreading across his face, he fully inserted a finger into the hole. When he withdrew it the finger dripped blood, and he raised it to his mouth and sucked it clean.

Revulsion swept over Daniel, strong enough to make him want to kill, anything, just to stop Cutter. The man was totally insane!

Cutter shuffled forward on all fours with canine eagerness. Daniel tightened his lips, raised the revolver and pulled the trigger. The hammer struck with a flat click. He hauled on the trigger twice more before he was forced to step quickly back to reload as Cutter lunged for his legs. With trembling fingers he cracked open the chamber and shook out the hulls, fumbled in his pocket for fresh shells and reloaded. Snapping shut the chamber he gave it a spin, then looked for the beast.

Cutter was on his knees, crawling like the wounded animal he was, still determined to attack. The wounds streamed blood, but his singleminded drive kept him moving onward. His burly arms embraced air, and his eyes beamed a venomous determination. He lunged again, but this time Daniel merely had to lift a foot to kick him onto his back. He stood over him, and for a few moments watched the vermin grovel in the mire. Daniel suddenly felt very awake, for he knew at last that he had the strength to relieve the beast of its life. Reason and human rationale would have to wait.

'You deserve this, Cutter,' he addressed the beast in a tone devoid of emotional inflection. 'All this and more, because I've been so afraid of you. And you know something else . . . ?' he jerked the trigger again. The blast took the beast squarely in the chest, knocking him onto his back. He writhed, grunting furiously and then, incredibly, powered by brute stubbornness, he clawed forward in the mud and forced himself upright. By now his breathing was horribly labored, and blood trickled from a corner of his mouth.

' . . . I believe it's getting easier.' Daniel aimed carefully, then blasted Cutter's right kneecap. The beast sprawled, whimpering, in the treacly mud.

'Yeah, I could get to like this.' Another shot, to the stomach this time. Cutter rolled onto his side and doubled up to stem the dreadful wounds.

Daniel's voice was high pitched with a mix of relief and elation. 'Fun, isn't it? I'd like to do to you what you did to Barbara, but I don't think I can quite get down to your level. Pity, really; simply dying is too good for you.' Another blast. Cutter clutched weakly at the fresh wound, then his hand dropped; his infamous strength had deserted him. He stared in desperation, mouth chomping and spraying spittle, eyes pleading.

Daniel drew back the trigger for the last time. Payback; he was actually enjoying watching the beast die! A look of horrified disbelief spread across Cutter's face as he realised what was happening. His rage had cleared and he knew it really was the end. He fell forward onto his face, frenzied movements slowing visibly as life escaped his clutching grasp. Daniel chuckled, and was surprised at the wickedness of the sound. He knew he ought to feel shame, or guilt, but he could not.

Cutter lay eternally still. With the tip of his shoe Daniel roughly kicked him onto his back. The head, apparently drained of blood, had turned a deathly, almost glowing white. A dark ragged rivulet traced a path across his chin.

Seeing the man he had grown to hate and fear lying dead at his feet was almost too wonderful. Payback; it felt good, and it had been easy after all.

* 24 *

In a daze he shambled along the treadpath, wandering numbly until, quite by chance, he stumbled upon his rental car — the one Turner had driven. Set a-trembling by the cold damp of the rain and the residue from adrenal surging, he stood by the car, pondering. His heart grew heavy as lucidity and recollection lowered their full weight upon him.

At last he snatched open the door and sat inside. The keys were in the dash, and lying on the passenger seat another bunch of assorted keys; David Turner's.

Starting the engine he mechanically reversed up the path, crushing bushes as he passed Cutter's car. He bounced onto the unlit stretch of turnpike. As he hit the road he felt lightheaded, elation doused him like a flood of cold wind. But it was a very temporary high, fast burning and soon extinguished.

To halt the onrush of despair he focused his energies on driving, and subsequently recalled nothing of the journey back to Barbara's apartment.

Sitting quietly in the gloom, he stared long and hard at the liquor bottle before finally filling the tumbler. He downed the burning spirit in a couple of draughts, then stumbled into the bedroom and collapsed onto the mattress.

It was a stormy night. Thunder rolled ponderously, with a resonance a score of timpani could not match. Daniel awoke and rolled onto his side, aware that the open window was flapping in the wind, striking the frame with a rhythmic, wooden slap. He got up and shut it, then returned shivering to the bed, drawing the duvet to his chin. The bedside clock glowed, 4:32. He struggled to sleep, but as his eyes grew heavy a sound from the next room jolted him wide awake once more. He sat up, knowing it was not the window that disturbed him after all.

Another sound, like someone crashing into furniture, set his nerves jangling. He cursed; the gun was in the other room. He had felt so *safe*! He tried to leave the bed but was too weak. His muscles were too drained to complete the effort. His head ached as if hung over. Straining, he began slowly to clamber from the bed, then he halted abruptly. It was too late.

The door crashed open, and in hurtled an ugly misshapen

beast of a man who launched himself at the bed. Senses frozen by panic, Daniel fell back, a cold clamp around his heart as the beast, bedraggled and filthy and inhumanly foul reached for his throat with stubby, muddy fingers. *CUTTER!!!*

'NO. NO!' Daniel cried through gritted teeth. Impossible! It could not be true but it was! Cutter was above him, heavy and solid and wet, and in the sudden illumination from a flash of sheet lightning glaring in through the window, Daniel saw the dead-white face, the gaping wounds. Cutter was snorting, his gargoyle head rocking intently as his fingers tightened.

Daniel felt the horrible squeezing on his neck, felt the throbbing of veins as he strained for breath. But in a series of gasps he was able to cry out: '*LEAVE ME ALONE!!!*'

Then bright sunlight burned at his eyes and he was thrashing alone on the bed, hands at his throat to fight off the imagined paws. He sat up, gazed around in wonder, quite unable to believe the attack had been only a dream, a nightmare. He held out a hand before him. It shook like a leaf in a gale.

A half dozen cups of sweet black coffee steadied his nerves, but the doubt remained. Had any of it happened? He needed to know. Impelled by fear and curiosity, and a vague feeling he owed it to Turner, he got into the hire car and set off.

He found the place and, perplexed, tramped the earth for over two hours, but though he found signs in the mud, trampled grasses and damaged branches, of the bodies and the cars there was no trace.

Someone had tidied up!

Greatly disturbed, he returned to the apartment where everything in sight was a painful reminder of Barbara, and where another shock awaited. A white envelope lay on the mat. It was sealed, but plain; no address, no name. He sat at the kitchen table to examine it. From the feel he guessed it contained a key . . . he tore it open to find his guess correct. A key with a numbered tag. Bus station locker.

There was something else, a magazine clipping, folded and crumpled, and stained in one corner with blood. But it was the picture, and the caption, that took his breath away. He read aloud: '*Senator Cyrus Galbraith . . . accompanied by his ward Miss Pamela Davis.*'

He had to read it twice, look hard and harder still, so difficult to overcome was his disbelief, his surety, that it was all some appalling mistake . . .

It was as though the world stood still. All he could feel and hear was the pounding of his heart. Pamela. Pamela. His Pamela . . . Galbraith's ward, part of his family. *She had known all along!* So how could she . . . how could . . . She had been Galbraith's line to Turner, to Daniel, to Newbolt.

'Oh Barbara,' the small cry crept from him.

He felt empty, betrayed, gutted. A gaping chasm occupied the space where his heart had lain. Slumping for the nearest chair he clawed at his hair in despair and frustration. Then he raised his head. The base of his stomach tilted queasily and he staggered to his feet. On a surge of anger he set out for the bus station.

The place was busy. It was designed for the transient, and the people traffic was constant. He passed the ticket offices, the queues waiting to board, the ranks of the disgruntled, the bums playing lucky dip in the trash cans, the fairies leaning provocatively by the men's john. He walked the carpet of cigarette butts, potato chips bags and plastic cups, he rounded the chicanes of heaped baggage and paused before the banked lockers. His approach from here on was wary; he expected to be intercepted at any moment. But not a move was made. Lifting a heavy case from a locker, he darted a last glance around then made for the exit. They must be watching, he told himself. It couldn't be that easy.

He did not return to the apartment. He dare not until he knew what the case contained. Checking into a seedy hotel close to the bus station, he climbed the stairs to the fourth floor room allocated him. It was the most basic imaginable, consisting of a bed, an open wardrobe fronted by a faded curtain, and a wash-basin that clung perilously to one wall.

Placing the case on the bed, he opened it and lifted out a fat file some seven inches thick, paper sheets crammed tight between worn velum covers.

He began to read, but so absorbing was the material he did not note the passing of the hours. When he next looked up to ease his aching eyes it was to find the room steeped in the golden brown patina of fading dusk. He put on the light, and paused to consider the dammingly awesome weight of the file — the incredible detail it contained; names, dates, pictures, sketches, depositions and transcripts. The locations of tapes even! Obtained who knew how. The complete story of the assassination of John Kennedy, told by one of the plotters. The full story, and what a satisfaction it was: How it had all been put together, and the great lengths gone to in order to mask the plot. The layers of deceit, the leaks, and the methods used to plug those leaks.

Contained in the file was a detailed breakdown of how the final day went, from the arrival of the shooters at the kill-zone, to the disposal, in a place named as the Brown House, of almost three quarters of the team used that day. Killed in a cellar which was later to be filled with concrete.

And the setting up of Oswald. How he had been a loose cannon for years. While he was in Russia his name and passport were used by a fake CIA company to buy equipment destined for the Bay of Pigs operation. J Edgar Hoover had written a memo about it! How Lee had been introduced as a public communist, a pro-Castro supporter, the only member of the New Orleans branch of the Fair Play for Cuba Committee. How his job depository was seen as crucial, the plotters knowing that to arrive at his luncheon destination, the Presidential car would leave downtown Dallas via Dealey Plaza.

Lee had been persuaded at one point, and for a different reason, to buy a supposedly untraceable rifle. This was to be the one used to kill JFK while Lee waited for the attaboy telephone call from his FBI contact, telling him that Kennedy was safe and the plotters tied up. There was a full breakdown of the way Oswald was taken to his lodgings by the four men in the station wagon, dropped off to change his clothes and leave for his so-called rendezvous.

But perhaps most astonishing of all was the way Oswald was trapped, and the way the evidence that might liberate him was ignored. After being spotted and reported for acting suspiciously, he was arrested in the Texas Theater and charged with the murder of police officer J D Tippett. And despite all the contrary evidence, the plotters got away with it . . . It was all there.

And then there was the why. The very month Kennedy had been sworn in as President, the CIA, unsure about his reliability, had begun to build a psychological profile designed to gauge how he would react to certain situations. Because of his father's wealth he did not need the traditional support of the establishment. He too was a loose cannon. After the Bay of Pigs he played both sides; unofficially sanctioning action against Cuba while plotting to make peace with Castro. He had an unofficial peace envoy in Cuba, visiting with Castro at the time of the assassination.

He had wanted to end the cold war. During the missile crisis of 1962, Kennedy had looked over the edge, seen the utter devastation that would result from an atomic spiral and realised that things had to change. Now he had become a threat to the intelligence infrastructure, and the experience the anti-Castro arm of the CIA had gained fixing wars abroad was turned upon the Commander in Chief.

But for the men who wielded secret power, Cuba was no longer enough. The rapacious military-industrial alliance, led by what intelligence specialist Colonel Fletcher Prouty called the Secret Team, and Turner had called the Octad, needed feeding. Cuba was too small. The CIA and the military-industrial alliance now had a juicier target in their sights: Vietnam.

Daniel turned on the light. He left the room and took a walk outside, his mind in a whirl. There was just so much to take in, so much to take in . . .

The file was a remarkable document. It had to be protected at all costs, that much was immediately plain. He began to wonder where on earth it had come from. From a diner he bought coffee and returned to the room. The night was deep, the place filled with eerie calm as he settled down and once more delved into the mass of information.

Names. Who was involved, who died, and who did the killing. The death of a senator, a man whose name Daniel recalled vaguely, who had been approached to join the plot, and on refusing had died in a mysterious aircrash. Johnny Rossi, mobster, killed by a man called Rama. A man referred to as Frank Rome who, along with Mather, was given the job of tidying up. There followed a complete and detailed list of those who they had tidied up.

His father was there. In a fever he rooted through masses of photographs. On the back of each picture was a name. He found one he recognised, flipped the picture over and read the scrawled inscription: *Frank Rome.*

The man who had visited his father, the man who had made the telephone calls. The man who had altered Daniel's life for ever. He felt despair cloak his heart, a sinking of his spirit.

He paused, drained the cup of the now cold coffee. The room too was cold, and he shivered. But nothing could divert him now, he had to know it all. Pulling on his jacket to ward off the chill, he returned to the file.

The compiler of the file had also done something similar to David Turner: created a family tree of the assassination.

This family tree showed how the names were knitted together, the branches and limbs that linked the CIA to the mob, to the FBI, to the plotters and the peripheral characters who provided the finishing touches. But the tree was more complete, for it traced the eventual fate of all of the characters, from the people who died between 1963 and 1968, when Mather and Rome traversed the country, seeking out and eliminating dissenters, to those who died just before being called before the House Select Committee for assassinations in the late 'seventies — among them Giancarlo Giometri, George de Mohrenschildt and Sam Giancana. There was a man who had died from five gunshots to the abdomen, and whose death certificate read suicide. There was the death of Frank Rome, former CIA contract agent, the shooter in the County Records building, who had been Mather's closest friend. He had died in the kitchen of his home one day before being called to testify before the House Select Committee on Assassinations. He was shot in the face, a half dozen neat bullet holes around his mouth. Listed too were others still alive, among them a high ranking Pentagon official, a Four Star General, and, of course, Cyrus Galbraith.

Here, Daniel found himself being surprised, for it appeared that Galbraith had been a peripheral player in this game — until after the assassination. Seeing how disposable the other footsoldiers were, he began manoeuvering himself into a position of strength. He struck a deal with Mather, and between them they disposed of those whom they considered a danger.

Vincent Industries, under Galbraith, became a favored investment of the Octad membership, reaping vast rewards from the Vietnam conflict. Ultimately, as older members of the Octad died to be replaced with those whom Galbraith could control, the number of people alive with knowledge of the assassination plot reduced, and Galbraith, through superb political instinct, found himself the sole keeper of the flame, the man destined to continue the work to keep America strong. . . .

As Daniel read on, he learned about Pamela. And what he read saddened him. She had been the daughter of Philip Davis, one of the footsoldiers, the man wearing the police uniform on the knoll, one of those who terrorised Harrison Baker. He felt choked; Pamela's father. What was it she said, lost at sea?

Her story was there too. She had a penchant for intrigue from an early age. And had trained professionally with Mather's old organisation, the suspected CIA front company, Metrotel. She was a good agent, rated CRO, a calm, reliable operator. A cool customer.

'God,' he muttered aloud, aghast at the many incestuous and intricate relationships between organisations and individuals. One big, dirty circle. And then of course there was the why, emphasised in a final, damming paragraph. Vietnam; mega-dollars. Contracts valued in billions. A sacriligeous collusion of industry and the military. No nuclear war — there was no money in it. But an arms race — now there was an argument for expansion!

Mather — Rama. Galbraith, the Executor, just as Turner had said. Names, so many names, and so many dead.

He closed the file after many hours reading. His eyes ached, but his mind was in overdrive and sleep was impossible. Pamela; he could not shake the idea. She deliberately deceived him, set him up. How, he puzzled, could she have seduced him, spent nights locked in passion and proclaimed so loudly her love for him if it had all been a lie?

Despite the hurt, the love he felt for her remained, but now it veered towards hate, and the pain, oh, the pain . . . He forced the feelings away. He could do that; he was stronger now.

He had to sleep. Had to force himself to sleep. He would be more rational after resting. He wanted to call Galbraith on the telephone, scream at him that the game was up, but he had found the strength to be patient. He was learning.

As he sank into sleep, he knew that he would have to be prepared when he faced the Senator, and this time he would need more than just a gun.

The whore.

Wracked by flashing, vivid horrors he somehow made it through the night.

The whore!

* 25 *

He was shivering, his breath expelled in wisps of frail mist that quickly shrivelled to nothing. He was seated in a brick-built gatehouse sited just inside the drive to Senator Galbraith's mansion house. The gloom was dense, unrelieved by the faint light cast from a wall lamp outside. Beyond the heavy wooden door, which had been locked to prevent him leaving, stood two armed guards, visible occasionally in silhouette as they moved past the window. He heard mumbled voices, and twice saw the flare from a match being struck.

He had been left alone in that cold dank room for some two hours, he estimated. Two hours during which his iron resolve, cooled by fear and uncertainty, had softened. Two hours since he had driven up to the gates and pushed the manuscript at one of the stone-faced guards.

'Get this to Senator Galbraith,' he had said with as much authority as he could muster. When this was met with a blank rebuttal he went on: 'Believe me, he will want to see this. I'll wait.'

He had been admitted through the gates and escorted into the gatehouse where he still waited. Another forty minutes passed before the door was thrust open, and three men in dark suits and armed with automatic weapons crowded in.

In silence, ignoring his questions, they escorted him along the drive and across the floodlit lawns to the house. He felt himself shrinking in the brilliant white glare as, heart in mouth and pulses throbbing, he crossed the tiled porch and entered through a set of open french windows. He was in a dining room. A dozen serious looking men were gathered in an anxious cluster around a table. Uneasy, hostile glances were directed at him, and as he passed them he heard someone mutter: 'I've never seen the old man so furious.'

His escort led him to the study where he had met Galbraith on his previous visit. The heavy oaken door was opened, and he entered. This time the atmosphere in the room was radically different. Gone was the soft comforting glow from the hearth, banished the soft lighting. All the lamps were on and the hearth cool. The effect was clinical, intimidating.

Cyrus Galbraith faced him across the room and without a word beckoned him nearer. The Senator still retained his matinee idol good looks and suave presence, but there was something shifting just beneath his calm surface. Daniel sensed it, and sensed too something else; danger. The Senator was cornered – and he was dangerous.

Galbraith sauntered to the bar. He looked cool, but the effort required to maintain an aura of control was draining. The silence between the two men persisted as they each gauged the other. Hunter and hunted, neither sure of his role.

The Senator helped himself to a brandy, then looked to Daniel, who declined. Accepting the refusal with a resigned tilt of his head, Galbraith took a sip. His lips moved in genteel appreciation. 'That's good, very good. Tell me Mr Baker, what are you looking for?'

Daniel stared blankly at him, his expression one of smouldering resentment. Unperturbed, Galbraith returned to his desk. 'Let me put all my cards on the table; what do you need? Money? I have plenty.'

'You couldn't afford it.'

'Oh you can speak then?' Galbraith snapped, malice seeping through his veil of control. He leaned forward, his fists on the desk. 'Try me.'

Daniel found himself short of words. The chase had been long and hard, all his efforts bent on reaching this point, on unearthing the truth and facing the enemy with it. His thoughts had not gone further than that. What exactly *did* he want? He started to feel cornered, to feel that Galbraith had a tighter grasp on the situation. Clenching his fists at his sides, he decided to confront him directly. 'You've read the file?'

'Most of it. Enough to realise its potency. Obviously denial would be pointless. There was some mention of tapes . . . ?'

'They are safe enough.'

'Then all that remains is the haggling. What is your price?'

Daniel scowled. 'I haven't done all this for money.'

'For what then? Justice? Somehow I don't think so. If that had been your aim you would have gone straight to the FBI, or the newspapers. You wouldn't have risked bringing your trump card into the lion's den, so to speak. This is a matter of a simple transaction. Come on man, I'm impatient. Name your price.'

Daniel strove to hold on to his temper. There was within him a growing realisation that his best survival tool might be anger, offensive anger. 'I don't want your money. Not a stinking red cent. I just wanted you to know you are no longer safe. You are blown. Through.'

Galbraith chuckled. 'In any other circumstance I might call your attitude laudable, but in the event I am simply surprised at your naiveté. You surely cannot believe we'll allow you to leave here?'

Daniel swooped with arrogance. 'The file you have is only a copy. If I don't get out of here you'll be going public a lot sooner than you think. There are other copies being looked after. If I do not appear they will be messengered to newspapers and TV stations.'

Galbraith was very calm, but even in the stillness the threat loomed. Daniel swallowed his fear. Galbraith inhaled, as though preparing to mount some obstacle. 'The copies I can suppress, the press I can fight, but if I let you walk out of here I've set free an unstable force. You may set about my destruction, and that I cannot permit. I have fought my way to the top. I'm not about to let all this be taken from me.'

'But you had the President killed!'

Galbraith effaced the attack with a shrug. 'I've made no secret of my ambitions. I want to be President, and I will *be* President, because I am the right man and because I have the support of those who matter. That's where Jack Kennedy and his old man took a wrong turn. Jack used his wealth to cut himself off from the body of true influence in this country, those who hold real power. A President cannot afford to do that if he wants to accomplish anything. They hate to be embarrassed. He knew the risks he was running. He had it coming.'

'You can't believe that.'

'Other Presidents made the same mistake. Nixon, Carter.'

Daniel snorted. 'What are you telling me? You're some kind of puppet?'

The barest pause. 'I have a line to walk. I either go with the stream or I drown. It's that simple.'

'You walk the line.' Dan sneered. 'You lead the Octad. You *are* the power!'

Galbraith was startled by this disclosure, but also quick to recover. 'It's true I hold a certain position, but with it comes a responsibility to the people who put me there. But I do not hold . . .' he cut himself off, knowing he was on the brink of indiscretion. 'Let's just say I sold my soul long ago. All these years I've played my part, now I'm about to be rewarded.'

'You sold your soul?'

Galbraith was amused by the puzzlement on Daniel's face. 'The story that is not in the file . . . of how, on the edge of insolvency, I fell into certain company, and found myself on the fringes of what I could see was a crime – and, incidentally a window of opportunity – of immense proportions. I had an insider's knowledge – a chance of a lifetime, and I snatched at it.' He sipped contentedly at his brandy. 'It has cost me, but by and large it has been an equitable arrangement. I have no complaints.'

'You were going bust . . . ? The SEC, the mysterious dropping of the investigation into your business. Is that what you mean?'

'You can make what I said mean anything you want it to mean, but don't ask me to be explicit. I'm too old a dog for that.'

'You found out about the plot and somehow got involved, and were rewarded by the stopping of the SEC? Who fixed that for you?' When Galbraith refused to be drawn, Daniel let his mind conjure up ideas. He decided on another tack. 'The people behind you. Are they still alive?'

Galbraith thought about this, then shook his head. 'Sadly, as years pass, friends get old and die.'

'So who have you been protecting? Who have you been tidying up for?' But even as the words left him he knew the answer. Galbraith had been protecting himself! The idea he had played with the previous night he now sensed was the truth. Somehow Galbraith had contrived to be the only one left. He had removed those below *and* above him. He was the Executor – and sole beneficiary. 'What a clever son of a bitch you've been.'

Galbraith was glowing. 'I have my good days. And you thought you could walk in here, knock the wind out of my sails and stroll out again.'

Daniel was tightlipped. He felt afraid. 'I left copies with friends and the master copy with a lawyer, remember? Can you take that chance?'

'Copies with a lawyer, with friends? I pride myself on being a man who knows a good risk when he sees one. You are new to New York. I ask myself, who would you know well enough to do such a special favor? I think I can take the chance.'

Daniel's throat was dry. 'I am not bluffing. The master is with a lawyer.'

'That old chestnut. The oldest trick in the book. Let me see now, that would be attorney at law Robert E Wiseman, wouldn't it?'

Daniel felt his world drop away from him, and he knew he was defenceless. He felt sick. Oh God, oh God.

Galbraith's smile widened. 'What did you imagine we had been occupied with these past three hours? This document is obviously a copy. I know you've seen movies enough to know you never go into the lion's den without protection. My deputy chief of security figured you would place the master somewhere safe and try to lever us with that knowledge. We simply contacted every lawyer in the book – and there are hundreds, believe me, and informed them that you were trying to blackmail me, and were expected to place the blackmail material in safekeeping. We simply said we would appreciate any information we could get. I'm a powerful voice in this town. To a man they were anxious to be of help. Your lawyer came to us.' He smirked. 'The master will be in our hands first thing tomorrow.' He had the look of a man about to tuck into his favorite meal.

'We are very practised at these things, Daniel. There are few corners we cannot reach into.'

Unnerved by the utter confidence of his adversary, Daniel raged inwardly. 'I'm leaving,' he snapped. 'Right now.' Impelled by the need to survive, he moved for the door. He had taken no more than three strides when he was halted by the Senator's warning: 'If you leave this room without my permission you will be shot dead before you cross the hall.'

Daniel halted, welded to the spot. A choking lump swelled in his throat. He glowered at his enemy.

'Sit down will you?' came the velvet invitation. 'Let's talk. Mather went out to meet you, I believe. I sent Cutter after him. What happened to them? Where did you get the file?'

Daniel moved nearer the desk but refused to sit. His voice, when he spoke, quivered with fear and exasperation. 'You've been clever,' he admitted, fighting back the feeling of helplessness that had been whittling away at his conviction. 'The way you set up the Assassination Bureau to control the flow of information was quite brilliant. But it's not over yet. You are too evil to live.'

Galbraith still smiled. 'Oh?'

The door burst open, then slammed shut, and Pamela stood with her back to it. She was breathless and her face was flushed.

Daniel almost swooned from the shock. He had believed he was ready to face her, but he had been wrong. The gaping chasm in his chest yawed open, and he felt his heart break anew.

Galbraith looked uncomfortable. He swallowed, then forced a smile. 'I believe you know my ward, Pamela.'

She swallowed. 'Hello Danny . . .' she began sheepishly.

'I heard the men talking, but I didn't believe it. I had to see . . .'

Pain gave way to emotion, then the two coalesced to create an invective fury that rose forcefully to the back of his throat. His jaw sprang taut; 'Bitch!' he hissed. He moved forward, and was gratified to see hurt flit across her face.

She adopted a humble posture, hands clasped to her navel, chin lowered, eyes staring dolefully at the carpet. 'I know how you must feel, Dan; no one likes to be betrayed, but there are things you don't understand —'

'SHUT UP!' Impelled by rage he turned from her. Tears burned his eyes but he found strength enough to quell them.

Straightening up, Pamela glanced to her guardian for assurance. He gave a small nod. Daniel turned in time to catch the exchange and was enraged by what he saw as their smug complicity. Bitterly he shook a fist in her face. 'Do you have any idea what you've done?'

She stared blankly. 'Here,' he snatched up the thick manuscript before Galbraith could stop him and thrust it at her. 'I've marked the pages. See for yourself!' In a fever he flipped pages. 'There . . .' he shoved it roughly into her hands. 'Read it for yourself. Your history. How you came to be here. Your father was on the knoll with Mather. Then he was killed – by Barry Mather, on the orders of your guardian. Read it! See what you've done!'

Galbraith walked around the desk. He moved to her but she shrank back. 'Pamela please . . .' he held out his hand for the file but she waved him away. She scanned the pages Daniel had marked, flipped one, two. Slowly the expression on her face hardened, and when she looked up, her eyes glimmered stonily.

'You had my father killed, and then adopted me?'

He squirmed, simpered in a conciliatory fashion. She referred quickly to the page. 'It says here that I was an unforeseen complication. You took me in to keep my mother quiet.'

Shamed, her guardian averted his face. This was a shock greater than anything he could have anticipated. Impatient, Pamela rounded on Daniel. 'Where did you get this?'

He explained; Mather, Turner, Cutter. The envelope on the mat. Galbraith listened in astonishment. 'I took steps to protect myself,' Daniel added, going on to explain about the copies he left with the lawyer. He thought she might faint, she was that still. Then weakly lifting a hand to her forehead, she asked him if he would wait outside. He agreed, but mindful of Galbraith's warning, asked her to talk to the guards.

In the hall he glanced around uneasily, avoiding the stony

looks from the armed men. Selecting a seat, he buried his head in his hands. Christ, what a mess!

Disbelief illuminated her eyes. 'I don't believe this. How could you? I believed you'd never do anything to hurt me.'

He stumbled out a tattered explanation but she cut him short. 'I love you. All my life I've called you father. But if all this is true . . . God, what a mess. Why did you have to get me involved?' She lapsed into disturbed silence, face still, masking the thought that whirled in her head. Then she faced him defiantly. 'He'll hate me now. He'll always hate me, and I deserve his loathing. You have to let him go. You have to. I can't be party to any more killing. If I'd known . . .'

He was apologetic. 'That was Cutter's doing. The man was unstable, but he's gone now. You heard Baker say he killed him. He will ruin me if I let him walk away. Please, Pamela, don't challenge me on this. Not on this . . .' He pleaded, but her expression remained stony. 'Pam, Pammy, the White House is within reach. The culmination of thirty years work. Look the other way this last time. I swear there will be no more.'

Her mouth curled sourly. 'There'll always be more. This can never end as long as you have something to hide. You'll have to bargain with him. Let him keep his file but promise to leave him alone. He's afraid, I'm sure he'd jump at the chance to get off the hook.' She paused. 'Daddy, he has to go free.'

Galbraith shook his head. 'I'm afraid too, sweetheart. I'm afraid of what might happen to us all if he leaves here. In the whole world now only we three know the truth about Dallas. After thirty years I can finally be safe. As for making a deal with Baker, I doubt very much he'd settle. He won't believe anything we tell him. In his shoes I certainly wouldn't. He'll see the deal as a way for us to take our time, picking him off.'

She was firm. 'He walks.'

Glumly he held her gaze, then shook his head. 'I'm sorry, honey. I can't take that chance.'

Her shoulders drooped, and her face narrowed into a look of resigned melancholy. She loosed a sigh. 'Then you'll have to kill me too. I love you daddy, but I love him too, and if one hair of his head is harmed I swear I will destroy you.'

The steel in her tone shook him. His voice, when he replied, was brittle. 'Don't do this Pamela. We are a family. Think what a quarrel between us would do to your mother. Her health is poor enough, if we let this come between us . . .'

'My mother?' She countered with a shrill cry. 'My mother? I love her too, of course I do. I don't want to hurt her, I don't want anyone to be hurt. But you can see the spot I'm in. And what about my real mother? Who was she, where is she now?'

His face was stilled, eyes turned downwards. She sensed he knew the answer to the question, and sensed too that nothing would induce him to tell. Anger and bitterness competed for her tongue and she swung to the attack once more: 'Daddy . . .' The slip hurt both of them. She drew a fatigued breath.

'I'm tired. Tired of it all. Tired of the pressure, tired of the deceit. You think I haven't seen your people following me? You think I don't know?'

He glanced up sharply. 'I've had no one following you.'

'Don't lie to me. No more lies.'

'I swear to you, I'm not lying.'

She gathered her resources. 'Just let Daniel go.' Her gaze bored into him with the unyielding force of toughened steel, and suddenly he too felt tired of the fight. He looked into the once-adoring eyes of his daughter, and knew he no longer had the strength to dominate this girl-turned-woman. He inhaled nasally, lips pursed tightly.

'Alright,' he mumbled. 'Just for you. Just this once.' The words were wrong, he felt; they were too forced, too falsely paternal, but they were all he could muster. He raised a finger in warning. 'But you better bargain with him for his silence, because if he does attempt to harm me —'

She nodded gratefully, knowing what it had cost him in pride to back down. He was a man unaccustomed to defeat, her father. She loved him. A rush of emotion brought a lump to her throat. She was glad he had not insisted on a battle; she was not sure she had the stomach for that.

As she stepped into the hall Daniel rose from his seat. They argued in hushed tones, she pleading, he haranguing her bitterly. Then realising the vulnerability of his position in the enemy camp, he ceded. Agreement voiced, he was allowed to storm out, and she dashed heartbroken to her room.

The door to the study opened, and Galbraith's newly promoted head of security entered. His name was Spector, and he was a tall, rangy individual, with neatly cropped greying hair, a thin, much lined face with an elongated jaw, and who spoke in a low, mid-western drawl. Galbraith was at the drinks cabinet, his face flushed. 'Has he gone?'

Spector nodded. 'And she's in her room.'

Galbraith took a swallow of brandy, and his mouth made small, chewing motions. 'Step up the surveillance on him.'

'It's already done.'

Galbraith nodded his approval. Spector would fit nicely into Mather's shoes. 'Good, but let's keep it subtle, shall we?'

Daniel.

He spent four days in a nervous and agitated state. Wherever he looked he seemed to spot the watchers; Galbraith's people. Them. He tried self reason — maybe he was getting paranoid, but he could not shake the feeling. Until he could be sure he was not being followed, he would act with the utmost caution.

All about him he seemed to find the marks of the Octad. Suspicious ads in the classifieds, a peculiar hollowness on the telephone line. On a couple of occasions he returned to the apartment positive that objects had been moved slightly. This frighened him, the feeling so intense he fidgetted constantly. He had taken to stroking his chin with his right hand, fingers drawing down his lips, and had begun to snap into rigid awareness at each untoward sound.

The pistol never left his person. He even carried it, along with spare ammunition, into the bathroom. But even then he did not feel safe, and slowly it dawned on him that the problem was not going to go away. Galbraith was still out there, and dangerously powerful. What lengths would he go to in order to win Daniel's silence? He thought he knew the answer.

An idea germinated in his mind; Action – blow the whole thing skyhigh. The effort might finish him, but it could be worth it.

He had decided on martyrdom.

Thus it was that he strode into a gunstore and asked to see a selection of hunting rifles.

Filled with a mixture of guilt and excitement he unpacked his chosen weapon and occupied himself by stripping and cleaning it, and familiarising himself with the component parts. His thoughts had closed in and focused on a single objective; finishing the affair quickly and finally. He had weighed the options and arrived at one simple conclusion; if he went about his day-to-day routines he would eventually have a fatal accident, and the mystery of the assassinations would be buried that bit deeper.

But if he struck before a large audience, and if when arrested he carried a copy of the damming file, the affair would explode. But to achieve all this.

He would have to assassinate Cyrus Galbraith.

His chest heaved with relief. Once the admission was made he felt calmness descend and cloak him. At last he could contribute something. At last he knew the true measure of his life. He need waste no more time.

* 26 *

The applause was thunderous. At the rostrum, Senator Cyrus Galbraith rewarded the adoring audience with a beaming smile. He left the stage, touching palms along the way, and emerged breathless but elated in the wings where his new Chief of Security waited. One glance at Spector's face was enough. 'He was here?'

Spector nodded. 'You make three public appearances in a week and he attends each one. He stays on the periphery, but he's out there.'

Galbraith looked about him at the crowded room, saw safety in numbers and allowed himself to relax slightly. He grimaced in exasperation.

'What the hell is he up to?'

Pamela.

Caught up in a whirlpool of ragged emotions, she had wandered the streets in a daze that first night and others since. Days she walked the parks. The revelation that her guardian, the man she had grown up calling Daddy, had been the man responsible for the death of her natural father, had gouged a hole in her that left a numbing ache in her breast.

She could not think straight! She had tried to hate him, but could not, for each time she tried some small memory of a loving considerate parent returned to haunt her.

If only she could put things right with Daniel. If only she knew what to do! If only she had someone to talk to . . .

'Oh mother,' the whimper slipped out. She sucked mournfully on her lower lip and closed her eyes as she fought the tears.

In a morose mood she walked to Central Park. The wind blustered in from the east, shaking the trees and tousling her sandy hair. She followed the path towards the bandstand. On the narrow ornamental bridge that spanned the stream she halted, attention drawn to a figure in a crumpled trenchcoat, watching her from a bench some fifty yards away. The face, the look! She was sure it was the man who had followed her in Florida! Immediately she set off in his direction. He saw her coming and hurried away.

Face suffused with anger, she started to run. 'Cyrus . . .' she muttered. 'If this is your doing . . .' Her hand went to the pocket where, for the past few days, she had carried a small .22 pistol. She was fit, and fast, and she soon closed in on the man in the trenchcoat. He was smaller than she, and his little legs pounded furiously, comically, with tiny, rapid steps. He was unfit, and as she gained on him she heard his struggling for breath. Grasping his collar, she pulled him to a halt and tucked the muzzle of the tiny weapon into the space behind his right ear. 'Hold it right there, my friend.'

He stopped dead. His head sank between his shoulders and his hands shot up in the air. 'What? What?' he bawled in a pronounced Bronx twang. 'You wanna mug me lady? Go ahead. I got maybe ten dollars and change. Right pocket. Right pocket.'

She smiled wryly. 'What I want is that you show me some ID. Then you can tell me why you are following me.'

He screeched. '*Followin' you?*' She smiled again. You had to love him. The act he'd worked up — playing the undersized

Jewish kid at school, defending himself with comedy, had a nice Woody Allen touch to it. Filing through his pockets she produced a wallet, which she flipped open. She murmured in satisfaction. 'Arnie Feldheim. Private investigator with the Bateman agency.'

'New York branch,' he admitted in a wincing tone — as if expecting to be punished for lying. 'So I'm discreet.'

'The wrong kind of discretion can get you in trouble, Arnie,' she muttered toughly. 'Come on, why are you following me?'

He squirmed. 'We're talking client-agency privilege here. You oughta respect that.'

'You ought to respect my privacy. Why are you following me?'

He sighed. 'I don't know. No, no really, that's the truth. I was engaged to find you, supply pictures and a record of movements, and send them on to my client. What he does with the information is none of my business.'

'And who is your client?'

Another sigh; world weary, leaked from the little man. 'Hell, I'm not paid to have a gun put to my head. The client is a law firm on the west coast. There's a business card in the wallet . . .'

She found the card, then withdrew the gun. She gave him a shove and ran, as fast as his legs would carry him, along the path and out through the gates. Grimfaced, she pocketed the gun and turned for home.

She had flown clear across the country to speak to the lawyer who had hired Arnie Feldheim. In his outer office, she gave her name to the receptionist and settled down to wait. Within the hour a flustered, middleaged man with a kind face and a sagging middle burst breathlessly in through the door.

'Busy morning in court.' He hastily apologised in a polite, Ivy League voice. 'Would you like to step into my office?'

He took off his jacket, rolled up his shirt sleeves, and slumped gratefully into a leather chair the other side of a vast oak desk. The desk top was incredibly neat and ordered, and the polished surface was burnished to a near golden ochre by the sunlight flooding in through the window. Pamela took her seat. Despite the anger that had propelled her across the country, she felt herself liking this gentle man.

He asked if she would like a drink. She declined politely. He nodded, then began to broach a difficult subject. 'Actually, I've been expecting you to call. I have been ever since Mr Feldheim filed his last report.' He opened his hands in a gesture of contrition. 'What can I say? I am terribly sorry for the embarrassment and inconvenience our actions may have caused you.'

'An explanation might help.'

He smiled, glad she had taken the intrusion so well. He drew in a breath, then cleared his throat. 'Of course. Tell me, what do you know of your family history?'

Taken aback, she considered for a moment how different her reply might have been had he asked her that question ten days earlier. In a little over a week her life had been turned inside out. Her real father had been a hired assassin, rubbed out because he knew too much.

She composed herself before answering. 'I know that the couple who raised me are not my natural parents. Is that what you mean?'

He looked slightly uncomfortable. 'Recently, one of our wealthiest clients passed away. We executed the estate. One item found amongst the personal effects was an envelope addressed to me. Inside the envelope was a note of instruction; we were to find and positively identify you, then hand you a letter.'

'A letter? From who?'

He loosened his tie, cleared his throat for the third time. 'Your real mother.'

She was still for a moment, then her heartbeat started to accelerate and she found herself short of breath. 'My real mother?'

He nodded. 'Additionally there is the matter of estate. She has left you a great deal of money and much property, but the main item, as far as she was concerned, was the letter. It was the greatest regret of her life that she never found the courage to come to you while she lived.'

'May I see it?' she asked timidly. Her mother! After all these years! And she was dead. Without a further word he unlocked a drawer in the desk and took out a plain white envelope. She accepted it with shaking fingers and stared in wonder at the words handwritten upon it.

Pamela Davis.

Her mother's hand. The first sign – ever! She was suddenly gripped by uncertainty, a disinclination to know the truth. Then alarm: 'This has been opened.'

'She left an instruction that I avail myself of the contents. For your sake, she said. You might need someone to talk to.'

'Did you know her long?'

He became sad. 'A very long time.'

She opened the envelope and took out a single sheet of paper. The handwriting was neat, and easily legible, and covered both sides of the paper. As she scanned the words, conscious of his gentle, watchful gaze, she felt mixed emotions stir in her heart. At last, tears brimming, she looked up from the letter.

'I know it's a great shock,' he said, 'And I want you to know that whatever happens, you can always call on me for help.'

In a broken voice she thanked him, then in silence reread the letter. A sob clutched her throat and tears misted her vision.

The awful, awful truth. They HAD killed her father!'

* 27 *

Galbraith had spent nights alone in his study. He had read and reread the file from beginning to end, and it scared him.

Turning his mind to the identity of the compiler, he concluded it had to be Mather. Only he had known the full story. Others knew of the circumstances behind the events at the Ambassador hotel, but they knew nothing of the earlier days – and Dallas. It had to be Mather.

Recalling those times brought a burn to the back of his throat; it still rankled that the man they hired to put that .22 bullet into Bobby Kennedy's skull had vanished before Mather could have him tidied up. He hated loose ends, like Daniel Baker.

There came a knock on the door and a senior PR aide entered. He was a slim, dapper man, who looked at the world through gold rimmed spectacles. He had slicked-down, old-fashioned styled hair, and was dressed into a square cut Brooks Brother's suit. The Senator disliked his company, and this showed in his manner when he returned the man's greeting. 'What do you have?'

The aide gave a breathless smile. He had the results of a poll in his hand. 'The overnights are very encouraging, sir.' He proferred the notes. Galbraith scanned them, then treated the man to an approving smile. 'You've done well.'

'Thank you sir. May I make a suggestion? Enjoy this next week, because from Monday you have barely a clear day for a year.'

'I'll try.'

His next visitor was Chief of Security Spector. The Senator frowned as he read the surveillance report. 'So, he buys a rifle and spends hours each day on the range. Sleeps in a different location each night. I see your point.'

Spector was ex-NSA, ex-Metrotel. He had spent four vital years under Mather's tutelage and had matured into a consummate professional. 'It appears he has decided offense is the best defense.'

'And you want to strike first?'

'I think it's an option we ought to consider.'

Galbraith swallowed. He looked to Spector. The man must at least suspect the reason for his recalcitrance; Pamela's involvement with Baker. 'The election is too close.' He sought to excuse his reluctance. 'We dare not risk it.'

'It can be done safely. I guarantee it.'

Galbraith was not so sure. He was on the brink of achieving everything he had worked for. One slip. . . . His nerve gave.

'I daren't risk it. We have to find another way. Money perhaps.'

Spector remained unconvinced, but then, Galbraith thought, he could afford to. He was a hired hand. He was not shooting for the biggest prize on earth.

'I don't believe he can be bought off,' Spector remarked. A look of pleading, of ill-concealed desperation, flitted across Galbraith's face. 'Let's try, shall we? Let's just try.'

Spector nodded, and left him. Galbraith glanced down at the thick file on his desk and once more cursed the stupidity of letting Pamela get involved. They had needed someone they could trust, Mather had insisted. Pammy was working at Metrotel, where Mather, through secret shareholdings, had a substantial say in the running of the company, and she was wasted. 'Give her a job worthy of her talents,' Mather had said, and Galbraith, weak through years of soft living, had let it all happen around him. And now things had gone too far. They had never anticipated the trail Baker followed leading to the Senator. Now he knew in his heart that between him and Pamela things could never be the same again. They could never ever be as close as they had been. The sense of fun that had existed between them had died. And now, he dare not risk her wrath. No telling what she might do. She was stubborn, like her father.

With a sigh the Senator turned to cognac for company.

Later that same day he and Spector clashed again. 'Baker is dangerous,' his Chief of Security insisted. 'At least call off your appearance at the Central Park benefit. You don't need that kind of exposure; it isn't our scene. Christ, there will be half a million people there. Any lunatic with a gun could take a shot —' He would have continued, but he was abruptly overridden.

'NO. We go ahead as planned. I understand what you are saying and I appreciate your concern, but when I become President I will have to go public, and I'll be running a bigger risk then. It will be alright . . .' he said, tone earnestly persuasive. 'Besides, we need support from every angle. We cannot afford a narrow victory.'

Snorting in disgust, the honest exasperation of an employee who knows what is right but is frustrated in his attempts to act correctly, Spector turned away. Galbraith sought to soothe him. 'I have every confidence in your abilities and feel perfectly secure in the knowledge that you will be handling the arrangements. If you cannot protect me, then no one on earth can. Don't worry, we'll make it.'

Later, when he was quite alone, Galbraith wondered at his own stubbornness. He knew in his heart that Spector was right; Saturday, and the rock concert, did feel wrong. So why wouldn't he cancel?

He wished he knew.

Thursday.

Daniel swept the razor down his cheek in a final pass, then washed the remaining traces of shaving foam from his skin. He dabbed himself dry with a small towel, tilting his head and examining himself critically in the mirror. The face looking back at him was gaunt, and he was surprised he had not noticed the change occurring. In recent days he had retreated within himself, begun to converse almost exclusively with himself, and to his surprise he realised that this did not worry him. Time was suddenly measured, his lifespan finite, set to end, effectively, the moment he pumped a bullet into Senator Cyrus Galbraith.

Motel rooms. He stood in the bathroom door and cynically surveyed the ubiquitous motel room style; crumpled bed, the open wardrobe, the over-filled ashtray on top of the TV. He had begun to view the world through a poisoned eye. It all looked so seedy, and unclean. The entire world epitomised by the shabby fittings in the motel room. The basic shape might differ, but the drabness was universal.

On the bed, in a well-prepared state of abeyance, lay the rifle. Crossing the room, he tucked a hand under the pillow and drew out the pistol. His fingers were trembling, but by closing them tightly around the butt he was able to halt the shaking. It had been a hard few days. Eating had been difficult; his stomach plagued by rashes of nervousness. Yet he could not quieten the hunger that raged inside him. He was forced to remind himself there was no other way. He had to remove the threat. That simple.

Dressing, he wrapped the rifle in a tattered blanket and packed his few belongings into a shabby case. He dropped the key at the desk and walked out to the parked Plymouth rental.

A ninety second slot on the morning TV had been devoted to the New Yorkers rock benefit to be staged in Central Park the coming Saturday. He was gratified to learn that Galbraith was still cued to perform the opening ceremony; he had been afraid they would guess at his intentions and break the Senator's itinerary.

As he seated himself behind the wheel he reviewed the past week. The row at Bob Wiseman's office, when he tried to retrieve the master copy of the damming file, had been fierce. He had been forced to draw his gun to persuade Wiseman to open the safe and return his property. The lawyer had threatened to call the police, and Daniel, with his new found aggression, invited him to go ahead. Wiseman, not knowing the contents of the file, but not wanting to cross Galbraith, had yielded, and Daniel had walked away with his pride intact.

Starting the engine he steered the Plymouth out onto the freeway. As he gathered speed he glanced in the rearview mirror and felt a chill steal over him as another vehicle, looked like a Buick, always a Buick, hauled out of the motel lot and settled behind him. His greatest fear blossomed, and the surge in his gut set his nerves aflame.

He put the hammer down and watched gratefully as the Buick receded into the distance. Relief ebbed at his heart, but the fear did not completely fade. He frowned as he concentrated on the road.

Pamela had taken to moving about the house in stealth. She was suspicious and afraid. She could not completely swallow her guardian's line about Daniel being left alone. It would be out of character for Cyrus to do that. She feared too that she was being watched. She had spotted no one — but then Spector's people would be too good for that. It was just that vague feeling.

She swept lightfooted down the curving staircase. The study door was open and, as she approached, she heard her guardian's raised voice. She ducked into a small alcove, close enough to bring her within earshot.

'No, for the last time no,' she heard Cyrus say. 'Where is he now?'

'We lost sight of him a couple of hours ago.' Spector replied. 'He's wise to the tailing and he's getting hard to follow. But he'll be at the range tonight as usual. He never misses that. We can pick him up there.' There was a pause, then Spector spoke again. 'The problem can be solved, if you let us handle things.'

She heard her adoptive father sigh. 'Just leave things as they are for now.'

She loved him for that. Then Spector was hurtling past her, moving soundlessly on the thick carpet he vanished into the kitchen.

She stepped into the study. Her guardian was at the window, his back to her, staring out over the vast expanse of lawn. He half turned his head, allowing her to study his profile. His lips were formed into a contemplative pout and his back was slightly bowed. He looked less vital than she had ever seen him. He looked . . . old. Despite the conflicting emotions warring within her, seeing him so vulnerable sent a wave of filial affection over her. 'Daddy.'

He turned suddenly. The exposed look on his face faded, and he brightened. 'Pammy. How are you?'

'Are you having Daniel watched?' Her directness came as a shock, even to her.

He had half expected the challenge. He was crestfallen for a moment, but then the tactician in him assumed control and he was on the defensive. 'I mean him no harm, Pamela, truly. I am simply protecting my interests. Once the election is over I plan to donate a substantial sum to his bank account and wish him well for the future.' He paused. 'I feel I owe him at least that.' Sensing her scepticism, he asked her if she believed him.

She swallowed. 'I want to.' Another pause. 'Yes.'

He looked self absorbed. 'Sometimes I wonder if it all isn't too high a price to pay for ambition.'

Seeing he was unguarded, she decided to unleash her curiosity. 'Would you talk to me about the assassination?'

He threw her a sharp glance. 'No, never.'

She stiffened. 'May I ask why not?'

He lifted a hand and slowly clenched it. 'I have spent the past thirty years in a vice. I've kept the jaws from closing by being quicker, by playing one opponent against another. It's a delicate balance, and it could easily tilt against me if I were to weaken or become careless. It's been a long haul, but I'm almost safe. Until I am safe, I dare not talk about this, and I don't ever want you involved.'

She protested. 'I befriended Daniel in order to report back to you through Mather. As luck would have it I fell for him, and if I hadn't he'd be dead now. I am involved.'

Obstinately he shook his head. 'That file Baker is carrying contains just about everything. So much so, I rather think Mather compiled it. Apart from myself, only he knew the whole story — and lived.'

'But if the file is so incriminating, why would he feel the need to do such a thing?'

He hesitated. This would be a difficult admission to make. 'This may be hard for you to believe, but he and I were never friends. We were always on the verge of becoming adversaries. All those years, the only thing that prevented me from having him removed was precisely the threat that it was all written down, taped and photographed. With him out of the way I would have been truly safe. I had managed to remove everyone else, there was just him remaining. But now he's gone, and the emergence of the file leads me to conclude he was telling the truth all along. Now I have to worry about Baker. He's afraid and unstable, and the slightest thing might send him over the edge. That's why he has to be watched, and you have to be kept clear.'

He returned his attention to the gardens beyond the window. She stared at him, her expression a mixture of anger and puzzlement. She was still finding it hard to believe that Galbraith, the kindly Senator, the beneficent industrialist, had been involved in the crime of the century, and had ordered the killing of her father.

She fought to keep her mixed feelings repressed; she was afraid how she might react if she spent too much time dwelling on the unsavory facts. She had surrounded herself with routines and followed them rigidly in order to preserve her sanity. She had to stay in control – until she knew what had to be done. Now, as she stared at her guardian, she knew she had to find Daniel. To explain to him that he was in real danger and to beg his forgiveness. But where could he possibly be?

Abruptly her face cleared. Of course! There was a renewed freshness to her step as she hurried out to her car.

Spector's people obligingly agreed not to follow her while she went to look for Daniel. She found him on the edge of the circuit that ringed the reservoir. During their telephone conversation after Barbara's death, he had told her of his loathing for the big city, and confided that the park was the only place in the entire metropolis even vaguely sane.

The park was an arena for poseurs. The late afternoon sun brought out the joggers and the dog walkers, the perverts watching the children playing and those who spied on the lovers clutched together in bushes. In the shade of a vast oak a black man in a kung-fu suit cavorted trancelike in a series of movements. Another nearby practised elaborate exercises with a Japanese sword.

Daniel was sprawled on a blanket spread in the deep shade of a tree. She sensed he was aware of her approach, yet he gave no sign. He kept simply staring across the parkland. She halted a metre away from him, and waited.

'Don't ignore me Daniel,' she said at last. 'I deserve better than that.'

He raised his head. His eyes seemed to stare right through her. 'I owe you nothing. You deserve nothing.'

She opened her mouth to speak, but nothing came. He hauled himself to his feet and faced her, chin to chin. He seemed to be straining to contain his anger, and, suddenly unsure, she took a step backwards. 'Daniel . . . ?'

'Do I have to keep repeating myself?' He overrode her. 'Read my lips; I want nothing to do with you. Barbara is dead because of you. My father is dead because of your natural father and your guardian. My entire life has been trashed by your family connections, but that wasn't enough for you, no . . .' he paused for breath. Wound up, his voice rose in pitch. 'You had to infiltrate my life. You let me fall for you, then you sold me out. You are scum!'

He edged closer, glowered beligerently at her, and she fell back. 'Why don't you turn right around and crawl back under your stone!'

Stung, she blinked back hot tears. She tried to explain but her trembling lips frustrated her effort. She clenched a fist until control was hers. 'I had hoped, that after these few days you might have softened.' A choked sob, lurking until that moment in the back of her throat, broke free, and she jerked.

'Softened!' Incredulity added fuel to his burning anger. 'You haven't the slightest idea how I feel. No idea!' His mouth opened and closed, and for a few moments he was too befuddled for words.

'In my entire life I never had anyone I could trust. No one. Can you imagine how lonely I was? Then you came along, and every ounce of pent up emotion, years of unused love, was focused on you. When you were there I felt I'd been rewarded for a lifetime of waiting. But then you turned around and set out to destroy me.'

'I know that!' she stormed. 'Don't you think I know that! And I am ashamed!' Her gaze implored him. 'I loved you. I still do, I never lied about that, and I want us to . . .' She broke off as a fat tear trickled down her cheek. She swallowed, tried again, but there was no climbing that last hurdle and she stamped her foot in frustration.

He turned away. She stared at his back, her heart aching until she wanted to scream. Emotion tugged downward the corners of her mouth, then recognising the futility of wishing, she spun on her heel and stumbled unsteadily down the shallow slope. Every step of the way hoping desperately that he would call to her. Then he did.

She halted — not too quickly; she was not sure what to expect.

He was standing lopsidedly on the slope, and when she saw the sorrow etched on his face she felt the faint stirrings of hope. He needed her. He jerked his head in to beckon her, and she approached gratefully.

He took her hands in his. 'I love you too,' he said softly. 'But we can't possibly go on. Two thirds of me desperately wants us back together, wants me to hold you and promise to put the past behind me. But the other third will never forgive. What happened will always be there, waiting to surface each time we argue, waiting to destroy us, and we both deserve better than that. We both ought to have the chance to start again. You do see that don't you?'

Dismally she nodded. He squeezed her hands gently, the lightly kissed her forehead.

They sat together on the blanket for the rest of the afternoon. Feeling, perhaps because of the imminent separation, much closer than before.

'You must let me help you,' she insisted. 'I have something important to give you. Where shall I send it?'

Despite his pressing her, she refused to tell him what the *something* was. Not sure whether his mail to the apartment might be intercepted, he told her to send it to the hotel where he had been employed. He had contacted his old boss and been assured his job awaited him.

She seemed brightened by the news. 'So, working at the hotel aside, what are your plans for the future? Do you have anything else in mind?'

He averted his head, and for the first time it seemed to her he was hiding something. 'I'm going to put the past in its place,' he said softly. 'I'm still taking life one day at a time.'

Soon afterwards they parted for the final time.

* 28 *

Friday.

The rifle action was smooth as silk, pleasing in its clean efficiency. Daniel squinted along the sight and drew a bead on the distant target. His finger met the pressure from the trigger, and the instant he was ready he gave it a gentle squeeze. The rifle bucked against his shoulder as it blasted. He steaded, aimed and fired again, and again. His action becoming a reflex as smooth and dependable as the rifle.

When the magazine clicked empty he lowered the weapon and fingered the button that activated the target mechanism. Suspended from an electrified pulley, the paper target crawled towards him along an overhead wire. He could see at a glance the ragged circles punched in a cluster around the centre. Good enough. He slipped off the ear mufflers and the protective glasses the club rules demanded he wear.

At the sound of footsteps he glanced up. One of the range masters, a stocky, iron-haired man wearing a sleeveless flak jacket with a National Rifle Association emblem displayed prominently on the breast, greeted him cordially. A look of approval was snapped at the target. 'Nice grouping.'

Daniel thanked him, then replaced the target and set the new one on its outward journey along the wire.

'You've been coming here a lot lately,' the man remarked conversationally. Daniel was immediately wary. He made a suitably guarded comment. The range master nodded at the weapon in Daniel's hands, saying: 'May I?'

The rifle was handed over, and hefted in a professional manner. Then the man snatched it to his shoulder and peered down the range. He murmured: 'Nice weapon.'

Daniel thanked him again and took repossession. The conversation had ground to a halt, yet the man did not move. He just stood, a half-inane grin on his face, watching as Daniel reloaded. He tried to keep the action as innocuous as possible, but he was uneasy. Was this the moment? he asked himself. Was he about to be hit?

'Y'know, coming up here every night an' all, you must want to be good with that thing real badly.' The probing was deliberately unsubtle; Daniel swallowed nervously.

The rifle was loaded. He worked a shell into the chamber. He straightened, and faced the man head-on. 'I have a lot of time on my hands right now, and I just like to shoot.'

The man worked his jaw as if pondering. His eyes gave away nothing. Abruptly he asked if Daniel planned any hunting.

It may have been imagination, Dan conceded, but he thought he detected the faintest glimmer of slyness in the other's eyes. A lump rose to his throat, and, imagined or not, he smelled danger:

'I might be.'

The man nodded. Daniel could almost hear the process of cogitation. Then pivoting on his flat shoes he waddled away along the corridor.

Daniel sagged with relief. He leaned against the wall and placed a hand over his heart. He had been scared! His shirt was clinging to his back.

Gathering his wits, he replaced his glasses and ear mufflers and turned to the gun alley. He fitted the rifle into his shoulder and fired a rapid salvo into the distant target.

Hunting? Tomorrow!!

Friday.

Cyrus Galbraith patted cologne onto his face, then studied himself in the dressing table mirror. The weak light from a nearby lamp made his face appear unnaturally pale. Why, he wondered, did the words *deathly pale* come to mind? There was an odd atmosphere in the house that night. One of foreboding. He could not shake it. With a nasal sigh he pulled tight the cord of his favorite robe; Chinese silk embroidered with golden dragons and circles. He smoothed the silk down with his palms, and walked slowly downstairs to the study.

He was sitting by the fire, warming a brandy glass between his hands when Spector entered the room. They began to talk, and Spector felt himself being manipulated towards a decision he did not want to make.

The Senator was staring into the fire. It was odd, he mused aloud, but he always liked to have a fire smouldering in the grate. It was one of his few peccadilloes.

Spector spoke up. 'Sir? Senator?'

Galbraith shucked off his dreamy mood. 'I'm sorry, what was that?'

'We lost track of Baker after he left the range tonight. He chose his moment to make a break for it. We won't find him now. He's gone underground — until tomorrow.'

'You are still convinced he's going to take a shot at me?'

Spector nodded gravely. 'More than ever.' The Senator sipped at his brandy. The effort it took to maintain the calm, unruffled facade was becoming almost too much, yet he dare not show his fear. His thoughts were focused on a day, thirty years earlier, when an enigmatic politician, despite all warnings, despite the filtering through of death threats, went ahead with a visit to Dallas. 'You know I cannot possibly cancel tomorrow. We can alter times, routes, entrances and exits, but I still have to appear.'

Spector allowed a calculated amount of annoyance to show. 'In the open air, surrounded by thousands of people, security can be a nightmare.'

Galbraith swallowed his apprehension. Positive Spector was right, he was at a loss to explain his own stubbornness. He ought to cancel. Why couldn't he? Finally, in a tone of resignation, he said: 'Do whatever you have to, short of cancelling. If I don't show I risk a massive dose of voter no-confidence. What good is a President who won't show his face? Do whatever you can, but I go on.'

Friday.

Pamela passed the night perched on the edge of her bed in a hypnotic stupor. Her body was tense, tilted forwards as if held on a straining leash, and there was a dull purpose in her eyes. She had the look of some fine thoroughbred animal poised at the starting line.

Infrequently her gaze would stray to the upright clock that stood with its back to the wall. She often liked to lie back with the light out, and be lulled to sleep by its sonorous ticking, but this night the sound had a different effect. The resonant and faintly hollow sound of the mechanism seemed only to make her muscles tighten, a winding effect that twisted her nerves like whipcord to snapping point. She swallowed, and was discomforted by the dryness of her throat.

Then as dawn broke, the chimes from the clock cut through the stupor. The well rounded reverberation from the notes hung in the air between beats. Then the sound faded, and she made her first movement in hours. She stood up. Her shoulders were aching, but she resisted the urge to ease them. It was important, somehow, that she contain all that tension. It was an energy she needed to conserve. She had to help Daniel, had to protect him, and to do that she would need all of her strength.

He had not slept. Nor had he shaved. Little seemed to matter anymore. His dramatic concentration upon a single goal had stripped him of all non-essential hindrances, and appearances were no longer of importance.

The rifle though was immaculate. No sloppiness there.

Looking dishevelled, and dressed in a crumpled raincoat, he shambled across the motel lot to the Plymouth. Just as well this was the last day; he had virtually no money left. A fine, out-of-season frost silvered the ground, and he shivered.

Clambering into the Plymouth he ran the engine with the heater on. He played with the radio controls until he found a weather report, and smiled without humor on hearing that the noon temperature outlook was promising.

He had begun smoking again. He had no idea when exactly he had resumed the habit; so much was a blur these days, but the cluster of crumpled Lucky Strike Packs on the dash called witness to the fervour with which the resumption had been made.

The rifle had been disassembled and packed with care into a small bag which he stored on the seat beside him. From deep in a pocket he unearthed a much folded, and greying, sheet of foolscap on which he had roughly sketched a plan of the park.

Relevant locations were marked with childishly large crosses. He studied the plan until the cigarette burned out, then on spinning tyres, and in a screeching roar, he sped out of the lot and headed downtown.

Galbraith awoke to a mood of supreme optimism. But over breakfast the mood inexplicably evaporated and his anxieties returned in full force. He scowled at a *New York Times* article criticising a recent address he had made on the imminent superpower summit. The older he grew, the less tolerant he became of liberalism. Fortunately, there was no one to hear his disgruntled mutterings.

Indigestion gnawed at him, and thrusting aside his meal he called for a Rolaid. A faint throbbing behind his eyes signalled the seeding of a monster headache; just what he needed to go to a rock concert!

Should he cancel? Dammit, he knew he should. But he could not avoid fate forever. He had to stand up, show he was not afraid. He would not let irrational and hysterical fears about Daniel Baker dictate the pattern of his life. He would not!

Restored to vigour by his anger, he strolled to the terrace and surveyed the gardens. Making a mental note to order alterations, he returned indoors to prepare for the day ahead.

The city was barely awake, yet the park was awash with activity. Apart from the thousands of fans, some of whom had camped in prime spots for days, there were teams of cops with dogs prowling the undergrowth, and security men in Brooks Brother's suits muttering importantly into walkie-talkies.

Hot dog vendors set up stalls, and on the vast stage the members of the sound crew burped the imposing mountain of speakers.

Daniel waited. Patience came hard – but he knew it to be an essential. The sun was climbing higher, the day warming and the crowd swelling towards the expected half million, when he took his courage in hand and joined the throng pouring in through the gates.

At an easy pace he threaded towards the spot in which he had decided to make his stand; a dense copse, bordered by a waist-high metal spike fence.

Spector was in the command post; a portable cabin sited at the top of a grassy crest. The entire park was overlooked by cameras, and at any given moment he had on offer a dozen views via a bank of TV monitors. Stoney-faced, he studied a view from a camera positioned high above ground on the towering point of a derrick. He expected trouble, and was determined to be ready for it.

One face, he sought. One face amongst thousands. An impossible task logic insisted, yet he had no other option. As he watched he repeatedly clenched and unclenched his hands, and each time he thought he caught that elusive glimpse of his quarry he would pound his left palm with his fist. Curses trickled from him, and he chainsmoked at an horrendous rate.

Daniel paused midway on his journey to buy a coke. Before drinking, he held the paper cup to his lips and let the mawkish odour of the drink infiltrate his nostrils. As he drank, he wondered if he would ever get to drink coke again. It was perfectly feasible his life might end in the park.

This simple acceptance did not move him, and he realised just how far he had come since that stormy night when he had faced the severed head of his friend and gone on to butcher Cutter. His outlook had narrowed, and, he observed wryly, he at last knew the true nature of obsession.

He reached the fence and managed, without drawing too much attention to himself, to slip over it and dive for the cover of nearby undergrowth. One thought echoed loudly in his head: *no going back.*

The crowd noise was muffled by the surrounding bush as he ploughed deeper into the copse. He had explored on a previous day and knew the tree he wanted. Following a path that was virtually invisible, he threaded towards the tree and was perspiring heavily by the time he arrived. He threw off his coat and slung the bag over his shoulder before starting up the thick, gnarled trunk.

In minutes he was high above ground and nestled securely in the thick green of the upper boughs. Settling himself in the fork of two strong branches, he swung the bag containing the rifle on to his knee and paused to catch his breath.

The heat from the sun increased as the morning wore on, yet

he stayed in his perch. He had come too far to quit now. High overhead a police helicopter buzzed. He eyed it nervously, keeping himself dead still despite the tickling of sweat as it coursed down his face. He had a full and uninterrupted view of the stage erected in the navel of the converging slopes, upon which were gathered the masses. Everything was perfect.

It was almost time. Taking a breath, he opened the bag and, one piece at a time, began carefully to assemble the rifle.

Pamela left her car and walked to the park. Spector had supplied her with a pass that would get her backstage. The nub of anxiety that had worried at her all night had grown in intensity until the pit of her belly was afire. The need to speak to Cyrus, to her . . . father, tightened with vice-like relentlessness. She had to reach him. It was vital she speak to him, to tell him, that she loved him. Once through the gates she began to struggle. The crowd was just too dense. And as she struggled the urge grew, and grew, almost to panic level, and she started to curse under her breath.

From above could be heard the buzzing of a helicopter. She glanced up and recognised the markings on the tail as it descended: Vincent Industries. Her father was arriving!

Daniel watched the helicopter, noted the markings, and felt satisfaction. Not long now. The rifle, grasped in hands slick with sweat, was calibrated and loaded. He was ready. From the stage came the sounds of instruments snarling discordantly as they were tuned prior to performance.

Plunging headlong into the crowd, she had the feeling she had hurled herself into some difficult sea. Despite her most strenuous efforts the mass delayed her, and within minutes she was whimpering in anger and frustration.

'Let me through!' she shrieked, the sound lost in the greater noise. Her single voice counting for nothing. 'You don't understand. Let me through!'

Desperation needled at the ulcer in Spector's gut. As time grew shorter he impatiently ordered more frequent camera sweeps of the crowd, and cursed crudely at the lack of success. 'He's out there,' he raged. 'I can smell him. The son of a bitch!'

The radio crackled. 'Red Fox to base. Come in.'

Spector touched the handset to his lips. 'Go ahead Red Fox.'

'Something shining in the treetops. Kinda like a mirror. Westfield area. Do you copy?'

Spector frowned. 'I copy, Red Fox. Can you be more specific?' From the base of his stomach rose a plume of excitement; it was coming.

'Intermittent reflection. Like a glass being moved. Over.'

'Could it be metal? Over.' Spector snapped. There was a pause. Red Fox was absorbing the implication. 'Er . . . could be. Do we have cover in that zone? Over.'

Spector's mind was racing. Ordering all cameras to concentrate on the pinpointed location, he stared at the screens. 'Red Fox, ground cover only in that area. Repeat, ground cover only. Maintain position. Over.' His eyes peered hard, until . . . 'THERE!' The word exploded from him with a force that startled the technician at the console. 'Got him!' Spector's nerves were stretched to full tolerance. 'All units close in on Westfield zone. Sniper in the treetops, repeat, sniper in the treetops. Shoot to kill. Repeat. Shoot to kill!'

At his side the technician remarked dryly. 'Let's hope we're not too late.'

When Spector glanced across to see what was meant by the remark, he gasped. For Cyrus Galbraith was walking on to the stage. In moments he would be alone at the microphone, wide open to the world.

'Shit!' Spector shrieked, 'Shit Shit Shit!!'

Daniel was unaware of the net closing around him. His entire attention was centred along the narrow telescopic sight; his whole world, past, present and future encompassed in that small black circle quartered by the crosshairs. He watched Galbraith step onto the stage, detach from the group of aides and approach the microphone to begin his address.

Taking a slow deep breath, Dan rolled the tension from his shoulders, and in a last nervous gesture, swallowed.

'Thank God!' Spector blurted out. He pushed a hand up his forehead and swept back his hair. 'Thank God!'

On screen the familiar figure of Barry Mather could be seen

clambering up to hasten to Galbraith's side. Galbraith saw him coming, and a wide smile broke across his face as he outstretched a hand to greet him.

'I never thought I'd be happy to see that son of a bitch.' Spector breathed. He had heard that Mather returned that morning, offering no explanation for his disappearance. 'Thank God.'

Viewing events through the 'scope, Daniel was puzzled by the sudden turning of Galbraith's head. He moved the scope slightly to see what was happening. He was not surprised at the sight of Mather — he was too far along the road to obsession to even wonder. From afar came the shouts of men struggling to force paths through the crowd. With a sinking heart he knew he was destined to be taken, but first, anger reignited, he trained the weapon once more. Now both men were circled in the scope. They were shaking hands. His finger took up the slack in the trigger.

What happened next shocked Daniel as much as it would later shock millions of television viewers around the world. With his free hand Barry Mather took a gun from his pocket and, still smiling, blew the Senator's brains out.

Uproar from the crowd. Stunned beyond belief by what he had seen, Daniel lowered the weapon.

Onstage, tension exploded into chaos. Screams of horror rose in a great wave from the crowd. The walkie-talkies of the men closing on the copse crackled urgently. Sniper forgotten, they ran for the stage.

In the command post, Spector stared transfixed at the monitor screens. At the multiplied image of Galbraith falling to the floor with blood jetting in weakening spurts from the side of his head. For the only time in his professional career he was speechless. Ignorant of the tumult he simply stood, rock-rigid, his face contorted into a mask of horrified disbelief.

Watching helplessly from the crowd, Pamela felt her heart break with the fragile ease of a cookie. Her forward thrust ceased — for she knew he was dead, and as his body slumped to the floor she followed suit, hoping with all her broken heart that she would drown in the sea of humanity that surrounded her.

There was an odd smile on Mather's face as, handcuffed to two uniformed police officers, he was bustled from the stage and towards a police vehicle that had bludgeoned a path through the crowd. Around him thousands of hostile faces stared, but he kept turning his head as though seeking a particular face.

Then as he hit the first step he jerked, appeared to stumble, as five gunshots ripped the air with scarcely a gap between them. He lurched forward, dragging the two cops down with him. And all eyes turned to the young woman standing at the front of the crowd, a smoking gun in her outstretched hands.

Florida.

Sea breeze, cool and fresh, filled the room. The curtains billowed softly. He sat at a table by the terrace window and thought back to the day in Central Park. How he'd had presence of mind enough to take apart the rifle and leave the park like any other good citizen, he would never know. His thoughts drifted further back, to the day he and Pamela had met at the reservoir. . . .

'It was all planned? All of it? But the mugging! What if I'd walked away?' He was incredulous.

'Our paths would have been made to cross elsewhere,' she had softly replied. Then she hinted that she had something important to give him.

The letter had been waiting for him at the hotel in Florida. Now, when he thought of her the image was distorted, a newspaper picture; slightly fuzzy, her pretty face contorted into a virulent snarl that burned from the page. Committed to vengeance.

'Poor Pamela.' Now he understood. With her mother's letter in his hands he understood. It filled the gaps. At last he felt he had the whole picture.

Her world had been hauled from under her three times in rapid succession. She was left with nothing, no one she could turn to, and he sympathised. He knew how easy it was to accept the pattern, to stumble into committing the ultimate violence. His own bitterness had been long sown, the roots had gone down deep, but already he believed he detected signs of healing. But for Pamela the world had ended, with the killing of her guardian, with her mother's letter. Again and again he read the letter, and was consistently awed by the truth.

Grieving for her mother – who had herself mourned the husband snatched away from her on the eve of a reconciliation. Grieving for her guardian, the man who loved and raised her. Grieving for the man her mother believed was her natural father. John Fitzgerald Kennedy.

For her mother had written. Told how she had been seduced by the President, then parted from her husband, Philip Davis, and learned she was pregnant. Told of her great fear, after the assassination, on hearing that her husband was dead. Told how she approached her husband's employer, Cyrus Galbraith. Phil Davis had let slip the name in conversation, and she had thrown herself on his mercy. Galbraith had paid her. Kept the child for his barren wife to raise.

Poor Pamela. Three fathers, each one killed by the man called Rama. Daniel understood. She had a right to vengeance. Mather; the manipulator, the plotter, the killer. To square the account he had to die too.

Payback.

On the surface, serenity, yet the pain was never far away. The balmy Atlantic breeze continued to flood in through the windows. The late afternoon sun had begun its descent towards the horizon, burnishing the great ocean to a brilliant mirror smoothness in the process.

At a leisurely pace he drafted a storyline. At first the imagination balked; the principals were all dead. Per Se, there was no longer a story.

Or was there? The idea would not go away.

The names would have to be changed.

It was nightfall when he settled behind the typewriter. Taking a breath, he struck the keys.

Love Field, Dallas, 22nd November 1963

There he paused, searching for a hook, a subtitle upon which to hang the opening paragraphs. Then, recalling something reportedly once said by Jackie Kennedy about her husband's favorite line from a favorite Broadway show, he decided on a neat paraphrasing:

'One brief dreadful moment . . .'

'There's the son of a bitch now.' Halstead said.